THE BAILIFF'S WIFE

THE BAILIFF'S WIFE

MAREN HALVORSEN

Cuidono • Brooklyn

The Bailiff's Wife
© 2025 Maren Halvorsen

Cover image: Jan Halvorsen

ISBN 9781944453282
eISBN 9781944453299

Cuidono Press
Brooklyn NY
publicity@cuidono.com
www.cuidono.com

For Jamie

And he spake a parable unto them to this end, that men ought always to pray, and not to faint; Saying, There was in a city a judge, which feared not God, neither regarded man: And there was a widow in that city; and she came unto him, saying, Avenge me of mine adversary. And he would not for a while; but afterward he said within himself, Though I fear not God, nor regard man; Yet because this widow troubleth me, I will avenge her, lest by her continual coming she weary me.

Luke 18:1–5 (King James Version)

You see by the foregoing Relation, how the Widow was left big with Child at the time when her Husband was murder'd, destitute of Friends and Money; which expos'd her afterwards to great Hardships: You see what Pains, Trouble, and Expence she underwent in enquiry after her Husband, in tracing out the Murderers, and in the Prosecution of them, having little or no Assistance or Advice but the Divine Providence, which assisted and directed her in the whole Series of this Affair... Thus we see how one Misfortune produces many. The Murder of the Father, and at the same time the loss of all his Writings, hath proved the occasion of this continual Trouble to his Posterity. And thus we see how just and faithful a Wife this Gentlewoman has been to her Husband, and how careful and indulgent a Mother she has been to her Daughter.

A True relation of a horrid murder committed upon the person of Thomas Kidderminster, of Tupsley in the county of Hereford, Gent., at the White-Horse Inn in Chelmsford, in the county of Essex, in the month of April, 1654. Published 1688.

They could hear her coming. Even as they stood there, minding their own business on the High Street, baskets on their arms, children under foot, they could hear her high-pitched, raucous voice, like a knife splitting the air in two. Anyone who came within sight of her was subject to her rant. She rounded the corner, her strides long and fast, her hands outstretched. It was a kind of madness, and they all feared it. The only thing to do was to turn away, flee into a shop, any shop, dragging your children as you went. Her skirts muddied, her red coat faded and frayed, her hair like a nest of weeds pushing its way from underneath her filthy coif, she flew down the street, searching for just one person to return her gaze and listen to her story.

"My name is Sarah Kidd," she cried. "My husband Nathaniel is buried in your graveyard, unmarked, no prayers said over his bones. Murdered here, in your village! The fortune he carried with him, coming home to me and our son, gone."

She reached the drunk Jewett, lying as he always did on the cheese-seller's porch. "I ask for justice," she implored him, hands out. "I ask only that the body be brought up, so that I can know it is my Nathaniel buried there. I ask only that his murderer be punished. Where can I find justice?"

Jewett opened his eyes and ran a shaky hand across his brow. Sarah Kidd came closer, until her skirts brushed up against his feet. Her voice grew soft, wheedling. "Will you help me? Perhaps you saw him, saw Nathaniel? Perhaps you saw the body when they found it, over by the inn?" She reached into her pocket and brought out the broadsheet, the one that told the story of the discovered remains, the skull bashed in, found in a field and hastily reburied in the village graveyard. She waved it at poor Jewett, like some kind of talisman.

"This tells of it, of the body and where it was found. Listen, please listen to me, I must see the body."

"I dunno know to read, milady, no more than you," said the drunk, no doubt hoping she would go on her way. The other villagers had gradually returned to their business, figuring she had found her victim for the day. Sarah Kidd stood her ground.

"You know this to be true," she hissed, "you and everyone in this village. There is someone here who profited by my husband's death. I mean to find him, and he will suffer for it. Do you hear me?"

"We—we do not know you, ma'am," responded Jewett, desperately trying to sit up so that he could move away from her. "You are not from here, you say you come from London. You have nobody here."

Sarah Kidd reached down and pushed him back, flat on the ground. This caused some people to wonder if they should come to the man's aid. And yet she was such a frail woman, her arms like sticks.

"I may be just a woman, alone, on my own, without my family about me," she said, her voice rising—she was speaking to the entire street, not just to Samuel Jewett—"but I swear to you, on my son's warm body, I will not leave your village until my husband is buried as a Christian man, and his murderer is hung from the gallows as a common criminal. I will be here, in the High Street, every day, until I can touch his bones."

Chapter One

———•◆•———

When Sarah Kidd came to the village of Chalfont St. James, alone, with no man alongside, she felt suspicion all around. She was aware of her insufficiency, a single woman in simple garment, no one to speak for her. It had been months since the constable, John Notkin, had ordered a stranger's body buried without ceremony in the graveyard. That she insisted the body be dug up, so that she could claim it as her husband's, was called insolent and worse. After all, this was the body of just some vagrant, found in the field beside Daniel Grinshaw's inn, come to a bad end.

With the King's Restoration just the year before, fear of vagrancy had somewhat receded, but still people were cautious with newcomers. That a woman should come, by herself, even leaving a child behind to be looked after by others, was criticized and condemned, and there was nothing she could do about it. People either stared at her with brazen impunity, or looked away as if she didn't exist. At first she tried to be soft, tried to persuade. She wept as she spoke of her husband and his disappearance, her eyes on the ground. But not one villager budged. They refused, with what seemed to her an unfortunate enthusiasm, to provide any help whatsoever. And so Sarah Kidd hardened, she spoke her mind, and she raised her voice.

The first place she stopped was at the inn, carefully counting out some coin to take a room there. The innkeeper's wife, Mrs. Grinshaw, was troubled by the presence of a woman all alone in her inn and said as much. That first morning, Mrs. Grinshaw didn't like serving her at breakfast and made sure that she just skimmed the thin surface of the potage bowl by the time she got round to

Mrs. Kidd. And yet the woman was no trouble: she sat pale and quiet at her table and waited.

"Why is she here?" Ellin Grinshaw grumbled as she made her way through the market, her basket weighed down by the butcher's fine sausages. "She's nothing to do with us. She's from London, she'll stir up trouble, that is what will happen. She may have the pennies to take a room but is she a good Christian woman? She best leave well enough alone, that's my view."

And yet Sarah stayed, and grew louder, not softer.

After a few days, she left the inn, her finances nearly exhausted. She wandered about the town, as the days passed, talking to anyone who would listen, demanding to see the body, to have it dug up. People avoided her, tiring of her harsh voice, her sharp face, her body shaking like the palsy as she made her way from person to person.

"Where can I find justice?" she would ask, her hands open. Her jacket became torn and disarranged, her skirts brown with mud, but she didn't take notice. She kept her mind on her work, which was to open the grave and see the bones.

She was aware that her story did not seem likely. Three years ago, her husband Nathaniel had disappeared while on his way home to her. He had served as a bailiff on a northern estate and was returning with the small fortune he had earned. But he never arrived. She had waited, with their infant son, in London, her situation becoming increasingly dire as Nathaniel did not come. She corresponded with friends, sought out acquaintances, but there was no help. The family's situation became desperate.

Friends of Nathaniel told Sarah that he had been seen in Norwich—there was talk of seeing him on a ship to Jamaica, an old friend had even told her he had seen him in a crowded church in Amsterdam. On she went, by boat, by coach, by foot, in search of her husband, never resting. She began to have visions: Nathaniel would appear at the foot of her bed, beseeching her, and she would cry out and reach for him. All there was to touch was thin air.

She never stopped, never even thought to wonder why a loving husband would go like that. She had to find him, for the sake of her child. She took work as a wetnurse to a merchant's family to support herself and the baby, since all she had was her milk to sell. Every moment was filled with her search. And now she had been told of a sensational broadsheet, telling of the case of the mysterious body found in Buckinghamshire. Nathaniel would have passed through Chalfont St. James on his way to London. So Sarah Kidd began the walk to Chalfont St. James, leaving her son in the care of others in London, to see the celebrated bones. By the time she arrived, the body had been back in the ground for some while, and as the weeks passed no one was eager to bring it up to please such a sad, sour woman as Sarah Kidd had become.

It had all started the winter before with the discovery of the body. John Adcock, busy with a new fence, had two men helping him with the work. The rains had started early and so the soil was soft and willing. Every muddy shovel dig brought with it its full complement of dirt, heaped high, and off to the side it went. Adcock worked alongside the two, anxious to be done with the post holes before dinner. It was then that his shovel met with bone and the round brown bowl of a skull came flying out of the hole. Down the hill it went, and the farmer thought that its bounce had a strangely light-hearted way about it. He ran down the hill after it. His two men paused in their work, their eyes following the journey of the skull to the ditch below.

As Adcock climbed back up the hillside, the skull in his hands, his two men set to digging once again, with more enthusiasm now, and very quickly the remains of a body were open to their wondering eyes. A crumbling skeleton, bits of cloth and button about it, a full-grown man. John let them all look at the skull as he cradled it in his big farmer's hands, and they could see the indentation on one side where none should be. Silently they looked at each other and then at John. There was, as they all knew and now remembered, the matter of the missing son-in-law, the drunken Ranter who had disappeared after a brief and miserable marriage to John's daughter Meg. It was widely thought that the two would come to blows, so when the young man turned up missing, the villagers only accepted John's explanation ("he must ha' gone away to London, gone down the road") out of neighborliness. They'd all known John Adcock for years and years, but the Ranter had been a wanderer and had no friend among them. Still, the gossips of the village kept busy with the story. Now there was a man's body, mostly just a skeleton, on John's land, and it was natural for the Ranter to come to mind.

But it was the farmer's suggestion that they take the remains to the constable, and so they carefully put the skull and bones, and the bits of cloth and button, into the small cart they had with them and made their way to the village. With only remnants of sinew to hold them together, the bones rattled about in the cart, a strange dance that made Adcock uneasy. It was a muddy slog, the wheels catching in the ruts along the road as they went. As they got to the inn, the nearest neighbor to Adcock's property, there came people about who looked in at the contents of the cart and began to contribute their own thoughts as to who the unfortunate was.

"Ah, it's a soldier from the War," was the decision of Samuel Jewett, but his lack of authority in the village—as a renowned drunk—made that opinion instantly derided and discarded. The village brewer ambled over and gave the corpse a good lookover. "Naw," he said with definition, "Too much meat still left on those bones. This ain't no soldier from the War. It's some poor misfortunate."

Will Porter was the next to come and have a look at the corpse. His knowledge as one who made his living as physician to all manner of livestock earned him a moment's silence as he considered the remains. "Could be he hit his head on somethin'," he suggested, his finger circling around the indentation. "Maybe fell down and hit a rock."

"That don't explain the burying of the body," insisted the brewer with a fierce shake of the head. "Somebody put it there, and unhallowed ground too." Porter just shrugged and moved back into the small crowd.

Finally the innkeeper himself, Daniel Grinshaw, made his way down the broad front steps of his tavern and over to see what the commotion was. The crowd parted deferentially for the man who held the most wealth of anyone in the village. He might not be well liked but he was respected, and there was a silence as the small group waited for his pronouncement.

"Naught but a vagrant," he said shortly. "Naught but a vagrant, not one of us. Put him back where you found him, for God's sake."

But the drunk had gone to get the constable, John Notkin, who now made this his business. And that was how it started.

The service had just ended and the villagers were making their way towards the door, having received, to their minds, their full complement of grace for the week. St. James' new clergyman was endowed with a fierce reforming spirit that reflected more the dying embers of the Cromwellian regime than the new, gentle warmth of Charles II's Church of England. His energy and devotion were unsurpassed. Nonetheless, he found it surprisingly hard to win over the congregation, who kept their beliefs to themselves but quite clearly showed little enthusiasm for all the changes he had introduced. For this congregation at Chalfont St. James was no little hotbed of religious controversy. Its people did not, generally speaking, gad about to the various conventicles and meetings held during the last years of the first Charles and the chaotic period of the Civil War. Even through Cromwell's Protectorate they stuck to their church, through thick and thin, and no matter what the ceremony or sermon, kept their own views to themselves. And so, even though Father Brunskill might go on and on about God's absolute, unknowable majesty and the predestination of the elect and the reprobate, the utter powerlessness of humanity, the members of his congregation were busy adding up their good and bad deeds for the week to see where they stood. As he watched them file out, so smug and satisfied, he felt a new and uncomfortable sensation of exhaustion, different from the outrage that had fueled much of his work in the village over the past year. It was discomfiting to consider how this ancient-minded congregation might be more of the coming world than his own carefully cultivated theology. He, who had been raised on Richard Sibbes and William Perkins, who had spent years in Cambridge waiting for his opportunity to preach the Word and bring others to his understanding, felt curiously part of a past world, and it was not right. The Restoration of the King had made the hoped-for godly revolution stillborn.

During his sermon—over which he had worked for days, only to have the congregation wink and nod throughout, slithering about on their benches—he had seen the visitor, the woman Sarah Kidd, standing a little apart from the rest, towards the back of the church, and it seemed to him that the air about her shimmered with tension as she stood there, eyes on him. As if he could do anything for her. For all his being the village priest, Brunskill was well aware that he had no real standing among the people there and it would never have occurred to him to intercede for the woman. So he watched her. The silent tears were rolling down her thin cheeks as she stood there, ignored, alone. There was something in her look, the fierceness of it, which told him they were tears of outrage, not sorrow. And throughout his sermon, as he labored his way through an arduous consideration of the meaning of *sacrifice* in this Lenten season, he felt her eyes. He tried to break away, to look at his congregation with their twitching and smirking and nodding, but kept coming back to Sarah Kidd, trembling there in her place.

His hands were damp against the pulpit. The light of the morning shifted as it found its way in through the grimy plain windows, sad replacements for the stained glass that had been shattered during the war. He gave himself a moment to clear his throat, and let his eyes drift across the congregation, from young Ann Barwell sitting solitary in her tidy brown cloak, to the innkeeper Grinshaw and his wife, whispering to each other in that intimate way that couples have: a single word from her, out of the corner of her mouth, and he would smile. There were Mr. and Mrs. Stroud as well, resplendent, local gentry, well known for their card-playing parties. More than one hapless guest had lost their fortune gambling at the Strouds' tables. Brunskill felt both envy and dislike as he finished the last of his sermon.

So now, as the parishioners stretched and yawned and went out into the cold, drowsy spring day, Brunskill waited for the woman to emerge. He stood there, by the entrance, observing the sharp contrast between the cool darkness of the church and the clear, hard light of the late morning.

Everyone had passed by, and still no Sarah Kidd. Puzzled to think that the widow had got past him, Brunskill re-entered the church, and was startled by her immediate presence on the other side of the door. She stared at him. Somehow it kept him silent, and they stood there, alone in the church, mute. He saw that she was a small woman, narrow and bony, her long face pale beneath the unhealthy splotches of red that mottled her cheeks and forehead. Her eyes were very dark, deepest brown, with lids that looked bruised in the filtered light of the church. She frightened him because he had no understanding of her, and felt that she might do anything, anything at all, her actions only limited by her physical strength and her purpose.

"You are a man of God," Sarah Kidd said, "you must see to God's justice." Her voice was rough, and she spoke rapidly. She didn't seem to care if he understood her or not. She continued, "He was my husband and he deserves a proper service. He was my husband and I mean to find out who murdered him. I am not just some weak-minded woman. I will stay here until I see the bones. I will stay here until the one who killed Nathaniel is found and punished. I will stay here until my fortune stolen from me is restored. I can feel God's presence and I know he will help me."

Brunskill took a deep breath. "Madam, I do see what you want and I would help you with all my heart, but you must see that I am not of any power in this town. I have no one's ear. The Constable is my parishioner and no more. No one will listen to me, any more than they listened to you." He kept his eyes on hers—she did not look away—and he could feel himself redden with the effort. His admission of powerlessness, as much as it might seem an excuse to the woman, was heartfelt and sad.

"You are a man of God," she repeated, "and you know that my husband deserves a burial with his name, a marked grave, he should have that. You cannot deny me." And now she clasped her hands together, long and bony with dirt etched into the lines, and repeated, "You cannot deny me." The words captured him, brought him to her place.

"I will put forth your case, but I cannot say that anything will come of it. Be comforted, Mistress Kidd." It was a plea, to get those eyes to look away, those hands to unclasp and return to her sides. But then, of course, she began to weep in earnest, and he felt that he had only pulled himself in deeper. There was no doubt in his mind that he was making a mistake. He needed to be ingratiating himself with this community, so that he might find a way to bring them closer to the Truth, not allying himself with this strange woman for whom the villagers felt nothing but contempt. But it also occurred to him, as he stood there watching her tears fall, that it was strange that the village was so set against Sarah Kidd, when they had been so curious about the body at the start. What had changed, and why weren't the villagers eager for a resolution to the mystery?

In taking the step to see Constable Notkin, Arthur Brunskill knew that he was not improving his position within the community. With Sarah Kidd marching at his side, he felt all eyes were upon him that morning, the day after the fateful meeting in the church. But he had agreed, out of sympathy. He wanted the body of her husband freed of its anonymous grave. So they walked along in the gentle light of the morning, the flapping of the widow's skirts their only accompaniment. As they walked along the Market Street, Brunskill wanted to take Sarah Kidd's arm, she looked so unsteady, but he knew she would not allow it. People paused about their business and looked up. Most of them looked away then, but there were a few whose eyes followed the priest and the supplicant down the road as they finished their journey to Constable Notkin's house, in the Lower Road.

John Notkin opened the door as if he had been expecting them. Perhaps a wind of rumor, pushed along by all those eyes and looks, had moved more swiftly than their feet and made it to his ears long before their knock on the door. He was a squat, untidy man, his shirt loose, his breeches slightly darkened with grease and soil.

For Notkin was a small freeholder, with a bit of land, paid to hold the office by those unwilling to take their turn as parish constable.

"Ah, Father, and I see you have Mistress Kidd along with you." His glance at the woman was a knowing one, as though they were old friends. "Come in, come in, and tell me what your business is today." He led the way back into the dark little house. They passed a small chamber, its door slightly ajar, and Brunskill could see, with a start, that there was a young man in there, shackles on his wrists, his eyes closed and his back hunched. The place had a slightly sour, stale smell, from the cooking of the day before. Arthur Brunskill felt oppressed. He could see that his companion was oblivious to the low character of their surroundings. He envied her that single-minded purpose.

They entered a long, narrow room that showed little in the way of comfort or warmth. There was a fireplace along one wall, warming the small grouping of chairs and a settee around it. Beyond that the room was empty of decoration or even furnishings, except for a low bed in one corner, covered with a dark brown woolen blanket. No rugs on the freshly swept floor, no hangings on the walls: it was a chilly room that did not encourage lingering. Notkin gestured to his guests, encouraging them to sit on the hard little settee by the fire, and Sarah Kidd took her place with little ceremony. After a moment's hesitation, Brunskill sat beside her, finding no other chair free for the purpose, one being occupied by the odious Notkin, the other by what looked to be a ledger of some kind. He felt the woman's skirts press up against him, smelled the woodsy scent in her hair (where was she sleeping now, the forest?). Regret that he had come this far took hold and kept him silent, until Notkin's gaze compelled him to speak.

"Sarah Kidd has a likely story," he said to the constable, who stood up quite suddenly, next to the fire, and looked serious. "Likely enough, it seems to me, that we should exhume the body and its effects to provide her with peace of mind. She has come all this way, and surely it would not be much trouble for some of the folk to bring the body up." It all sounded so sensible, that any re-fusal on Notkin's part would surely be suspicious. Brunskill relaxed a bit as he sat there, feeling relieved. They were nearly done, and he could return to his business. All Notkin needed, really, was a man to speak up for the widow.

The constable stared at the woman, from top to bottom, making clear his view. "It is an astonishment to me, Mr. Brunskill, that you should be speaking for this woman. She is naught to us here, naught but a vagrant. Who is to say her story is true? This talk of a husband and child? She's a Londoner! She could be a mischief-maker, a trouble-maker." The firmness of his tone belied the weakness of his argument. Brunskill could only wonder at why someone would choose to come and camp in a town, desiring a body to be dug up, for "mischief."

Sarah Kidd did not flinch. She stared hard at the constable. "You are no Christian, to deny me this." She turned and grimaced at Arthur Brunskill, as though she had eaten something gone rank. "Who can say why the constable denies me this request." Again she turned her eyes to the offending official, her face pale with concentration, in an effort to weaken him with a look. But their war of wills had gone on for weeks and he was not to be so easily intimidated. The priest sighed, knowing that this would be no easy task, to bring the body up. Perhaps if the woman had been more sweetness and less gloom, things might have gone better with the constable. Resentfully, his gaze averted from the woman picking at her coat sleeve next to him, Brunskill tried again.

"John Notkin, you must see that this woman will not leave until we do something. She will be here, at your doorstep, day in and day out, and will not stop until you do this." This line of argument had little effect: Notkin looked at her with disgust, as he would a stray cat dying at his front gate. Brunskill took a breath and found his way down a different path. He put a finger to his nose and half-smiled, as though in deep thought. "I do wonder if this matter is yours to consider, by the by. The body is in the town cemetery plot, and there are other officials we can ask, perhaps John Stroud…"

The mention of the justice of the peace's name sent Notkin into a fury. "Ah, naw, you may not bring him into it! This was a felony committed, a murder plain and simple, that's for me to decide about the body!" Face reddened, the man stepped forward and shook his fist at Brunskill. Sarah Kidd looked on, sharply, seeing a crack in the wall.

The rivalry between the Justice of the Peace and the Constable was honored by time and the particular personalities of the two men involved. Justice of the Peace Stroud, a gentleman, thought of Notkin primarily as a jailer. Notkin, however, had a sharp view of the dignity of his office and felt it under attack by the Justice. Arthur Brunskill had not learned a great deal about this town in his year there, but he had learned that much. It was with barely concealed relief that he wondered aloud about Mr. Stroud's immediate whereabouts, and soon had Notkin agreeing to an exhumation.

A small look of satisfaction on Sarah Kidd's face as the arrangements were made was all the gratitude he collected for his efforts, but he did not expect more. He escorted the woman back out into the road, and she left him then, without a word but with a nod, her face composed and her step slow.

The next day turned warm and breezy, the tail-end of a stormy April, daffodils and crocuses in full-throated song all across the field. To see the small crowd of folk there about, it could have been a somewhat festive occasion, all looking on with great interest: among them the constable, his gray jacket surprisingly clean; Father Brunskill, showing more color in his face than the winter had allowed; the two laborers, same as the ones who first dug out the body with farmer Adcock, jacketless, their sleeves rolled up, ready to work with their shovels. The only darkness in the scene was that of Sarah Kidd, wrapped in her worn red coat, her face shuttered, remote. Her hands were straight and limp at her sides. The narrow grave was a plain one, with a small wood marker atop it, somewhat at a remove from the other graves in the yard, a stranger to be kept apart.

As the shovels began to dig, the soil yielding soft and damp to the pressure, the small crowd stepped back, to allow for bits of dirt to come this way and that. There was just the sound of the grating of iron against sod and then the soft wind of the lift, the dirt falling in a heap behind the gravediggers. Nobody spoke. Eyes wandered from the grave to the dim blue sky of early morning. Notkin, his arms crossed as he stood there, was clearly and stubbornly unhappy with the proceedings, shifting his weight from one foot to the other, heaving a loud sigh now and again as the shovels made contact with the ground.

Arthur Brunskill found himself standing next to Sarah Kidd and wondered how she would greet the bones once the coffin had been pried open. He was uncomfortable being in such close proximity to something so unpredictable. Would he be expected to comfort her? Was there any chance at all that this wasn't her long-lost husband, that she would turn away from the bones and effects, and leave them to put the body back into the ground, leave the village without a word? He gave a sidelong glance at the woman, who stood there absolutely still. He wanted to reach over and straighten her cap.

The shovels made contact with wood and gradually the coffin took shape before their eyes. The diggers looked triumphant, as though they had found something long lost. The work went faster now, with a communal intake of breath as the men reached down and pulled up the wooden coffin, using all their strength, groaning dramatically as they thrust the flimsy wood box on to the ground at Sarah Kidd's feet. Nothing seemed to unsettle her. She stood there, unmoving, and waited patiently for Constable Notkin to walk over with his tools to pry the lid open. He took his time.

It did not come open easily. The constable cursed softly as he put more muscle into his work. Finally, after a few more long moments, the lid came off and fell to the side with a clatter. They all gathered round and looked in at the pile of bones with the bits of cloth and button alongside. Then their eyes all traveled up to meet those of the woman.

As she gazed upon the bones, Sarah Kidd's face took on an expression of quiet satisfaction. There was even a small, thin smile on her lips as she bent down to touch the bones which were clearly, to her mind, her husband's. She reached in and caressed the bit of cloth, soft and worn, with the button attached. Then she knelt in the wet earth and began to whisper, her eyes closed, and Brunskill could see that she was praying.

The priest knew the story was far from over, even as he watched Sarah Kidd kneel beside the opened grave. It was interesting, he thought as he stood there looking at her crouching form, how he felt an exhilaration, a not-altogether pleasant sensation, intense and painful, at the prospect of the next inevitable scene. It was as though he had been holding his breath for a long time and suddenly it freed itself. He saw himself thrown to the winds even as he stood there, so still and straight, that improbable bundle of dank cloth and hair beside him, immovable in its misery.

After a short while the widow rose stiffly and turned to the constable, pronouncing the corpse to be that of her husband. Then, of course, "Where is the fortune that my husband was carrying with him?" This said in a harsh, knowing voice, for she was aware of how Notkin would answer.

The man had been already moving away from the grave, his job distastefully done. He stopped short at the widow's words. "Woman, he's been in the ground for too long—how are we to know what happened?" Then he smiled, a slow dirty smile—"and is it your word, widow, that he had money at all?"

In spite of himself Brunskill reached out and put his hand on the woman's shoulder. He felt nothing but a bit of cloth over the bone, and that only for a moment before she flew forward, to put herself in the constable's path. The rage in her voice sent it even lower. "It's all I have, all my child has in the world. If you do nothing, you have stolen the money yourself."

Notkin, not much caring about her opinion of him, stepped aside and went around the woman, continuing his march away from the grave. The small crowd had melted away, and the two gravediggers looked at Brunskill for instructions. The priest went over to the widow and moved to face her.

"Mistress Kidd, we must see to the proper burial of your husband." Brunskill nodded at the gravediggers, who moved a few paces away, shovels at the ready. "If you would care to, I could conduct the service now and rebury the body with the help of these men." The widow reached out her hand and, in touching his arm, gave her weary assent.

"I am the resurrection and the life…" he began, and Sarah Kidd gave a soft shudder as she listened.

"Know that my redeemer liveth, and that I shall rise out of the earth in the last day, and shall be covered again with my skin, and shall see God in my flesh: yea, and I myself shall behold him, not with other, but with the same eyes." Brunskill thought on this as he spoke it, thinking of the small nest of bones in front of him, and what kind of man this once was, a man who had loved his wife Sarah, had begotten a child with her, and had set off for home with a fortune to see to their needs.

As though reading his thoughts, the widow began to softly cry again, the tears falling down already-wet cheeks, perhaps imagining that once vital husband and the future that was now denied them. He realized, immersed as he was in these thoughts, that he should be thinking less worldly ones, that surely to think on regret and life in this world was to deny the very words he was speaking. There was something in the nearness of her that was corrupting him. This was the first time he had had that thought, in all his dealings with Sarah Kidd, and it shook him.

"And that is born of woman hath but a short time to live, and is full of misery; he cometh up, and is cut down like a flower, he flyeth as it were a shadow, and never continueth in one stay."

At this, Sarah Kidd put her hand to her mouth and bit fiercely. Perhaps it was to keep herself quiet: she made no sound as a small trickle of blood began to spread across the back of her thin, wasted hand. Brunskill could not take his eyes off the hand, as he intoned the well-known passages from the Prayer Book.

"The last enemy that shall be destroyed is death…"

He continued reciting the lesson, his mind now a blank except for the image of Sarah's small hand, a sacrifice to her silence. It was as he found his way to the passage thanking the Lord for his deliverance, as the gravediggers readied their charge, that she joined his voice with hers.

"We give the hearty thanks for that it hath pleased thee to deliver this Nathaniel our brother, out of the miseries of this sinful world beseeching thee that it may please thee of thy gracious goodness, shortly to accomplish the number of thy elect, and to haste thy kingdom, that we with this our brother, and all other departed in the true faith of thy holy name, may have our perfect consummation and bliss, both in body and soul in thy eternal and everlasting glory. Amen."

And he saw that she was dead to the world and its constraints, and that was why she could deny herself everything in her search for justice and her child's fortune.

As the pair left the gravesite, freshly darkened with the turned earth, Sarah felt herself gain in strength and energy, and she began to talk of the fortune lost. In some way, the finality of the Prayer Book's ritual had allowed something to pass through and from her, so that she felt, for the moment, freed of the burden of her dead husband. She looked ahead, looked for revenge. She knew that she would have to be strong to see it through.

"We must now seek out the murderer," she said to Brunskill. "This is our task. For he has profited by my husband's death, to the detriment of our child, and I will see him answer for that."

Brunskill sighed with visible irritation that such an assumption could be made, that they were now partners. Two days had passed since their meeting at the church, and he was clearly ready to be part of her past.

"Mistress Kidd," the priest said in his most reassuringly hearty tone, "you have done much in finding your husband and making sure of a Christian burial. Be pleased with that, and go on your way. Your child waits for you in London. There is no hope of finding the one who did this deed, nor the fortune you speak of. Surely the money would be spent by now, so that even if we were to discover the villain we would not see anything for our pains, and even so, how are we to find the culprit after this long a time?"

"I am always told to go away," Sarah said with urgency, "and yet I have found my husband and buried him after all these years. I can find the murderer and the fortune too. He is here in this village. I know who he is. Master Brunskill," and here she looked up at him, her reddened eyes narrow with calculation, "you have been my only friend, and you know the doings of this village. You can help me with this. We will pursue him, chase him, seek him out and he will be punished. I know him, I know him to be a sinful man, proud and with avarice."

"And who is it, who could have done such a thing?" Brunskill asked with great reluctance.

"Ah," she said with a dark smile, "it is someone here who is known to all as friend and fellow Christian. And yet he is not. I will not say his name, not yet. No one will listen to me, not yet."

They were coming upon the village now, attracting the usual curious looks, others even hostile, young Tom Maltman looking away and spitting as they passed by. Sarah Kidd thought nothing of it. She was at ease with dismissal and disregard. But she could see that the priest was made uncomfortable by it and wished that he were stronger. And yet he was all she had.

They came to the church, and she turned to walk away. Suddenly the priest reached out and touched her arm.

"And where do you sleep, Mistress Kidd?"

She looked straight at him. "I have not had much of that, sir, not in all the days and nights I have spent since my husband died."

A short, awkward pause, and he let go of her arm. She let it fall back, flat against her side. "Then stay here in the church," he told her. "We can make up a bed for you in the storeroom, we do that for—well, for unfortunates." He did not like that word, but that was what she was, unfortunate.

Sarah thought, here is a small kindness, and it would be wrong to ignore it. He is all that I have.

"I will stay here for now," she said with a nod, looking for all the world as though she were the one extending the favor, and walked with him into the church.

Chapter Two

———•◆•———

The field was a brilliant milky white, shining under the dark sky, as if the moon had dropped from its distant perch and become liquid. Each blade of grass stood stark and white, drenched in the moon, glowing. At the edge of the field stood a mass of folk, all different, old men and small children, husbands and wives clinging to one another, and all were afraid. How she knew this was unclear. They had no words. They stood there silently and gazed across the field at her. Then one man separated himself from the rest and moved into the field, and yet remained unchanged, the moon did not touch him, he was all dark. He slowly made his way across as the folk stood and watched, and she felt that he was moving towards her.

Suddenly she was in her room, the shutters ajar, the bedding all askew, and Frances knew it had been a dream, a private vision for her to wonder at. The pounding of her heart took time to abate. She sat up and let her feet touch the icy floor, and moved across the room slowly and carefully to close the shutters. She looked out across to the fields: this was a night for the full moon, so all was bright and defined, and she thought about the dark man.

She could not go back to sleep, but remained sitting in her bed for a time, unsettled. This would have been a time for her husband to wake and to comfort her, and she missed him. No doubt he would have seen much in her experience, and they would have prayed together, earnestly, new each time. Instead she sat here in the dark, the shutters now closed, the room still and unyielding. The practical side of her nature told her this was a mistake, that the day would be so hard without sleep, but she could not help it. She rose, opened the shutters again, and in the early-morning grayness dressed herself. The woolen nightshirt, warm against her body, was replaced by a linen shift and petticoat, followed by her blue day-gown, all cold and stiff, only gradually softening and shaping themselves to her skin as she moved about. Making her way to the soft, decayed embers of the fireplace, she lit her candle and pulled open the door to the hall. The door to her daughters' chamber was shut—Eliza and Jane were asleep. The still of the morning made her footsteps on the cold plank floor seem all the more pronounced. Even Deborah, whose job it was to be up earli-est, to have everything ready for the family, was not about. All was dim and cold. A part of Frances liked this very much, the way all seemed different, and hers alone to see. She made her way with a candle down the stairs to the kitchen, where she set about the fire and made the kettle ready. She was not above Deborah's work, not about to lie abed waiting for her maidservant to make things cozy and easy.

Frances thought about the man as she moved about the room, feeling her skirts warm about her, bringing a cup down from the shelf. What could this mean? It was so dark, so somber, and left her with an intense foreboding. Perhaps at Meeting the answer would come to her, God's thoughts would be revealed to her mind. How could there be such darkness when she struggled so hard and long to do right? It was a mystery, and she thought on it as she sipped her small cup of watered wine and waited.

The room was small, but Frances was inordinately proud of it, of the yellow tapestries and the thick wool carpets. It was her little bit of comfort, warm and intimate, nestled within the cold, drafty house. She saw this room as her past world, before she found the Society of Friends: it was luxurious and worldly. And it showed her, in her anxious maintenance of it, how hard it was to give up that world for the more godly, less comfortable world of the Friends. So there was a little guilt, and a silent prayer for strength, as she sat there and watched her brother-in-law Richard Bright settle into his comfortable chair. The dream of the night before was still very present in her mind, but she put it from her with some determination.

Richard was tall and broad, and filled the chair to its fullest extent, his legs stretched out awkwardly in front of him. His largeness made his eyes and nose seem all the smaller, perched there in miniature, sharp and thin, with delicately fine eyebrows, almost as though a second, separate person were imprisoned within that fleshy, rambling frame. He did not take after the Brights generally. While his brother, Frances' late husband, Matthew, had shared with father and sister the large, slightly bulbous sky-blue eyes and dark curling hair that were seen as Bright family requirements, Richard instead took after his mother with his thin brown hair and green eyes, and shared her wayward spirit (as did all of her children, although they exhibited it in different ways). He had shocked his Puritan family by a sudden conversion to Roman Catholicism as a young man, followed by a journey to Rome to take training as a Jesuit. During that period he was cut off from all family except for Matthew, who undertook a letter campaign to win him back to the Protestant fold. Their letters, filled with theological argument, flew back and forth between London and Rome, and finally Matthew met with some success: the younger brother returned, foreswore his conversion, and joined the parents at the pew in London's St. Mary Aldermanbury. He could not find his way those few additional but crucial steps to his brother's Quaker faith, and this had remained a defeat for Matthew. Nonetheless he had been a frequent visitor to Matthew and Frances' home, the Grove, in Chalfont St. James, during Matthew's final years. Frances appreciated his thoughtful, serious conversation, and saw him as a fellow seeker. He was not an easy man and there was a coldness about him, but nonetheless his mind was restless and unsparing in its search for the truth. He and Matthew would wander the garden paths, deep in godly conversation, never raising their voices against each other but rather inclining the ear to listen, followed by a gentle response. Frances liked that Richard still felt at ease here, after his brother's passing, and would come and visit, taking time from his work as a merchant in London to look after his dead brother's family. She enjoyed clos-eting herself with him before supper, the two of them, talking of faith, of politics, of family. Their conversation was never trivial, always went to the heart of things. They had their disagreements, and she could never quite feel comfortable with him—at times his temperament seemed of the choleric, a quickness and temper that could strike without a moment's notice. But nonetheless her own need for conversation overcame these reservations and she felt it to be a treat, to have him with her for an evening.

A pause in the conversation as Frances rose and poked the fire. The early spring days were still chilly and damp. Again, her love of this room—love was the word for it, she knew, abashed—lent her a feeling of contentment. The carpet soft beneath her feet, the good draw of the tiled fireplace. She sat back and turned the conversa-tion in a new direction.

"Richard, what of your father? Is there any hope of pardon?" The elder Bright had fallen far. As a leader in the City, and a promi-nent Puritan, he had been one of those whose decisions led to the execution of King Charles I for treason after the king's capture by the Parliamentary forces, and as a sad result he was currently a resident of the Tower for what was now declared to be an act of regicide rather than patriotism. All of his property had been forfeit to the Crown. His likely punishment would be death, meted out in all justice by the dead King's son, returned to his throne just three years before. His wife, Matthew and Richard's mother, Mary, spent her days weeping and praying, in much reduced circumstances.

"You know my father," Richard said glumly. "He will not recant, he will always declare his act to have been right and just. There is nothing in it for the King to pardon him; he is no longer a power-ful man. He will remain stubbornly as he is, and the King will see to his death."

Frances remembered the senior Bright as a man to whom all things seemed to come naturally and easily. Men looked to him for advice and approval. His fishmongering business thrived and his household prospered. To his fellow Calvinists, he had seemed one of the Elect, his sign of election revealed by earthly success. It must be strange for him to find himself in a small, leaky cell, gawked at by the jailers, his requests for visitors ignored. He suffered in silence, cut off from them all. So different from years past when truly John Bright was the center of an orderly Puritan universe. His only disappointment had been his children—one who became a Quaker, another a Papist (and in the most violent way, seeking to join the Church Militant, the Jesuits!), and the third, living in London, a daughter of whom no family member spoke and who from all outside accounts seemed to be without any religion at all. It was said that the clever Samuel Pepys, new in the Admiralty, brought her barrels of oysters in return for her favors, and that he was but one of many. A family of seekers, each a different path.

"I am very sorry," she said to Richard, "I will pray for him," not really sure that her father-in-law would welcome the prayers of a Quaker. Perhaps by now he was less certain of his own version of the truth, and might well welcome all prayer short of a Moor's.

Richard shifted in his chair and she knew this signaled another turn in their conversation. The light had faded, Deborah had come in to light the lamps, and soon there would be supper to attend to. She felt the warmth of the evening together, the family all sharing the meal, the continued good conversation, and loved all of it, felt content. But the smile of anticipation on her face faded with Richard's words.

"I must talk of a serious matter with you, sister Frances," he said, his voice deepening with every word. "My father's imprisonment has meant that I am now the head of the family, and as such there is something I would like to address. This house," his eyes wandered the room, landing for a brief but full moment on the yellow curtains and the warm tiles framing the fireplace, "this house was given by my father to his son Matthew, my brother. It is a house that has been in the Bright family for generations. Now, it must stay within the family, must be a home for the Brights. Matthew's only child is a daughter, and she will marry away. She will belong to another family and her children will bear their name. It is my intent to see if there is an entail on this property, requiring that it pass to the nearest male heir, which would be me." He ended with a flourish, rising from his chair and beginning to pace around the room. Frances felt oppressed by his size, a giant playing in a doll's house. "And," he continued, "if there is no entail, then I shall challenge Matthew's will in court. It is not right that the house should pass out of the family, because I am the male heir."

Frances rose from her seat as well and her chair tipped backward, falling against the curtains with a soft thud. "What are you saying," she said, trying to keep an even tone to her voice, to keep it from wavering like a woman's. "This was Matthew's and my house. We have improved it and made it as you see it now, and it is for Eliza to have one day. She is enough of a Bright."

Perhaps he had expected tears rather than unseemly anger. He turned his back on her and faced the fire, and spoke to it. "It is not my purpose to upset you, Frances, and I am surprised that you do not see this as I do, as anyone would. It is extraordinary that your daughter should inherit our ancestral home. This may well be the home that—" and here a pause, as he tried to find a way to say it—"that my father might come to if the King finds it in his heart to be merciful. Where his father and grandfather both were raised, where Brights have lived for two centuries."

This truly angered her. "You have just spoken to me of your father's fate," she said with energy. "And you know, you must know that if Father Bright is released from the Tower, he will be quite welcome here, he and Mother Bright. I would take it as an honor to care for them." And she really thought this, in her heart, although it had never occurred to her before, the old man and his wife needing her. They had always been so removed from the ordinary sufferings of others, she had always viewed them almost as statuary, impervious to winds or weather. But now all was different.

He turned and there was a half-smile, shy, on his lips. "Naturally, dear sister, you would offer that. And perhaps it will come to pass, for I offer you now the residence of this place, even as I own it." A pause, and then: "You understand, Frances, that for many, your marriage to my brother was never within the law of Church or man."

She stared at him, wordless, for a moment, and then moved to right the chair. It gave her a moment to consider her response.

He watched her as she stood there, sharp-edged and small against the drapery. She was not a beautiful woman, but she did have a presence, her slender face framed by firm brown eyebrows and a fine-boned jaw that met a now quivering chin. Her almond-shaped brown eyes sparkled, wet.

"Your brother left me this house, to care for, as Eliza's inheritance," she said. "It is mine, and will be mine. You may take this to court if you wish but it is mine." She had no learned arguments, nothing to offer beyond this. The words repeated themselves over and over in her mind, "it is mine," as Richard lost his smile and bowed his head. "I have cared for it and seen to it," she stumbled on. Bitterly, she thought of how she came to this house, given to her and Matthew by his father, the "ancestral home" of the Brights: eaves rotting, rain coming in through the roof, the garden a mire of mud and weed, the kitchen a horror. It was a sign of the Brights' humble beginnings in Buckinghamshire, before the grandfather made the remarkable decision to try his luck in London and enter trade. It had been kept out of sentiment, and given to Matthew. Practical and thrifty, she had cared for it all the years of their marriage and the years since Matthew's death. She had raised her two children there: one, Jane, born while fresh in her first widowhood, the other, Eliza, near her second and but a small child. She had done it all, the repairs, the care, the yellow drapery. It was too much to bear.

"And," she said with finality, "my marriage to Matthew, the two of us saying our vows before God, was just as lawful as any marriage done before a priest. We were as married as your parents were."

The maid Deborah entered and declared supper to be on the table. Richard reached out his arm to Frances who paused for just a moment before taking it.

After she saw Richard off on his journey back to London, Frances took herself out into the garden to look for early flowers to cut. She found solace in her everyday tasks as she thought about Richard and his demands. She had been there but a short time when her younger daughter came toddling in her direction. Eliza was panting with excitement and effort. She held out the prize to her mother, who took it gently from those hot, muddy hands.

"What's this? Oh—" Frances touched the dry moss and the sticks and saw how they were shoved together into a large mass. What was it? She turned the object around and peered at it. "Where did you find this?" Then she saw the small opening and peered inside: waxy soft beaks, four or five, and a slight movement. "Ah, Eliza, look!"

The little girl stretched as her mother leaned down to her and they both looked in the opening. Frances had a sinking feeling— where was the mother? What would happen to these babies? But Eliza was lost in the wonder of the moment, and was entirely thrilled, her little hand reaching up to touch them. "No, Eliza, don't touch." A gentle taking of the hand, and the little girl stood there and held her breath as she gazed upon the newborns.

It was hopeless, of course, but with Eliza's childish help, Frances took the nest and propped it in a branch of the apple tree, wondering if the mother were hovering about. Even if she were, what could she do to save the nest? Was she watching from the fence, would she watch as it fell once more and broke apart on the ground, the babies helpless? Or would she turn away, indifferent, and begin again? How long would it take to build such a nest as this? Frances fled inside the house, Eliza in her wake.

Through the back door and into the hall, and then she paused, the little girl breathing beside her. Calm, calm. She took Eliza's hand and they made their way to the stairs, to go up to the nursery. She was startled to see the flash of a skirt in the doorway to the main room, so after giving a little nudge to Eliza to make her own way to the nursery she turned from the stairs and into the chamber. She nearly collided with her mysterious guest. The woman was pacing the room like a mad person. All thought of birds disappeared from Frances. She had a tidy mind and now turned to greet Susan Harp.

"Susan, how good to see you," she managed, her hand outstretched in greeting. Susan, absorbed in her own thoughts, jumped, and the eyes that met Frances' were wild. She shakily extended her own hand and muttered something about "nobody about" when she had arrived, and thus her presence in the drawing room. Frances, however, knew it had more to do with Susan's inquisitive nature than with the lack of response to the knock on the door. She was one of the more celebrated gossips of the town, and despite her Quaker conversion remained firmly immersed in the worldly doings of Chalfont St. James.

Despite Frances' nodding towards the comfortable chairs in a corner of the room, Susan without ceremony launched into her story as she stood her ground. It took some prodding to get her to take one of the chairs and sit. She was agitated and at first her words were jumbled, so that it was hard for Frances to follow her meaning. This was not unusual for Susan, under any circumstances, but her clear distress only made it worse.

"It's all so horrible, I can't see what to do, Frances, what should I tell the widow? You have to tell me—I heard this horrible cry— but it was a long, long time ago. Should I talk to the constable about it? I heard this noise, you see, this uproar, I remember it well, it frighted me, and I never said naught about it until now, to you..." She was peering at Frances with her short-sighted eyes, her round face unusually drawn and pale. She was a short, strongly built woman, but also one who did not seem to care much about her own person. Her clothes always had a brownish, dirty tinge to them. Wringing her hands as she stood before Frances, Susan was almost babbling. Frances reached out a hand and took hold of her right hand. Susan's solitude was such that Frances knew such a touch was a rare thing and startling enough to stop her fussing.

"Now, Susan, sit you down. I will have something to drink brought to you, maybe some ale?—and you can begin your story again. I'm sure that I cannot understand anything said so far." She called to Deborah, who stepped away from her work to see to things.

This brought a long pause as Susan's pale, watery eyes lifted and met Frances', and Frances had the distinct and somewhat unpleasant impression of a burden lifting from Susan's narrow shoulders on to her own.

"You are right, Frances. I will start at the beginning." A deep breath, representing much suffering.

"It was nearly three years ago. Something has come back to my mind. It's because of the widow Kidd, and her—her talk of her husband. It happened years ago but it is something I've thought about since. I am troubled by it." The woman took another breath, holding it for a moment before exhaling and starting her story. "I was out late one eve, having gone to visit old Katherine Ball, you know, she was beginning to fail then, and her daughter, remember, she married that traveler—the one that mended fences—weren't in the village anymore. So I had gone to see to her needs, and got her settled for the night. Afterward I walked my way home, up along the road to Seer Green. I am not one who minds being out at night in the dark. It is all welcome to me, quiet and peaceful, so I can think. The moon was full and helped me make my way." She was breathing more slowly now, obviously relishing the story as it unfolded. Frances smiled and let go of her hand. She could understand, but not quite believe, Susan's announced desire for quiet. The woman was constantly going about, looking after (indeed, for?) sick folk, running here and there, almost as though she found her own good health so tedious that she must seek out the illness of others.

"I was passing by the inn, you must know, Daniel Grinshaw's place, which isn't a place I like to walk by at night, strangers often about. Some clouds moved over the moon, and I was having trouble seeing my way, but the inn was there and there was a light on, I could see it. All was quiet. The place were closed up, but then I heard this—" she paused, her face scrunching up with the strain of remembering—"this yelling, someone crying 'Help me, help me,' distinctly, not very loud it was, but then cut off before it was done, if you take my meaning."

Frances kept still and waited, and after yet another deep breath, taking some satisfaction in the drama of her tale, Susan continued.

"I didn't know what to think—the crying stopped, but then I heard more voices, a clatter, and then all was quiet. I was rooted to the spot, I was, and didn't know what to do or think. I was all alone there, with no one about, and no one heard it but me. I—I thought on it a moment, and then began to wonder if I had heard it at all, things was so quiet that I waited there in the shadows, I was so frightened! After a short time I saw the back door open, the one off the kitchen, and I saw two men—I could not see them well, they were in the shadows—dragging something between them. I didn't know for sure what it was—but now I think it was a body. I was so afraid they would see me! So then I went ahead and I—I went home, as fast as I could." Susan's face was flushed, and she looked at Frances, to hear her verdict. "Should I have stopped them, asked them about the scream for help? What would you have done, Frances?"

Frances stood and walked over to the window, gazing out across the garden out to the road, the same road to Seer Green, quiet and in shadow. "What did you think happened, Susan?"

"Well, what I thought then is what I think now—someone was murdered there!"

There was a stunned silence between them, as if Susan had said something blasphemous. The floodgates opened. "And now, there's this body, buried next to the inn, and this widow here to see to it, and something happened to him—I'm sure it was him, Frances, I'm sure! Somebody killed him at the inn and then buried the body. I heard it, I did hear it, I saw it, no mistake! What do I do now?" More tears fell. "I couldn't have done anything then, the deed was done, and I am just a poor little woman, if I had gone to the inn I'd have been buried alongside that man!"

Frances turned and bent down to Susan, putting her arms around the woman's heaving shoulders. "It's all right, you did the right thing. It's certain you could not have gone to the inn. That would have been foolish. But who knows what that noise was, whether those were the words said? Perhaps in memory it has become louder? In the dark of night, too, you know, noises seem louder than they are in daytime, and words can be misunderstood. And as for the men, it was dark, perhaps you mistook a burden for a body. Be comforted." Deborah came in and handed a cup of warmed ale to Frances, who placed it carefully in Susan's hand. The woman paused in her weeping long enough to take a sip, then, finding it good, a long draught.

"Ah, nutmeg, very good, Frances." An appreciative pause, then, "I know what I heard. It filled me with horror. And now, to find this body, buried not fifty feet away on John Adcock's land! There is no doubt in my mind that those are the bones of—of that man that was murdered in Grinshaw's inn." Past the guilt, Susan was now on to the murder and its clear connection, in her mind, to the bones found on the farmer's land. And Frances had to admit that the connection seemed possible.

"Have you told anyone of this? The constable?"

Susan looked stricken. "I never told anyone, I felt so ashamed that I did nothing. I couldn't talk about it. How can I talk to the constable now?" A pause, her voice quavering. "Could you tell him, Frances?" Hopeful, quiet.

"I don't think that would be enough—I wasn't there, Susan. The constable would surely hear me out but he would want to speak with you."

It was clear that Susan had thought about this a great deal. She took another draught from her cup and shuddered slightly. "But—wouldn't that mean accusing someone? And being in a court, and taking the—taking an oath?"

This made Frances pause. Of course, there was the requirement of oath-taking when one takes the witness stand. Any prosecution would make use of it. Indeed, such would no doubt be part of her conflict with her brother-in-law, and a possible reason he felt he could pursue his recent interest in the house. Members of the Society of Friends did not take the Lord's name, not in a worldly court of law.

"It may not come to that, Susan. Perhaps someone else heard the cry? Surely others were staying in the inn that night?"

"I don't know, but Frances, you know as well as I do that Daniel Grinshaw is the kind of man that could do such a thing. Not that I like to speak ill of anyone," she ended weakly. "He is intemperate— his quarrel with Friend Salter, you know." Susan looked pleadingly at Frances.

"It is one thing to threaten, another to carry out," Frances said mildly.

"But you see what I mean, Frances, he's a man who talks of violence. He's a man with a temper." Susan suddenly stood. "I know I can't say a word—but I know that I should!"

Frances thought for a moment. "Have you seen the widow, the woman who is asking about the body?"

"I have seen her, everyone has," replied Susan with a small bit of testiness. "She is always in the road, asking. She stands in front of John Notkin's house and waits for him to come out, to talk to him. She is always about. But Frances, I have not spoken with her, I am afraid."

"I have seen her in the village," said Frances, thinking back to her own brief encounter with Sarah Kidd. She had been struck by the woman's powerful stride, as she walked through the main thoroughfare of the town, on her way to make yet another demand. Her skirts dragging in the dirt, her coat hanging open from her thin shoulders, she walked on, looking neither to one side or the other. Frances had come face to face with her, but the woman looked past her, and Frances had had the uncomfortable, rare feeling that she was invisible and did not matter.

Susan brought her back. She had risen from her chair and stood with her arms hanging at her sides. "Please, Frances, I need your counsel."

Frances gazed at her with affection. She wanted to have an answer for the woman but could only provide her with the comfort of a Quaker: "Listen to the Seed within, Susan, that is far better than any advice I can give." But she knew, as she said it, that it would not be enough.

That night, as she lay in her bed, her thoughts on the day that had passed, she found herself moving into a vision, back into the field with all the people shining in the moonlight. She saw the man, dark and tall, and she tried to see his face, staring hard at his dark form. In spite of the brilliant light of the moon it was obscured, in shadow, but whence the shadow came she could not tell. She could not keep herself from struggling to recognize him, put a name to him, even as she could see him moving slowly across the field, even as she knew, with finality, that she should move away, fall back into the darkness of the house behind her. She could feel herself standing at the near edge of the field, opposite all the people, no longer in her room, and this startled her when she realized it. She was cold, and the night was so still as the man moved closer. His strides were long and purposeful. There was no sound.

Suddenly she was in her bed, the covers on the floor, shivering in the dark night air. Frances lay there, frightened, for the only way to interpret the message was to see it as a warning. She felt nothing good in the man. He was dark and he filled her with foreboding. Once again the early, early morning stretched before her. This time, overwhelmed with fatigue, she reached down for the counterpane and fell back into a deep, dreamless sleep.

She was awakened later by Ann, moving about her room, warming it with the fire. The homeliness of her movements was reassuring and comforting. Later, as she set about her morning tasks, Frances reflected on how to make sense of this vision. The only way in which it could be understood was in the realm of faith—perhaps this was a threatened temptation. And yet the man was so frightening, not seductive at all. She did not feel tempted in the vision. She felt fear.

As she sat there, going over her accounts in the study, lost in the vision and its meaning, she was suddenly alert to the crying of Eliza, outside. She found her under the apple tree, her face red and moist, her hands in the dirt.

"What is it, Eliza?" She looked hard at the ground, where Eliza's tears were falling. It took a moment, but then she saw it: three little beaks, the tiny bodies almost indistinguishable from the dirt, featherless and soft, dissolving into the soil. A few steps away lay the nest, broken and torn, now empty.

Frances stood in her small work-chamber towards the end of the day, her table arranged with mortar and pestle, various bowls of different sizes, and a neat row of jars, labeled carefully in her own cramped hand. Baskets encircled the swept floor, some of them empty, some overflowing with dried grasses and leaves. The room was fragrant with dried lavender, as well as cinnamon and sage, a warm heady mixture that always made her feel at home. This was a favorite place for her, and rarely did anyone else pay a visit.

She set about her task, for she had promised Katherine Ball something to ease the dropsy which had bothered her for a long while. She took the tops off some red mint, mingled them with nettles and sage, and then crushed them to extract a small liquid. It took some time to come up with a sufficient quantity, which she then strained and transferred into a small jar. A few drops in her ale would be all that Mrs. Ball would require. Frances was supremely confident of her skills, and while she did not possess a real cure for what ailed Mrs. Ball (who did?), she could at least ease her troubles.

As she worked, she mulled over her conversation with Susan. It made her very uneasy. When she had taken up with the Friends, the demands placed on her, in the giving up of oaths and other articles of the faith, only made her conversion more appealing. To be asked to live one's faith in the world, day to day, was something powerful and even exhilarating. The Friends asked this of her in a way unlike any other sect—certainly unlike the Church of England, in which she had been raised. She was asked to be plain and simple, to speak to all as equals, and to live the Scripture in her life, which included giving up all oath-taking.

It was never easy, never meant to be. At times she found it painful and hard, to give up her life in London society, to hold her tongue when a witty remark crept upon her (and they so often did!), to ignore the invitations to dinners and all sorts of gatherings. To give up games and music. When she met her future husband Matthew at Meeting, she was struck by his complete and utter surrender to the new faith. They had had long talks about their shared delight in the transformation that came from their conversion, the closeness to the Light, the sense of wholeness and purpose. Their marriage, the two of them before the Meeting, had been for Frances a transcendent moment, one of unity and homecoming both. But afterward their experience had parted ways. Unlike her own occasional struggles, Matthew had never found it hard to leave behind worldly temptations, despite his high rank in society. He had simply retreated into his study to read the Scripture and write lengthy, thoughtful commentaries on it, completely at peace with himself and at a distance from the world. He would write and write with the door closed. And then he would come out, and refuse to doff his hat to the Duke, or attend a Meeting that was then closed down by the authorities, and end up in a very cold prison cell for six months at a time, returning home afterward as calmly and peaceably as ever, if a little worse for wear. Back into the study, opening up the book where he had left off, and dipping the pen into the well. No matter how close to the Light she felt, Frances never felt that complete and utter equanimity in the face of such punishment.

It was George Fox, in the beginning, who had helped her to see past the physical poverty of the Friends, to the spirit. His own manner was not well-bred: he was rough and impetuous and spoke whatever was on his mind. There was a wildness about him. Frances had to admit that this wildness excited her.

It had not been easy, not easy at all. To be in the Church of England meant only to attend services on Sunday and be baptized. To be a Friend required a daily rejection of much of the world around her. The Society refused to use the conventional addresses of respect and treated all the same as before God. They rejected the traditional use of the days of the week, instead referring to the days in a less pagan way, as First, Second, and Third day. Frances had long ago given up much frivolity, from dances to games, and so that part was familiar to her and necessary. She still felt a pang as she had given up the dinner parties, replacing them with more somber, simple dinners made up of prayerful, godly talk. London friends fell away. Matthew Bright had replaced that world, and for her it had been enough. She and Matthew made the decision to remove here to Chalfont St. James, to take a house away from the distractions of the city, the house given to them, somewhat reluctantly, by Matthew's father. Here, at the Grove, Matthew had lost himself amid his books and writings, seemingly oblivious to the repair work undertaken by his capable wife. And here their daughter Eliza was born.

They had made new friends and found a community in the little band of Friends that lived hereabouts, including Susan Harp. Now Susan was to have her own faith tested: Scripture forbade the taking of the Lord's name in an oath, and yet here she was, on the road to finding herself in a courtroom, testifying as a witness to a murder. Where was the answer to be found for this? Frances turned once again to her salves and powders, and set to work.

> *As I walked forth one summer's day,*
> *To view the meadows green and gay*
> *A pleasant bower I espied*
> *Standing fast by the river side,*
> *And in't a maiden I heard cry:*
> *Alas! alas! there's none e'er loved as I.*

Nathaniel loved to sing as he walked. It being high summer, he remembered a song he would sing to Sarah as they went walking along the Thames. It had seemed incongruous, there in the foul streets of London, and amusing to sing. Sarah had seemed ever puzzled by it—the idea of meadows and flowers, as they stood on some smell-laden wharf, watching the barges move past. As he walked through the countryside now, it lacked that power to amuse but provided some comfort in his memory of Sarah.

> *Then round the meadow did she walk,*
> *Catching each flower by the stalk*
> *Such flow'rs as in the meadow grew,*
> *The Dead Man's Thumb, an herb all blue;*
> *And as she pull'd them still cried she:*
> *Alas! alas! there's none e'er loved as I.*

He kept up the tune even as he climbed a rise that made the burden on his back feel all the heavier. Singing kept him moving. He was justly proud of his voice and, even though there was no one to hear him, finished the tune with a flourish, repeating the last line a few times for good measure.

> *When she had fill'd her apron full*
> *Of such green things as she could cull,*
> *The green things served her for her bed,*
> *The flow'rs were the pillows for her head;*
> *Then down she laid her, ne'er more did speak;*
> *Alas! alas! with love her heart did break.*

As he reached the end he topped the rise and found himself on a gratifying downward slope. The view before him was wide and various: small nests of forest interspersed with fields, his own road meandering through, meeting up with a stream about midway across the expanse. The landscape was dotted with clusters of slow-moving sheep. At this distance he could not make out any shepherds, and he felt like the only man in the world.

He had left his position in the North in good standing with the estate owner for whom he worked, having managed the estate and its people as bailiff for the past year. He knew himself to be an efficient, honest manager, and there was no doubt that Lord Delancey had been well-satisfied. His newborn son was a central reason for Nathaniel's departure. If he had stayed another six months, all the more fortune he could have brought back to his wife and child. But what he had was good enough. He had been frugal and put all of it aside so that he would be welcome in his wife's family's house as someone who could provide for her.

On the downward side he picked up his pace and felt the sun burning against his hat as it came from behind a cloud. Summer had been late in arriving this year and no doubt another hard winter was soon on its way, so these few days of heat and dust weren't so bad in his view. Better than fighting his way through snowdrifts. He was always one to appreciate what he had. Sarah was always the fearful one, thinking ahead to fresh troubles, never content with what was. She had told him of her dreams, dreams where she looked for him but could find him nowhere. She was so afraid that he would not return to her. And yet here he was, almost within shouting distance of London, just a few more days. With money in his pocket. Nathaniel laughed out loud, imagining her face as he made his appearance at her door. She would cry, and reach out to touch him, to make sure he was real, not just another of her dreams.

Nathaniel kept up his march, making good time, running through a few more of his favorite songs as he crossed the bridge over the small stream. He paused—the stream was crystal clear, one of those fine chalk-streams the region was known for—and filled his small flask with water that would last him until he reached Chalfont St. James. Still no sign of others on the road. He loved the peace of it. He liked his fellow man just fine, but too often on the open road there was need for caution. This was an easy part of his journey, just he alone in the middle of Buckinghamshire. He sat himself down by the stream and pulled out a bit of bread from his bag. He cut off the green parts with his knife and enjoyed the rest.

Chapter Three

———•◆•———

That night, in the bed she shared with Eliza, Jane was having her own thoughts. She tried to keep awake, to enjoy her moment of solitude, as Eliza breathed softly next to her. She fought sleep, treated it as the enemy, pushed it away. Always, the struggle ended in defeat, and she would wake in the morning to the gray light and Eliza's prattle, aware and angry that precious hours had been given up to sleep.

She sat up in the bed, careful not to disturb her sister, and slipped out on to the smooth cold floor, settling herself down on her knees. At first this had been hard to do but now it came naturally and she found no reason to complain. Her woolen night-gown kept her warm enough as she knelt there, thinking. She was busy with thought. To have her hands empty, with nothing to do, felt good. Her knees hard against the floor kept her awake, kept her mind in pursuit of those subjects she needed to consider.

Sometimes she spent these nights thinking about what would happen to her—both in this life and what would come next. She could now imagine living apart from her mother, could even imagine children of her own. She felt ready. Once, when she was quite small, her great-aunt Preston had cheerily told her about this future, of leaving her home and being with a husband, with children, and she had burst into tears at the thought. But now it seemed her due, and she considered what it would be like to no longer share Eliza's bed but someone else's.

The floor gave off a chill that made its way up into her bones. She felt this with pleasure, the cold sharpening her mind. What she had planned to think about was, of course, Samuel Prosper. She let herself whisper his name, softly, eyeing her sister as she did so. She desperately wanted to conjure him up, to have him kneel next to her here. She wondered where he might be. Perhaps on the road back to her, to fetch her as he promised. A fortune to be won, and then her. Now she was sixteen. When he had left she had been just a child, but now all was different.

The back of his neck, white and vast, as he sat there facing away from her. Vulnerable and open, the strands of damp hair like thin veins crisscrossing the white skin. His hand, the fingertips ink-stained, the nails carefully trimmed as if it mattered. The feel of his hand on top of hers, warm and soft, large, encompassing all of hers so that none of her flesh could be seen. She imagined him in the bed next to her now: he would crowd her, his large frame spilling over, she nearly crushed beneath his weight. As her knees began to go numb she thought of that.

When she had first met Samuel, standing tall in the doorway, her mother had said here is your new tutor, obey him in every way. He was to teach her so that she could be able to read God's Holy Word for herself, and so that, once she became mistress of a house, she could manage its accounts without leaving that to a husband (she had seen how her stepfather Matthew relied upon her mother, that it was she who managed it all, Matthew with no thought to tomorrow). At first Jane had done so reluctantly, not charmed by the tutor. His slow way of talking and the smile that would steal across his face whenever she spoke unnerved her.

But as time went on she began to expect, and wish for, his eyes on her as she worked. Her own vanity troubled her, but she could not help herself. She had always felt disregarded, and to have this man so interested in everything about her made her proud. She lived through it again, how she would look up from her book to see him gazing at her, making her feel that every inch of her were something new and important for him to learn about.

Eliza gave a great sigh and whimpered softly as she turned over in the bed. Jane worried that she was seeking the warmth of her sister, but the little girl settled. She was running out of time, and she could feel her thoughts become loose and wild, as she thought about the way his lips curled and the curve of his nose as it dipped down to meet them.

The next day was First Day, the day of the Friends' Meeting. It was always perilous, to come together, given the King's hostility to religious sects and to Quakers in particular. But the Friends continued to gather, at a small house near Frances' property, a small storage building owned by a farmer who had joined the Friends a year or so before. Frances could walk there with ease in the morning. It was a dark, mean little house, and it took some doing to feel a connection to the divine as they stood in a circle in its one room. Still, that was part of the experience, to transcend the earthly darkness and find the Light, the Light hidden from view, intangible, only present within. Frances felt a warm satisfaction as she walked there on this fresh spring morning, feeling the moist earth beneath her feet giving way with each step. The primrose pushed out along the path, exuberant and frothy with bloom. The almost cloying, dense smell of wet grass made her dizzy. Eliza trotted behind her, and she could hear the little feet stop every once in a while as her daughter became entranced with some new flower or buzzing bee. Then the feet would start again, from a distance, as the child came to her senses and saw how far ahead her mother and sister were.

Frances walked up the front step, followed obediently by Jane and, somewhat behind, Eliza, and entered the large, low-ceilinged room. It was empty except for a couple of benches for the infirm and a table in one corner. The small windows were open to the air.

There were several people already there, nearly twenty, standing in a circle in the middle of the wide-planked floor. There was Susan Harp, standing by old Joan Sharpton, holding her hand and nodding at whatever the old woman was muttering. Susan had a look of restless distress about her, agitation even, straining with all her might to remain still. Frances hoped that the Meeting might provide some small respite from her suffering. People continued to enter, and stood expectantly, in silence. They all well knew that the authorities could choose to come and take them all to jail, for such meetings were forbidden, and this perhaps contributed to the heightened sense of expectation. Martyrdom, when viewed in the momentary abstract, can be appealing, thought Frances ruefully. Jane and Eliza stood on either side of her, quietly, very still. This unnatural stillness contributed to an atmosphere charged with anticipation, as the small group stood there, waiting.

The room had still some cold to it, and Frances was preoccupied with keeping herself from noticeably shivering. This annoyed her, because it was such an obvious distraction, physical and petty, from God's voice. She turned her mind inward and allowed herself to be cold. She felt the darkness of her mind, warm and shadowy, and put her thoughts to the Light, to illumination, to God. Her eyes half-closed, and the room began to feel far away, gray and insubstantial. The silence was absolute. Her shivering ceased of its own.

Suddenly there was a movement, a shifting, as Susan Harp roused herself. Frances could see her, a solid block of a woman, with her woolen dress hanging on her, shapeless, gray. Her shoulders were heaving, and her voice was distorted with tears.

"Our Lord looks within us, examines our souls, and knows that it is so hard sometimes"—her voice broke, and there was a short pause—"hard to remain true to our faith, to remain true to what he wills us to be. He does test us, and it can be unbearable, to see suffering around us and do nothing because of his will." Up to this point, Susan was uncharacteristically ordered and clear in her thinking, so that Frances wondered at it—perhaps this was indeed God speaking through His instrument. She had her eyes closed, tears rolling down her pale cheeks. "It is too much to bear, so much murder and mayhem, and we can do nothing, we must wait for God's justice, but it is—it is unbearable, I can't help but think about the dead and the ones who mourn them—" Susan's voice became thin with effort as she tried to keep herself steady, but it was no good. She began to weep in earnest, and stood there, holding everyone captive to her tears.

This went on for several minutes, the weeping, everyone else in the room silent. Then the crying fell off, and Susan said in a final voice, low, thick with tears, in anguish, "There is a murderer in this town and it is my fault. He is loose among us, free to do his evil, unpunished for what he did." She pushed past poor old Joan, who began muttering wildly, and fled the room.

All was silent again, except for Joan, whose words made no sense and were so soft that few could hear them. Frances felt that somehow the Meeting had been stopped cold, that God had departed, and they were all alone with their earthly thoughts. Susan's sad words had broken the small, narrow, glowing ribbon that Frances always imagined in her mind as the link between herself and the divine.

She turned and whispered to her daughters to stay, and went off in pursuit of Susan. Nothing else to be done for it. As she made her way down the front steps, she saw Susan up ahead, running away along the path, her shoulders heaving, her head bent down, lost in misery. Without thinking, she hitched up her skirts and trotted behind, slowly advancing because Susan kept pausing to wipe her nose with her sleeve. As she closed in on her, Frances reached out, touching the woman's arm, and said, urgently, "Susan, please stop now!" At first Susan kept going, shaking her head, the sobs coming even more fiercely, but after another touch on the arm she slowed, and then quickly crumpled to the ground, there in the common, and looked up at her friend with despair.

In the quiet of the common, Frances knelt down and cupped Susan's downcast face in her hands, feeling the warm, tear-slicked cheeks beneath her own dry fingers. "Be still, Susan, be still. Calm yourself. We must get you home and talk about this. I know you are disturbed, but you are not forsaken." These words, low and soft, made Susan look up into Frances' eyes with gratitude. The burden was to be fully shared.

It was no easy matter for Frances to talk with Sarah Kidd. The widow resided, it seemed, in a storeroom at the church, but did not spend much time there. There was, therefore, no formal place to call. She could have sent an invitation for Sarah to call on her but was not confident of the reply. And so she set out the next afternoon as the weather cleared of the morning drizzle, to the graveyard behind the church, where quite naturally she found Sarah sitting on a small stool beside the grave of her husband.

When she had seen the widow in the village before the body had been exhumed, during the days when the fierce battle over the body raged, Sarah had seemed a very tall woman filled with energy and purpose. She had had the stride of someone who needed to cover long distances quickly. Now, she appeared much smaller, the bones in her face making shadows where none should be. Her dress was loose about her. There were rips in the fabric of the skirt, and the collar and cuffs were soiled nearly to match the darker color of the bodice. The red coat still gave her presence, but it too had suffered from time and weather. Frances tried to ignore the odor that held close around Sarah, full and ripe.

When she saw Frances approach, Sarah rose from her stool and turned towards her, but her look was flat and disinterested. No doubt this was an unlooked-for interruption of her communion with her husband. Frances held out her hand and introduced herself.

"Good morning, I am Frances Bright," she said with a warm look. "Please accept my sympathies for the loss of your husband. I am sure it brings you some peace of mind to have this knowledge now, of his passing, as hard as it is." She gestured for the woman to sit back down on her stool; she looked so frail. Sarah continued standing.

"Good morning, Mistress Bright," she replied, "I am glad to know you. This is indeed the only place where I feel comfort, to be next to him here. Were it only that his murderer were here too, I would be well pleased."

Frances thought this a hard thing to say. She sighed, and looked off at the graves that surrounded them. "That is something we leave to God and his merciful justice—his will be done in this world and the next." As she said this, something so easy and effortless, she found her own mind at variance, for it had become an interest of hers to find the guilty man. This was not, of course, leaving it to

God but rather inserting herself into the affairs of others. Surely it was not her place to meddle in this, a mistake.

"God's justice is all well and good," the widow declared, plopping herself back down on her stool and arranging her skirts about her. "But we are charged with seeing to justice in this world, with all our judges and constables and the like. That is their duty, to fulfill God's will here on this earth, to see to the punishment of the guilty. And they do a mighty poor job of it. As far as the next world, I will not wait until then to see my fortune returned, and that of my child." She nodded her head vigorously, rocking a bit on her stool.

Frances took some time to reply. She was in conflict within herself over this matter, and desired to know the widow's intentions. "Dear Mistress Kidd, how shall you see to this matter here, you a solitary widow with no one at your side? How shall you see to justice, if no constable or justice is there to help you? By what means shall you discover guilt?"

"I have a friend here," said the widow proudly, "I am not alone. I know the villain, as well, so I shall put myself before him, I shall pursue him, I shall cause him to be unsettled in his mind and body, I shall pronounce him my husband's murderer. I shall do that and bring him before the constable. The priest is my advocate. He has been my only friend in this village." She looked up at Frances, her eyes dry and tired. "My husband was dear to me and all I could ask for. He and I were together for too short a time, as he made his fortune for us. His son will never know him and will go out into the world without a father's help. We are unprotected. To restore the fortune will be to make us secure in the world and that is what his father would want."

"Who is the man you seek, Mistress Kidd? And what is your certainty of guilt?"

"I am not afraid now to say his name. It is the innkeeper, Daniel Grinshaw. A man traveling with gold can be a strong temptation to a greedy innkeeper. I have seen Grinshaw, and his is the countenance of a thief and a murderer. I have"—a slight hesitation, then a lift of the head—"I have been where the crime was committed,

I have seen it in my mind, God sent the vision to me. I will not wait for God to punish Master Grinshaw, I will see to it myself." Sarah grimaced, her nose high in the air, a look of aggrieved rectitude.

"Well," said Frances, not surprised by the indictment, "that is fine, indeed, but without evidence the accusation will not stand. There are enough wretched characters about but few of them are murderers. Do you know that your husband stayed at the inn?" She thought of Susan Harp and the problem of witness.

"I know it," Sarah said firmly, "but the innkeeper denies it. And yet, the first night I stayed in this village, I stayed at his inn. I had to know the place. I got a room and slept there." She looked sharply at Frances. "He came to me in the night, my husband, and stood at the foot of my bed."

Frances shuddered in spite of herself. "Ah, a dream," she said.

"Oh no, it was more," said the widow. "It was he, standing there, pale and struggling for breath. He looked at me with all the sorrow in the world, all of it, and said not a word. It was like someone were taking the breath from him at that very moment, as I watched. I could not speak. I was unable to move. I could not even say a word of comfort. After a time I closed my eyes but for a moment and he was gone. And that was how I knew he had been murdered at the inn, by this Grinshaw. My husband is waiting for me to see to his punishment."

"A dreadful night you must have passed," said Frances with all sympathy, wondering at her own visions and their meaning. "And yet for murder to be shown, your husband's ghostly presence will not suffice."

"I am not a fool," said Sarah Kidd. "But it was that night that assured me of the crime. As for the courts, there was a person who saw my husband about the village, I spoke with him. His name is Samuel Jewett. He has said to me that he spoke with Nathaniel as he entered the village and asked the whereabouts of the inn. They talked of the dryness of the weather and the poor crops hereabout. It was Master Brunskill who found Master Jewett and spoke with him first. I am but a poor woman, no one need answer my questions."

Samuel Jewett, as Frances knew him, was a man given to drink and one who made his living in the shadows of the village. He was a day laborer but was not known for his strength or skill. She had passed him on the village square, drunk and asleep, with a regularity that made clear his habits. His word was trusted by no one. Mistress Kidd would need more help, if this were the case she had built against Grinshaw.

"I am but a poor widow," went on Sarah, her voice fading. "The truth lies all around me and yet there is no one to listen. There is a path to justice but it is so steep and bad. I will stay here and follow it as far as I can, for my child, for my husband."

Frances knew what her answer to this must be. "You have me as your friend as well," she said, holding out her hand once more. "We share a widowhood, you and I, we both know what it is to sit by our husbands' graves. We care for fatherless children. We lie alone in our beds and must face the world on our own. Please allow me to help you, and call on me at my home. It is known as the Grove and is where I live with my two daughters. You must accept my offer to help."

And so Sarah Kidd rose, and the two widows clasped hands together there in the graveyard as the sun struggled through the trees.

Arthur Brunskill was gratified, the next Sunday, to see the widow in his congregation. He hoped that at the very least this discovery of her husband's body would strengthen her faith and help her to see past revenge. The fourth Sunday of Lent was not one of his favorite services: the traditions of Mothering Sunday seemed to overwhelm the lessons of somber Lent. He had no patience for flowers and simnel cakes, surely the Word should be enough. But he could see, as he looked out over his distracted congregation, that everyone there was thinking of their cake and the tedious little rituals they pretended were Christian, rather than his own sober reflections on Corinthians 5:16. And in spite of himself, he had a moment's thought for the child of Sarah Kidd, without patrimony, without his mother, growing up among strangers.

His gaze turned to the Grinshaws in their front pew. No simnel cake awaiting there: Ellin Grimshaw was barren, having married her husband when nearly past her childbearing years. She was no Sarah, to be blessed with a miracle in her later years. But despite the lack of children there was no doubt that it was a happy marriage for both. Mrs. Grinshaw had been a prosperous widow, new to the town, when the innkeeper began to court her, and their mutual interests and high regard for each other had led to a quick wedding. Ever since they had been a contented pair, with no ill word spoken, despite Daniel Grinshaw's well-known temper. She seemed to know how to manage him. Even as they sat there, the wife's busy eyes, after taking in the room, would settle on her husband with a small, satisfied smile.

All the village's leading citizens made a show of coming to St. James during Lent, culminating at Easter, and then as summer came attendance tended to fall off. Brunskill had a full house today—farmer Adcock was nodding off next to his wife and daughter, and behind them the brewer Benett with his five motherless children. No sign of the drunk Jewett, no doubt sleeping it off behind the mill. The pew where once the Bright family had sat was now given over to the Strouds. Mr. Stroud was involved in all sorts of trade and property, and his house was one of the more imposing in the region. He was well known, too, as a gambling man, and often hosted card games which were the ruin of his neighbors and friends. Brunskill's predecessor had seen nothing wrong with joining in from time to time, but even though gaming was not prohibited within the Church, Brunskill could find no value in it. His single attendance had confirmed this view. No doubt it was part of his estrangement from the village, this refusal to join in. Well—the Strouds had chosen not to attend this Sunday, perhaps, thought Brunskill uncharitably, too tired from their cards the night before.

This pew could, of course, have been claimed by the returning Brights, Matthew and Frances, but their conversion to the Quakers had left it for the Strouds. Brunskill thought about Frances in her somber meeting house, no song or sermon to be had. He would have liked to visit it sometime but of course the very idea was dangerous. It was bad enough that he was escorting Sarah Kidd about town. If he were to associate himself in any way with the Friends, it would be the end of his tenure at St. James. But as he readied the incense with his usual reluctance he wondered if that would be a bad thing.

He could see the widow Kidd again in the back of the room, standing behind the last pew. She did not seem to want to make herself comfortable. Standing erect, her arms straight at her sides, she was not looking at him but rather at the people in the pews, the villagers who so carefully ignored her. Her eyes wandered restlessly over them all, from one to the next. He had the sense that she was readying herself, that something was about to happen. Brunskill had to look away so that he could keep his mind on his work.

But as he provided the final benediction there was a commotion in the back, and Sarah Kidd came striding forward down the center aisle. All faces turned to her in unison as she made her way to the front pews and took her place in front of the surprised Grinshaws, her back to Brunskill. He watched helplessly as she raised her hands and waved them in the air.

"This declaration I do make," she said with a loud voice, full and resonant. "I have made this accusation to the constable of your village, Master Notkin, but he will do nothing. So I come to this place of God, to this people of God, to ask that you hear me. I throw myself upon your mercy and judgment. My husband was foully murdered here, in Chalfont St. James, and his fortune stolen from him—*my* fortune, and that of my son. I have your priest, Father Brunskill, to thank for the burial of my husband under his own name. Now I beseech all of you to prosecute and condemn his murderer and restore to me what I have lost." She paused for a long moment as the Grinshaws sat frozen in front of her, and all was perfectly silent in the room. Then she continued, her voice rising even higher.

"I accuse Daniel Grinshaw of murdering my husband, out of greed and the wish to do evil. My husband stayed at his inn, and once Daniel Grinshaw saw what wealth my husband carried with him from his bailiff's position, he resolved to carry out a horrible plot of murder. Thus my husband was found, buried in a shallow grave next to the inn, the victim of violence and malice. Thus Master Grinshaw has profited by his actions and seen only prosperity come of his evil deed. He must now be punished for this crime, and my fortune restored. I ask the people of this village to see to this justice."

Brunskill held his breath throughout the woman's speech, as though he could silence her through his own asphyxiation. The room dissolved into disorder as people cried for the widow's removal, and Brunskill saw the constable Notkin making his way to the front of the church where she still stood. The priest left the altar and went down to Sarah Kidd's side to help steady her. The Grinshaws, clearly outraged but in full awareness of the support of the villagers around them, stood to one side, and Daniel Grinshaw began to speak. The crowd quieted as his voice grew in strength.

"I will not stand for this, Notkin," Grinshaw said, addressing his words to the constable and pointedly ignoring Sarah Kidd. "These flagrant accusations, without any grounds, nothing! Charge this woman with making mischief and be done with it. She cannot walk about saying such things! I am not the one with malice, she is! She is eager for this fortune, and she has chosen me as one to provide it. She chooses well—I am a prosperous man—and that is why she accuses me. There are no witnesses to this crime, and this village serves as witness to my character. I will not allow this to affect my business here. You must put a stop to it, Notkin."

Brunskill could feel the tension in Sarah Kidd as eyes turned to the constable. But he had to speak, this unseemly conflict so misplaced in his church. "I ask of you all, please talk no further here, in our church. This has to do with earthly justice and this is not the fitting place for it."

He might as well not have not spoken at all. Little Notkin puffed up with importance. "We will hear no more slander, Widow Kidd," he announced, his cheeks glistening red with perspiration. "No more, or else I will have to take measures. You have no grounds. These are empty words and so you must stop. Master Grinshaw is an important man in our village and has earned the respect of everyone here. You are but *a vagrant, a woman, from London*, and we don't know you." This was spoken as though it were the highest crime imaginable.

"Ah, you know Master Grinshaw about as well as you know me," spat the widow, stepping away from Brunskill. "You think you know him but you are in willful ignorance. This is not the only crime he has committed. How many other innocents have helped him to prosper? How many other bodies are buried hereabout?"

It was at this moment that the Grinshaws turned on their heels and left the church, the crowd parting for them as they went.

"If you say one more word," cried the constable, "I will put you in chains, Widow Kidd!"

The woman slumped against Brunskill. Her last outburst had taken what remained of her strength. His own feelings were in tumult as he stood there, his arm bracing her back. She was so wrong, so misguided. And yet he found himself more in sympathy with her, as she stood there trembling, than with his entire congregation as they looked upon him with a mix of satisfaction and disgust.

Chapter Four

———◆———

The Grove was known far and wide as a house of elegant proportion, well-maintained both in structure and grounds. As she walked past the gardens towards the chicken coop, Frances felt great satisfaction. When she and her husband had arrived at this place, refugees from the tumults in London, it had been hardly fit for habitation. The roof leaked everywhere, floors were rotted, and the garden was nothing but weeds. There were ferrets in the cellar and birds in the attics. No one had lived in the place for a generation. Frances remembered her tears, as her husband settled in to his work, having found a dry room to serve as his study. He had been puzzled, really, by her emotions, for all he needed was a fire and a table at which to write and he was happy. Perhaps that is why he survived so well those months in jail, for that is what he had: a table at which to write. He simply replicated that at the Grove, as his wife set about repairs.

She had hired workmen to repair the roof, replace floors, clear chimneys of debris. She had brought in servants to scour and clean the muck off the walls and windows. She had laid plans for the property, clearing fields, rebuilding the scattered sheds and barns, restoring paths, planting flowers that pleased her. Everything done with an eye to economy and saving, so it had all taken longer than was comfortable. Now all was in order. The fields were rented out, the chickens were giving her eggs for her market-women to sell, the kitchen garden gave her vegetables to put on the table and to preserve. With careful pruning the fruit trees were producing again and she had planted more. Old dying trees had been chopped down and used for firewood and yet enough remained to give the place a stately air. She had been busy with it, as her husband came and went from jail, as he wrote his pamphlets and printed them in London only to find himself in prison again. She would be standing with one of her men, discussing whether it was practical to try to put in a grape arbor, when she would look up at his window and think of him there in the silence of his room. There was no doubt in her mind, that he was close to God in that room and that he remained closely nestled into the Presence. And yet, when he had been near death, during that last illness, he had cried out the most terrible cries and she wondered how one going to God could sound so terrified and in such pain, even one such as her husband who had known God as a close and dear friend. The cries were terrible.

Well, one's mind moves along and one cannot make it stop, she reflected as she reached the chickens, from the happiness of being in one's home to the horrors of death. And these are a worthy distraction, listening to the clucking chickens, gold and brown and white, pecking at the dirt. It was a fine day, making one think ahead to summer, with the sunshine warm against her back. She herself did not feel the same intimacy with God as her husband had. For her it was an intermittent, fragile link, like a flickering candle, all too easily lost for long periods of time, leaving her dry and alone. But the moments of light that she did experience were what she lived for. It was not unlike that warm sun on her skin, making the cloth of her dress damp against her, a sensation of shared experience. For Matthew it had happened in the privacy of his study, but for her it was more common when she was with the Friends, in Meeting, a communal link. The Grove itself, with its busy servants and the comings and goings of family, was part of that communion. It was not simply the worldly comforts of the Grove and her own accomplishments thereof that gave her such happiness but rather the wonderful sense of orderliness and rightness about it, forging a link between herself, her fellows and her God.

She could feel Eliza behind her even before she heard the little girl's soft "Mama," the breathing, radiating warmth of her. The child's small hands grasped on to Frances' skirts, and she laughed at the chickens as they ran about. Frances thought of Sarah's young son and what it must be like to be separated. For Sarah, it was entirely to help her child that she left him back in London to be cared for by strangers. She sought his birthright and fortune. Frances' eyes swept over the Grove, beyond the smiling eyes of Eliza, and thought of her own struggle to keep it, for her daughter's sake.

Picking her daughter up, she began to make her way back to the house. The sound of hooves and the clatter of gear made her put Eliza down and walk quickly round to the front of the house. There was a fine dust obscuring the arrival of a small group of horsemen. Frances shielded her eyes as sun and dust filled the air around her. When it cleared, she saw with great delight her visitor and rushed forward to greet him.

"Ah, George, I did not know you were hereabouts," she cried, as the first man in the group dismounted and gave her a broad smile. His hat was dusty and stained over wild hair, his face thin and worn. His companions, three men, all dismounted alongside him and stood brushing the dirt from their coats as George Fox took Frances' hand. "We come from Amersham," he said to her, "and must stop with you awhile. We'll be moving towards London soon. Do you have room for us, Frances?"

"Yes, yes," she replied eagerly, smiling at his companions whom Fox introduced as Friends Talbot, Taylor, and Stubbs. They all made their way into the house as Frances' boy handled the horses and took them off to the stable. Once they had removed their cloaks and hats and gone into the kitchen to wash the grime off their necks and arms, she ushered them into the larger parlor, not quite as well-appointed as her favorite but spacious and accommodating to such a group. In many ways, with the guilt she felt over her drapery and tiles, this more spare room with its simple chairs and time-worn rugs was more suitable to her guests. The servant Deborah went to get refreshment for the men.

"How is it with the Friends here?" asked George, with his usual directness, angling himself into one of the smaller chairs. By this was meant, were any Friends in prison, and were meetings still held. Frances took an undeserved pride in her answer, given the state of things generally in the country.

"We have not been intruded upon here of late," she said. "I do not know the reason, but we have been allowed to have our meeting without interruption. I am glad of that; it means that there is less fear and so more families come." Deborah entered with a generously proportioned pitcher of ale and several cups on a tray. The men took their filled cups with gratitude.

Fox seemed pleased, and they talked of Friends elsewhere who were not so fortunate. "Mistress Fell has been arrested," he said with some gloom, "near Swarthmore, at a meeting. Her daughters have gone to London to plead with the King. She, meanwhile, goes about her business in jail, writing letters and conversing with the other Friends there." Fox himself, of course, had spent months at a time in prison, and so was well aware of the privations and dangers. Frances counted herself very fortunate for not having undergone such a test, though at times she wondered if it lowered her in Fox's eyes, that she had not had to make that sacrifice.

The conversation went on, much of it concerning Fox's missions and his plan to go to Ireland, into the very jaws of that monster, Papism. Eventually, as the three silent Friends became restive, he asked about her own life here at the Grove and how she was. She made a choice, then, to speak of Susan and her conflict, and the matter of the murdered man, because it was so much on her mind. As she told the story, Fox's face remained still. He had this way about him, this complete and utter concentration that made it seem that he was alone in the room with you. She wanted to know how to talk with Susan, to keep her in the Life but also to be sure that justice was done. She had always looked to Fox to be her guide. He was the essential spark in her conversion, and she trusted him utterly.

"I ask your advice," she said finally. "Susan's struggle has such import, for this woman and her child. I have spoken with Mistress Kidd and am convinced that she is in great need of help, and so will do what I can, but the matter of testimony is something that cannot be got around. I do not know what to say to Susan."

It was true that Fox was not one to spend time on the matters of this world. He was indifferent to his own comfort and had
no steady place of abode. He ate and drank for sustenance only
and did not talk of much beyond his fervent desire to bring more
people to the Light, and to preserve those already there. Matters of
inheritance, even of murder, were not things he found at all interesting. To him, they were indicators of how far mankind had fallen
and were things that could only be cured through conversion to the
faith. There was a long pause before he spoke.

"There is no question here, Frances. Susan knows what she
must do, to remain in the Life, which provides everything. You
must not encourage her to have doubt. There is no doubt. These
people will sort out their business, and God's will shall be done.
The only way for that is for the Friends to remain in the Truth
and not to waver, even when it might seem a good deed. It is not
a good deed, it is wrong, and not only that but might well lead to
an overweening pride in Susan, to see herself as so important in
this matter." He paused, and took a drink. Frances felt dissatisfied.
It was upsetting in its own right, to feel this unhappiness while
George Fox sat in her chamber conversing with her. She wrestled
with the feeling, understanding that in part it came from her own
attachment to worldly things, and her own anxiety about the fate
of her house and her daughter's fortune. This was not entirely
about Susan.

He went on, "Perhaps I should have a moment to meet with
Susan Harp, if I am still here on First Day. I will speak with her
then." This offer made, they returned to their discourse of Friends
far afield, and doings in London, and Fox's hope to go soon to
Ireland. As they spoke, Frances had word sent to other Friends in
the village, so that as usual Fox's visit would become a long parade
of visitors. This was Fox's way wherever he traveled, to meet with
local Friends. He was there to raise their spirits, to encourage them,
to listen to their concerns and give his advice, just as he had for
Frances. She didn't mind; it was what he needed to do, and she was
to help him in that in every way she could. Particularly given her
unworthy thoughts.

It occurred to her, as she had Fox and the others shown to their rooms, that this holding of audiences, so much an ingredient in any Fox visit, would free her to pursue her own concerns. As much as she longed for his presence and felt that it provided an essential sustenance to her vulnerable faith, she felt a very strong pull towards the mistress Kidd and her concerns. She could not leave it.

That night, Frances found sleep elusive. She lay there and felt ill at ease even as she warmed to the soft, worn sheets. The mattress itself needed restuffing, having grown hard and solid in a way that made her feel to be all edges and sharp bones. But that was not the difficulty. She found that she kept circling around the matter of the murder and the mystery of it. And then, as she forced her mind away, it found another circle to wind round and round, and that was the puzzle of her own faith and how to keep herself in it. How could she think of murder, sitting there next to George? Why could she not allow herself to think on the Seed and how to grow it? For that was wholly George's concern—he had spent the entirety of their evening meal talking of it—and he was able to bend his mind to it always. These circlings of hers went on, it seemed, for hours.

There was no staying in bed. Lighting a candle with the embers in her fireplace, she slipped on a woolen dressing-gown and made her way to the hall and down the stairs. As she entered the main hall, she was surprised by a light in the small parlor. It was very late. She knew, however, right away who it was. Fox was known for his restless nights, perhaps just the other side of the coin of his immense personal energy.

He looked up as she entered. He was sitting with a candle of his own on the table next to him, flickering, waxing and waning, with his hands in his lap. He had no book nor paper. The room was cold, with no fire, and the dark shadows made it seem colder still. He was dressed in the same plain britches and shirt that he had worn at supper, but without the ceremony of a vest or collar. Frances was painfully aware of the informality of her own garment, the woolen dressing gown, her hair pulled back into a thick braid down the back. She was embarrassed at her own temerity, opening the door when she knew full well who was behind it, when she should have just crept back up the stairs and into her room. What must he think of her.

But Fox was not someone who was at all interested in codes of behavior or dress, beyond what the Scripture called for. He greeted her simply and indicated a stool next to his chair. She set her candle on the other side of the table from his. They sat in silence for several minutes.

"I could not sleep," she said at last. "Perhaps it was the excitement of today, your arrival and our evening together. My mind is so busy, there is nothing for it but to forget sleep for a time. I sometimes come down here when I cannot sleep, and sit and read, or write letters. I can see that you are much the same."

"Not at all," he replied, his face serious, the shadows creeping around about him. "Not at all, dear Frances. I am not defeated by my thoughts, I seek them out and so come down here to be awake. That is my wish. My days are filled with sweet conversation with Friends, but this is where I am restored, not by sleep."

Fox never stooped to be agreeable or to ease others, Frances knew this. She was sorry that she had come, for here he was now, forced into conversation with her, away from what he had come downstairs to do. And yet he had gestured her in. She fought a small fierce feeling of annoyance, mingled with dismay, trapped as she was on her little stool.

Fox continued, "Stay awhile with me, Frances, you've something to talk about with me," and this invitation made her regret her annoyance. His voice was rough and thin from having spent the evening talking at supper. She felt uneasily that he saw into her mind.

"I am sorry to disturb you," she said softly. "I can remain sleepless in my chamber as much as here, and truly I do not want my troubles to weigh upon you. My matter is still the one we spoke of earlier today, of the widow and her need of help, and poor Susan Harp. I know that it is a matter for earthly justice, and it is, without doubt, a matter of very worldly things, of fortunes and misfortunes, but it is very strong in me, the desire to be of help to them both." She paused, and then plunged on. "We Friends are still in this world, George, and surely the Light is there to illuminate more than just our own souls."

"Frances," he said in nearly a whisper, "Above all, you must keep to the Seed, to the Light within, and allow it to guide you. Sometimes there are voices that push you away from the Light, that are false. They can be very persuasive. It is hard, sometimes, to remain in the Truth." He looked pained as he watched her face.

"I cannot think that this is a false voice I hear," she insisted. "It is in keeping with all that I believe. This woman has suffered a grievous wrong, and there is an evildoer who is not punished. And yes, I do know that he will meet God's judgment, but I cannot bear the suffering that this woman and her child must endure because of the evil."

"Stiff pride," he said firmly. "That is what it is. You must resist it. Foolish pride, to think that you as a woman here in this village can discover the murderer and bring him to justice. Why do you think so? Why do you think it is your place to do this, and not for someone else? You are a mere woman, you are not the constable, nor do you hold any office that would make you responsible or provide you with powers to do this task."

His honesty and directness, something she had grown accustomed to, was disconcerting when directed at herself. His wide-open eyes held hers, and they did not waver in the least. He had never in his life, she thought, known a moment of doubt. He was on his path and never looked to the right nor to the left. She, however, felt herself veering this way and that, never sure, always seeking and stumbling. She wanted so much to grab on to his hand and allow him to pull her along in his wake. But she could not.

"I understand your words, Friend George," she said warmly. "And they are words with which most of our people would agree. I know I am wayward, but I feel such sympathy for Sarah Kidd. I will help her, even if it is in a small way. I know too that I am a weak woman, so that my help may not be enough, but perhaps I can be of some use to her." She did not talk of her aspiration to speak with the constable, for she knew what George would say to that. She wondered at herself, such defiance, towards someone she loved so dearly and admired so much.

The intimacy of this moment, the two of them close with candles burning low, the chill of the room, all conspired to create a certain strangeness of which Frances was more and more aware. Fox did not reply to her arguments, and they fell into silence there in the flickering darkness. She could see that his thoughts were drifting in a different direction, away from her, and she found this to be a relief. She rose slowly, nodded to him, took her candle and returned to her bedchamber.

Once settled back into bed, she fell into a troubled sleep. A dream captured her. The field rose up around her, and all was black and gray. She could feel the wet grass against her bare feet as she stood there, felt a cold breeze through her dressing gown, pressing the gown against her legs. She was alone, but then there was a presence. It was a darkness even darker than that all around her, a living presence, a threat. She could hear its steady breathing, heavy and low. At first it seemed far across the field from her, but then suddenly it was up close, and she felt the brush of something against her back.

Counterpane off the bed, she was sat straight up and gasped for air. Gray light seeped through the shutters. The night was done.

The dream caught Nathaniel unawares. He was not much one for dreaming, falling into a deep, dreamless sleep most nights. Sarah would share with him, each morning, her nocturnal adventures, believing they were all forecasts of the future, heavy with the weight of all her hopes and fears. But for him, the night's sleep was empty, dark and solitary. So to lie beside the stream, nestled in amongst the roots of a widespread willow tree, and be caught up in a moment from his past, felt like a visitation.

The sight of her again, the lift of her chin and the way she would purse her lips when considering something of importance, was too rich a reminder. Sarah's youthful face, soft and round, and the expressions that flitted across it as he spoke with her. In the dream, she stood there beside the stream and looked at him, a small smile dancing on her lips. As she gazed on him, her hat pushed back on her head and her coat too warm for the summer, he reached out to take her hand. She gave him such a look then and turned away.

He awoke, solitary, only the soft sound of sheep murmuring in the distance. It would be a long walk today, but he hoped to make it to Chalfont St. James. He gave no further thought to the dream, and distracted himself with another favorite song.

> It was a maid of my country
> As she came by a hawthorn tree,
> As full of flow'rs as might be seen
> She marvel'd to see the tree so green...

Perhaps when they were together again he would take Sarah away from London, to some small village, where he could get a living. Away from the filth and the crowds. He'd been a Londoner by accident, having come there as a young boy to find his way in the world, but it was the fields and the forests that felt like home to him. Maybe he could return to his home in Leominster, after all these years, and make his way there. The thought fed his mind for the next few miles as he began the climb up over the next hill.

Midway up he took another long view of what had come before, the rolling fields and the stream, and let himself catch his breath. He could see down below a figure walking at a pace quicker than his own, equipped with walking stick. Perhaps he had come on to the road at Amersham. Nathaniel paused. He was not sure of company, but he felt it unfriendly to turn around and keep walking with this man right behind him, they two the only travelers on this road. The man waved in greeting and picked up his pace even more as Nathaniel waited impatiently.

"Hello," said the man as he came close. Nathaniel could see he was a large young man, fleshy and strong, and there was something soft about him in the curve of his eyes and his nose. He was dressed for travel, a light coat to catch the dirt of the road and sturdy boots. He had a friendly smile which seemed at odds with his eyes, darting this way and that. Nathaniel was cautious.

"I am traveling to Chalfont St. James," continued the man with a heartiness that seemed too much for the moment. "Samuel Prosper, in the household at the Grove."

"I don't know the Grove," replied Nathaniel with a shrug. "I'm not from this part of the country. I am called Nathaniel Kidd, returning home to London after some time away. I have been on the road for many days."

"Ah then, we can walk together," the man said inevitably, and Nathaniel's heart sank a little. "I will be your guide, Nathaniel Kidd, for I know this country. I was off to Amersham to visit my old father, and am glad to be returning to the Chalfonts. London, heh?" He fell intro stride with Nathaniel as they continued their walk south. "That is a place where much happens."

"Aye," said Nathaniel. He tried to be as close-mouthed as possible when traveling with strangers, but this one made that hard. "It's a busy place. And now, with—well, all unsettled"—he didn't know the man's politics, after all—"it can be dangerous as well."

"So you have family there?" asked Samuel, relentless in his quest for information.

"Yes, I have a family," replied Nathaniel, walking a bit faster. They were now at the crest of the hill and could look down to the rolling fields around the Chalfonts and the wandering of the Misbourne shining like a silver ribbon through the green. "It will be good to be at home."

"Ah, a family of your own," said the man with a short laugh, and Nathaniel began to see that he would get to know Samuel. "I would be a happy man with that. But I am only a tutor in the Grove household, tutoring two little girls in their grammar, so my fortune is yet to be made. It's a hard life for those of us who have nothing. I saw my father in the hope that he would give me something with which to make a start for London, but he was unwilling."

They were now on the downward slope, picking their way carefully through the dusty ruts in the road. A wagon was up ahead, heading in their direction. As they approached the town, the road came to life. He considered lapsing into silence, perhaps that would put an end to Samuel's complaining. But he found he had something to say.

"I went to London first as a boy," he reminisced, "with nothing but pennies in my pocket. I found work soon enough, on the wharves, and worked hard. Those were bad times, for sure, with the War—I could have been caught up by either side, I knew that. I stayed away from trouble. Work was hard to find, and I was but a small boy. But here I am, with much to be thankful for. I earn my keep and that of my wife and child." He patted his bag with some satisfaction.

The two men moved to the side of the road to let the wagon pass. The driver was an old man in a filthy shirt, and the wagon was heavy with barrels rolling recklessly about. This was not someone who cared about his work, thought Nathaniel. Once it was past, they took to the road again. The pace of the tutor seemed to slow as they approached the town. His conversation was relentless.

"Some of us have God's ear and others not," said Samuel, his smile now entirely gone. "I am a good Christian, but I think about why trials are my lot where others have it easy. As I say, I am a good Christian and I do right by others in this world, and yet I see those who are lost to God's grace go about and grab on to riches with a laugh. My father says I must make my own money, and make my own way, but he is but a mean, unfeeling man whose own religion has nothing to do with the Word of God." The last words were almost spat, but then the young man drew himself up and paused in his walk. "I am sorry, Nathaniel Kidd, I mean not to show disrespect to my father. I do not know what I am saying."

Nathaniel allowed a silence to fall between them, clearly more welcome to him than to his companion. They continued their walk until a small grove of trees encouraged escape from the summer sun and a midday meal. Nathaniel shared his bread, and the tutor's contribution, a bit of dried meat, was meager but welcome. They took long draughts from their water-flasks and allowed themselves to lie out under the trees' shade for a rest.

"If I could but keep on going after Chalfont St. James, I would," Samuel declared, his eyes closed, his pack underneath his head. "But I have promised Mistress Bright that I will serve her for the year, and it is my hope she might provide me with more payment so that I can then leave in good conscience." He coughed. "They say London is in much excitement now, that the Protector is ill and won't be long for this world. There is talk of a change. Living in this village, I will not be a part of any of it."

"Ah, I've no need to be in the midst of that disorder," Nathaniel smiled. "Whether it be those Fifth Monarchists or the Quakers or those who want to bring back the king, it's none of my business and I stay clear of it. My people were for the Parliament, and so was I. Now we've no Parliament and just Master Cromwell to lead us. Most men be fools." He closed his eyes to discourage further talk but Prosper did not seem to notice.

"You're a man of wealth," he said almost accusingly, touching Nathaniel's bag. "How did you come by it?"

Nathaniel told him about the bailiff's position and the work he had done on the estate. "'Tis nothing marvelous about it, my friend," he finished, "I found the position and I worked hard. What I earned is for my family, and our life together."

The tutor did not seem persuaded and simply guffawed. They fell into silence, for which Nathaniel was grateful. After a short time they roused themselves and continued on the road.

Now more people were about, a farmer leading an elderly horse, two tall women with baskets and a brisk walk. Cottages began to break up the monotony of the fields. As the day grew late, Prosper gestured to a road that veered off to the west.

"Here is where I leave you, friend," he said somewhat ostentatiously with a tap of his hat. "This way is shorter to the Grove, but you will want to continue straight on into the village, not too many miles ahead. Get yourself to Grinshaw's inn. Perhaps we will meet again." And with that he turned and set off down his road. Nathaniel felt relief as he turned to continue towards the village.

He was coming up now on a small bridge over the Misbourne, the stream shallow here, clear and cool. He decided to stop for a time and wash his feet in the stream. Even with the earlier rest, he felt unusually tired. Perhaps it was his companion, troubled with some matter, that had wearied him. Plunging his feet into the fresh clean water, he soaked the dirt of the road off before stretching them out in the sun to dry. The warmth of the sun did its work and before too long he had drifted off again into sleep.

Chapter Five

———•◆•———

Preparing his sermon was the part of his work that Arthur Brunskill loved best. He loved the very act of it, sitting down at his worn oak table early in the morning, a table that had served many priests before him, and settling in his chair. He loved getting out the paper, folding it neatly, his pen damp with ink and poised in the air. A few essential texts sat on the far edge of the table, available for ready reference, including the New Testament that he had taken with him to Cambridge. He would always begin by writing, at the top of the sheaf of paper, the date and the citation for the biblical text he was to gloss. Then he would sit there for hours, writing in bursts followed by long periods of thought. It was all very enjoyable, all of it, and what he was made for.

He would have liked to remain at Cambridge and teach, but that was not his calling, at least according to his teachers there. They advocated for pastoral work, and felt it would suit him. He had his doubts—he loved the library, loved reading and writing, loved tutorials—but he did as they told him and here he was, a fortunate man, in a much-coveted post. And yet the congregation interested him not at all. He found their visits, their problems and their worries, beyond his understanding. He knew what to do with a sermon, since it followed a familiar, never-varying outline, relied upon authority, and provided a lesson to be learned. But what to do with a man who is convinced that his neighbor is a witch and has been making his cow refuse to give milk? What to do with a woman sick with misery because she rolled over on her infant during the night, smothering the life out of him? The husband and wife who refuse to live together any longer? The deaf child, whose father abandons him by the road? It went on and on, the endless round of misery, the need for answers. He had none. He could write a thorough and intelligent gloss of Paul's understanding of grace, but he could not answer the people most in need of that very thing.

Now, as he sat there and touched the coarse paper, watching the ink soak in as he began to write, he did not feel quite the usual degree of satisfaction. Too much of his mind was elsewhere, with the woman who lodged in his storeroom. He was not at all sure that his visit to the Grinshaws had yielded anything but discord. This was not a good thing, he knew, as much as he wanted to be honest and open with all. He had made a mistake, a mistake that could be very important to the widow who depended upon him. Why had she chosen him, what could have possessed her? No doubt because there was no one else to serve as her fool.

With all of this occupying his mind, there was a sharp sense of frustration as he contemplated the nearly empty sheet of paper in front of him. This was not going well, not well at all. His life was disrupted, the things that gave him pleasure were empty of it now, and he was plagued by a constant sense of being inadequate to the requirements of his office. He blamed the widow and her troubles for a good part of this. If she were not here he would have written a full page by now, and be deep into the words of Paul to the Ephesians.

He heard knocking on the door to the rectory and the soft footsteps of his housekeeper, the ample Mrs. Corning, as she made her way to the entrance. Then, a short time later, the shuffling of feet in his direction (it nearly drove him mad, this shuffling, day in and day out). She tapped on the door and then came in before he had time to respond (again, maddening). Mistress Bright was announced, and so again the shuffling of the feet, there and back again, as the lady was escorted to his small study.

He had of course seen her about the town, and admitted to a certain degree of curiosity, given her social place in the community and her conversion to Quakerism. He thought her a fine-looking woman, slender and upright, with a clear gaze and a nicely proportioned face within the confines of her hat and veil. The elegance of her dress seemed at odds with what little he knew of Quakers: the dress was fashionable and, while simple, it was made of good material, a pretty sky blue with dark gray trim. She moved into the room gracefully and he rose and took her hand, gesturing to her to sit down on the one good chair in the room, his own. He moved to settle himself upon a bench. Mrs. Corning slowly beat her retreat after unsuccessfully urging upon Mistress Bright some refreshment.

"I hope that I am not intruding upon your work, Master Brunskill," the lady said with a sad smile. "I know too that we have not been formally introduced, so I hope you will not be shocked by my visit. I feel we have something to talk about."

"Indeed?" he asked, surprised. He was not sure he was up to converting a Quaker.

"Yes," she looked slightly discomfited, as though she knew what he was thinking. "It is my understanding that you have been look-ing after Mistress Sarah Kidd, in her difficulties here in Chalfont St. James. You have been a good friend to her, Master Brunskill, much to your credit. I too have come to know Mistress Kidd, and I would like to be of service to her as well. I find her situation to be quite unjust, for both her and her child." She spoke warmly, urgently, her eyes never leaving his face. "I know that you and I are from—well, we think differently on some matters, but I hope that we can find a common bond in providing aid to Mistress Kidd."

Brunskill was relieved. While he felt confident in his faith and in his theological arsenal, he had heard that Quakers were wily and knowledgeable enough of Scripture to make any kind of reli-gious debate a hard-fought battle with no certainty of victory. Truly Scripture had a wax nose, as Luther had said, and those schooled just a little were the most dangerous in its abuse. Women especially could be troublesome, their animal spirits and childishness getting in the way of true understanding. But this was a matter of Sarah Kidd and her accusation, and this he could manage.

"Let us talk then," he said, "for it is clear we have much more in common than one might have thought."

Their conversation was long and with a degree of sympathy that neither Frances nor Brunskill would have predicted beforehand.

They compared notes as to their view of Sarah, their understanding of the matter, and what actions they had each taken up to this point. They considered the possible guilt of Grinshaw and his wife. The talk spilled over into the afternoon, so pleased were both to find someone with whom to explore the various aspects of the matter. Towards the end of their talk, Frances, being of a practical turn of mind, asked about how they were to move forward, to uncover what had actually happened to Nathaniel and thus to resolve the matter to everyone's satisfaction.

"If indeed something happened at the inn that night, or if Nathaniel Kidd were a guest there, surely the servants would know," Brunskill said slowly. "If someone were to speak to them..."

"If they be not too affrighted of their master and mistress," Frances interjected. "They have said naught up to now. It would seem unlikely they would freely talk with you or me, Master Brunskill." She thought for a moment. "Ah, but perhaps if one of my servants could converse with them, more would be readily shared. There's a thought." She smiled, thinking of her servant Ann Barwell with her ready laugh and round figure. She knew that George Fox would not approve, not in the least. Here she was, closeted with a Church of England priest, planning a secret campaign of truth-gathering having to do with a murder. She wondered that she did not feel badly about it. She had thoroughly enjoyed conversing with the priest.

They agreed upon this plan and Brunskill saw her out, Mrs. Corning lurking ineffectually in the background. He had no doubt that the whole village would know of this visit and come to their own conclusions as to its purpose. A meeting with a Quaker woman. It was no matter to him, what any of them thought. He returned to his tidy desk, to the thick paper and dark ink, and to his thoughts on Paul.

A spring storm was blowing in when Sarah Kidd made her way towards the Grinshaws' inn that evening. The rain had not yet begun but the wind was up. She kept pushing the strands of hair that had escaped her scarf from her eyes and mouth as she made her way along the Market Street of Chalfont St. James. She could, of course, feel the eyes of the villagers upon her, as she rounded the turn and headed up the road that would take her to the inn. They were all idiots, she thought fiercely, fools, stupid cattle who feasted upon the miseries of others. They did not care that one of their own had carried out a horrible crime, because the victim was a stranger, not known to them. They were blind, mucking about their little village. She had seen much in her brief life and wanted no part of this paltry existence. She longed for London. She had been born and raised there, and loved its web of streets where one could get lost in an hour. She loved the Babel-like frenzy of voices at the shops, she loved that when she listened in she could hear the full array of humanity, from students to tradespeople to beggars. Music, to her. Here, in this village, the notes were thin and few, and constantly repeating. It was driving her mad.

The approach to the inn was neat and tidy as always. Someone must be out sweeping the walk more than once a day, she thought angrily as she made her way along the path. She had spent her first night in the village in this inn and had had her encounter with Nathaniel as she lay in bed sleepless. Now, she returned, because she wished to be with him again, even just his spirit. She couldn't do this alone. Simply to see him gaze upon her as she lay there, both of them silent, would be the refreshment she so desperately needed. She still had a small sum, and now that she was in the priest's care could use it for purposes other than feeding herself. This would allow her the precious night with Nathaniel.

She strode up alongside the inn and saw the Grinshaws' boy Tom taking a bucket of food scraps out the kitchen door, to the side of the building. She slipped in front of him, so that he could not avoid her.

"Good day," she said in her best, friendly tone, "I will be needing a room again tonight—are there rooms free at the inn?" She hoped that her voice was suitably light and easy. She knew that her appearance was anything but that.

The boy, a thin awkward young man with hair so dirty it was hard to determine its color, visibly shook as he saw her and tried to brush past, the contents of his pail spilling over on to his none-too-clean trousers. She put her arm out in front of him so that he could go no further, and he shook all the more. What did he think she was, a demon?

"Tell me, now, are there rooms to let? I must know," her voice was tougher now, stronger. Her eyes sought out his and he could not help but look at her.

"Aye, the lodgers from yesterday have cleared out, but for one," he said quickly, as though by saying this as speedily as possible he could pretend not having said it at all. He was incapable of lying to this woman, she was so frightening to him. He did not want her to touch him. He thought perhaps she was a witch. She had the persistence and stubbornness of one. His life was hard enough without a witch interested in him.

Sarah left him then and returned to the path leading to the front entrance. As she pulled at the front door the first splattering of rain hit the porch. The entrance hall seemed crowded with people but once she had adjusted her eyes to the dimness she realized it was one large man, alongside Daniel Grinshaw. She didn't like the look of him. He was big, broad, with hard dark eyes and a large nose surrounded by broken veins. His clothes were of fine quality and clean, which made him somewhat conspicuous. He stared at her without apology, but then she was used to this in the village. She knew that she gave people something to stare at and felt no need for an apology on either end.

Grinshaw, of course, was furious at her appearance and began to shout. "Get away from here, woman! Go back to your hole! Go back to London, you are not welcome in this place!" He moved toward her, but the large man put his hand on his arm and pulled him back. "Peace, Grinshaw, you could have the constable here before long."

Sarah smiled grimly; an odd defender, this strange man. She was not afraid of Grinshaw or his violence. Indeed, she wanted to encourage it, to let everyone see this side to his nature. She had no need of this big man, no wish for him to come to her aid.

"I am here as a paying lodger," she said in as strong a voice as she could muster. "I would like a room for the night. I have stayed here before, it is a very comfortable inn." She could see the rise in color on Grinshaw's face, and saw, with a certain amount of pleasure, his hands turn into fists.

"We have no rooms!" he exploded, "We are full, there is no room for you here."

"I know this is not true," she returned. "I have just come from speaking with your boy, and he says the inn is empty except for one guest." She turned her eyes upon the large man. "No doubt that is you, sir."

"Aye," he acknowledged, "The boy speaks the truth."

"My coin is good," Sarah said to Grinshaw, who was breathing heavily. "I have done you no harm, Master Grinshaw, and surely my spending a night under your roof cannot be frightening to you. I am but a small woman with nothing, with no one. All I ask is for a bed for the night, a place to rest for one night."

"Ah I am not frighted of you, woman, but you speak of me to all as a murderer. And in church! I will not stand for it, I won't. I don't have to give you a room, even if you rain coin down on me."

The big man seemed amused by this struggle between the two and clapped the innkeeper on the shoulder. "Give her the room, Grinshaw, there's a good man. It will make you look all the more generous, and let people know you care little what this widow says or what anybody thinks." He laughed and gave Grinshaw a little shove. Sarah thought it all very strange, but she was quite willing to accept the man as her brief champion. He seemed to be enjoying himself.

There was a long moment of silence as Sarah Kidd stared at Grinshaw, motionless. He finally stepped to one side, to allow her in. "I will let Mr. Stroud vouch for you. Take a room, if that's what you want, though if you bring any vermin into this house, it will cost you," he said with a kind of defeat. "Sally!" he roared for the maidservant, who came tumbling down the stairs within a minute in answer to his bellow. Sarah could see she had won and felt a moment's satisfaction, mingled with the warm anticipation of seeing Nathaniel.

"Any chamber," the innkeeper ordered the maidservant, and Sarah was escorted up the stairs as the two men watched from the hall. She was ready for her night.

Ann Barwell was still considered a recent addition to the village of Chalfont St. James, even though she had arrived there, with her father, fifteen years before. She had no memory of any other place. From the little her father later told her, they had traveled from a good-sized village near Oxford after the deaths of her mother and baby brother. Those deaths had caused some sort of unsettling in her father's mind, and he gave up a good living as a bricklayer to take to the road. Joseph Barwell never spoke of his wife and son.

She and he lived in a small cottage to the south of the village, and he took up day-laboring on nearby farms. He was a short man inclined to muscle or fat depending on the circumstance. He did not go with her to church but sent her every Sunday, walking with their neighbors the Satterbees. She could contrive a small list of things that she knew about him, such as these, but that was all. Their discourse was by habit brief and practical. She took care, from an early age, of the kitchen fire and the cooking, and had planted a small kitchen garden to the side of the house. He would go off to whatever work there was, sometimes stopping off on the way home at the Satterbee house (he and Ben Satterbee got along well), have her serve him his dinner and then sit in the corner mending this or that or staring into the fire. Such was their life together.

During her days now, of course, she was at the Grove. She had been taken on as general maidservant a couple of years before. There were those in the community who were reluctant to hire on at the Grove, because the Brights were Quakers. She felt no such reluctance, being eager for the work, eager to get out of the cottage and to be with people. She found Mistress Bright to be a generously minded mistress, especially since this was Ann's first position and so she did not know anything when she started. She knew how to keep a kitchen, and could take on whatever small chore was asked of her, but at first she needed much direction. Mistress Bright was always careful with her, never sharp, even when Ann could see a brief flash of impatience in her eyes. She had grown used to a quick cuff around the ear from her father when something did not go right, so this kind of forbearance was strange and wonderful. After a time she stopped flinching.

Now, she felt a great attachment to the Bright family. There was a small bit of pride as she walked up to the big house, admiring its lawns and gardens like she had anything to do with them. She took pleasure in watching Eliza play amongst the chicks, and helping Jane tend to her sewing. Ann had known Matthew Bright, of course, but he was a distant figure, kindly enough but his pastimes and work seemed to revolve around his study. She remembered once watching Matthew and Frances Bright walking in the garden, the mistress reaching out and taking her husband's hand, shaking it gently, he turning his face to her and smiling. But for the most part they seemed to walk in a solitary silence, his continual reverie cloaking the two of them in a thoughtful remove.

She felt she would devote herself to Frances Bright and her children and call that a satisfying life. She did all that the mistress asked of her and did it to the best of her ability. She knew that she had become better at her work, that she was a true help to the household. Now, Mistress Bright was asking something else of her, and it made her uneasy.

Her mistress had come upon her in the early afternoon as she busied herself with sweeping the main floor rooms. She found this task the most unsatisfying, in that it had to be repeated frequently and the results of her labor were so transitory. It only took an afternoon for the floors to look as they had before she swept. She rather wished she could keep everyone out of these rooms. As she swept, humming to herself a little song that Elizabeth Satterbee had taught her, Frances Bright came up to her and stilled her broom.

She had said it all in a very every-day sort of voice, that made one feel that this was just a usual task, but it clearly was not. As Ann walked along to the Grinshaws' inn, bearing with her a carefully packed basket of eggs, she wondered at her own agreement to the task. Mistress Bright had asked her to take the eggs to the maidservant at the inn, and to then inquire about whether that poor man who had been murdered had ever stayed at the inn. She was to simply ask that direct question and observe the maidservant, taking her answer back to Mistress Bright.

"You see, Ann," said Frances with a friendly look, "I would very much like to ask that question of the girl, but she would be afraid of me and would no doubt not say a word. Her response to me would have more to do with who I am rather than what I was asking. I am interested in the answer, for reasons of my own, but I know that you are more likely to gain it than me. There is no harm in asking such a question. The whole village is talking about this. I am trying to be a help to the poor widow of the murdered man and to help her find the answers she seeks. Can I ask for your help in this?"

Ann had seen no other way but to agree. She was simply to ask a question. But it made her uneasy.

The lane was empty except for her, tromping along with her eggs. Another clear blue day, harbinger of summer, and the air was heavy with the scent of grass. Waves of birds made their way from one bushy shrub to another, clogging the branches and making the plants seem alive, in movement.

She turned onto a small track that was a shortcut to the inn. She wouldn't mind altogether if she came across Tom Maltman, the Grinshaws' boy. He was worth taking a look at. He was a couple of years younger than she, but there weren't that many boys in the village to choose from. One time an old woman, the one they called Mother Grime, had looked at her and said she'd marry late, which worried her.

As she rounded a corner and came out of a small copse of woods, there in fact stood the boy, standing by the pigpen throwing in some slop. His shirt was filthy and he reeked. Clearly it had already been a long day of such work for him. He looked over at her and grinned. There was a dab of damp mud that ran from a corner of his mouth to his ear which made the smile look all the greater. She waved at him and held up her basket.

"We had a great laying of eggs," she said, "and you know they don't keep. It isn't the day for Mary Stout to carry the eggs to market, so Mistress Bright asked that I bring these over, figuring the inn could always use them."

Tom looked at the basket. "I'll fetch Sally," he said, turning to go. Ann quickly reached out and touched his arm.

"No, there's no need," she said hastily, "I can walk them to the kitchen myself." This stopped Tom, but he stood there waiting, expecting her to begin marching towards the house. She stood where she was, pretending she had all the time in the world. She found she didn't quite know how to do this.

"So," she said in a lingering sort of way, digging one of her feet toes-first into the dirt, "Do you have a great many lodgers now?"

Tom looked knowingly at her and chuckled. He knew what she was about. "Oh no, we're nearly empty," he shrugged. "Just the widow. The master weren't too happy about that!"

Ann felt that luck, for once, was with her. Suddenly this became very, very easy. "The widow?"

"Aye, she's troubling us once again. You know, she stayed with us when she first came to the village, one night. We didn't know who she was then, a'course. We as sure as pie know now!" He chuckled again and leaned against the pigpen fence, getting comfortable, telling the story. "She showed up early today, scared me to death, she's something of the witch about her. I didn't want to talk to her. I don't scare like that very much, but she's not one of us. Nobody talks to her but the priest." A pause, and then, "Well, I weren't all that scared, she's but a woman."

"Why is she staying at the inn?"

"God knows. Or maybe it's the Devil who knows. The master gave her the room, that's all I can say." Done with the story, Tom turned to go. "I must get on with my tasks," he said apologetically.

"I know," said Ann, "but I wonder, did the murdered man ever stay at this inn? Do you know? For sure," she continued hastily, "your master had naught to do with his death, but it could be that the man was here for awhile before it—it happened."

Tom stared at her. "Who else says he did, besides the widow?

Are there those talking to you, Miss Ann? Or have you been talking with the widow? Curiosity killed the cat, you know—women and their talk!" He spit out the last words in disgust. "You won't hear any talk from me, that you won't!" And then he turned and stomped off in the direction of the road. Ann trembled as he walked away. All pleasurable thoughts of him taking her hand, and other things, were swept away in that moment.

But then, as she began to walk back to the Grove, completely forgetting the mission of the eggs, she thought, there it is, he didn't say No.

Sarah Kidd lay herself down on the bed and felt her body ease into the mattress. The faded blue coverlet was worn and soft. It was like lying on what she imagined velvet to feel like. There was a rickety table in the corner of the room with a washbasin and pitcher, and a simple chair beside it. A chest was at the foot of the bed, for any belongings she wished to stow there. The floor was swept and there was a tidy stack of candles in a basket by the small fireplace. No one had come to light the fire yet, but it was a warm spring day and so she did not mind. The afternoon was waning and she had nothing to do but lie here and think about Nathaniel.

She missed her small son, whose name was John Edward, but he did not come to her as vividly as Nathaniel. An infant has no presence, there is just the desire to hold and to love, but nothing, really, to remember the small child by. But as for Nathaniel, her memory was rich with him, full of him, and even though she had seen his bones he felt alive to her. They had not seen one another for nearly seven months when he began his journey back to London, and their life together as man and wife before that had been brief. But it encompassed her life as a grown woman, and she accorded it importance.

She sat up and removed her shoes, throwing them onto the floor with a clatter. After that she laid herself down again, leaning back into the coverlet, spreading her arms wide across the bed. Her memories of Nathaniel came flooding over her as she lay there. She knew that he was present in this room, and looked forward to the night when he would make himself known to her. She thought of him as she had met him, when her older brother Ned had clapped him on the back in the family's small kitchen, smiled at her and said this here is our Sarah, and Nathaniel Kidd had brazenly looked at her with those startling green eyes. Ned and Nathaniel had found work together, on the docks of London, loading and unloading barges. They had taken to walking home together, since Nathaniel roomed with a family down the road from the small place that Sarah and Ned shared with their mother. Sarah began to find herself out front, washing the front steps, at the very time when the men came down the lane after their work was done.

The two of them started to walk together of an evening, and he told her about his earlier life, in Leominster. He could have had a living there but was restless. A friend had made his way in London, and so that was where Nathaniel went to make his fortune.

Sarah had listened to this and thought, here was a man who had been unafraid to go out into the world beyond his town. She liked his green eyes, his dark, resonant voice, the way in which he would hold her hand as though each finger were precious cargo. His skin was a warm shade of olive, in the way of Welshmen, and his hair black and curly. Not a tall man but alive and strong, he had steady work on the barges. His humor was light, and he had friends. There was no one to speak ill of him.

She thought of their wedding day, and the night that followed. In spite of all her mother's warnings, it had all been so easy, so loving.

Now, as she lay on the bed by herself, she could feel the warmth that Nathaniel always brought about in her. When the maidservant knocked and came in to light the fire she realized it had grown dark outside and that the night had begun. She observed the maid, a slight blond thing who had an angry look to her, and waited until the servant had shut the door behind her before lying herself back down on the bed. It was like she would never leave it, ever.

Chapter Six

———•◆•———

The house had been full of Friends that day. Frances, alert to Ann's return, found herself distracted by the comings and goings of all these Friends, all of them eager for a moment with the man everyone saw as the leader of the Society. She found the constant visitors a strain as they made their way into the hall, boots stomping their way into the parlor, endless hospitality required, the monotonous sound of voices in conversation. Fox's nasal, clear voice carried above all, exhorting his followers to stay with the faith, to see to its nourishment. Everyone found it very inspirational, but Frances was tired. As well, there was always the risk that the authorities would decide that Fox's audiences comprised an illegal gathering and that they would be descended upon and taken to jail. This kind of harassment was capricious, unpredictable, which made it all the more terrifying. Up to now, Frances had always escaped its threat, but she was aware of its possibility. As she moved about the kitchen, giving directions to the cook Meg and her girl Betty, she found herself listening for the sound of horses' hooves on the pebbly drive out front. Whether it be yet more eager Friends or soldiers bristling with weapons, both were a trial and tribulation.

Suddenly Fox appeared in the doorway to the kitchen. He looked tentative, so she gestured for him to come in.

"Frances, a moment to talk with you would be welcome," Fox said quietly, and they drew off to the side of the room to sit on the bench together. "Your girls, Frances—they need a tutor, or so I hear. The last one that was here for your older daughter—"

Frances interrupted quickly, "Yes, we haven't had a tutor for a few years now," not wanting to go into the details of the story.

"I know that you need someone to help with their education. I have someone in mind, a young man, a Friend, completely trustworthy and with some small experience as a tutor. He has a good understanding of Latin, some of Greek, and can tutor in English grammar and also arithmetic. His name is Nicholas Brown. I think you would find him quite satisfactory, and he is in need of a position."

She could not really deny George this, as much as she had begun to think of ending Jane's education altogether, troubling as the incident had been with the last tutor, and teaching Eliza herself. She didn't like that this tutor was a young man, preferring someone old and stooped.

"Of course, please send him to me," she replied. "I am very grateful for this. I will be glad to bring Mr. Brown into our household here."

Fox coughed. "Good, good. Now, there is the matter of which you spoke to me the other night." He looked over to see that the cook and her girl were deep into soaping the dishes at the other end of the kitchen and then continued, "I know you want to do good in the world, Frances, it's your nature. But I ask you to be careful in this matter. It is one where you could find yourself far from the principles that shape our faith. Far indeed." He warmed to his topic. "Beware of the whore's cup, Frances, the worldly ways of the nations, and stay true to the everlasting gospel. That is what I say to you."

Again she had the uncomfortable feeling that he could see into her mind, and she had a moment of worry that Ann would choose this moment to appear and spill forth her conversation with the inn's maidservant. Tumbling along with those thoughts a great fear of wishing to deceive George, which then made her circle back to his words, giving them weight.

"I thank you for your care for me," she replied. "I also am glad of your instruction in the dangers this matter presents for me. I will be careful, Friend George." She decided to not go any further, but to look him right in the eye with her own version of the truth.

There was the sound of pounding feet and the rustle of skirts as Ann burst into the room, her face flushed. She looked down at her basket of eggs and carefully lowered them on to a table before turning to her mistress. It was hard to say how many of them had survived the trip to the inn and back again. Seeing Frances there with Fox, she hesitated, put her hand to her mouth, did a slight curtsy and made her way back out of the kitchen.

"Now Frances. It is not an easy thing for a woman to head a household. I hope that if you bring this young man Brown into your home, he will be a help to you and guide your girls. He is strong in the faith. You must stay low and quiet with the truth, Frances, do not let your sympathies get in the way of that." Then he rose, gave her his hand so that she might rise too. "The people of your town have been most, most welcoming to me. It is of course my hope that this terrible event of which you spoke is resolved peaceably." He gave her one more searching look, which caused her much pain, and then turned and left the kitchen to return to the gathering in the parlor. She waited a moment or two before going in search of Ann.

The room had darkened. Sarah had left the curtains open but there was no moon. It had become cold, as the fire began to turn into embers, so she had undone and removed her dress and pulled the counterpane and coverlet both up over herself. She thought about the Grinshaws, husband and wife, sleeping in this very house, found it disgusting to think of them pawing at each other, snoring, the night's spittle running down their chins, nightclothes crumpled and damp with their sweat as they tossed and turned. She was so very lonely now. She had grown up sharing a bed—an older sister, who had died of a terrible brain fever when Sarah was twelve—and of course it wasn't too many years after that that she began sharing one with Nathaniel as her husband. She was used to having someone next to her, warm, turning in the night, softly breathing, feet touching. Her thoughts moved to poor Arthur Brunskill, alone in his own bed, no goodly priest's wife yet to share it with, and the lady Frances Bright, a widow like herself. All of them sharing this same night, perhaps looking out their own windows at the starry darkness.

But then, she did have someone. She lay there and hoped to conjure him up from nothing. His unsettled ghost, compelled to stay where the body had separated from the soul. She was certain of what Brunskill would say to that. It was a silly notion, one that old wives told, and boys who knew nothing. She knew where his body lay, she had seen to that. But where was Nathaniel now, his spirit? Resting with God, or in some sort of sleep until the Final Judgment? If even theologians could disagree about that, then she could imagine him here, in this house, waiting for the justice he deserved.

She began to softly say his name, letting the syllables rest on her tongue, as she closed her eyes. She knew when she opened them again he would be there, at the foot of the bed. She felt the familiar ache, the physical need for him, sharp and insistent. Her hands felt for the warm places, moved with ease and she began to feel herself expand and open. After a time, thoughts became confused and her mind's images of her husband began to flow into one another. She lost herself. Cushioned, soft, warm in the bed, the usual creakings and mutterings of the house seeming to fade away as she lay there. Her breathing came and went, came and went. The bedding folded and refolded to move as she did. She began to feel too warm and pushed away at it.

Then she felt something come at her, resisting her pushing hands, surrounding her. Suddenly she was awake, and Nathaniel seemed far away as she felt the thick pillow pushed against her face. She could not move it. There was a presence in the room, a heaviness, and she could hear someone grunting. Heavy hands against the pillow, pressing down on her. Her breath was rapid and shallow but then she was struggling with it, could not get a breath out, as the pressure continued against her. She fought against it, her arms flailing about in the darkness, touching nothing but air, as the pressing on her face continued relentlessly, almost soundlessly. Her struggle came even as she knew (and thought about this later) that she was dying. It was as though her body were separate from her mind, going about what it must do to stay alive. She had no say in it.

Time slowed, she exhausted herself, and she could do naught but let her arms rest on the bed, feeling herself to be falling, falling, as the pillow was held tight against her. Then, some sort of racket outside, the sound of horses' hooves in the sandy yard, a man's voice, muffled so that she could not hear the words, even as she felt herself falling, but she could hear the urgency.

The pillow fell away, she heard the door shut, and she noisily gasped for breath as she threw the covers off the bed.

No more sleep was to be had that night. Sarah Kidd lay there, her eyes on the door, and listened to the sounds of arrival and settling in swell and fade. A new guest at the inn, she could tell, who had arrived at the moment of her death. She lay there feeling her breath go in and out, in and out, with a fresh appreciation. God had spared her.

As the light filtered in through the curtains, she rose and washed her face. The cold water gave her strength, and she felt she could now take on the task of what had to be done. This attack would be made known and this innkeeper and his evil ways exposed to the community. She could see that it would not be easy to make the accusation, but then such qualms had not stopped her before. She carefully put her dress back on, smoothed its wrinkled skirts, and pulled her red coat across her thin shoulders. She let her hair down, brushed it with a bored disregard for where it caught in knots big and small, and then pulled it back into place. She knew she had become an old, dull woman, far from the creature who had tempted Nathaniel and laughed in his bed. She was also now a woman without fear, though she knew that was not the same thing as courage.

Downstairs the inn was bustling. There were customers in the dining room, breakfasting, and she could see the boy carrying in firewood to keep the morning chill away. There was noise and conversation, men's voices. The place was warm with the men, and

Sarah as she moved about them wondered which one was the midnight arrival who had saved her life.

Across the room stood Grinshaw, wiping down tables. He was silent, watchful, his eyes moving about the room as he worked. She knew that he had already seen her, from the moment she had come down the stairs. She made her way over to him through the maze of tables and stools. Men scooted in their stools as she passed and looked upon her without curiosity. No doubt they all felt they knew as much about her as they cared to.

Sarah thought about what she would say once she reached Grinshaw—she would accuse him to his face and demand satisfaction, demand he turn himself in to the authorities—but as she was making her way across the room out of the corner of her eye she saw a movement, an entrance, a brilliant mingling of color. Skirts rustling, the lady laid eyes on Grinshaw and made directly for him. Sarah fell back, her moment lost.

"Innkeeper," the lady said with relish, every syllable clearly enunciated. "I want to apologize for my late arrival last night, I am quite certain that I woke all of your good guests. My arrival from London is inconvenient, with the house repairs my husband has undertaken not yet complete. I appreciate your hospitality. You are so kind." She towered over him, smiling, and Grinshaw, no doubt relieved to avoid the confrontation with Sarah, ostentatiously threw himself into the role of genial host. He walked the lady to the table at which her husband was engaged in his breakfast. Sarah recognized him as the man from yesterday afternoon, Mr. Stroud. The three of them shared a laugh, Grinshaw's eyes sliding over to Sarah as she sat on a stool fuming. She could not bear it. They were laughing at her, the whole room knew her humiliation. The man who pushed a pillow over her face, in a murder attempt, now free and easy among friends. A murderer in their midst, laughing and being made much of, as she sat there alone on her stool with no one. She had to do something.

Rising so that the stool fell over, making such a noise that people quieted and turned towards her, Sarah pointed her finger at Grinshaw where he sat at table, and declared in a voice trembling with anger, "He tried to murder me in my bed last night. He murdered my husband and now he tried to silence me in the same room in which he killed Nathaniel. You all bear witness to my declaring." As she spoke, Grinshaw sat motionless, glaring, but the lady next to him fell to the floor without uttering a sound, her skirts crumpling around her, cushioning her fall. Lips bloodless, her face still and white, she lay there as both men jumped up to her aid. Sarah was again left alone as the lady in her distress occupied all present. She had no choice but to flee the room.

As Frances prepared herself for Meeting, she felt the familiar apprehension that came with every First Day. As a child, church attendance had been a gesture of civic duty more than anything else, and she was rather sure that was how her Uncle and Aunt Preston continued to see it. The family made a quiet show of it on Sundays, walking to church in their best, sitting in pews they had paid for, the common villagers standing at the back with hats in their hands. It had seemed all good and right, for a time, before she began her own questioning and then found her way alongside Matthew. To be separated out, each according to his or her rank in society, part of the great Chain of Being, was understandable and even satisfying, and she had had enough of the selfishness of a child to think that the people crowded in the back all felt as she did. She had later been surprised to see people all pell-mell together at the meetings of Friends. As she read her Testament with fresh eyes, she saw her early acceptance of rank as something horrible. The truth was simple, so clear and so present, that she was shocked by her own delay in understanding. At Meeting, all stood together and the Light was within all, in equal measure if they would but see it.

She wrapped her shawl around her, for the morning was sharp, and went downstairs. Jane and Eliza were already there, sitting on stools and listening to Fox who was speaking in a low voice. It was charming, really, to see them both so intent, and he so at ease with them. The girls stood as she entered and George looked over at her, smiling.

"Your daughters are close to God," he said. "You have kept them close in the Seed, Frances, and they are both strong in their discernment." This comment surprised Frances, more about Eliza than Jane. Eliza, with her round eyes and lips always on the verge of a smile, a little child, not inclined to matters spiritual. Jane was another matter, a young woman much as she herself had been. The thought suddenly worried her, as she held out her hands for her daughters to take.

The sun had come out from behind the clouds and the day began to warm immediately. The woolen shawl that Frances had wound about her shoulders now felt scratchy and heavy. But the sun felt good on her face and she smiled at the girls as they walked. Perhaps they would be allowed to worship in peace this day. For some time now there had been no disturbance. But Fox, much as he was an attraction for the Friends (there were bound to be many more than usual at this Meeting) was also a draw for the authorities and so Frances worried about the possible disruption and its effect on her daughters. Far worse it would have been to remain at home, hiding. Fox would not have allowed it.

She looked over at him as he walked by her side along the path. His face was weathered and lined prematurely, from his constant travels and frequent imprisonments. This made his eyes seem all the brighter. No doubt being out and walking was nowadays his natural state, and she could see that he was trying to slow his pace to match hers. His coat was dusty and his trousers had seen better days. She wondered at her own selfishness, not to have noted this before. She would have to see to his laundry once they returned from Meeting. The thought gave her pleasure, to be able to do something for him before he set out on his travels once again.

Eliza began to fall behind, struggling to keep up with all the adults around her. Fox reached down and picked her up, something she agreed to with a surprising equanimity. They made their way through the copse and out into the field facing the little house where they would all gather. A wide blue sky had opened, cloudless, above them. There was already a crowd of people, more than usual, making their way through the door. It would be close and warm in the room. Frances paused before entering and removed, with some irritation, her woolen shawl. Fox set Eliza down and was immediately surrounded by a number of Friends, who welcomed their leader with visible joy and excitement. Susan Harp was there, hanging back a little, with a shyness that seemed excessive, even dramatic. That was perhaps for the best, thought Frances, given Fox's attitude about Susan's dilemma. She moved with the girls toward an open window where she could get some air.

There was then one of those moments when everyone tacitly agrees to be silent. The crowd around Fox dissolved and people took up positions in the room, quietly standing with arms at their sides, some with eyes closed, some staring straight ahead. Frances glanced over at Fox to see that he too was still, his eyes closed, his hands together, at rest and yet alert. Waiting. She looked at her two daughters, both with their eyes closed (Eliza's scrunched shut, with dreadful effort), heads slightly bent. The air was dense and warm in spite of the open window, and Frances did not know how long she could stand there. She felt very empty of the Light, and strangely hollow and brittle, sensitive to every worldly discomfort. Her woolen shawl was a damp, heavy bundle in her arms.

Someone began to speak: it was a man Frances did not know, a stranger who had no doubt traveled to be here this morning with George Fox, not of their community. He was a tall scraggly man with a fine but threadbare coat and discolored breeches, his boots so worn the toes had opened to reveal thin, bloodied stockings. She could not follow his words, which were disjointed and disturbed. He rambled on, his thin raspy voice growing louder as he went. And then there was silence again, for which Frances was entirely thankful. After that a number of people spoke, some of them with wisdom that Frances acknowledged and admired. They spoke of their struggles and how God reached within them and lit a candle and opened them to a true understanding. Their daily woes were drawn on a large canvas, given meaning and power. She was envious, and knew that this day was lost for her. She looked over at Fox and saw that he had a small smile on his face, his eyes open and staring straight ahead as the members of the congregation spoke.

No doubt he would report to others, the delight he took in this company, the closeness to God that he felt, the seeking after the Light so strong.

Everyone expected Fox to speak and of course he did. For who else would be as likely among them all to feel the Light, the touch of God, at Meeting? But he bided his time, and the silence grew until Frances thought she would herself become emotional, just from the weight of all that silence. Tears, laughter, something. She grasped her shawl more tightly and waited. His quiet tormented them, made them wait, built the silence until it was an impossible burden that only he could lift.

He broke the quiet with soft words that gradually grew in strength. The tension in the room eased. "All have peace and life, as ye dwell in the blessed Seed, wherein all is blessed, over that which brought the curse; where all shortness and narrowness of spirit, brittleness and peevishness are." A long pause. "We must keep in this blessed Seed. Whatever bustlings and trouble, tumults and outrages, quarrels and strife, arise in the world, we must keep out of them all; we must concern not ourselves with them, but keep in the Lord's power and peaceable truth, that is over all such things. Live in the love which God has shed abroad in your hearts through Christ Jesus; in which nothing, nothing is able to separate you from God and Christ, no outward thing, nor to hinder or break your heavenly fellowship in the light, gospel, and Spirit of Christ, nor your holy communion in the Holy Ghost, that proceeds from the Father and the Son, withal that you have fellowship with the Father and the Son, and with one another." Out of breath, Fox paused again, and looked around the room, slowly, into people's eyes, drawing them in. "This is it which links and joins Christ's church together, to Him the heavenly and spiritual head, in unity with his Spirit." What had begun in a small voice was now filling the room.

Another pause, everyone quietly breathing around him. Fox turned his gaze on one Friend after another as he continued to speak. "Keep in true humility, and in the true love of God, which do edify his body, that the true nourishment from the head, the refreshings, and springs, and rivers of water, and bread of life, may be known and felt amongst you." His voice faded again, soft and slender, as he retreated within himself and left nothing behind.

Frances had closed her eyes, not wanting to meet his, and was torn between seeing his words as aimed at her yet also the selfishness of thinking this was true. Humility—oh, she was far from that, far indeed! And as for the world, she was right in the middle of it, deep in the muck, gadding about with priests and fancying herself a defender of disinherited women. And there she was, fighting for the Grove, foolishly thinking it mattered at all. Why did she not throw herself on the ground this moment, and allow the forgiveness of Christ to open her to the Light? Why did she stand here, suffocating, stubborn and closed, saying nothing?

At that moment she heard the approach of horses and turned to look out the window, her daughters turning with her as with one mind. They knew what this was. Her heart pounding, Frances turned again to look at Fox, who seemed lost in his own thought, eyes once again closed, still. She knew better. She knew he was listening for the sound, indeed had been listening for it all along. The Friends all stood where they were, frozen, following his example. This was to be a test.

Frances reached down and pulled Eliza close as the horsemen trampled across the field and arrayed themselves in front of the door. She could see their faces, cold and bare, hard. There was the clatter of weapons and the neighing of horses as they dismounted and moved towards the house. All around her people stood silently, even Susan Harp, so apt to weep. Here, steadied by Fox's example, the poor woman merely took the hand of her neighbor and remained quiet. The silence in the room made the noise of the soldiers all the greater. As they entered, the men placed themselves immediately around the door as their leader strode forward and made his way to Fox.

"I am Captain Harris," said the man, his tone surprisingly smooth and almost gentle. "Are you the Quaker George Fox, the leader of these people?"

"I am he," said Fox with a slight smile. "But these people are led by Christ Jesus."

The officer turned to the crowd. "Be it known that you are gathered here in disobedience to the King's law which forbids treasonous meetings against the King and the Church of England." His voice was strong, filled with confidence, the kind of confidence backed by strong men with sufficient weaponry.

Fox, of course, had his speech ready, one that he gave on all such occasions. He looked up at the captain and tensed his shoulders. His hat stayed firmly on his head, as always. "We are not here to disobey the King or to do wrong by him, this you know. We are a peaceable people, met together in worship, we do not seek to harm the King or the law."

The soldiers had their orders, and so the officer spoke, "So you say, Mr. Fox, but we are charged here to take you into our custody, along with other leaders among you, and take you to the constable for jailing until the next assizes. If, as you say, you are peaceable, you will come with me now." He looked about and decided that the four or five people most closely clustered by Fox should come too. He was not going to take them all, there were too many. He pointed to Fox's traveling companions, and then to a couple of men standing next to them, a farmer by the name of Parrott and the old Welshman, John Williams. But other people began to crowd forth and ask to be arrested. They would not let Fox be taken and remain standing there doing nothing. The officers had a time of it, roughly pushing the Quakers back into the room as they escorted Fox and the others out onto the field. Fox went willingly, as always, his face composed and his step measured. Frances watched as she held tight to her daughters.

Suddenly one hand squirmed out of hers and Jane darted through the doorway before Frances could do anything. A blur of blue skirt and burnt-red hair, and she was out the door and pushing her way to stand beside Fox, her pale face flashing bright in the sunlight. Frances let go of Eliza and ran after her. She could hear Jane talking to the Captain, who looked annoyed. On Fox's face there was no expression.

"Go back to your family, Quakeress," said the officer, a nod of his head towards the house. "The jailhouse is no place for you. And this man"—a glance at Fox—"he is in no way deserving of your faith. Go to your mother." For by this time Frances, her breath coming fast and short, was standing next to Jane.

The girl stood her ground. "Christ speaks to me in my heart and I am where he wants me to be," she said with a fierceness that surprised Frances but which did not even make Fox look up. "We are the people of the Lamb, and we are to be sacrificed."

This made Fox stir, which was a relief to Frances. She could do nothing, and the captain was clearly unwilling to pick Jane up and move her out of the way. She stood in the midst of the horsemen, close to Fox. He looked up and seemed to speak with great reluctance.

"You are not in the habit of jailing children, are you Captain?" he said roughly, not looking at Jane. "I will give her over to her mother, as is proper." And then he turned, touched Jane's arm with his hand, and moved her towards Frances. It almost seemed, to Frances, that Jane was going to resist. There was something about her expression, something set. But she allowed Fox to maneuver her over to Frances and she stood there, quiet but not complacent.

"You would cause your mother great sorrow, coming with us, Jane," Fox said, "you must think of others, not just yourself."

Jane's face reddened and she looked to be on the verge of tears. Frances swiftly put her arm around her and moved her away from the soldiers who all looked on in brazen curiosity. "Let us go home." She began to walk with Jane back to the meeting house. The rest of the Friends stood there and watched Fox and his fellow prisoners walk away, surrounded by the men on horseback. The captain turned his horse and looked back at the Quakers. "Disperse, go to your homes, or you be in defiance of the King's law." He nodded at three of his men who turned and dismounted, moving once again towards the house. Frances was at the doorway by now and ran inside to find Eliza and pull her close. She found her next to Susan Harp, holding her hand. The soldiers entered and roughly put their hands on the backs of the Quakers, pushing them towards the door if they hesitated. Frances kept hold of Eliza as the crowd surged forward to the door, propelled by the soldiers with their threat of weaponry and their strong arms. As much as their faith preached pacifism, nonetheless some of the men could be heard angrily protesting as their wives cried out. Frances felt herself shoved by other bodies toward the door and began to be afraid of the crush through the narrow opening. She picked up Eliza and threw the shawl around her as they were moved in a wave, shoving in their turn the young couple in front of them. She had lost sight of Jane, having left her in the field.

Eliza was crying in her arms. They tumbled out into the field, almost falling, a rush of bodies flailing about in the noon sunshine. The young couple in front of them fell flat on their backs in the grass, stunned. Frances rushed forward with Eliza, looking for her elder daughter, who was nowhere to be seen.

Jane kept herself hidden. She followed the little group of soldiers and Quakers at a decent distance, through the wood, using paths she knew. She knew where they were headed, and she planned to move in amongst them at the right moment. She had an endless appetite for penance, it seemed, and this would only be the start. She longed for the cell, imagined herself sitting next to Fox on a broken-down old bench, the two of them waiting for their thin soup, saltless and greasy, as evening drew on. Praying together with the other prisoners, softly but making sure their jailers could hear. Finding a small dry place to sleep on the stone floor, pushing bits of straw here and there to make a bed, feeling the cold stone against her back. That was what she wanted.

She could see Fox, surrounded by the soldiers on horseback. He of course would know what jail was like. His travels throughout England were punctuated by such stays. He had described one such stay to Jane and her mother, and it had remained with Jane as evidence of just how removed Fox was from her own experience. He told her how he had been placed in an upstairs room that was missing an exterior wall. The winds and the rain blew in as he sat there in chains. He was never dry, never warm. The rains soaked his food, his clothes, his bed, as he lay there. Then the sun would beat in and cause him to blister and burn. Months he spent, prey to the elements, and he nearly died by the end of it. And yet here he was, having put himself in harm's way again at Meeting, a prize for new jailers.

Jane moved through the trees, keeping herself in shadow, as the party made its way along the road to Amersham, where the accommodations were more capacious than with the constable in Chalfont St. James. It was not an easy thing for her to keep up with men on horseback. The Quakers slowed them down a little, but they were going at a steady clip. Jane's shoes were not meant for such steady and fast walking and so she found herself stumbling from time to time, catching herself before a fall many times. The woods had their paths, and so she was able to keep out of the brush, but it was not easy. She had to keep the party in sight, so that when they arrived in Amersham she could become part of them.

By mid-afternoon they were approaching the town. More folk were out and about on the road and gazed upon the troop of soldiers with their prisoners with curiosity and even humor, tossing taunts at the Quakers as they passed by. The prisoners remained silent, following the lead of Fox whose demeanor was unchanged throughout the journey. Despite the King's fear of these stubborn subjects of his, the public's view seemed to be less fearful and more amused. Fools these were, nothing more, to risk their freedom for their own strange view of Scripture. Times had changed from the early days of the century, and people now seemed eager for a return to the old ways, King and Church together. These Quakers were obstinate and to be pitied.

The day had turned very warm and Jane could feel the sweat trickling down her arms as she moved quickly through the town, following the cart as it made its cumbersome way to the jail. No one paid her any mind, a young maid in a plain wool dress, cap securely covering most of her flaming hair, walking like she knew where she was going. No one said anything to her as she moved along, dodging young couples a-courting on a Sunday afternoon, their somber parents strolling along in that peaceful emptiness that followed a good sermon. She had no trouble keeping up with the Quakers, since the streets were narrow and slowed the soldiers. Some people had decided to follow along, too, interested in the whole proceeding, and so she found herself to be part of a procession, of men, women and children, eager to see the Quakers put into jail.

She saw her chance as the soldiers were pushing the Quakers towards the jail, roughly and without ceremony, Fox the first. A mob surrounded them, and she found it easy to make her way through the jostling crowd and place herself in front of a soldier who, his eyes on the Quaker in front of him, proceeded to shove the two of them through the doors and into a large empty room with no windows. She found herself standing next to the old farmer John Williams and his wife Faith. They looked at her with some surprise. "Where did you come from, little one?" Faith took her by the hand.

In front of them a man sat a desk with a ledger, taking names as the Quakers were escorted back to the cells. Jane placed herself behind the Williams couple, so that Fox could not see her. There was the tall Farmer Parrott behind her. She approached the man with the ledger and drew herself up, saying her name to him with a clear voice. "I am Jane Lyndal, Quakeress." The man began to write but then, looking up at her, stopped and lifted his pen. It was then that Fox came forward, "this is but a child," with the ledger-keeper nodding and saying, "yes indeed she cannot be here, send her home." There was noise all about, Quakers declaring it wrong that the authorities had rounded up a child, the ledger-keeper and the soldiers replying that they had done no such thing. Fox took her aside in the midst of all this and shook his head.

"Why are you here, child?"

Jane could not tell him how much she longed for sacrifice. That would be selfish in his eyes.

"Where you go, so shall I," she said with energy. This was something familiar to him, the loyalty of a follower. He smiled at her and touched her shoulder.

"Except here," he said with finality. "You are not your own, you belong to your mother, and it is her suffering you should be thinking on. She does not know where you are and is no doubt looking for you. Go to your mother and tell her for me that we are well." He then turned from her and joined the others as they were escorted into their cell. Jane was left to stand in the foyer with the clerk, who had blotted out her name and closed his book.

Chapter Seven

———•◆•———

With the arrest of Fox, the Grove fell into stunned silence. Frances found herself sitting for long periods over the next many days in her parlor, a text in her hand (more often than not one of Fox's treatises—he was a prolific author) but her eyes on the fire or sometimes, with the fineness of the spring weather, out the window to the garden. All those visitors, with their comings and goings, had taken her strength with them when they left. Now Fox languished in his cell, a lock on the door as he awaited trial. Frances made the strenuous journey to see him as often as she could, but whether she actually saw him was up to the whim of his jailer: one day she was allowed to visit for a few minutes, the next not at all.

Fox himself seemed in good spirits, used to this kind of thing, used to the bad food and the gloomy surroundings. He seemed so at home in the mean little room, his fellow prisoners sitting about on stools and the floor, the air foul and close. She wondered at him. Was he mad, to be so at ease here, with no care in the world? The place only made Frances angry, to see such a good man treated like a common criminal. He might sit there, talking with his fellows or reading quietly in his Bible, but she wanted to pound on the door and demand justice.

Jane had returned, sullen and quiet, her skirts muddied and her pale face smeared with dirt and tears. Frances knew better than to talk with her then. She was sent to her room with no supper as punishment for her disobedience, but that was all. Frances felt Jane to be a mystery, closed and distant, but when she thought of it a different way there was a familiarity that was almost harder than the distance.

During these days, her servants knew better than to trouble her. They went about their business, and the little farm continued as it always had. Both daughters spent time with her, doing their bit of sewing, or Jane reading alongside her with an occasional anxious sidelong glance. Frances felt burdened, weighed down, and her nights were now entirely dreamless.

The unlikely event that brought her out of her low state was another visit from her brother-in-law. It was late in the afternoon, the day still bright and the sky cloudless. She had a small fire in the grate and was turning the pages of a letter published by Margaret Fell, seeing but not reading.

Richard made his way into the room in a manner that made Frances think of a landlord, sure and easy. He handed a small basket of Spanish lemons to Deborah, with a flourish. "For the household," he said with a smile. He then made his way to the comfortable chair he was so fond of. Frances rose and he took her hand as he sat down heavily. "Ah, Frances, it is good to see you," he said, but she did not believe him. He was truly here to see the property, she felt, but she could not say that. Instead she offered him a cup of ale, and he accepted with a speed that surprised her. It made her worry that he was settling in for a period of time. This was not to be a short visit.

"Please do stay for our supper, and if you wish the night," she said to him, not wanting to be shamed into being hospitable. "You've arrived late in the day, you do not want to start your journey back after dark."

Richard smiled slightly. "I thank you, Frances. I am sorry to catch you by surprise. I was determined to come and visit with you and your family. It was Matthew's clear wish that I look in on you from time to time, and I am honoring that as best I can." He took a sip of the ale. "Know you of what they drink in London these days? Beer, finished with hops, a strong bitter flavor, much favored by Londoners. I have enjoyed it." He looked at his own cup doubtfully.

Matthew had wished her to be closer to his brother. Despite their differences, Matthew had always loved Richard and treasured their closeness. She had seen it as part of Matthew's utterly complete and admirable lack of pride, that he never seemed to notice what she saw so clearly as the younger brother's condescension. As much as she had enjoyed her discourse with Richard, she always saw this chill in him. She knew it to be an easier path in the world, not to be so aware of other people's faults, and wished her eye were less acute.

Richard began to talk, in a desultory fashion, of the events of the day, the King, the changes in London. It seemed to Frances that he had only come for idle conversation, or else he had decided to save his attack until later. She was a prisoner to this conversation, not liking it nor wishing to rush ahead to the inevitable argument, but she did find that their talk brought her out of her lethargy. For this she was grateful, and she steeled herself to join in small conversation with her brother-in-law until supper was ready. As the sky grew darker her daughters made their way to the parlor and sat on the rug, listening as Richard began to share memories of Matthew, their childhood together, those strange days before the War when every family's table was dominated by talk of Minister or Archbishop, Parliament or King. He ranged from simple moments of Matthew reading to him, to grand moments of Cromwell's army marching through the city streets and his own flight to Rome. Frances let him talk, interested in the stories of the past he shared with Matthew in spite of her impatience with the way in which he assumed her interest. The girls sat silently, absorbed, for this was a past new to them.

Supper was served, and so they moved to the table in the main room. There was an awkward moment as Frances quickly bowed her head, grasped the hands of her daughters, and led grace. Her words were infused with the language of the Friends—she spoke of the Light, and the Seed, and above all Love—and she could see that, as innocent as each word was, as a whole Richard was disturbed by what they signified. No doubt too he felt that as the head of the family he should be the one leading grace, but she was not about to allow a former Jesuit to speak for her.

Throughout supper the same conversation continued, safe in the presence of the girls. They were silent, as children should be, listening to their uncle talk on and on of his dead brother. In spite of herself Frances loved these stories, these small portraits of her Matthew that revealed much to her even now.

Richard took another sip of the decent wine that he always found at Frances' table. "I was the child who always got into trouble," he said with a half-smile. "It was I who would run through the house in muddy shoes, who would not have my lessons done. And it was Matthew, more often than not, who would intercede for me with our very strict father." The smile faded. "You girls do not know your grandfather well, and that is a sad thing. He is a man worth knowing. When I was a little boy, I remember how he would come into a room and there would seem to be no one else in it. He was in those days a leading man in the City, one that everyone looked to for advice. We were all afraid of him, as we should be. Your father Matthew, however, was not so afraid, and when at times punishment came my way for all my many misdeeds it was often Matthew who stepped forward and asked my father to stay his hand." He paused and gazed at his glass as if it held the scene he imagined. "Perhaps that sparing of the rod spoiled me, indeed, but at the time I was very grateful to my brother. He was the only one, barring none, to whom my father would listen. The only one."

Frances herself had never been at ease with the senior Bright, but her thoughts of him now were filled with sympathy. As one of the regicides, those who had decided for the death of Charles I, he now languished in the Tower of London, his lands and property confiscated, his fortune gone, his life barely hanging in the balance. There was nothing to be done for him now. He was an unrepentant Puritan and Parliament man, who showed no remorse for what he had seen as the godly path, the necessary death of a king, one of the reprobate, brought down by the prophets of God. Frances had not seen him since Matthew's passing, on the eve of the return of the dead king's son Charles II. He had been the center of the family, powerful during the Interregnum, someone who mattered. And yet, it had always seemed strange to Frances that none of his three children remained with his faith nor, in fact, did any of them please him. Richard had become, briefly, a Jesuit, and had been cut off from the family (except for Matthew's letters) for that period of time. Their sister—well, no one talked of her and Frances had not seen her since her own wedding to Matthew. And of course there was Matthew himself, the beloved son, who turned his back on his father's faith and became a Quaker. How hard it must have been for the old man to look around him and see only dust where he had hoped to build a city.

Richard fell into silence and they all sat there, finishing their meal in the growing darkness. Candlelight swept their faces with a fragile warmth, flickering in the drafts that Frances, for all her daubing and caulking, could not prevent in this leaky house. The chill of the evening settled on them as the servant Deborah cleared the table. The girls then rose, curtsied before their uncle and received his hand in blessing before they left the room for bed. Frances and Richard were alone.

Neither made a movement to go into the warmer parlor. Frances had to admit that she wanted to encourage an early bedtime and did not relish being closeted with Richard for the remainder of the evening. All had been spoiled by his demand for her home. She contemplated a candle by her bed and one of her few, dear books in her lap. She supposed that at this very moment Jane was upstairs, reading softly to her younger sister, and that led her to imagine Richard, as a small boy, with Matthew next to him in a chair, reading from the family's Bible. So strange that the two boys would come to read it in such different ways.

"Dear Frances," Richard opened, clearly past the reminiscences, "I am sorry that our previous meeting was so strained. I did not mean to be so hard with you, and am sorry if my words were harsh. It was not my intent to upset you, or to turn you out of this house."

"I thank you for your generous words," replied Frances with some caution, "but I prefer the honesty of words harshly spoken. Unless your purpose here is to change your view of the ownership of this house, then the sweetness of how you it say means nothing to me."

He looked startled, but then laughed and said, "Oh, so you do battle against my Jesuitical subtleties with your firm Quaker honesty! Yay or nay, as your man Fox says. My purpose, dear Frances, is the same, in that I do intend to own this house. But I have an offer to make to you that I hope will make this prospect less, well, miserable for you. I cannot see you thrust out of this house, homeless. Will you hear my proposal?"

"Of course."

There was a long pause as her brother-in-law considered his words. "I wish the house to remain within the family, and it is mine by right of being the male heir. However, I would very much dislike removing you and your daughters from it, and would feel it oppressive to my conscience. Your elder daughter Jane is of age and I would find it very satisfactory if she would be my wife, with all of you remaining here with me. I ask for your agreement to this, as the girl's mother, though of course I will talk with your uncle Preston as well."

"She is your *niece*," was all Frances could manage. Suddenly she felt dizzy and her hands grasped at the tablecloth in an effort to remain seated.

"She is, but only by marriage, Frances, and that is not prohibited. We are not blood relations. She is your daughter by your first husband and no relation to the Brights, none at all. The Church will permit it."

Frances let the silence linger and expand. They both remained in their seats, the candles ebbing. Richard's face now in shadow, inscrutable. She wanted to think through her words. Her wish was to make him leave the house, that very moment, to go out into the night. But she knew that to be an impossible request, and so allowed herself a moment to think, knowing that all the while his discomfort grew. She felt strangely hopeful. Perhaps his unspeakable proposal was the result of desperation, knowing his suit to be unlikely of success. And his was a request, for once, that was within her power to grant or deny. She knew that her uncle Preston would never go against her wishes in this matter.

"Richard, you must see that this proposal is one to which I will never agree." Her tone was even, and she was surprised by her own strength. "I will choose to see it in the most beneficent light, that you only wish our well-being, and that you see this as a way to insure the happiness of us all. Understand that this would not be the case. I cannot give my daughter to you. She is a member of the Society of Friends, and she will marry within our faith. To marry someone who was not a Friend would only serve to cast her out. That alone prevents such a union. I will also say"—and here her voice began to shake a little—"that I would rather my daughter were not the instrument in a plot to gain property. Her marriage will be one of sober deliberation and will reflect God's will, not man's selfish desires." With this she stood, her chair scraping against the floor. "Please remain here as long as you wish and retire as you please. I am very tired and will say good night."

Richard's expression was neutral and did not reveal whether he had expected this reply or not. He simply gazed at her, his eyes hooded and remote, and slowly nodded. It was not a gesture of defeat but one of deferment.

Although her mistress seemed well pleased with her report, Ann herself felt there was more to be got out of Tom. She didn't know quite what, but she knew herself as someone in whom people confided (with the exception of her taciturn father), and if there was more to the story she would eventually get it out of the boy. She liked doing things for Frances and felt that she had something to offer. Today she found herself along the path to the inn, in the midst of errands to the village, and decided she would stop awhile and get to know Tom a bit better.

The day was bright and warm, promising summer, and it lifted her spirits after the sobriety of winter. Even though the Grove was a comfortable home and far better than the small home she had been raised in, it had its drafts and damp, and one never felt completely at ease. This was the time of year when it was warm in the sun and cold in the shade, and she sought out every particle of sunshine as she danced along, this way and that, to avoid the shade of the leafing trees. She approached the inn and saw that Tom was in his customary place, looking after the animals. She waved at him like they were old friends. He waved back uncertainly, as he tried to maneuver a large, over-full bucket of scraps to the trough for the pigs. He was not a big fellow and so it took some straining and heaving to hoist the bucket over the top of the trough. She watched him in admiration.

"Hallo, there, Tom," she said smiling, trying not to let the smell of the pigs and their habits dismay her. "What news today?"

"What do you mean?" he asked suspiciously, flinging the bucket down hard on the ground as the pigs ran about. "Go find the women to gossip with, if that's what you're about." The pigs snorted in the background, rubbing their fat rears up against the boy's legs, the little piglets squealing and keeping close to their mother. Ann took a deep breath, despite the odor. Something must have happened, and the boy was afraid to talk.

"I'm no gossip," said she. "There's a difference, Tom, between the news and talk. I've not the time, nor have you, to tell stories and say things about folk. Surely it's a Christian duty, to know the doings of neighbors? Surely that's a courtesy, to ask how things are?" Ann let her face show some disappointment as Tom picked up the bucket again and turned to leave. But then he paused.

"Ah, I know that," he said slowly, setting down the bucket and brushing his hands on his trousers as he climbed out of the pen. "There's folks, though, that talk about us—well, talk about my master—and every time I walk into the village I see all of 'em staring at me, with all that talk. I don't like it, I don't, and if that's what you're about I don't want any part of it. I keep myself honest."

"I know you do, Tom," Ann said warmly, moving toward a patch of sun next to him. "I think it's too bad, how there's such talk, and how you are blamed alongside your master for whatever happened. Whatever it was," she added hastily, "it's a mystery. I know you to be an honest man, and you would never hide anything about a good Christian's murder. We all know that's what they talk of, that body and how it came to be there. Some day the truth will be known, and you won't have to worry about the stories being told in the village. Whoever did it will be found out, that's

God's will, and any that helped him will meet justice too, if not in this life then in the next, at the Judgment."

The two of them were silent as they stood there, in the quiet of the yard, looking at the pigs contentedly pushing their snouts around the trough. The inn itself loomed over them, in silent threat. Tom stood there so close and still, Ann thought about the warmth of his skin beneath the threadbare shirt and vest. It was like everything, even time itself, had stopped. His hand reached out and grasped her arm, and he swiftly leaned down and kissed her, a quick touch of the lips. He seemed as startled as she as they looked at each other. When he leaned down again she was ready.

The arrival of Nick Brown at the Grove was anticipated with much excitement by Frances' daughters, each in their own way. A small room off the kitchen was prepared for his lodging, and the nursery was transformed once again by a table and chairs to be a place of intellectual pursuit.

After all this anticipation, which also involved a fair amount of imaginative picturing of the young man, his arrival could not possibly meet all expectations. Frances desired someone plain and severe, but for Jane there were more vivid images matching the previous tutor's impetuous recitations of poetry. As for Eliza, all that was asked for was a friendly gaze. None of these things came to be, as they all greeted the young man at the door. He was dusty and tired from his journey. He took no notice of the girls, but rather centered his attention on Frances, and made clear that the Grove was not so easy a place to find, in part because the good townspeople of Chalfont St. James were remarkably taciturn and unwelcoming. It was all Frances could do to distract him from this perceived series of slights and get him settled in his chamber to clean off the dirt of travel. She thought she heard him continue with his plaints behind the closed door, muttering as he splashed water on his face, the words hard to distinguish as she sat there in the kitchen. It might be just as well to have a tutor short on charm. Jane and Eliza hovered in the background, intimidated by his brusqueness but compelled to remain, filled with anxious curiosity.

The young man looked startled when he emerged from his room to find the three female Brights sitting there at the kitchen table, smiling nervously at him. He coughed, smoothed his vest and it seemed to Frances that his smile was a weak one. He bowed his head towards her and apologized for his rough appearance.

"Too much travel," he said by way of apology, "has made my manner short. I hope that you will forgive that, Friend Frances." The intimacy of his tone seemed jarring to her, though as fellow Friends they were of course equals. There was something about the ease of it, that he had not even thought to hesitate, that bothered her.

Curling brown hair, dusty with the road, circled around his face, which had a softness about it that added to his youth. A short pert nose above a mouth that slipped into a half-smile with little effort made him all the more boyish. He had dimples, round brown eyes, and thick quizzically shaped eyebrows that seemed too weighty for his face. Frances knew exactly what he must have looked like as a child.

The girls were eager to show him the schoolroom, and so she let them go. The young man affected a stately gait behind the girls' swirling skirts as they disappeared up the stairs. Frances stayed seated in the kitchen with this rare moment of solitude.

The knocker at the front door sounded and she heard the soft footsteps of Deborah as she went to greet the visitor. Frances knew she should rise, to find out the business, but she felt suddenly, warmly tired. She would let Deborah come to her.

It wasn't Deborah but the guest who showed herself into the kitchen, leading the way as Deborah ran behind her, announcing her presence to Frances well after Sarah Kidd had planted herself in front of her hostess.

If anything, the woman looked more bedraggled than ever. Frances knew that she was sleeping at the church, and so at least had a bed to lie in each night. Evidently no change of clothes nor bath were to be had. She was as thin as a shadow, her dress sitting on her as it would a coatrack. Frances could hardly bear to look at her. The woman certainly did not stand on ceremony. She sat herself down on the bench next to Frances and sighed. Frances felt another wave of fatigue as they gazed at each other.

"I am grateful for your offer to help," Sarah said. "For a lady such as yourself to put out your hand to me is unlooked-for, a kindness. I have had such a terrible time of it, from the very moment when Nathaniel left his bailiff's post to now. It is hard to think that I was not there when he died, to be of help to him against those who robbed and murdered him, truly." Her eyes were on Frances, close and unblinking. Frances wondered what she had been like, before this tragedy, whether she had been soft and light or the same as she was now, so rough and full of duty. A young Sarah, just beginning a life with her husband, knowing that all would go well for them. The thought brought to mind her own early marriage: because she had had no experience of what could go wrong, she had been filled with the promise of future delights. It had all gone wrong. He had died an early death, in the midst of war, and left her with a small child.

"There is no need to thank me," said Frances with warmth. "I have not done anything as yet. There is little any of us can do without more evidence to support your case. Master Grinshaw is innocent until we show that he might be otherwise. Indeed, we would not want to subject a man to trial without such cause, we must know our view of the crime to be right." She wondered what had become of Ann and her fact-finding mission and decided that she would have to question the maidservant closely this evening.

This naturally brought Sarah to full attention. "I do not wait," she said firmly. "My own life will be taken if I do not take action. Just a few nights past, Mistress Bright, I was accosted in my chamber at the inn. The innkeeper came and tried to smother me in my bed. I was only saved by the commotion of a new arrival at the inn, so that he fled. God was watching over me, else I would have perished, and no one would have known my fate, just as they did not know Nathaniel's. I would have been a-buried on the farmer's land, no doubt deep in the ground. You all would have gone about your business, sure that I had given up my suit." She had a dry, spindly laugh.

Frances, horrified, reached out and took the widow's hand, clasping it in both her own. "Now you have your witness, Sarah, it is yourself!"

The woman shrugged her shoulders and took back her hand. "No, truly, I did not see his face, though I know it was him. The next morning I confronted him and he did not deny it. He said nothing as I accused him, nothing."

What to do with the miserable Sarah Kidd but ask her to stay for dinner. The widow had to be pressed, but then she assented, and the two of them went into the sitting room to talk more and consider how best to proceed. Frances persuaded her to have a small portion of raspberry wine, and the poor woman's face flushed with the unaccustomed warmth of the drink. There were many tasks waiting Frances' hand, but she could not leave the widow alone. They talked on as the room brightened with the light of noontime, as Sarah, adrift with the wine, shared her memories of the life she had led before Nathaniel's death.

As she listened, with sympathy and yet with wandering mind, Frances found herself thinking back to her own young marriage and the way in which it had come to an end with her husband's untimely death during the war.

Sarah gazed at her, eyes full, tears blurred across her face. "I know it is sinful but I thought a moment of dying that night at the inn," she said to Frances. "I know it is wrong, but it is hard to be in the world. Something in me wants to return to where it happened, to return to that room."

"No," replied Frances, now pulled back through the years, "that is not what you want." And with that she smiled and stood. "Let us go and see about the dinner, and join in company with our new tutor Master Brown. You will meet my daughters, and they will cheer you." She made her tone more lighthearted than she felt.

Chapter Eight

———•◆•———

Frances walked Sarah back to the village in the afternoon, the day proving to be unusually warm and fresh. Their conversation concerned the constable and whether they had a case to bring to him. Sarah, convinced of her assailant's identity, argued fiercely for yet another confrontation but in the end, by the time they reached the church-door, Frances had prevailed. They parted, and Frances, enjoying the peace that comes from being alone in a crowd, walked back down the High Street past the shops. Chalfont St. James was thriving, and so the shops were busy. Frances took pleasure in observing the women with their baskets, children clutching at skirts as they walked along the road. She did not know these women, and yet they would dip their heads to her, out of respect, as she passed.

Just past the butcher's shop she saw Mrs. Stroud, a very tall woman with a stately air moving along much as a ship would as it entered a harbor. Slow and majestic, her skirts lifted to keep clear of the dirt, her head high with a straight gaze, confident of her feet finding their way around the puddles. Her dress was fine, a clear sky-blue, and her hat, of a richer, darker hue, perched atop banks of perfect curls. The woman's face was long and narrow, the chin nearly as long as the nose, the eyes with a downward pull. She had no doubt been a beauty in her day but every feature had become exaggerated well beyond loveliness with her years. In the time that Frances had lived in Chalfont St. James, she had rarely seen Mrs. Stroud in the village, and their social lives had not crossed. Frances was naturally social but her status as a Quaker set her apart.

Alongside her, arm-in-arm, strode Mr. Stroud, of equal height and larger girth, but just as well-dressed. Frances was struck by how fine everyone looked these days, now that the King had returned, the vaguely military puritanism of Cromwell no longer the fashion. Vests with slashes of color, the more the better, wigs cascading across shoulders. Men and women alike with their lace collars and colorful ribbons. She thought of Matthew and his insistence on a plain coat, with hair cropped close to his head and no wig. Perhaps life was simply more serious then, the war and the end of the world seemingly at hand (indeed, many hoped for it). Now it seemed they had gone back forty years, to the ostentatious frivolity of the Stuart Court. How could they have come so close, only to lose their way now?

The gentleman and his lady were just turning the corner on to the Market Street when a commotion sent a young boy out of a shop and into the street, flat into Mrs. Stroud. He was holding a wrapped cheese, and the impact against the woman threw her to the ground, the wet cheese resting next to her head. She lay there in surprise as the boy scrambled to his feet, snatched the cheese, and ran towards the common, the storekeeper after him. Frances reached down her hand as Mrs. Stroud sat up, her hands flying quickly to her wig.

"Please let me help you," she said. The fallen woman gratefully took her hand and, with the help of her husband (who had leaped back at the fast approach of the boy, getting safely out of reach), stood up, wobbly in her fashionable shoes. A handkerchief quickly came to the aid of the dirtied skirt, and both women were occupied for a time with straightening and shaking off the mud of the road.

Mr. Stroud bowed. "Many thanks for your help, Mrs. Bright. You are too kind."

Frances nodded and smiled. She knew little of Mr. Stroud, only that he was Justice of the Peace, and that he was of an old family. She had heard rumors of gaming at his home, and that this had been the ruin of some local men. This had been part of the reason she had not included the Strouds, even if they had wished it, in her small social circle. But now, as she gazed upon them, she wondered if this might be an opportunity to put forth the suit of Mrs. Kidd and win them to her side.

"Mr. and Mrs. Stroud, it has been my fault, and now must be remedied," she said. "We know little of each other, and yet have long been residents in Chalfont St. James. I would like to invite you both to the Grove, please feel welcome to call."

"Thank you, dear Mrs. Bright," said Mr. Stroud after only a moment's hesitation. "We will indeed call, perhaps tomorrow? We are returning to our home tonight. The necessity of repairs to the kitchen have kept us at the inn." Mrs. Stroud looked away, smoothing her skirts with energy.

As they spoke, Frances saw Arthur Brunskill turn on to the road, a book in his hand. He seemed lost in thought, his expression pensive and even sad as he walked along, and it was clear that he had not seen her. She moved across the road and greeted him. He raised his eyes and the smile that resulted was gratifying to her. He nodded to the Strouds.

"So you are staying at the inn," he said hesitantly. "I have been told there was something of a scene there this morning, as guests were breakfasting."

Mrs. Stroud turned pale as her husband turned red. "My goodness, people talk in this village," she said haughtily, "one must watch one's step." She looked hard at Brunskill. "It was an embarrassment to me, and I would rather not talk of it here in the street."

"I apologize," the priest said hastily, "I meant no disrespect, Mrs. Stroud. I do not mean to carry stories. I only mention this because of the coincidence, that I should hear of the episode and then come upon you here in the road. It is no matter, we need not talk of it further." This seemed to satisfy the Strouds, who then nodded to Frances, agreed to come calling, and went on their way as before, only a little worse for wear. Frances remained with Brunskill.

"Was it a matter that had to do with Sarah Kidd?" she asked him quietly as they moved to the side of the road, away from other ears. He nodded. And as he described the event to her, she realized that Sarah had only told her part of the story of the confrontation with Grinshaw. As seemed to be usual for Sarah, she had reduced the moment to a solitary confrontation between herself and the innkeeper. Now the landscape broadened, but as the scene was peopled and expanded it was all the more confusing to Frances.

They conferred for a time in the road, and Frances urged upon Brunskill an invitation to her home the next day, for further conversation with the Strouds. He accepted, welcoming any opportunity to avoid his parishioners in favor of what would be, no doubt, a conversation devoid of petty sins and small grievances. He began to see his life here in the village taking on a more complicated social dimension, which lifted his mood and made him unnaturally cheerful as he made his way home.

Haec civitas longe plurimum totius Galliae equitatu valet magnasque habet copias peditum Rhenumque, ut supra demonstravimus, tangit. In ea civitate duo de principatu inter se contendebant, Indutiomarus et Vercingetorix; e quibus alter, simul atque de Caesaris legionumque adventu cognitum est...

Weighed down by the serious girth of the passage, those solid Romans with their literalness and their practicality, Jane felt on the verge of tears. This of course made her angry. She would not cry, not over Caesar. The descriptions of battles with wily Vercingetorix, the portraits of the Gauls, the earnest explanations of military fortifications, moved her not at all. She longed for the sonnets she had read under the tutelage of Samuel Prosper, the flight of language, the sweet images that came to mind as she spoke the words. He would smile at her, and then when she had finished her recitation, he would put his hand to his heart to calm it. Nothing of this, of course, with Mr. Brown, who usually had his back to her as she dutifully recited from the *Gallic Wars*.

Samuel had been aware of her, fully aware at every moment. They had walked in the garden together, as he told her of going to plays in London (whispering, for it was not something to be talked of in the Bright household). Proudly he told her of his association with society in Chalfont St. James, especially the Strouds and their glittering evenings of gaming, another thing not to be mentioned to her mother. And then there was that day in the classroom when he reached out and touched where her heart must be, felt her warm under his hand, and then she let him undo her buttons and run his hand across her belly. She held her breath as his hand stopped, and then he leaped to his feet and walked quickly from the room. She knew it would happen again, and it did. She never touched him, she felt no desire for that. To have his hand upon her and his gaze fully in hers was enough.

Now, as she made her way across the heartless landscape of ancient Gaul, she smiled at the thought of those hands, and how they trembled, the power she had over Samuel. He waited on her, he followed her. They would walk down to the Misbourne for their botany lesson and they would talk of their future life together. He proposed marriage as they stood on the footbridge, the water slipping away beneath their feet. She was but a child and yet she had made a man feel this way about her. It was no small thing.

Always, though, the strangest part—for all the loveliness of the moment, the anticipation, the soft touching, the soft words—always, as they walked back to the Grove, he would seem almost angry, holding himself tight, apart from her. He would talk of his poverty and how her mother must view him, and she learned not to dispute this for he would only become angrier. It did not un-do what had gone before but it left her confused.

Now here with Caesar, wondering where Samuel Prosper was out in the world, wondering when he would come back for her. She knew he would. She had that last night to remember. She had astonished herself that night, a cold winter's night, all clear and dry without, her breath white as she walked the narrow halls of the house to his room. That she had never done before. But she had seen an invitation in his eyes that day as they had read Catullus together and she could not bear another night apart when she knew he lay there in his bed waiting for her patiently. And so she had thrown on her wrap and made her way with candle in hand, her breath shallow and sharp. Tapping on the door, wanting to weep with excitement.

He had taken time to open the door. When he did cautiously crack it open, she could see that he was as excited as she, his eyes wide and a fine sheen of perspiration on his pale face. And yet he told her, with fierceness, to go back to her room.

"No, I cannot," she had said to him with certainty, not to be treated like a child. Not when they had known each other as they had. "I am here for you."

He stared at her for a long moment and then shook his head. The door shut, and she was left standing in the hall.

The next night was the night he left and she had not seen him since. And yet she still waited. Her sleepless nights were for him.

In the dark of her small room, Sarah lay on the bed and took turns opening her eyes and keeping them shut. The darkness of the chamber, with no window to disturb it, was complete, and so it made no difference, open or shut. She supposed if she kept her eyes open for long enough, she might be able to discern the different objects in the room: the low cot on which she slept, the trunks and baskets pushed up against the walls, the worn carpet by the door (a small homely effort to turn the storeroom into a guest chamber). She spent a good part of each day here now, thinking. Mrs. Corning was always after her, with plates of stew, to persuade her that eating was something worth her while. She was not interested, but she did find that her weakness required that she lie here and rest. In one part of her mind she understood the connection between her lack of sustenance and her weakness, but she refused to act on that connection. She did not know why, other than that it did free her time for thinking.

A light tap on the door pulled her from her imaginings. Arthur Brunskill stood in the doorway. She must have seemed even more disheveled than usual, because the look on his face was one of dismay, mingled with something else that she couldn't quite read.

"I would like to invite you in for supper," he said. "I understand from Mrs. Corning that you have yet to eat anything today. Mrs. Corning has some very good fish stew for me, and I would like to share it with you." He reached out his hand to her, making clear that there was to be no discussion. Sarah felt irritated, and tired, and did not feel she had the strength to walk to the rectory, much less to put a spoon to her mouth of the good Mrs. Corning's stew.

But he would not be moved. He stood in the doorway until she had managed to put her shoes on, and then they walked together to the rectory in the early evening light. Mrs. Corning had the table set for the two of them and set about filling their plates with the hot stew and slicing bread to go alongside. She stood to one side as they sat down to eat; Sarah could see that she did not feel it right to leave them alone. It was amusing, really, because she had no concerns of her own in that regard. She cared nothing of what others thought. But of course Mrs. Corning was there for the priest, not for her.

Their conversation, given the good housekeeper's presence, was shallow and thin on the ground, and it was clear that Brunskill was annoyed by this. He continued to look over at the old woman, sighing, and then would move into yet another topic, from the weather to the sermon this coming Sunday to the weather again. Sarah put all her attention to her food. It was hard to swallow, and she seemed to have no room in her for even the most meager of spoonfuls. She forced herself to eat, to match every two slurps by her host to one of her own. The flavor seemed strong, the smell nauseating to her. Greasy chunks of fish in a warm broth, laced with turnips and greens. She saw it as yet another trial she must perform, before she would be released back to her room.

But she was not to be released so easily. His plate scraped clean, and after a final swig of the rather good ale, Brunskill turned to Mrs. Corning and asked her to clear the table and finish up the things in the kitchen. He then smiled at Sarah and asked if she would join him for a sit by the fire in the parlor. This made Mrs. Corning flush with anger as she began to stack the dishes on to a tray. Sarah thought, well, I can lie on the floor in his parlor, I am so tired.

She propped herself up in one of the two chairs fronting the fire. The small room was warm and the fire robust as they sat before it. There was a long silence between them. They could hear the clatter of dishes in the kitchen, the boiling of the kettle, as the plates were manhandled by the housekeeper.

Finally the noise in the kitchen abated and it was clear that Mrs. Corning had taken herself off to her chamber. Brunskill and Sarah sat before the fire, on and on, but Sarah knew it was only a matter of time before he spoke and she would have to pull herself up. She didn't mind the sitting here, in the warm dimness, the fire constantly shifting its shape. She looked over at the priest. His face was in repose, soft and contemplative, and she was certain that these were the moments when he felt most at home, to be quiet by the fire. She surprised herself by being the first to speak.

"I am grateful for the food," she said hesitantly, still looking at the fire, "and the bed. It is a kindness. You are good at such things. But I need to know how to bring this man to trial, so that I can discover where Nathaniel's fortune be. I cannot just stay here and live in your storeroom, away from my child, and be the laughingstock of the village whilst that man walks free and easy." Her tone began soft but became harsher by the end. She couldn't help herself; she was not a soft woman. This was what she was now, hard and cold.

"You need a better ally," Brunskill said thoughtfully. "I have no influence in this village, you have seen that. I know that you have spoken with Mrs. Bright, and she is someone to reckon with, though as a Quaker she is viewed with some distrust. Unwarranted, of course. I find her to be of good manner and with virtue. Still, you need to make friends in the village and make yourself into someone the constable must pay mind to. There must be people who know what happened, and they will come forward if you are a person of sympathy."

Sarah laughed miserably. "Oh yes, I am a sad creature, they all see that. Do not these garments and these tears tell a story, which would raise the sympathy of any man?" She looked down at her poor dress, the smeared mud of many days' walking a permanent part of its hem.

Brunskill thought on the fine gentleman and his lady early in the day, striding along the High Street. He was quiet for a moment, but then turned to her and smiled. He rose, hastened over to a large wardrobe and pulled out a quilt. "We will start with your clothes," he said firmly. "You must disrobe, Mrs. Kidd, and I will see to the washing." He laughed abruptly, threw her the blanket, and then shut the door behind him as he made his way to the kitchen to set the large pot to boiling on the fire.

Sarah thought perhaps he had gone mad. She couldn't remember the last time her clothes had been washed, and thought of the priest washing her woolen stockings. It was all too strange. In some way she had become part of what she wore, so that it was hard to imagine peeling it off, much as it would be to peel off her skin. She stood and eyed the quilt as it lay there warming by the fire.

Brunskill made an appearance, his face flushed and his sleeves rolled up. "Your clothes will dry by the fire, Mrs. Kidd, and be ready for you to wear in the morning. They are but thin bits of wool. I promise you that I shall not observe the clothing, merely stir it in the water so that it becomes clean." He fluttered his hands at the quilt. "Please." And then back into the kitchen, the door shutting discreetly behind him.

She found herself smiling, in embarrassment, as she shed her clothes, once the priest had safely removed himself into the kitchen. In the firelight she gazed down upon her body—her wasted belly, her thin bony legs, her feet a mass of callouses and sores. Dirt in the creases of her elbows and knees. Too much walking, and her shoes nearly gone. It was good to feel the fire's heat directly on her skin. Her skirt and blouse on the floor, the black stockings stretched out and worn. As thin as she was, and yet they had all started out together thick and soft. Now she and her clothes both but shadows.

The quilt was large and she lost herself in it. She gave in to the moment, sat herself back down in the chair and watched Brunskill pick up the pile of clothing and make his way back into the kitchen without a word. The clothes would be nicely cooked in the cauldron, and she could imagine him in there with a large spoon stirring and stirring, the dirt sliding away into the water. Gray, black, and white, her garments all awash, and no going back for they would take time to dry.

Brunskill emerged again and set a rack by the fire, on the tiles. The air would soon become dense with drying wool. He lay the garments one by one on the rack, with care, and she was ashamed of their paltry nature. But the priest seemed, if anything, to delight in his ordinary task, humming a bit as he moved the rack closer to the warmth. The room was silent except for the crackling of the fire and the dripping on to the tiles. Just a simple blouse, a skirt and under-skirt, with a short vest and her thin red coat. Stockings draped to the side. They settled back in their chairs. He was gazing at her and she wondered what he thought of her, this filthy woman from London, wrapped in a quilt.

"You must stop looking at me," she said quietly, and he did as he was told and turned his eyes to the fire.

"You have my sympathy, utterly," he said with feeling. She thought he was going to continue but he stopped, perhaps content with what he had said. She rearranged herself for comfort, being careful to keep the quilt close about her. Then he said, "Nathaniel must have been a very good husband to you."

"Nathaniel was good to me," she said, "and he left me alone only so that he could earn a fortune for us and our son. He was a good Christian. We were content with each other."

"I have never known that," admitted Brunskill with a small sad smile. He looked at her again. "I have never known the contentment of a wife and family. Indeed, my own family was filled with disagreement and discord." He told her of his parents, still no doubt at odds with each other, over in Croxley Green, never a quiet moment between the two of them. He remembered hiding behind the house with his brothers so often that there was a small bare patch of ground there where he had nestled as a child, hard up against the wall, waiting for the quiet. Sometimes, on the winter days, he had gone out to the chicken coop and, amid the feathers and kitchen scraps, fallen asleep there. His father was a prosperous man, important in their town, but always dissatisfied, always seeing the wrong in things. His mother had her peculiar thoughts about religion and her unnatural interest in the Scripture, reading much into the words, making it all too clear why women should not set themselves to reading.

"Nathaniel and I never quarreled, not once," Sarah said. "And we were well-matched. He was good to my mother and my brother, and took care of all of us. What would we have argued about?" A long pause. "That is something to hope for, a wife to bring ease to your days, with no quarrels." She felt her own days were done, in this regard.

Brunskill put another log on to the fire, which responded with a crackle and spark. "Well, that is unlikely in Chalfont St. James," he said with a laugh, returning to that strange giddiness that had overtaken him with the laundry. "The very idea is distressing to me. Ah, yes, you were a fortunate bride, Mrs. Kidd." His gaze returned to her and they smiled at each other. For the first time since her arrival in the village, Sarah felt safe. She reached out her hand and he took it. The warmth of his hand surprised her, and she imagined him as he had been in the kitchen, sleeves rolled up to his elbows, vigorously churning at the wash water with his large spoon. She let him touch her face with his other hand and soon he was kneeling next to her, cupping her face and kissing her. There was no sound other than the fire. She let her lips part and drew him in.

Chapter Nine

———— • ◆ • ————

The quails were dripping with lard, smeared with flour and thus ready for the pot, where they would meet up with pungent nutmeg and apples retrieved from the larder. Ann loved to watch the cook, Meg Cathcart, move about the kitchen. She was an economical woman, every move calculated to achieve two or more tasks. With one hand she shoved the quails into the pot, with the other sprinkled some nutmeg over them followed by a small spoonful of salt. Her eyes, meanwhile, were already at the fire, making sure at a glance that the heat was right, and she seemed to have eyes in the back of her head regarding the girl Betty, telling her to be sharp about it and punch down that dough.

Ann's own work was less aromatic. She was on her way with the kitchen scraps, to feed them to the pigs, which made her think of Tom. Usually this would be Betty's task, but with the bread-making and other chores she had asked of Ann this favor. Ann was not above doing such work. She did it all the time at home.

In return, Betty had agreed to take on some of Ann's work this afternoon, as she was to slip out soon to meet Tom down by the old footbridge. There would be the sweeping of the stairs, and the setting of the table for the evening meal, as well as the mending that Miss Jane played at but never really accomplished. Ann felt that her small holiday was a deserved one, since she was hoping to learn something for Mrs. Bright along with the pleasure of being courted by her Tom.

By afternoon, the day had turned a bit overcast which threw something of a pall over the rich green grasses of the fields. As she walked close to the honeysuckle she could hear the bees, always at work. The path down to the little Misbourne River was dry and easy, and she tripped along at a good speed. She had taken extra care with her dress that morning, putting on a clean skirt, and searching until she found the stockings that did not have holes in the heels. She wore her mother's small coat, the soft green one, and knew it made one notice her hazel eyes. Her father had been safely gone to a day's work when she dug around for it in the big chest and carefully draped it over her shoulders. She did not know what Deborah or Mrs. Cathcart thought of her fine things, and did not care.

Having passed through the Chantry Wood, she had but a small part of the journey ahead of her. Her mind turned from her own finery to Tom, already imagining what they would talk about as they strolled the riverside, what she would talk to him of (for he was generally a boy of few words and she knew she would have to take charge of the talking), how he would take her hand and might lead her towards the Hogtrough Wood with its dank little paths and shadowy glades. She had not quite decided what might happen there, and had imagined it in different ways just to try them out.

Finally the path dipped down and there was the little stream, running higher this time of year. It became a trickle in the height of summer, but with the winter rains had risen to the brink of its most ambitious banks. In the summer one could see the entirety of the drowned footbridge, decrepit and broken as the water lapped up against it. This time of year, only the link to the shore was visible, dropping down under the waters almost immediately, never to be seen again. There had been no replacement for the bridge. Whatever traffic had encouraged its original construction, many years ago, had long since disappeared. Ann found it troubling to contemplate, that ruin of a bridge beneath the dark water, hiding there.

"Hallo," Tom startled her by coming out from behind one of the elms that hung over the stream. He was smiling, with a long stem of grass sticking out from between his teeth. He gave it a suck then discarded it as he approached her. She noticed that his shirt was clean, and that there was not the usual reek about him. This pleased her, that he had gone to some trouble. She had never seen herself as a girl likely to be courted and so this entire turn of events made her heart beat fast as she stood there.

"Hallo," she said back shyly, taking his lead. She was surprised by his kiss, light on the lips, pulling back right away to grin at her. His hand on her arm. She had heard such tales—her neighbor Mrs. Satterbee talked often enough of her own rough courtship and the many babies that followed, to the point where Ann wanted to cover her ears—so this gentleness was unexpected. They began to walk along the riverside, and she could see that they weren't going to try to cross over into the Wood despite the piles of rocks here and there that would have aided in their crossing. Tom kept them moving south, where the path alongside the Misbourne grew wide and smooth. At first their talk was of small things, the weather (wasn't it fine?), a pedlar who had come through the village yesterday, the fact that the Quaker George Fox had come to the Grove and now was in jail awaiting the assizes, and other such news. Tom talked of his aches and pains (which again surprised her, in just a boy, something she was accustomed to hear from her father but not in one so young), the chores he had ahead for himself in the afternoon. Ann kept busy with listening, something she felt comfortable doing. This was a new side of Tom, this talkativeness, and it made it easy on her.

As they were moving south, away from the village, the path narrowed again and expanses of open field were interspersed with small copses of elms along the shore. Nobody was about, except for an occasional fisherman, dejectedly watching his line move with the soft eddies of the stream. Of course, these men were known to Ann—there was Will Porter, tall and thin and red, ready to launch into one of his ranting speeches if they had paused—and she to them, as well as Tom, so if they were prone to gossip all the village would know about the courting before long.

Tom fell silent and they walked a bit further, his hand ever tighter over hers. She would have liked to have stopped and found a dry place to sit and talk of small things (this was an image that pleased her) but she waited for Tom to do the choosing. She noticed the freckles that littered his cheeks, the small roundness of his ears concealed beneath his wild hair. Now his arm moved in against hers as they walked, touching now and then, sleeves rubbing against each other.

Their pace slowed as they rounded a curve in the river. The Misbourne became as narrow as a ditch though the winter-fed water still surged up to the top of the banks. Tom's pace slowed as they made their way to a small berm overlooking the stream, sheltered by a trio of small trees. She wondered if he had had this destination in mind from the start, or had simply wandered this way with her, not knowing. Men were mysterious. Sometimes she felt that she was somehow blind, that things others saw as plain as day were invisible to her. She was lucky just to find the ground her feet walked on, that's what her father told her.

Then it all happened very quickly. It was clear that Tom knew what he was about, Ann thought with relief. The kisses came fast and warm. They lay back on the berm, and she worried for a moment about the damp ruining her mother's coat, but soon all thoughts were gone and she was caught up in Tom's need. This went on for some little time, but Ann came to herself as Tom's hand moved its way up under her skirt. She remembered Mrs. Satterbee and all those children about, and the look of angry dissatisfaction on the woman's face as she thrust another babe on her shoulder to be burped. She did not know much but she knew what could come of this, and hastily pushed his hand away. This action on her part, after lying there so pleasantly passive for him, made Tom start. He reared back on his elbows and looked at her as though he were seeing her for the first time.

"Not yet, Tom," she said softly. "Let us talk awhile, look the sun is out now." The overcast had burned off to reveal a strong afternoon sun and she felt it warm on her face.

"Ah, we been talking," he said with some heat. "I thought we be done with that now." Then a long pause as he seemed to consider. "You're a pretty thing, Ann," he said by way of courting.

She gave him a smile. He was breathing more slowly now and shared in the view with her.

And so they talked in a desultory way, speaking of this and that. He found his way to touching first her arm and then her belly as she lounged there on the berm. Small kisses to her neck which tickled her and made her laugh. Then he suddenly leaped up, exclaiming about the work waiting for him back at the inn. "Master Grinshaw, he'll be after me, no doubt," he said with anxiety. Ann awkwardly got to her feet (no help from the newly distracted Tom) and they began to return the way they had come, except with greater speed.

"So Tom," she said to him as they marched back, hardly touching, "surely Master Grinshaw is a good master? He knows you to be a good worker and he won't be angry with you this one time."

"You don't know the man. He's a rough master, for sure, I've felt his hand many times and have not deserved it. He's come after me with a stick, he has, and with the mistress cheering him on." Shaking his head in disbelief at his own words, Tom looked at Ann. "You've got but the Quaker lady. You know nothing of how it is."

She had to agree with that, and felt herself fortunate. She asked him why he stayed, if the innkeeper so abused him.

By that time they were nearly back to their starting-point, so swift was their march. Tom shrugged. "There not be many masters around here, and the man pays me," he said simply. "I figure to put away my coin and then when my fortune is enough, take the road to London."

That's what everyone says, thought Ann. Everyone is going to London, one of these days. "This Mr. Grinshaw," she said slowly, "he's got a temper, no doubt, from what you say. Have you ever known him to truly harm someone? Does he make you afraid?"

The boy stopped in his tracks and looked at her. "Do I look afraid?" he asked fiercely. "If it comes to that, I can defend myself as much as any man. As for the master, well"—and here there was a long pause—"to kill a man is nothing to him." He eyed her as he spoke, his face still, the very fact that his employer was a man of violence lending him a certain amount of gravity.

She had no answer to that, and chose merely to lift her face to his for a goodbye kiss. His lips were cool and he did not touch her otherwise. They parted soberly, as if she were sending him off to war.

Frances could not get an answer out of little Betty as to where her Ann was. She could have used the help. The Strouds and Mr. Brunskill were all to place demands on her hospitality that afternoon. She had gone into the kitchen just past noon only to find Mrs. Cathcart berating Betty for not having brought up the stepony from the cellar. The little girl was hastily trying to haul the bottles into the kitchen as the cook leaned over her as a threat. The kitchen had not been swept and there was a small pile of greens to be cleaned. Betty, overwhelmed, was near tears.

The guests were expected soon, and so Frances gave up her search for Ann and instead turned her attention to the stepony, to make sure it had been prepared correctly. She took some pride in this preparation, having added to the recipe her aunt had given her so that it was something her own. Having set it to boil yesterday, the lemons (fresh from London, Richard's gift) and raisins combining with the water to fill the kitchen with its scent, she had had it stored carefully in the cellar to cool and combine for use today. It was there, leaning over the bottles and pouring a sip for herself, that Deborah found her, to announce that the Strouds and Mr. Brunskill had arrived. Stopping off at the classroom to ask Mr. Brown to join them, Frances made her way to the parlor.

Deborah brought in the stepony with the cups on a pretty little tray and set it ceremoniously on a small round table which was placed in the center of the room. Frances shared with her guests the story of how she came to the Grove and Chalfont St. James. This carried the conversation for a short time, with mainly the Strouds holding up the other end. Brunskill seemed lost in his own thoughts, and they did not seem to be happy ones.

It was Nick Brown who then took the conversation in a new direction. "Dear Mrs. Stroud," he said, perhaps in a kind effort to bring her more into the talk, "I would like to know your view of the village. I have not had an opportunity to become acquainted with many of its residents, my duties here at the Grove keeping me close." Frances thought his tone pompous, as one might speak to a large gathering rather than in this intimate space. She wondered at George Fox's opinion of him.

Mrs. Stroud had a way of holding herself so that she always seemed to be looking down from a great height. Sitting there on the settee, her rich skirts circling around her, she filled the room with fabric, scent and the soft gleam of the pearls that covered her bosom. She had a habit, Frances saw, of making people wait on her word. There was a small, expectant silence.

"My husband and I enjoy our life here," she said slowly, taking another sip of the stepony. "We take pride in this village, and my husband plays no small role in its security, as our Justice of the Peace. Its people are sound, good people." And there she stopped.

The tutor pressed on. "There was something of a stir, was there not, when you returned from London? I had heard such—from one of my charges here—that a deranged woman caused you some distress. I am so sorry for that, and hope that there were some sort of consequence for her." He looked pleased with himself, but the reaction from the lady was anything but pleasant.

"Must we speak of that? Must everyone remind me of it?" she said. "I was frightened to death by that woman. Please say no more." She took her handkerchief from her pocket and unsteadily touched her powdered cheeks with it, looking rather like she was about to faint again.

"Please, Mr. Brown," Mr. Stroud said with firmness, "this is not proper talk for our gathering here. My dear wife is still indisposed as a result of that unfortunate meeting. That woman was violent towards my wife. Surely she is possessed, or perhaps has lost her mind."

Brunskill looked quickly at the two and seemed to wake from his somnolence by the fire. "I am sorry for it," he said, "but you may have misunderstood the lady's purpose. She is not unsettled in her mind, but rather in great distress over the loss of her husband and her fortune. You cannot know the facts of the matter, and truly the lady did not intend to cause Mrs. Stroud to faint away. Mrs. Kidd was attacked that night at the inn, and she was speaking out of fear. I, for one, see her actions as perfectly understandable."

The Strouds were united in their response to Brunskill's contribution. Color filled the lady's cheeks as Mr. Stroud sat forward on the settee as though ready to launch himself at the priest. "It is my view," he said with feeling, "that to allow such violent persons to wander the village, to cause mischief, is a danger and a folly. This woman seems to be a vagrant, someone wandering the highways, who has made her way to this village to no good end."

"I do not mean to dispute with you, but she is not a vagrant," replied Brunskill hotly. "She rather came to Chalfont St. James quite intentionally, to find her husband. She did find him, and buried him. Now her task is to find the fortune he had with him when he died, and thereby find his murderer, seeing that justice is done."

The tutor seemed oblivious to the argument he had engendered with his innocent query. He had the affect of someone at a delightful party. Frances, on the other hand, was in great pain over the turn of the conversation but had no idea of how to restore the fragile good feeling of a few minutes before. She felt as though she were looking through a window at a great storm, the trees shaking in the wind, the fury of the rain hitting the glass.

She could but try. "Dear Mr. Brunskill," she said, offering the bottle of stepony again, "please let me refill your cup. I think that we are all in agreement that this is a trial for all concerned, that Mrs. Kidd's distress has had an unfortunate effect on others. And we all share the hope that she is able to meet satisfaction and return to London and to her child." Surely that would stop the rain.

Mrs. Stroud was as dark as a thundercloud. "The woman did great harm to me," she said with conviction. "I hope never to cross paths with her again."

"I am sure that would be her wish as well," said Brunskill with a low fierceness.

This was enough for the Strouds. They rose as one and, nodding to their hostess, thanked her for a lovely visit. Their exit was swift. Frances allowed a silence to fall in the room, wishing for her own solitude. Taking the hint, yet ever oblivious to his role in the abbreviated visit, Mr. Brown stood, bowed, and returned to the classroom. Frances was now alone with the priest.

"I have a great favor to ask," the priest said after a prolonged silence, finally meeting Frances' eyes. "I am aware that you hardly know me, and that what I must ask is something you should in fact refuse."

Frances sat herself down opposite him and tried to look encouraging. "I am glad that you see me as someone who might help you," she said. "I am used to being either shunned or attacked by priests, as my people always are. Your welcoming me into your home was surprising enough; to have you here is even more so. You are a very different kind of clergyman, Mr. Brunskill."

He gave her a small sad smile. "I know that well, Mrs. Bright. That seems to be what I am, indeed." A shrug, perhaps trying to persuade himself that it didn't matter. "Here is what I must ask of you. I think it harms Mrs. Kidd's case to live in the church next— next to my home. For her to be seen much with me, with the kind of intimacy that living closely brings, does only damage to her and no good. I ask that you might take her in and allow her to stay here with you at the Grove. I know this is too much to ask." His customary pallor was now awash in pink, which Frances thought helped his appearance considerably, but she felt very sorry for him.

Frances did not hesitate. "Of course, Mr. Brunskill, she must get out of that little storeroom. I do not know why I did not think of it before. We have room to spare here. Please send her to me." She would later wonder at it, wonder at the responsibility she had taken on, with such a woman as Sarah Kidd, a woman of the town, and nearly of the street. She would also wonder, a little, about the priest's clear urgency.

The stool's legs sank a little into the ground as Sarah placed it next to the grave. The rain showers of the night before had loosened the dirt. When Sarah sat, light as she was, the stool sank still further, and she looked ruefully at her fresh-washed skirts now damp and smudged with soil. Soon it would be as if the priest had never washed them, much as everything else from that night would be put away and forgotten. She adjusted the stool still further to place herself under the shade of the oak tree and settled in for what was left of the afternoon.

She had to work hard to think about Nathaniel. Easy as it had been to think of him in the room at the inn, here at his grave, with his bones so near, he proved elusive. The little wooden marker gave her something to look at as she spoke to him, but even as she said the words she had no confidence of his presence.

"Maybe I should have let it be," she said to him softly, "let the man smother me as I slept. Why did I fight, Nathaniel? I would be with you now, sweet and quiet, you and I. But I fought it, and even worse has happened." She fell silent and thought about the days when Nathaniel worked in the North, her own concern that he would never return, perhaps in favor of some Northern woman who caught his fancy. She knew that men would lift a skirt as easy as say hello, and had no illusions about that. The worry had been that he would not come back to her. She never thought of any other while she was Nathaniel's wife. His leaving took all her desire with him. There was the child, too, who was so needy and so close. But here, in this forsaken village, her son far away, she had gone untouched for so long it had been a shock to feel the priest's hand upon her.

How he had fumbled with her, he almost seemed frightened. She had had to put her arms around him and calm him, hold him close to steady him. A touch of her breast had sent him all trembling again. She had regretted her welcome almost as soon as he kissed her, seeing how it would be, all wrong. They were both overthrown by the moment, carried into it, and very soon he fell away onto the rug nearly senseless. Afterward she was surprised by how little she remembered of it. He had fled the room and left her there to curl up in her quilt and fall asleep next to the fire, what she had wanted to do all along.

But now, she could not talk of this with her dead husband. She let her mind wander, let it circle about and move this way and that, outside her own will. She thought of her child for a moment, small John Edward, with his green eyes, no doubt forgetting her as he was cared for each day by her neighbors. They had been none too happy to take on the task and she worried that they would find him too much a burden. That when she returned, triumphant, to London, her son would no longer be with the Martins or that they themselves might be gone. There was no counting on people nowadays. They came and they went. She was doing all of this entirely for John Edward and yet he was a phantom in her mind, a ghostly child with no substance.

She looked down at the plain wood slab and felt nothing but doubt. She had come to Chalfont St. James in late winter, determined to find the fate of her husband, to avenge his death by bringing his murderer to justice, to find the coin he had earned as bailiff. Now, as the days lengthened towards summer, she had accomplished but one of these tasks. She had managed to find friends, such as Mrs. Bright, but had thrown over her strongest advocate in a single night. Most people viewed her with hostility and if she were to pass from this earth tomorrow no one would grieve. The loss of her brother in an accident on the wharf had followed fast on the heels of her mother's passing. She had no one but John Edward, and this man in the grave before her.

A breeze picked up and played with her hat as she sat there. She felt close to leaving, to returning to London to find her child and make her way as best she could. But the prospect was so unsettling, so unlike what she had hoped for herself, that she could not bear it. As much as she loved the streets of London, she knew them to be heartless. She and her child would find themselves without a crust of bread between them. With Nathaniel's earnings, they would be able to have a life.

"You are too much alone here," said a familiar voice, and she turned to see Arthur Brunskill standing behind the oak, perhaps not sure of a welcome. He held himself warily, ready to flee at the least sign from her.

She shook her head. "I am not alone. Indeed, I am less alone here than in all other places in the world." Even as she said this, knowing it to be untrue, she discovered in herself a will to make others uncomfortable.

An awkward silence. "Well," he said with a false heartiness as he moved closer, "I came here with a purpose, Mrs. Kidd. Your friend and ally Mrs. Bright has offered to take you in. It is her feeling, and I quite concur, that the storeroom in the church is not fit habitation for a woman such as yourself. We both feel we should have done something about this earlier"—a deep flush—"but it would be well for you to find your shelter with her in the more spacious quarters of the Grove. You are indeed very fortunate to have a friend such as Mrs. Bright."

Sarah felt her face burn with shame. To think of the priest and Mrs. Bright, conferring together, what to do about this inconvenient widow. She could not bear to think of them talking of her with such pity and concern. No doubt they had wrung their hands together over the poor Mrs. Kidd. The only way in which he could rid himself of her was to find a new place for her to stay.

She would like him to have said more, about how he had abused her trust, but knew him to be incapable. It was even possible he did not see it that way, that he saw her as a filthy temptress who had found her way into his home. She was not even sure of her own view of what happened. Now he was telling her to leave. He stood there, she thought angrily, waiting for her reply, her *gratitude*.

She took her time, looking down at the grave, trying to capture her will and not say something she would later regret. So easy to just get up and walk away. She had to keep her eye on her plan, and not allow this anger to put an end to it. She needed Mrs. Bright's help and perhaps in many ways the Quaker would be more useful than this priest had been. Without looking up, she gave him her answer.

Frances was once again in her work chamber, collecting and combining to make a small dose of spiced water to ease the breathing trouble of one of the imprisoned Quakers. She was confident, absorbed in her work as she mingled the nutmeg, mace and ginger together with galingal to make a fragrant liquid. She had learned much of this from her Aunt Preston, whose own medicinal skills were legendary, later adding to her store of knowledge through experiment. There were a few texts on her table that provided her with even more cures and palliatives. The ones she turned to most frequently were William Turner's *A Newe Herball* and of course Oswald Croll's *Basilica Chymica*, recently translated into English (though, and Frances was quite proud of this, she could also read it in the original Latin). These she read carefully, sometimes agreeing, sometimes not. She would have liked to have been at a table with one of these writers, to work together and discuss the various treatments, to find out why such and such an ingredient must be included in this or that recipe. Sometimes what she perceived as the reasoning behind a dose seemed flawed. Some authors were in disagreement with each other: there seemed to be a debate between those who followed Galen's understanding of the humors, and based treatment on the idea that a condition or illness represented the imbalance of the entire body, and those who argued for a more "chemical" basis in treatment, treating just the immediate area or symptom rather than the body as a whole. She did not know whom to believe, though she had always trusted the ancients and so Galen was her touchstone. Still, sometimes the traditional medicines did not seem to do much good, and she would have liked to understand more fully the basis of the formulations.

She measured and stirred and thought on the matter of Richard and the house. It was best to do that kind of thinking here, when she was calm and could be alone to sort it all out. She had not heard from him for a time and was worried that plans were afoot, that she would be caught by surprise. She did not know what to do, how to fight back, in order to secure her home. Perhaps she would have to travel to London, to be advised as to the law of the matter.

Sunlight seeped in through the window panes, frail and transitory. It warmed the wood of her table as she let her hands rest, the draught mixed. She listened around her to the silence of the house: the girls were reading their lesson, perhaps Mr. Brown was out for one of his long solitary walks. The cook was no doubt at work in the kitchen, rolling out dough for the evening's meat pie, the girl Ann sweeping out the parlor, Deborah seeing to the arrangements for Mrs. Kidd's stay. One task after another, everyone about their work. They were all connected by this house, her shelter and solace. She tried to imagine leaving it, tried to be practical rather than emotional, thinking of where she would go with her limited income and the children. Perhaps another, smaller house in the neighborhood would suit. She had no wish to return to London and that world, especially now that the nature of the place had changed so much with the Restoration.

She rose to go to the side table and inspect her jug of Dr. Stephens' Water. Dr. Stephens was famous for having lived into his dotage, drinking this concoction, and so she had seen to the recipe and kept it as a regular part of the family's medicinal supplies. She had first heard of it during her time in London, early in her marriage to Matthew. It was a rich mixture of spices, sack, ale, and herbs, all aged in a large jug and then distilled in a limbeck. She had known it to cure the stone, a disease much feared, and to take care of stomach ailments. It had secured her popularity as a healer in the community and allowed her to play a role here in Chalfont St. James. People might look askance at a Quaker but when she came with bottle and spoon in hand, she was welcomed more often than not. The aches and pains of daily life, not even to consider those deadly diseases that took one's loved ones so quickly and without warning, were what bound her to the people of this village. Susan Harp might gad about, commiserating, rearranging blankets and listening to the litany of woes, but it was Frances and her healing knowledge that found the most welcome.

No answer regarding Richard and his plans came to her as she stood there. Annoyed, she began to wipe down the table, finished for the day. In this room, she felt so powerful and helpful. Out in the world she was but a woman and had to wait upon the man.

A knock on the door brought Deborah into the room, telling her that Sarah Kidd had arrived. Frances had arranged for a small bed to be placed in Matthew's old study, a way to bring the room back into use. She did not mind having the widow here, though she admitted to a slight feeling of uneasiness about how Sarah would be at table with her daughters. Such a grim woman, with no conversing, no interest in anything other than her search. Perhaps I would be like that too, thought Frances, with so much at stake.

She followed Deborah down the hall and stairs to the front entrance. Sarah stood just inside the door, holding a small bag. She looked a little cleaner than she had of late, but the same sad air hung around her like a shroud. Frances greeted her warmly, taking the widow's cold hands in her own.

"Welcome, Sarah," she said, "I am glad to have you here with us. You must let me know how we can make you most comfortable. I have a room ready for you, let us get you settled."

Sarah looked somehow peeved as she stood there, her brow low and her mouth a thin line. She nodded curtly and followed Frances to Matthew's study, walking a step or two behind Frances as though she were a servant. Frances tried to slow and meet up with Sarah only to find the widow slow further and remain at a distance. This was going to be difficult.

The chamber was small but inviting. Its white-washed walls, scrubbed wood floor and the window looking east all served to create an atmosphere of warmth and light. Matthew's walnut table was still in the corner, with its Bible and bottle of dried ink. A hooked rug, in blues and grays, from Frances' own childhood home, was spread in front of the bed. There was an imposing chest below the window, with room enough for Sarah's things. The fireplace was set with kindling. This was a very real improvement over the storeroom at the church.

Sarah knew enough to say so. "I thank you, Mrs. Bright," she said quietly, placing her bag on top of the chest with a casualness that betrayed the paltry nature of her belongings. "You are very kind to make room for me in your home. I hope for your sake, and my own, that my stay will not be overlong."

"Oh, you must not think of leaving just as you arrive," cried Frances impulsively, "let this be your home for now. This was my husband's study and has had no good use since his passing, until now. I am glad to have you here." She reached out to touch Sarah's arm, caught up in the moment, only to have the woman flinch and retreat. "Well then," she added in a lower key, "I will leave you to rest now, but we will talk more at dinner."

When next he woke, Nathaniel wondered at it, that he had fallen asleep in the full sun of a summer's afternoon. Likely the many days on the road had added to his fatigue. It was now well into dusk. He was hungry and ready for shelter. He hastily checked his bag to ensure that he had not been robbed as he foolishly slept so close to the road. The sight of his coin comforted him, and it was with satisfaction that he felt its weight as he heaved himself up and put his shoes back on for the next stage in the journey.

The road was visible in the evening light and he could hope that with the rising of the moon he could arrive in Chalfont St. James. He generally avoided travel at night, both because of the threat of robbery but also the threat of peacekeepers, the night watchmen who looked with suspicion on anyone who entered their village past sunset. Yet the road from Aylesbury to London was well-traveled and so he had hope that the local watchmen would have a less parochial view, and that the robbers, common as they might be in the far reaches of Northumberland, might be thinner on the ground here. He kept up a steady pace, undeterred by lengthening shadows, and began to hope he'd be in sight of the village before too long.

As he walked, he thought on the tutor, whose dissatisfaction seemed so steeped in an envy of others. Fearful, too, to feel he needed a full purse to make his way in London. Why, Nathaniel had arrived with little beyond his own strong arms, and had made his way, finding himself a wife in the bargain. He shook his head as he walked—fear and envy. That tutor was never going anywhere.

Under the darkening sky, before the rise of the moon, Nathaniel slowed as he walked, noting the increase in small cottages off to the side of the road. He must be coming to Chalfont St. James. The cottages were dark except for an occasional flicker of a candle or the low glow of a fireplace. No one was about. Country folk found their way to bed early. He was wide awake, having slept so soundly by the stream, and found the somnolent mood of the village somehow discordant.

"Hallo there," said a voice, high-pitched for a man, out of nowhere. Nathaniel followed the voice by turning his head and looking behind him. There stood a grim-faced fellow, pale face rising out of the darkness. "Tell your name and your business, to be out on such a night."

Nathaniel readily gave his name. "On my way to London, man," he said, shifting his bag on to his other shoulder for relief. "You need have no fear of me or my intent. My only design is to find a bed for the night."

The watchman cleared his throat and widened his stance in the road. "So you say. I have tidings that there is a robber on the road hereabouts, having done violence to one of our people here in the Chalfonts."

"I've had no worries," replied Nathaniel easily. "I have seen no one to be suspicious of. Though with your news, I'll be all the more glad to find my way to a room and a bed. Could you point me towards your inn if there is one?"

"You take much care with that bag of yours," the man said, and his expression was resolutely unfriendly.

Nathaniel took a deep breath. The watchman was clearly not going to let him be on his way without more questions. He tightened his grip on the bag. "I do take care," he said slowly, "for it holds all that I have."

There was a long silence as the watchman moved his gaze from Nathaniel to the bag and back again. "Put it on the ground and open it," he finally said, moving a few inches closer.

"That I will not do," Nathaniel replied with some force. "There be no reason. I am a traveler, with nothing to do with this village, trying to get home to London. Your suspicion is not in keeping with the manner of things. Let me pass, watchman, before I must move you aside." He knew, as he said it, what the result of this would be. The watchman's face turned darker and he moved in close to Nathaniel.

"Now then, you will indeed find the inn, for that is where I will take you to be questioned," he said firmly, reaching out and taking hold of Nathaniel's right arm. "I am the watch of this village and you must do as I say." The last sentence was very loud. It prompted another voice in the darkness and a man loomed into view. Nathaniel could see the tip of the moon on the tops of the trees nearby and was grateful for it. This darkness was a threat.

The second man approached. He was a tall, lanky man, his jacket not tailored with his size in mind, his bare wrists hanging down from tattered sleeves. But his shirt was good, and he wore boots that looked new. Nathaniel waited, the watchman's hand still on his arm.

"Will," said the watchman, "there's a robber about, and here's this traveler in the road at night. A stranger. I'm taking him to the inn so that we can get to the truth of it. Can you get folks together?"

The tall man nodded his head as he stared at Nathaniel. "Caught him, have we?" He made a sound that was either a cough or a laugh, or maybe both. "Enough of these ruffians, stealing and troubling our people. I'll go get who I can, and we'll have some hard questions for this stranger." Again the laugh-cough as he made his way off.

Nathaniel gave the hand on his arm a shake but the watchman held on all the tighter. Nathaniel knew that he could fight his way through this, and escape without much harm, but he needed a place for the night and didn't relish having to watch his back all the way to London. Surely these people were a reasonable sort and would see that he was no brigand.

"I will answer your questions, as I am fully innocent of whatever harm you think I have committed," he said to the watchman. "I have nothing to hide from you. All I want is a bed."

"We will see about that," said the watchman, with a rough pull at Nathaniel's arm. "The man that was robbed will get a good look at you and your bag, and we will see about that."

Chapter Ten

————•◆•————

Nick Brown shielded his eyes from the sun and looked across the field at the nearby woods, and thought how far less menacing, and even inviting, they looked in the warm spring sunshine. This pleased him, for it seemed to represent his experience at Chalfont St. James: what had seemed forbidding and difficult now seemed easy and inviting. He had established himself as the tutor of the two girls, who obeyed him without question, and he had been part of small social gatherings which, he felt, he had carried off with skill and even talent. No doubt more social invitations would follow, and he would begin to be a member of the community. The tutoring would be but a way station, on his way to greater things, and he hoped to move on to some new position within the year. In the meantime, the girls were quite tractable and he felt he did right by them.

He entered the wood with an intention to make his way down to the Misbourne on the other side. The sun retreated before the deep shade of the elms, and he found that it had been a mistake to leave his coat behind. The complete solitude, however, was what he sought, and he took his time winding through the paths. Birds made the bushes shiver as he walked past and here and there he spied a small rodent or a rabbit darting into a hiding-place. One of the aspects of Quakerism that had spoken most emphatically to him was its engagement with the natural world. It was George Fox's argument that the best way to educate a child was to take him out into the fields and the forests, to move about in God's Creation. Nick was torn about this, being much in love with Latin and his small collection of books, but here in the forest he could feel it so strongly, the touch of God, warm and green and wild. It was in places such as this, more than in Meeting, that he felt God's Light within. He considered that he should be introducing the Bright girls to this world, but then solitude was part of the experience and he was not eager to share it. He wondered if it was the very solitude itself, more than the natural garden around him, which brought about this religious experience. Perhaps he could have been a monk in a cell just as much as a Quaker in the woods.

At last he made his way out into a clearing and then down to the banks of the river. The narrow path was muddy and slick as he walked along, aiming for the submerged old footbridge as a place to sit on some streamside rocks and read the little book that rested in his pocket. He knew that he should be reading the edifying work of, say, Isaac Penington or George Fox, but instead he had secured a copy of Cicero's orations and preferred that. He felt he had a great deal in common with Cicero. A great intelligence and eloquence, so much wisdom, and yet no one listened to Cicero, not as they should. His death was the result of his determination to tell the truth. He was not a wise man, politically, but surely admirable.

There it was, the wood slats just showing below the water line on the shore. There was a small stand of birch trees right there, and some large smooth rocks to perch on. The sun felt quite warm now and the chill of the forest was completely gone from him as he sat down and propped his feet on a smaller stone. He pulled out his book and turned to his favorite oration, "Against Catiline," breathing a long, full sigh of contentment. For a time he was absorbed in Cicero's phrasing, finding himself saying the words aloud in all their Latin simplicity. So much said in so few words, and so well.

He had nearly memorized the piece and so his eyes drifted off the page as he continued to recite the passage. As they drifted they met with a strange sight below him in the water, nestled in against the footbridge. It was a flash of white, rippling and winking in the sunlight. As he looked he realized it was more than that, and in his horror Cicero was thrown into the deep. For there, moving gently to and fro in the water, caught beneath the bridge, was the body of a young man.

As the two men pulled the body from the water, the constable stood on the shore with a look of studied seriousness on his face. The corpse, slick with weeds and weighed down with water, made for an awkward struggle for the men. The boy's face was blank of all expression, eyes and mouth open. He had not been dead long, even to the inexpert eyes of the priest, who had been called alongside the constable to give the moment its due gravity.

Nick Brown stood beside Brunskill and shuddered. "Who is he?" The clothing suggested a poor laborer, no one of note, but he was naturally curious and felt strangely responsible for the dead boy. Brunskill made the sign of the cross.

"He is Tom, I believe Tom Maltman, the innkeeper's servant," he said. "How 'tis possible to drown in this stream, I am sure I don't know. The boy was not known for drunkenness, and knew his way about."

None of this had any meaning for Brown. He began to think about his lost Cicero, and resisted the urge to return to the stream in search of it. Meanwhile the constable made a show of inspecting the body, peering into the eyes and mouth. "Drowned in the Misbourne," he said definitively. "A shame. Someone must be telling Daniel Grinshaw, it will be hard on the man to lose his servant."

"When was the last time somebody drowned in this stream?" asked Brunskill suddenly, with force. "Why, it is bare three feet deep at the middle! Surely there is another cause for death, Mr. Notkin, that we must ascertain. The poor boy."

Notkin, of course, had other plans for the rest of his day, and did not agree with Brunskill's assessment. "The boy had no parents, no kin hereabouts," he said with finality. "Who is there to concern himself with how he died? It's a sad thing, one so young, but I cannot say that it is murder. No witnesses, heh?" He looked about him at the small gathering and paused. "No, this is over and done with, Father, we can bury this boy."

The body was heaved into a cart, to be taken and prepared for burial. As they all began their slow trudge away from the stream, there was the sound of quick footsteps and a girl emerged out of the woods. She ran as fast as her skirts could allow and, when she saw the cart with the weight of a body in it, paused and slowed, stumbling as she made her way to it. Stopping next to the cart, she reached out to touch the boy's sodden hair, then pulled her hand back with a small cry.

"Naught but a dead servant boy," said the constable roughly. "None of your business, Miss Ann." Brunskill thought him unnecessarily cruel. The whole village knew of the courtship of Ann and Tom. He walked over to the girl and touched her arm.

"We will have a proper service for him, Miss Ann," he said to her with feeling. "He has gone to his Creator now and is at peace. It was not a hard death for him, he did not suffer long." How he knew this, he had no idea, but he felt it needed to be said to her, by way of comfort. How, after all, had the boy died? Perhaps a blow to the head, before being pushed into the stream? Strangled, choked? Why would someone do that—what did the boy have that anyone else might want? The questions came to him, but no answers, as he walked alongside the girl, behind the cart with its unfortunate burden.

When Frances went next to visit Fox in Aylesbury, she found that he and his fellow Friends had been removed to another building outside of the town. The assizes were, as was customary, scheduled for Midsummer, and so there was need of a place that could house them until then, since the local jail was for the holding of lesser criminals who could be tried by the local justice of the peace. She suspected, as she rode along to their prison, that other reasons were involved in their transport. Quakers did not, generally, provide the kinds of bribes that jailers took as a matter of course, and as a result often found that their habitation deteriorated over time.

Her fears were realized as she entered the low, dark building. In the recent past it had served as a barn. The stench was unbearable.

Even in the hall, before she entered the Quakers' chamber, she was nearly overcome. The jailer, from his post outside the door, nodded to her and allowed her entrance before retreating to his own chamber. She had never been in such a place before. Her eyes took time to adjust in the darkness, but the smell was so strong that she had to hold on to the wall to keep herself steady. It was the smell of excrement, rich and foul.

"Friend Frances," said a murmur of voices, and in the gloom she could make out Farmer Parrott, the Williams couple, the trio of Taylor, Stubbs and Talbot, and then of course George Fox, all standing in one corner near a small open window, the shutters nearly off the hinges. There were a few chairs scattered about, a plain table with an unlit candle, and two narrow beds, a dirty blanket on each. They had to take turns with their sleep, apparently. To Frances' horror, she could now see that the entire floor was covered in animal excrement. Holding her skirts up, she made careful steps at first but then, seeing it made no difference, she resigned herself to simply putting one foot in front of the other until she came to the circle of Friends. They watched with concern for her, but she knew they were not ashamed of their circumstances. Rather, they knew it to be a consequence of their belief and so utterly necessary.

She held out her basket, which had in it a salve for John Williams' stye, and a tightly sealed jar of ale mixed with honey for Farmer Parrott's persistent cough. Looking at the small band of Quakers, she realized she should have brought more, for they all looked as though they were wasting away. It was clearly difficult to take sustenance in these conditions. And yet they were all smiling at her, their shoes covered in shit.

"Thank you for this, Friend Frances," said Fox, his voice a whisper. "We would like to ask for shoes, come our day of trial, so that we need not wear these—" he laughed ruefully at his feet— "out of respect for the court. They say Midsummer, which is but weeks away."

Frances did not think she could be as cheerful as these folk managed to be. She suspected it was all Fox, and that the others kept up the pretense out of love for him. She knew herself well enough to imagine her shoes off and herself cowering on one of the beds, out of the muck, holding her nose.

She set the basket on the table and ignored the soft squishy sounds her feet made as she walked back and forth. "And how is it that they put you in such a place?"

Fox looked around. "As you can see, we have been flooded. It seems this used to be a barn, and that until recently animals were kept in the next chamber—when we arrived the place was dry and habitable, but then there was a rain and it flooded both chambers, mingling all together. The animals were removed, to dry quarters, but we of course remain." He shrugged. "It is our punishment, not unlike ones I have experienced before. We are more sorry for the lack of writing materials and books."

Frances was not sure if the others shared this sentiment. They seemed so miserable as they stood there, faces toward the window to get what fresh air there was to be had. She did notice that after a time the odor was less strong. With all the gaps in the walls, there was no lack of breeze, which helped to move the bad air.

"Please pray with us, Friend Frances," said Fox, and so they all bent their heads and clasped their hands together. Fox began to speak, in a frail, worn voice, expressing hope that their jailers would be witness to the Light within them and change their ways, allowing the Friends to go free to worship as they were called to do. Frances let her mind wander along Fox's trail, up and down the glades of his thought. She did not feel the warmth of the Light here in this barn, and so the journey was something of an arid one, but she did feel love for Fox, for the purity of his belief. He was so at peace with his God, so completely immersed in the Light.

Fox fell silent and all of them stood there, in that drafty, malodorous barn, their eyes closed as they waited. Frances knew it was of no use for her, this time, but she patiently waited as the others found their peace.

Slowly, one by one, her fellow Quakers opened their eyes, and they all smiled at one another. "Thank you for this sweet fellowship," said Frances with feeling, knowing that they had taken this moment for her, so that she could share in their experience. "I will return in two days. I am sure your eye will be better then, Friend John, and the cough will be nearly gone, Friend Samuel." The two men looked at her with smiles on their faces. They were lit from within, and even happy, in this cold barn filled with animal waste. Frances couldn't wait to leave.

"And, Frances," said Fox, "how is your matter with the widow? Has she made her way back to London?" His gaze was open, honest.

She hesitated, and hated herself for it. "No, she has not gone, not yet. I have opened my house to her. It was asked of me, and I saw the reason for it. A church storeroom is no place for a woman to live, alone and without friends or family."

Fox looked startled, as if he did not know her at all, she thought. Of course she would offer up her home to the widow. How could she do otherwise? And yet he seemed surprised, expecting a completely different answer. Perhaps he would have wished for her to personally have loaded Mistress Kidd on to a wagon and sent her back to where she came from, at his request.

"That is a good act, to provide a warm bed for a poor widow," he said quietly, "though there is much behind it, I think, that has little to do with charity. You must pray on this, Frances, and ask for enlightenment. I see your mind is clouded with your own wishes. The darkness keeps out the Light." His gaze was steady and unblinking. Not even a small cluster of errant lice escaping from his hair down to his neck moved him. He stood still, willing her to be the one to look away. Which she did, picking up her basket once more.

"It has been good to see all of you here, so refreshed in the Light," Frances said with finality. "As I have said, I will return in two days and bring more for you. I will take care of you all."

"*Hoc proelio facto, reliquas copias Helvetiorum ut consequi posset, ponte in Arari faciendum curat atque ita exercitum traducit...*" Jane could hardly bear it, as she escorted Caesar's troops in their war against the Helvetians, though she wasn't sure that was how their name translated. No doubt the tutor would tell her. There were no soft words in Caesar, no dusky locks or honeyed lips. All was hard and cold, marching across the wild landscape of places she did not care about. She couldn't help herself, she wanted the Gallic barbarian Vercingetorix to be victorious, to send Caesar and his legions back home and out of Gaul. Vercingetorix seemed passionate, clever, and mysterious, compared with methodical Caesar. Indeed, she thought wildly as she sat there in her chair, the tutor's eyes upon her, she was ever grateful to the betrayal of Brutus, so that Caesar did not write more.

"You may stop reading now," the tutor declared, closing his own book as Jane closed hers. "Please work on your translation of that page for tomorrow's lesson." He stood and brushed off his trousers, giving her a curt nod as he left the room. She noticed how he constantly sought solitude, escape, removal from her and Eliza. There were no conversations, he knew nothing of her and she less than that of him. She felt the poverty of it.

She placed her book, closed, on a corner of her desk and then prepared to leave. She hoped to spend the remainder of the afternoon with her mother, learning some of the less complicated medicines that Frances compounded in her workroom. She enjoyed those lessons, working side by side with her mother, who encouraged her no matter what mistakes she made in proportion or dose. She had ruined entire batches of tonics through her mistakes and carelessness. Her mother would simply sigh and heave the entire contents into a pail to be disposed of later. Then they would start over, and she would do better.

As she closed the door behind her she could hear something, muffled, low, in the next room, a closet not currently in use. She listened to what became clear to her was the sound of quiet weeping. Opening the door, she saw Ann Barwell sitting there on a stool, tears running down her pretty face and soaking the collar of her dress. "Oh dear," she said, quickly kneeling beside the girl. "Poor thing, poor thing." She did not know what else to say. She knew of Tom's death and had heard that Tom and Ann were expected to marry. This was far more interesting to her than Caesar's legions.

Ann was flustered. She was supposed to be hard at work, seeing to the cleaning. Instead here she was, caught in tears by her mistress's daughter. She stood up quickly, knocking Jane back on to the floor, and then just as quickly apologized and pulled the young woman up to her feet. They stood there looking at each other.

"I must be about my work, miss," she said with an energy that she did not feel. "Please excuse me."

Jane was horrified. "Oh no, no! Do not be sorry. You have lost the man who was to be your husband, and that is a terrible thing. He so young, and who knows by whose hand! I feel such sorrow for you, it is so sad." Her own eyes filled with tears, which led to more flowing on the part of Ann. Back she fell back onto the stool, giving in to a fresh torrent of tears. Jane slipped once more to the floor.

For some time the two girls sat there, Ann on her stool and Jane on the floor, both of them in tears. It felt good to Jane, to let her tears come, without much thought as to the reason. It felt good, that was enough, and being secreted away in this little closet made it all the better.

Ann wiped her own face with her smudged, stained apron, and sniffed. "I am so ashamed for you to find me here, away from my work." And she stood, tipped her head to Jane, and slipped out of the room. Jane was sorry to see her go.

She sat herself down on Ann's stool and wondered at the way of things, that it had all come to this, the violent death of Tom, a boy who had done no man harm. She knew well enough that God's ways were inscrutable, but she had also heard her share of stories of just retribution, miraculous and satisfying, evil men and women struck down as visible signs of God's justice. Many times George Fox had told stories of those who had wronged him and later found misfortune. It all gave her much to wonder at. Tom's death had meaning, but she had to take time to discover it.

As they all took their places around the table that evening for supper, Frances found some satisfaction in the way the candlelight warmed the table, casting it all in a soft, burnished gold. She sat at the head of the table, the young tutor Nick at the other end, her daughters and Sarah Kidd on either side. Bread with butter, a bowl of roasted parsnips, and a chicken soup fragrant with thyme and onion were all passed hand to hand.

Frances noticed that Jane did not look well. Her pale skin was mottled, her eyes reddened, and she took little onto her plate. The girl seemed never at peace with herself, always suffering in some way, as though there were a small hard stone within her, impossible to soften, that made her remote and unknowable. This had been true since she was a baby, thought Frances with resignation. She had thought, as a mother, that she would have an instinct as to how to quiet her crying child or bring comfort to her, but that had never been true with Jane. And yet at the same time, this unknowable child was much as she herself had been at the same age.

Sarah Kidd, her hands cleaner than Frances had yet seen them, helped herself to most of the bread and ate with determination. Frances hoped she would not be sick. The woman seemed to be making an effort to respect her new surroundings. Her collar was clear of grime and her hair was pulled back from her face in a way that was almost pleasing.

Frances told them of her visit to Fox and the other prisoners, taking care not to describe the conditions at the barn but rather to talk of the devotion and love that had been present there. She knew as she spoke that Mrs. Kidd had little or no interest in the Friends, as the woman helped herself to more soup, clattering the dishes and asking for more salt. Nick, on the other hand, seemed embarrassed, perhaps realizing that while she had been ministering to the prisoners he had been pleasantly wandering in the woods. He loudly insisted that he would accompany her on her next visit to the barn.

A silence fell. Suddenly Jane looked at Frances and put down her spoon. "Ma'am, I must ask this of you. I would like to attend the burial of Tom Maltman. It is to be tomorrow, in the morning. I would like to stand there with our servant, Ann." She looked down at her plate.

"Did you know the boy, Jane?" asked Frances, puzzled by this request and a little worried. "This has nothing to do with us, or with you. We are all very sorry, and I understand that he was a friend of Ann's, but that is all." She looked over at the tutor. "And such a hard thing for you, Nicholas, to have found the young man."

"I do not know that I can ever visit the Misbourne again without seeing him there, below the water," said the tutor. He quickly glanced at Eliza who was following his every word with concentration. "I will say no more here about it, a terrible death for that young man."

Jane ignored him and kept her eyes on Frances. "It is important that I go," she said with finality. "I want to be there as a help to Ann. I must do it, I must go."

Frances knew that Jane would go even if she were forbidden. In this, she was much like her mother. "You have my agreement in this," she said quietly. "You may go as a help to our servant Ann. You will go as a representative of our family."

Jane nodded, and then asked to be excused from the table. Frances felt helpless in the face of such strength of will. The girl left a full bowl of soup and bread behind her as she slid out of the room.

"She is a strong one," said Sarah Kidd suddenly, looking up from her own nearly empty bowl. "She will always get what she wants."

It rained again during the night, a hard rain unusual for this time of year. When it rained like this, Frances was prone to lie awake and think of leaks in the roof. The pounding made her imagine rivulets seeping through the shingles, feeding small streams in the attic, seeking out cracks in the walls and floor to sluice down into the house. And yet always, after such a night, she would make her way carefully up into the attic of the house only to find it dry. Late, past midnight she thought, she heard one of her daughters cry out. She lit her candle and made her way, stumbling, down the cold-floored hall, opening their chamber door with a loud squeak of hinges, only to see the two of them side by side breathing softly in the bed. She crept over to them, unable to resist such a moment of repose. Even Jane, one arm thrown over Eliza, looked at peace, her features relaxed, her hair damp against the blanket.

The next morning Frances made her way to her work chamber. She found Sarah Kidd already there, picking up first this jar and then that pot, examining the contents with a curiosity new to her. When she saw Frances she smiled crookedly and gestured at the row of boxes and jars, already disarranged through her careless groping. "You have a large store of medicines, I see. You must have a gift for tending the sick."

Frances was annoyed and began moving the containers, restoring them to their original order. Sarah watched for a moment, then shrugged and sat in the only chair in the room. "How did you come by this? I have never seen the like. In London, we have shops with such things in them, and one pays handsomely for the privilege of a medicine."

"My medicines work or they don't," said Frances with humility. "Sometimes the body wants it, and sometimes it doesn't." She thought of Mary Fields, with the sickness of the head, which had not responded even to her most extreme efforts. "One tries different things. That is what is most important, to try new combinations." She felt herself enthusiastic in spite of everything. Rarely did she get an opportunity to talk about her art. "I have the old recipes, the ones my aunt taught me and that I have learned from others. Sometimes they need to be altered, and so then I consult my books—" she pointed in the direction of a low shelf, with her favorite texts neatly stacked on it—"and consider what could be changed, and to what effect."

Sarah stared at the books. "You are a scholar, then," she said with a small voice.

Frances laughed. "Oh no, I am no scholar, I leave that for the men. I can read, and I can think, and I want to be of service. So that is what I do." She began to open a large jar that stood on a corner of the table, took a sniff and then nodded approvingly. "Things cook away in here, settle and mix, and I am the mistress of it."

There was a smile in return. "I will watch you as you work," said Sarah with a note of pleasure in her voice. "We shall talk of the matter, and you shall work."

"The matter," repeated Frances as she began to lay out her instruments and mixtures. "I have no thought for what we can do now. Poor Ann and her Tom."

"Yes, but you see, don't you, that it is Tom who is leading us to the truth." Sarah settled herself more comfortably in the chair. "He was in the employ of the innkeeper during that time of my husband's murder, and his death is part of it."

Frances' hands fell to her sides as she contemplated the boy's death and its connection to her and to Ann. It was possible, then, that her own meddling, sending Ann to talk with the boy, might have led to his death. Why this had not occurred to her before this moment she could not say.

Sarah, however, seemed to find this a lucky turn. "This will lead us to the truth," she said with energy. "We're almost there, he has done it for us. It is thanks to this that the murderer has shown his hand. I can see it, I can see him at his business, as though it were happening before my very eyes."

"You do not mean that," cried Frances, though she knew she did. "The poor boy, gone because of my curiosity! This is what George meant about my meddling, thinking I am rescuing someone when really I let that boy die." She felt sick, a dense feeling in her chest. What evil she had done.

The widow ignored her, standing and going to the window, thoughtful in the face of Frances' wildness. "I will go to the burial of the boy today, with your daughter Jane. I will see if the guilty murderer comes, and I will watch for a sign. I will call him out, challenge him, he will not be able to escape me." She leaned against the windowsill and looked back at Frances with some satisfaction. "I wonder if he will dare to show his face."

The two women gazed at each other, but they each might as well have been alone in that chamber. Sarah's eyes were full of the murderer, the shame in his eyes as he looked back at her. And Frances was looking upon the dead body of a boy, the fresh face gone slack and empty.

Chapter Eleven

———◆———

Brunskill felt that half his life seemed to be spent with the dead. This did not bother him, for in so many ways they were easier than the living. A small crowd of whom gathered round him, looking to him to give the moment, and the boy, their due. There was young Jane Lyndal, enshrouded in her coal grey cloak, shadows under her eyes as she stood there contemplating the gaping hole as the digging progressed. Next to her was Sarah Kidd, of all people, her red coat a flash of color in the dull brown of the landscape. Round little Ann Barwell stood close by Jane, almost hiding behind her, afraid to see what was to become of her Tom. Her face was still as a smooth stone, her eyes wide and bright.

Other than that, there was just a small number of villagers, here for either the sights or because they had run across Tom in some dealings over the years. Tom had no family, so no mother stood weeping by the grave. For everyone here, he had been but a passer-by, briefly regarded as he moved across the scene. Brunskill thought about what Tom's future would have been, married to Ann at some time when his fortune allowed for a wife, with children, finding work in the fields, perhaps, or opening some sort of shop. Then he would have been one of the villagers here, known all too well, self-important, gossipy, standing at some poor servant boy's grave.

It came time for the coffin to be lowered into the ground, which the men did with little ceremony. Brunskill stepped forward to provide his service, but as he opened the book he was interrupted by the arrival of another, this time the large presence of the innkeeper Daniel Grinshaw. Striding across the field, looking grim and uncomfortable in his ill-fitting jacket, the man kept his eyes low as he negotiated the muddy path. It was only as he fell in with the group, clustered around the grave that his eyes lit on Sarah Kidd, which made him visibly startle. She had not taken her eyes off him from the moment he had appeared over the rise. He had hesitated for a moment, once her presence was known to him, but then resolutely marched forward. He was not to be stopped by this widow. Standing next to Brunskill, putting himself in charge of the whole matter, he nodded his head, and the priest continued his service.

At least Sarah allowed him that much, Brunskill thought as he brought the brief ceremony to a close. She had let him finish. The boy was now with God, and he had had this small dignity, this brief recognition. The priest felt a sense of relief even as he witnessed the shoveling of the dirt and gradual disappearance of the coffin.

"Come to see your handiwork," said Sarah Kidd in a high voice, looking straight at Grinshaw. "The poor boy, dead at your hand." She walked over to him, with a look of triumph on her wasted face. "God will strike you dead. Who will be next, this poor girl?" She turned and pointed to the terrified Ann Barwell. "Perhaps he told her all your nasty secrets, you can't be too sure!"

The villagers all stood stock still, waiting for the innkeeper's reply. Grinshaw was at first silent as he listened to her, staring over her head at some far distant object. But then he laughed, a brutal, hard laugh, and stepped close so that he was almost touching the widow. Unafraid. "What's a servant boy know of me?" he asked. "He was naught but my boy, and the most he could talk of were pigs and firewood." He laughed again, a harsh sound. "Look for your murderer somewhere else in this village, Mistress Kidd."

Sarah Kidd refused to look away. Her eyes kept seeking his, almost desperately. "I will find you out," she said. "I will find you out."

Then she turned and walked away across the field, not bothering to raise her skirts above the muck, to the tune of Ann Barwell's hysterical weeping. Jane, her arm across the girl's shoulder, turned her gaze on the innkeeper as he stood there triumphant.

"Master Grinshaw, if what she says be true, you must not come near this girl here," she said with a loud voice. "She is an innocent, in truth, far from all these concerns. She but cared for the boy."

Brunskill was surprised by her steadiness, this thin little girl, imagining herself as some sort of guardian for her maidservant. While he himself had been struck dumb by Sarah's attack, here was Jane Lyndal, speaking up for poor Ann. Talking to Daniel Grinshaw, with whom she had never exchanged a word before in her life. Her words seemed to have a powerful effect on the man, more so than those of the widow.

"Miss Lyndal, never would I touch a hair on the head of that girl, and you must know that I am innocent of all that has been said against me by that woman. It is all her imaginings, you can be sure. The devil has taken her over and made her say such things. There is no truth in it, nor does any other man or woman speak ill of me." And then Grinshaw turned and made his way along the path, having said farewell to his servant boy.

The villagers gathered themselves and began to follow him, the grave now a fresh mound of dirt. Brunskill went to Jane and Ann, but there was no more consoling to be done. The young women turned from him and followed the villagers, arm in arm. They were allies in this and he was, still, an outsider.

Frances opened the letter, unable to breathe. From Richard, she imagined it to be yet another attack on her ownership of the Grove. It saved her the pain of his actual presence, but also worried her in its formality. Richard rarely wrote to her. That had been his custom with Matthew, a constant stream of letters, but with her he had never taken to the pen. She sat herself down to read. The house was quiet, the girls at their study. There was only the sound of Ann's broom, sweeping the stairs.

But it was not a letter of demand. It was very brief.

> *Dear Sister,*
>
> *On the second of June, my Father left this World. He died in the Cell in which they had placed him, fulfilling his Punishment. He suffered greatly but no more. May God give him rest. Please give this news to Eliza as his only Grandchild. I hope that this letter finds you all well.*
> *With Regard,*
> *Richard*

Frances knew that Matthew and Richard's father had no love for her. He blamed her for Matthew's conversion to the Friends and could never forgive her for that. He had been so strong in his own faith, his son's apostasy always salt in the wound, so to blame Frances made it all easier. Never mind that his other son became a Jesuit and his daughter a kept woman known far and wide all over London, thought Frances with some bitterness. The man's complete belief in himself and in his faith was unshakeable even in the face of such rebellion. He remained, always, certain of his decision to condemn the King to death, and never wavered thereafter. Too much his own man to work well with Lord Protector Cromwell, he had eventually found himself isolated and ignored by those in power, which had been the beginning of his long decline. Frances and Matthew, even when they had lived in London, had not visited the elder Brights with any regularity, pained by their many differences. Frances' most vivid memories of the couple were of the way in which they both would look over her head as she spoke, perhaps thinking she should be taller. Amid the great size of the Brights she always felt a child, to be lectured at and ignored.

She would have to write a note in return, with proper condolence, to her brother-in-law. She did not mean to attend the funeral, if there were one. Since the deceased was a disgraced regicide, there might be a graveside prayer and no more. She couldn't help wondering what this latest turn in events would mean regarding the Grove. As a prisoner with a life-sentence, Bright had forfeited all his property to the Crown, and thus impoverished his heirs. The fact that the Grove had escaped this fate by the father's signing it over to his son some years previously made it particularly precious to the remaining family. She could not simply wait for Richard to take her to court. She must take action herself, even if it meant compromise. Compromise not including Jane, she thought with anger, but surely something that would keep Richard away from the Grove.

Frances got up from her table and moved to the window, looking out at the front garden that stretched all the way to the small pond and then the road. She found herself on the alert for any sign of a horse in the lane, worried that Richard was headed here this moment. But all was quiet. It was a warm morning, the sun strong in a cloudless sky as it turned the pond to burnt gold, making her look away. But not before she noticed the two figures at its northern end.

Mr. Brunskill and Sarah Kidd were standing close together, in serious conversation. Then they moved apart, the widow starting to walk on the path circumnavigating the pond, the priest pausing for a moment before running to catch up. It was like that for the next ten minutes as Frances watched: two figures close together, then the widow moving away only to have the priest, after a moment of doubt, trot after her. It was most interesting.

It seemed the proper thing to do, thought Arthur Brunskill as he made his way to the Grove after the burial. Having asked Mrs. Bright to look after the widow Kidd, it was his duty to see how it was all settled, and to show his gratitude once again to Frances for her good deed of hospitality. Indeed, not to do so would be noticed and would have grieved both Mrs. Bright and Mrs. Kidd. It was his obligation. So he told himself, over and over, as he walked the short distance from the village vicarage to the Grove. And yet he still had this uneasy feeling, the overwrought, sick feeling he always got as a child when he knew that he was going to be punished for what he still, almost helplessly, had settled on to do.

It was a beautiful day, warm enough that he tossed his coat over his shoulder. After the long, wet winter, filled with rain and snow, he could feel the dampness leach out of his bones as the sun settled on him. Walking was a pleasure on a day like this. The English summer was a frail thing, hesitant in arrival and fickle enough to leave on a whim.

As he approached the Grove, he admired the pond, a pleasingly oval body of water fed by a spring. Marshy grasses grew around its edges. A path encircled it before running off to join the main path to the house. A contingent of mallards paddled around the southern half of the pond, and curlews settled in the grasses. Brunskill gave a sigh of delight as he moved closer. That was when he noticed Sarah Kidd, alone on the solitary bench that cupped the northern tip of the pond, her eyes closed as the sun warmed her face.

"Dear Mrs. Kidd," he said softly, not knowing if she had dozed off. "Dear Mrs. Kidd." He stood before her as she slowly opened her eyes, reluctant, perhaps coming out of a dream she didn't want to leave.

"Mr. Brunskill," she cried, standing up hastily. "You must excuse me, you've surprised me." She smoothed her skirts and touched her coif, yet remained clearly uncomfortable. She was, for once, without the red coat, instead wearing a light blue cloak that had no doubt been given her by Mrs. Bright. "The sun is quite warm this morning."

"Yes, our summer has come," the priest said heartily, "Truly a blessing, after the rain of the spring." He coughed gently. "I am glad to see you looking so well, Mrs. Kidd. Mrs. Bright must be taking good care of you." He was relieved at the discourse, happy to know that he and the widow could carry on a greeting without difficulties. Perhaps all the awkwardness could be forgotten. He felt a slow flush cover his face, with the memory. Awareness of it just made the blush all the deeper.

Mrs. Kidd looked away, mortified. "I thank you once again for providing shelter to me, Mr. Brunskill, and for persuading Mrs. Bright to take me in. Your kindness will not soon be forgotten. I am now able to pursue my business here without the cares that would otherwise be my lot. You are a good man."

He felt this to be a cruel remark, and his flush deepened further. "I am not good, Sarah, not at all, I am not good," he said before he could stop himself. "I must ask your forgiveness. I took advantage of one who is without protection and so did great wrong. I—"

The woman moved away as he spoke, perhaps frightened by his words. She struck out fast along the path. He stayed a moment, not understanding, but then found himself trotting to catch up with her. "Please, Sarah, stop with me a moment."

She turned to him, her eyes filled with angry tears.

"It doesn't matter, it doesn't matter. You think on it more than I do. I am indifferent. It may be important to you, as you mull over your sins and virtues, but there is no such comfort for me. I am empty, and to touch me is to touch nothing at all."

"I do not believe that, Sarah," he said, insisting on her first name in a way that no doubt galled her. "I know that I harmed you, I can see it now, and for that I am sorry. I must say it. Believe me, it is little comfort to either of us. I ask your forgiveness."

She moved away again, more slowly this time. He followed her, insistent, for surely she must know that as a Christian it was her duty to forgive. They stood close together at the water's edge. Suddenly Sarah's face changed, became remote and stern, and she raised a thin hand to quickly wipe tears from her face. "Mrs. Bright," she said softly to Brunskill. He turned to see their hostess skimming along the path from the house, smiling and now calling to them.

"I am so happy to find both of you here," Frances said cheerily, "on such a fine day too. Ah, Mr. Brunskill—" she took his hand warmly—"and Mrs. Kidd," again a warm grasp of the widow's icy hand. What followed was a brief awkward silence.

"I am visiting in order to thank you for your care for Mrs. Kidd," said the priest with some formality, "and I was fortunate in that I found Mrs. Kidd here by your pond." His voice was running high, as it always did when he was nervous. "Truly, Mrs. Bright, your hospitality is timely and generous."

Mrs. Kidd, meanwhile, seemed to be struggling with her composure. She looked down at the ground. "Really," she said in a low voice, "Mr. Brunskill, you need not have taken the trouble. You must think me a child, to feel you need to express my gratitude to Mrs. Bright."

Brunskill looked as though he had been struck. There was a long silence, but Frances could not bear it.

"I am sure, Mrs. Kidd, that Mr. Brunskill meant no disrespect," she said with energy. "No doubt it was simply an excuse to visit us here at the Grove. Dear Mr. Brunskill, please know in future that you need not have a reason to visit. We are always delighted to see you. Now, please, let us go to the house and sit together awhile. I am always glad of company."

She thought she might have to take the two by the hand and lead them to the house, but after a moment's hesitation they followed her in silence. She could not understand their difficulty with each other. It was clear to her that the priest cared about Mrs. Kidd, perhaps more than was seemly, but Sarah Kidd's anger was unexpected. She was a strange woman.

Brunskill, for his part, was in despair. It seemed nothing he said could ease this chill between himself and the widow. He was well aware that she had not forgiven him, leaving it all unfinished and sore, something his mind went to on sleepless nights. She was hard on him, but there was a part of him that felt he deserved it.

Having insisted that Mr. Brunskill stay for dinner, Frances presided over a table that was unusually quiet. Jane was, as usual, lost in her own thoughts, and Eliza had been sent to her room after spilling her soup. The tutor had been nowhere to be found, no doubt off on one of his rambles. The priest and the widow sat at opposite ends of the table, so that Frances found herself taking turns, first making remarks to Brunskill and then eliciting comments from Sarah Kidd. The very good pigeon pie, savory and surprisingly tender, seemed wasted on both of her guests as they picked at their plates. Frances had even served some of her better wine in the hope of bringing some warmth to the table, to no avail.

Deborah appeared in the doorway in the midst of the meal. "Mistress Harp here to see you, ma'am."

The good woman was of course asked to join them at their dinner, and sat herself down with alacrity, having no doubt come from her own meager, ill-prepared dinner. A large slice of pigeon pie was placed in front of her alongside a gratifying glass of Frances' wine. At least now there might be some conversation, thought Frances, though it will be Quakerish and no doubt would not suit her other guests.

"I give thanks to God for this good meal," said Susan as she dug her spoon into the pie. "I am sorry to have interrupted at this time, your dinner is later than most, Frances."

As Susan enjoyed her dinner, Frances introduced her to Mrs. Kidd and the priest.

"It is good to meet you, Mrs. Kidd," Susan said, ignoring the priest. "I was pleased to hear of Frances' generosity. I—I think it terribly kind of her." Then, after a short pause, she continued, looking only at Sarah.

"There's nothing to be done, is there?" she said. "It's over and done with, your husband gone, nothing more. It is good that he is now in hallowed ground, buried as is proper. That is good." She nodded, seeming to reassure herself.

There was a long pause.

"Dear Mrs. Harp," said Sarah Kidd, "Thank you for your concern about my good husband. But the matter is not done. It is not. There must be justice, there must be punishment. Nathaniel's murderer will be brought to trial and his fortune returned to me and my son. My son, who has not a penny to his name, and yet his fortune was taken from him, along with his father. You cannot tell me that it is done. Who are you to know?"

Susan turned white. Sarah continued. "It is kind for the people of this good village to have sympathy for me, and to be so glad of my husband's burial, which I assure you delights me as well. But it passes understanding why these same people are willing to allow a murderer to go free, unjudged, living among them here in Chalfont St. James. He has murdered two good Christians now. He has tried to murder me in my bed. Those who do not help me in my search for justice are in league with the murderer. It is as though they killed poor Nathaniel, and that poor boy Tom, with their own hands. They are bloody with it. They are"—and here Sarah's voice went high—"they are murderers themselves, every one of them, sitting quiet in their little houses, saying their prayers every night, thinking they are talking to God. Their prayers are empty, they do not reach God's ears, not while the murderer is free in this village. They are all excommunicated, out of reach of God's grace. They are to be judged: they will stand side by side with Daniel Grinshaw as they face their Final Judgment. And they will be thrown into the very darkness of Hell."

"I heard him cry out," whispered Susan, her own hell here on earth as tears filled her eyes. "I heard him, Mrs. Kidd. He cried out, for help, I could hear as clear as though he were sitting at this table. I heard his cry and I ran away, I could not help him."

Frances reached over and took Susan's trembling hand. "Now Susan, do not trouble yourself."

"Ah," said Sarah, "so you were there, Mrs. Harp? You witnessed my husband's murder? Tell me more, what you saw, what you heard!" She was excited, had pushed her plate away and could hardly keep herself still in her chair.

Susan took a deep breath, all eyes upon her. She told her story with a surprising coherence, having practiced it over and over in her mind, imagining herself in a court of law, addressing a judge with the weight of the King's justice behind him. When done, she sat back in her chair and took a deep breath, exhausted. There was a long silence.

Jane could not stop herself. "Oh, Mrs. Harp, so is Mr. Grinshaw the—is he guilty?"

Susan Harp put her hand over her mouth for a moment before speaking. "Oh no, little one, I cannot say. I heard the scream. I saw—I saw a dark form in a doorway. Then some sort of bundle being carried from the house. I cannot say whether poor Mr. Kidd was the one in danger that night, we can't know for sure. No more, no more."

"Dear Mrs. Harp," said Sarah Kidd, "dear Mrs. Harp! Your story—we must take it to the constable. I have another witness, who can place my Nathaniel in this village at a time and place, if your memory be with his then we have evidence, we have evidence."

"I do not know the day," said Susan slowly, "but I know the year and the season. And it was a full moon, I know that too, so that I could find my way in the dark."

"I'm sure," said Frances, "that your other witness's memory is not more precise than that. Indeed, I am surprised he remembers this meeting at all. Susan, you understand the meaning of going to the constable?"

Susan looked like a child in trouble, her pigeon pie grown cold on her plate. "Oh yes, I do, Frances, you know that. I may be asked to testify in a court, and take—an oath. I do know that."

Jane interjected a remark once more, determined to play a part in these decisions. For certainly, in her mind, this had to do with Tom Maltman as well, and poor Ann Barwell, for whom she felt somehow responsible. "The oath is a small matter compared with a man's life," she said with finality. "Indeed, the lives of two men. Surely, Mother, we Friends would agree to the punishment of such a sinner as Mr. Grinshaw is."

"I cannot pretend to know the Friends and their views on oaths," said Mr. Brunskill, drawn out of his thoughtful silence. "But it seems to me it would be a hard thing to live with, to not come forward with such evidence when a widow and her child's future is at stake." He looked at Sarah Kidd with a small, hopeful smile. "This may be the answer to your prayers, ma'am."

They all had lost interest in the dinner. There was nothing to be done for it, thought Frances with resignation. Susan's secret would now become part of the story of Nathaniel Kidd and his murder.

Frances woke to the sound of rain hitting the shutters and sighed with some irritation. Today was her journey, a visit to her mother-in-law in London to pay her respects, but also in the hope of putting an end to Richard's suit. Fortunately, as she descended to the dining room for her breakfast the rain sputtered to an end, and she was greeted by wan sunshine as Deborah opened the curtains and pushed open the shutters.

On his last visit, along with the precious lemons, Richard had brought chocolate, which was all the rage in London. Frances delighted in the drink as a morning draught, extravagant though she knew it to be. The cook had at first been suspicious but had followed Richard's instructions to the letter. Convinced, however, that it was dangerous, she had refused to taste it.

Eliza and Jane joined Frances before she had finished. They preferred their simple milk with bread, and sat in companionable silence as Frances finished the last of the chocolate. Probably no more where that came from, she thought ruefully. She would miss Richard's largesse of London goods. She tried to see this in the most useful way, that these were troublesome seductions and indulgences that he brought, which only served to weaken her. Thus it was all to the good that he would no longer come bearing gifts.

Her two horses were brought round and there was young Stephen from the village, mounted already, both excited and frightened of the journey. Stephen had never been farther than five miles from Chalfont St. James, and was troubled by the very thought of a town the size of London. It amazed him, how so many people could be gathered in one place. Someone, a traveler, had once told him of being "lost" in London, and he wondered at that as well. He had always known where he was. What would it feel like, to be unsure about something so vital? How would you find your way in a town, if you were lost? It almost made him stop breathing, just the mere thought of it.

As they settled themselves, Sarah Kidd emerged from the house. She strode up to Frances' horse and reached for Frances' hand awkwardly, with a moment's hesitation.

"Mrs. Bright," she asked, her eyes imploring, "I know you've business in London that will occupy you, but I ask that you visit my son when you are there. I need to know if he is all right. He is with my neighbors, in Boo Lane, you can find them above the shop that sells tobacco and such, they are Mr. and Mrs. Thompson." She tightened her grip. "I must know if he is alive and well, I left him as such a small one."

Frances could answer in no other way. "Yes, Mrs. Kidd, I will do as you ask. Do not cause yourself more worry."

The road was clear and the weather dry, and they made good time. Frances gazed at the alternating fields and woods, the day warming to high summer as they went along. She thought about her mother-in-law, the imposing Mrs. Bright, sure and silent. She could not imagine her with children, with a small Matthew on her knee. So austere a woman as she would keep children at a distance. Matthew had used nothing but loving words about his mother, as someone who had taught him right from wrong, who had served as an exemplar of devotion and goodness. Frances tried hard to see this in the old woman when they saw each other but failed each time. She thought it was perhaps because she thought of goodness as kindness, and these two did not meet in Mrs. Bright.

It was midday as they approached Hillingdon, and they stopped by the side of the road so that they could take some nourishment. Frances had brought bread, cheese, and a small jar of preserved plums. She and Stephen sat together in the grass and ate silently, watching the occasional horse and wayfarer go by. The road had become more populated as they came closer to London. Stephen could not stop staring. The parade of people he did not know, all strangers to him, their eyes on the road ahead, held him in thrall. Frances, busy with the work of eating, hardly looked up. She still had Matthew's mother Mary in her mind, thinking over what she must say to her. What had seemed a very hopeful journey began to seem foolhardy as she imagined the old woman's response to her. Surely she would take Richard's side as her only living son and the only child with whom she remained in communication. Richard would eventually marry—not to Jane, God forbid—and his children would, in Mary's eyes, be the rightful heirs to the Bright property. Eliza would eventually lose her name to that of her husband, and her children would thus be one step removed from the direct Bright line.

And yet, and yet. She put away the unfinished jar of plums and nodded to Stephen. They shook the grass off their clothing and climbed back on to their horses, Stephen not knowing enough to help her up, which made her smile. For the remainder of the trip she thought about her arguments, about Eliza and the home that was theirs. In her imaginings the old lady began to soften.

Chapter Twelve

———·◆·———

Jane decided that at the very least, she was now allowed to sit at the head of the table, in her mother's chair. As the household gathered around and seated themselves for the evening meal, she took some small satisfaction in nodding to Deborah. The loaf of bread made its way around the table followed by a hot gruel to which Jane had a strong aversion. She took her serving and felt closer to God as she swallowed.

"Let me ask something of you," said Mrs. Kidd in a lighter tone than Jane had come to expect from her. "I do not think it is too much to ask. Your care for Ann Barwell, so evident at the burial of the boy, whence comes that? It is not something usual between mistress and servant, not in my eyes."

"The Friends believe that all are the same before God, and that master and servant are the same in this world as they are in the next," said Jane with conviction. "I saw her troubled, with your words at the burial, and I wanted to comfort her. She has no one now: her father doesn't care for her. You frightened her, Mrs. Kidd, and I did my best to ease her worries." There was no note of accusation in Jane's voice but her eyes were fierce.

Sarah Kidd thought for a moment as she chewed her bread. Finally, "I did not mean to frighten the girl. I meant to frighten the murderer, someone whom everyone lets go free to walk about and do as he pleases, from murdering my husband in his bed to murdering a poor boy who knew of his villainy. Ann Barwell has naught to fear from me. If Tom Maltman told her anything of the innkeeper's doings, she might have something to fear from that man. I wanted to say that, for all to hear."

Jane admired Sarah Kidd's sense of purpose. She said things and took actions that, no matter the outcome, never troubled her conscience. No apparent self-doubt to weaken her. It was something to which Jane aspired but felt that her own Quaker faith undermined, with its constant introspection and unworldly demands.

"I know that I can be of help to you," she cried out impetuously, as Mrs. Kidd finished the last of her gruel.

"Perhaps you can, even one so young as you," Sarah said. "You are now the mistress here, in your mother's absence."

Mr. Brown broke in. "I feel there is a misunderstanding here. Miss Jane is not the mistress in her mother's absence. She is here to see to her younger sister, but we as her elders are to be obeyed in all things. I cannot countenance any actions that this child may undertake of her own will." He looked severely at Jane, who put aside her gruel and stood. But before she could say anything Mrs. Kidd coughed.

"How is it that you can help?"

Redirected, Jane sat herself down once more and looked at Mrs. Kidd. "I will help you find what you need to bring a case against the innkeeper. Might he not have, in that house of his, some things belonging to your husband? Were all things with your husband in his grave, or would there be possessions that would be kept aside by the murderer?"

Sarah Kidd thought for a moment. "All that was with him was his bones," she said, "and a button from his coat. Of course he had his fortune with him, that which was taken." A small, bitter laugh. "Poor Nathaniel, he had little else, but I was sorry not to see a small box that he always carried with him. It was of pewter and carried a small"—she blushed heavily—"belonging of mine that he kept by him. I never thought I would see it again."

"Well then," said Jane with enthusiasm, "where that box resides, resides the murderer. I wouldn't wonder if Mrs. Grinshaw keeps it on her bedtable."

"This is too much," declared the tutor. "You cannot go asking for a little box. You will bring evil consequences onto this family and this house. You are but making mischief." He took a deep breath. "Miss Jane, I must ask that you not leave this house while your mother is away."

I am like Sarah Kidd, thought Jane, *I can say things and not feel sorry. I can do as I please.*

"Dear Mr. Brown," she said with a smile, looking over at Mrs. Kidd to be sure she had her full attention. "This is not your concern. Caesar is your concern, as is Cicero perhaps, and certainly the Scripture. But you are not to direct me in other matters." And she got up from her chair and left the room, leaving silence behind her.

Frances' arrival in London was a slow, grinding affair as they wound their way on the busy road, dodging carts and coaches, making their way to Old Fish Street. Having come down in the world from the great heights of the Interregnum, Frances' mother-in-law now resided in this crowded, gloomy lane of small houses near the Thames. As they brought their horses up to the front stoop of Mrs. Bright's home, Frances was aware of a richer array of odors than she, even on a farm, was used to. The intense acrid smell of urine was cut by the sweetish odors of animal waste that on this summer day seemed to cover everything with a fine dust. Along with this came the reek of the river, foul with summer's stink. Stephen took the horses to a nearby stable to be kept. Covering her nose with a handkerchief, Frances made her way up the stairs to her mother-in-law's front door and was greeted by the old lady's maidservant. Now old herself and bent nearly double with age, Margaret brought Frances inside into the hall.

Frances was aware immediately of the consequences of an aging if loyal staff. As the elderly Margaret shuffled ahead of her, she moved past dark furnishings sticky with grime, the floor swept but with a light touch. The house had the sour, warm smell of age. It saddened her, remembering as she did the large and finely appointed home of the Brights' younger years. The contrast between the home of a prosperous civic leader and that of the widow of a disgraced regicide was painful to witness. She was led, via the faltering steps of the maidservant, into a small chamber crowded with heavy furniture. She could see the old woman by the window's filtered light, a book open in her lap. The elder Mrs. Bright was unusual in her literacy and her life-long devotion to her own well-worn copy of the Bible. She knew her place and said not a word in church, but Frances had a suspicion that entire sermons, wise and erudite, lay stillborn in her head.

The lady did not rise, the infirmity of age keeping her to her chair. She held out a hand to Frances and nodded for her to take a seat beside her.

"It is a surprise to see you, my dear," she said, her voice firm and clear. "We have not visited in some years."

"Not since Matthew's passing," replied Frances with some embarrassment. "I was very sad to hear of Father Bright's death, and have come to give you my condolences." She found that there was, indeed, a small drop of sympathy in her heart for the old woman, in spite of everything. "I see you are all alone here with Margaret. I am here to offer you my home, to live with me and my daughters. Margaret is welcome too."

A sharp look from the old woman. Then silence for a time as Margaret brought in a jug of cider and poured a small cup for their guest. It was delicious after such a long journey, and Frances was suddenly aware of how tired she was. Then Mrs. Bright reached over and rapped Frances' knee. Meant, perhaps, affectionately, it also felt like a demand for attention.

"You are good to offer," the widow said, "as a daughter should. I have lived here alone since my husband's imprisonment, and I am at ease here. Chalfont St. James is too far."

Frances fully expected that answer, and indeed a part of her acknowledged that she would not have made her offer at all if another answer had been likely. Not a nice thing to know about herself, of course. She had hoped that her invitation would elicit some commentary from her mother-in-law about Richard and his claim, but the woman fell into silence once more. Frances finished her cider and poured herself another cup.

"You will stay here tonight," Mrs. Bright said with a note of resignation. "Are you to return to the Grove tomorrow? Or is your stay a longer one?"

"I plan to return to the Grove in a few days," said Frances, "I do have some other business to see to before I leave. I thank you for your hospitality, Mother Bright."

The old woman nodded: yes, this was indeed a great deal to ask. "I take my supper early," she said, "and at that time you and I will talk of Richard and his request of you. He has told me of it, and I can see that it is on your mind. You will now excuse me." She sat motionless in her chair as Frances rose and turned to find old Margaret waiting by in the doorway, ready to show her to her room. Once there she lay down on the narrow bed and fell asleep within minutes.

The old woman was true to her word as she and a somewhat re-vived Frances sat down to their evening meal. The room was dark and dingy, the dishes not as clean as Frances would have liked, but she took a deep breath and thought no more of it. Margaret stumbled about and served them the evening soup, a thin concoc-tion in which floated pale vegetables and small bits of bone and pigeon-meat. Her eyesight was poor and her hand infirm, so that the ladle of soup dribbled from pot to bowl, joining a long visible history of sticky stains from previous meals. There was a strongly flavored bread and butter, along with a fresh, milky cheese. Frances bowed her head as the elderly Mrs. Bright thanked God for their meal and for Frances' safe arrival in London. A world of women, Frances thought to herself as Mrs. Bright raised her head, eyes still closed. Sitting alone at our tables, leading prayer. The men all gone. Her mind travelled to Sarah Kidd and Ann Barwell.

"My table is not as it once was," said the old lady. "I am sorry that I cannot serve you better, but nothing can be done about it. The King, as is his right, has taken everything. I am left with this lodging and these few things around me, as you see. I have learned about pride and its consequences."

"It has not to do with your pride, Mother Bright, but with events outside of you and me," replied Frances with energy. "The Kingdom of God seemed at hand. How could we have been so mistaken, the signs seemed so clear. And yet here we are." *And with a Catholic as heir to the throne*, but Frances left those somewhat treasonous words unspoken.

They sat silently for a time, eating their meal, the candles flickering low in their bowls. Mrs. Bright was slow and careful with her spoonfuls, and had to gum the bread into submission, having lost many teeth to age. Frances decided it was best to wait for her to bring up the matter of Richard. At long last the bread was finished and the old lady looked up from her plate.

"Richard has told me of his request, that you give up the house to him," she said. "It is an honorable request, and I do not understand your stubbornness, Frances. If Matthew had had a son, things would be different, but we must keep the house in the Bright family. This was always my husband's intention, even as he gave Matthew the house. At least we didn't lose it to the Crown. It is the only thing left. It is of a time before the family came to London and made its fortune." She took a small sip of ale. "All that my husband built has now come to nothing. All we have is what we came from, in Chalfont St. James. When Richard marries and his wife gives him a son, the line will continue there."

"Does he have plans to marry, Mother Bright?" asked Frances, carefully.

Mrs. Bright shook her head slowly. "Naught that I know of, but then Richard does not confide in me. I do not know in whom he confides. He has little to say to me. It has always been so. He caused his father much unhappiness in his life. His has always been a restless soul—I do not know to what church he goes now. The godly have fallen away. The priests all look to the King before saying a word these days." Her eyes lifted from her soup and gazed at Frances, grief-stricken.

Frances sighed. The old woman had moved past Richard, to the ways of the world in which she found herself, the inexplicable retreat of the godly. But Frances knew that she had to talk with

Mother Bright about Richard and the house, even as she also knew what the old woman would say in reply. She had come all this way.

"Mother Bright," she said, "Richard's request of me goes against Matthew's own will. You know this to be true. My husband's will left the house to Eliza, and I am her guardian. There is no mention of Richard in Matthew's will other than the love he bore him."

"Matthew was never one to think of the family," replied the old woman with finality. "It had no meaning to him. Isn't that the way of your religion, to neglect all earthly obligations? He flouted his father, ran away from his faith, derided our position in the world. Here was his father, a leader of the godly of London, having given all to his sons in raising them, only to see his eldest flee amongst the rabble, those mean Quakers and their lot. His child, our only grandchild, unbaptized! At least Richard has returned, has given up on his youthful mistakes, and shows due respect to his family. He understands that the Grove is all that is left for the Brights." Her voice rose with every word. Margaret appeared in the doorway, looking alarmed, before edging backwards into the shadows of the hall.

Frances gathered herself together. The old lady was hard. "As is true of all in your family, Matthew sought God before all else. So did Richard. You and your husband as well." She could not bring herself, of course, to mention their sister, not yet. "Surely you do not begrudge him his search, even as it took him far from you. Mother Bright, you taught Matthew as a small child"—and here she pictured in her mind the frayed Bible in the old woman's lap—"to seek God however he might. To read the Scripture for what he would find there. His journey took him far from his family and yet he remained very close to all of you. He did not undertake his search in defiance of his father, he undertook it in honor of you." Here, of course, was the crux of the Bright family experience: the father austere and outward, seeking his name in the city, the mother at home with her Bible, three children clustered about her. All of whom came to grief with their father.

Mother Bright looked away for a moment before speaking. "I stand by Richard in this matter, Frances. Now let us talk of it no more. I am very tired." She rose from her chair and took Frances' hand. "I would sit up with you for a time but I am afraid these old bones seek their slumber. Please rest easy tonight, and we will see each other tomorrow."

In spite of her day of travel, Frances felt awake and anxious as she found her way to her chamber. This time she was more observant of her surroundings: the bed was damp and smelled of mildew, the room sparsely furnished and the window high up and grimy with the dirt of neglect. Even the long shadows created by the single candle did nothing to conceal the poverty of it. She could see that the old woman was simply waiting it out, waiting for her own death. With no possibility of God's Kingdom here in this world it was purely a matter of looking towards the next.

The matter of the small box was all that Jane could think about as she lay in bed that night, tossing about, poor Eliza scrunched over in a corner of the bed in an effort to escape her sister's restless movements and fall asleep. She could almost see it, on Mrs. Grinshaw's bedtable, near the candle, glowing softly as the woman made her preparations for bed. The woman would pause and reach over, touch its lid, and smile as she climbed into bed beside her husband. Jane did not know what was inside it but knew it to be something precious. A reliquary of a kind, sacred to the two of them, Nathaniel and Sarah. The innkeeper's wife kept it out of avarice, to have it amongst her things, not thinking of the blood that was spilled so that she could have it. Jane could see herself in that room, as the woman slept, reaching down and picking up the box, still warm from the candle's light, placing it gently in her pocket and retreating, not making a sound. To steal into someone's home in the night and take away such a thing, that would be wrong, but surely in the eyes of God to return such a possession to its rightful owner was a good act. She could see it all.

Eliza groaned in her sleep and turned to lie closer to Jane, her body radiating heat as she nestled in. This was often a time when Jane thought of Samuel Prosper, but tonight all thoughts were of

Sarah Kidd and the mystery of the murder. The pewter box would be the answer. It would show the constable what needed to be done. As she warmed to the idea of her own trespass, she began to consider how it might be accomplished. Her mother found her way into homes all through the village because of her healing medicines. Perhaps she could do the same, offer something to the innkeeper's wife. She would need to find out what ailed her—something always ailed women—and then it would be a simple matter to visit Mrs. Grinshaw and seek out her bedchamber. She would find the box herself. Not to take it, of course, for now Jane's imagination went to her own leading of the constable into the bedchamber, the identification of the box, the tears of the innkeeper's wife and the triumph of Sarah Kidd.

And then she pulled herself from Eliza's warmth, slid to the cold floor, and set herself free to think of her absent tutor.

The room he was brought to was large with many tables and benches scattered about. He had indeed been brought to the inn, thought Nathaniel ruefully, so close to a bed for the night and yet as far as he could be. The watchman made him sit on a bench at one end of the room as a few people filed in, led by the tall thin man. He kept his bag close next to him, uneasy. In his many travels this had happened before, but he had always been able to charm the watchman and be on his way. This turn of events surprised him and left him wondering. The last thing he wanted right now was to spend a night in jail, with the very real prospect of parting with at least a portion of the fortune in his bag.

The small group was a strange representation of the town. There was a tall man with a gruff aspect, heavy dark eyebrows low over his sleep-ridden eyes. Next to him was a neatly dressed, delicately plump woman, clearly his wife as they sat companionably together. She too had a grim affect, mouth with a downward cast, eyes puffy with sleep, but her dress was tidy and well-made, everything in its place. There was a boy behind them, possibly their son or servant, in clothes far too big for him, someone's hand-me-downs. Two other men on a second bench: one had a slippery look, his skin luminous with an unhealthy pallor, but his girth indicating good, regular meals. The other, a scrawny gray fellow, had his arms crossed, with an anxious mien. Finally, an old woman, to whom all others deferred as she slowly made her way into the chamber, cloaked against the summer night chill, her eyes milky with age. This group, thought Nathaniel, was to be his jury.

The watchman stood in the center of the room and cleared his throat. "I am grateful to all of you for coming out on this summer's night," he said with ceremony, including a fussy little bow in the direction of the married couple. "And to Mr. and Mrs. Grinshaw, to allow use of their inn. We have a stranger here, who not only be traveling about at night, but on a night when we know there to be a robber about. We must put questions to this man, to find whether he is the robber that is frightening folk here about. If he is, then our constable here, Mr. Notkin, will keep him in jail for the assizes upcoming. If not, then we can let him be on his way, no harm done."

No harm, thought Nathaniel, except an innocent man being kept from his bed. He stood up and faced the group. "I'm no robber," he said to the group. "I am just a wayfarer trying to return to my family in London. You must look elsewhere for your robber." Back down he sat, as the villagers stared at him without speaking. There was a long silence. Finally, the watchman stepped forward, walked over to Nathaniel and opened his bag, removing Nathaniel's hand with no ceremony.

"Your bag," he said, "is heavy with coin. How come you by such a fortune?"

There was a rustling in the group, everyone shifting position, clearly impressed with this turn of events. The old woman shared a moist cough.

"I earned it by honest work, as a bailiff in the North on Lord Delancey's estate. Let me swear on a Bible, this is the truth."

"There's something," said the little pale man. "Where's a Bible to be had? We're good followers of the Church of England, we've no need to have a Bible in every chamber. It's in the church where it belongs." His laugh had a threatening tinge to it. "Are you one of those dissenters?"

Nathaniel knew better than to reply to this sally. "I will swear on it," he repeated.

"Save that for the assizes," replied the pale man, standing up taller. "They've a Bible for that very purpose there. We'll do no oath-taking here tonight." As though it were some sort of lewd suggestion on his part, thought Nathaniel with despair.

"Go get the man that was robbed," said the tall man, "That will decide the matter. We know not who this man is, nor even if the oath matters to him. Fetch the witness."

The boy standing behind the couple took off with a nod from the man. Nathaniel felt more at ease now. Surely the victim would fail to recognize him, and he would be freed. He relaxed, though his grip on his bag was restored. This would take some time, but in the end he would have his bed.

There were some idle, curious looks as Ann found her way to the inn's kitchen door, so that she felt very aware of every step she took. Jane Lyndal had sent her on this mission, to inquire after Mrs. Grinshaw's health, since village gossip had it that the inn-keeper's wife had once again taken to her bed. Ann repeated her previous ruse, bringing eggs to share with the Grinshaws' cook. The heat radiated out of the room as she entered, the fireplace ablaze, a chicken roasting over the coals. The making of food never stopped at an inn. There was a large pot of what looked to be vegetable stew on the table, the rich broth sending forth an aroma that made Ann's mouth water. Their own cook did not possess nearly the skills of the inn's Mrs. Neale. Next to the stewpot rested two loaves of brown bread, soft with heat, alongside a bowl of radishes, scrubbed clean of all their garden dirt. It was a warm, inviting picture, the table laden with food, the fireplace aglow. Ann stopped and gazed at it.

THE BAILIFF'S WIFE

"What are you bringing us this time?" It was Mrs. Neale, noting the basket on Ann's arm. "This is what started your seeing young Tom, wasn't it then? The eggs?" She was not unfriendly but there was a tone in her voice that Ann did not like.

"Yes, ma'am, we have so many," she replied weakly, reluctant to hand them over and thus lose her opportunity to talk with Sally. But there was no choice. She placed the basket on the table, next to the radishes. "We cannot eat them all, they are very fresh. It's not market day or Mrs. Baker would take them to the market for us." She looked around the kitchen, as if she would find Sally hiding behind a chair.

"Our thanks to you, and to Mrs. Bright," said the cook briskly. "Your chickens do better than ours. Maybe it's the quiet of the Grove. Here at the inn, so much coming and going. Puts them off their laying." She paused and looked at the girl. "Now off with you, I'm sure you have got your work waiting for you."

"Yes, that I do," said Ann slowly. "Do you need some help here, maybe? I don't see Mrs. Grinshaw." Usually, she knew from Tom, Mrs. Grinshaw had her hand in everything to do at the inn and spent much of her day in the kitchen hectoring the cook.

The cook smiled briefly. "Off to her bed," she said with satisfaction. "It's the flux with her. There's something not right with it. That's why she's barren. It comes at strange times and puts her to bed for days each time." A sigh that showed she was tired of talking of it, and then the obligatory "poor woman." The cook herself had six children, of which four were living, and she worried about them as she went about her work.

"You must miss her help in the kitchen," said Ann. "Is there nothing I could help with?"

"Oh no," laughed the cook. "I get twice the work done when the mistress is in bed, that is the truth. Off with you now, believe me your own cook can use your help more than I."

Ann quickly took herself off without a backward glance. She had got what she came for, and rather hoped that she'd not be asked to come this way again.

Chapter Thirteen

———•◆•———

Frances knew better than to tell her mother-in-law of her errand that morning. In any case it was not likely to meet with any kind of success, so it was not worth the trouble of upsetting the old woman. Still, she thought it important to make every effort, and so she had Stephen bring the horses round. She could see that the city was hard for him: as they made their way through the narrow, crowded streets, people dashing this way and that, his shoulders were hunched with concentration. The horses themselves, country horses, were easily frightened by the noise. It was all they could do to keep them moving forward. Frances was heartily tired of the noise and smells of the streets by the time they arrived in front of her sister-in-law's house.

It was in a better street than Mrs. Bright's lodging, the houses well-kept, Joan's door freshly painted a dark, glossy red. The place had a solid look about it, tidy and welcoming. A hard knock brought a young maidservant to the door, skittering down the passageway and greeting Frances with a small curtsy and a smile.

She waited while the maid rushed up the stairs with the necessary introduction. All was well-appointed and clean, the floor freshly swept, the small table with its oil lamp shined and dusted. Quiet, cool and dark, restful. Frances sat herself down in a chair that matched the gloss of the table, with a soft blue cushion as a seat. The luxury of it.

Soon the maidservant came clattering down the stairs and smiled at Frances, nodding at her to follow. Up the stairs they went, and down another hall into an airy, pretty room that was clearly Joan's bedchamber. Frances' sister-in-law sat on a small, delicate bench at a matching table, a loose silken dress gathered round her slight frame. It was a room filled with color, from the soft pink of Joan's dress to the blue of the counterpane and the cream mixed with gold on the tapestried walls. Frances could see that in the several years since their last meeting, Joan had aged, but this had refined rather than lessened her beauty. She still had, of course, the wide blue eyes of the family and her dark hair was thick along her shoulders. But there was a translucency to the skin around her eyes, and an etching of fine lines around her mouth, that gave the passage of time its due.

Joan rose from her chair and held out her hand to Frances. "Welcome," she said in that light, high-pitched voice of hers. "Welcome, Frances. I have not seen you for—well, years it's been, since you and my brother departed London. I was sorry to hear of his death, after all those imprisonments and privations, poor man. My parents would not have permitted my presence, and so I chose to stay away. So young he was. I hope that you have remained well." She sat back down and gestured to a chair next to hers. Frances made herself comfortable.

The maid appeared again with a pot of brewed coffee and two cups. Frances had heard of the concoction and its popularity in London but had not seen it before or tasted it. She was not surprised that Joan would be with the fashion. That had always been her way. The drink was dark brown, nearly black, in color, and had a slightly granular look to it. Its taste was bitter, with a slight burnt aftertaste, but not unpleasant, perhaps due to its heat. At least she had been given a very small amount, Frances thought with relief.

"I am well, Joan, and I am glad to see you. Matthew prayed for you, you know." She thought this a kindness to say, but she could see from Joan's expression that this may have been a mistake.

"You are staying with my mother?" the younger woman asked with a smoothness that belied the look in her eyes. "How is she, my mother?"

"She is frail and her house is not in good order," admitted Frances. "I am sorry for that. She will not come to the Grove, she wants to remain in her house, such as it is. Margaret is with her."

Joan laughed and finished off her own coffee with enthusiasm. "Oh yes, Margaret will always be with her. That is her family now, that old hag."

"Well, there is Richard," Frances said quickly, her own last bit of coffee cool in the cup. "Have you seen Richard? He visits the Grove." She kept herself from saying more, wanting to hear Joan talk of her brother.

"Frances dear, no one in my family will talk with me. They think I am godless and lost. Perhaps I am, perhaps I need your prayers after all. I am a weak woman, and on my own. Once upon a time, I would have been shut away into a nunnery. But here I am, to everyone's displeasure, with my London house and entertainments. My mother always said I was a wayward child, disobedient and frivolous, and so I am still. Because of my waywardness, I have no family. But I have friends who care for me and look after me, and so I am content." A knowing smile for Frances, as she arranged her brushes on the table. "So now, Frances, tell me why you have come."

"A fool's errand," Frances said before she could stop herself. "I hoped that you and Richard, now that your father has died, had renewed your ties to one another. I had always thought it was your father who kept you apart. And so, because I am in need of someone to persuade Richard to drop his suit against me, I thought I would talk with you. You—you understand, dear Joan, what it is to be a woman on her own." At that moment there were fast footsteps up the stairs and the door burst open. It was the maid, flushed and smiling. "A barrel of oysters has been delivered, ma'am, shall I take them to the kitchen?"

"And who might they be from?" asked her mistress with a greedy smile.

"Oh, that young secretary in the Admiralty, Mr. Pepys," called the maid as she turned and ran back down the stairs, to deal with the barrel and its contents. Joan turned to Frances again. "Not completely on my own, dear Frances," she said with a shrug.

Frances tried not to think too much about what this entailed. Shifting the conversation back to her problem, she took a last, ill-advised, sip of coffee (now cold and extremely bitter). "Dear

Joan, your brother has engaged a suit against me, to challenge Matthew's will. He is demanding the Grove. By all rights, the house is Eliza's inheritance, but Richard is claiming it as his own, as the male heir. This—" she wanted to use the word 'betrayal' but knew it to be too large a word—"this act on Richard's part has caused me much sorrow and unhappiness. Perhaps you have some influence with him and might be able to deter him from his path."

"Dear sister," said Joan, clearly distracted by the delicious oysters and the amusements sure to follow, "I cannot think of anyone less able to influence Richard than myself. He's still a little Jesuit at heart, you see. If he could take *my* house away, as proof of my sin, he would. He has no mercy in him. Perhaps he will win this case, perhaps not. If he forces you out of the Grove, you are welcome here, with Jane and Eliza, there is plenty of room. We can be a house of women, unto ourselves."

Frances felt the malice there, the petty satisfaction of someone else's misfortune. The realization made her stand abruptly and extend her hand. "I am so sorry that I troubled you today," she said stiffly, Joan's cool hand in hers. "I made a mistake by asking you. Even so, dear Joan, I am glad to have renewed our bond, for surely we are one family."

Joan rose, the folds of her lovely dress shimmering around her. "Yes indeed, sister, we are in this family, such as it is. I wish you well on your journey back home."

As Frances made her way down the stairs to the waiting Stephen, she could hear Joan behind her, giving instructions as to the dinner and the guests she expected to follow swiftly upon the oysters.

Entering her mother's workroom, Jane felt a shiver of trespass. It had been one of her mother's most certain, yet never spoken, rules: no one was to enter this room without permission. To simply stand in the room, alone, was a transgression. Jane examined the various jars and bowls on her mother's work table, picking them up one by one and setting them down. Powders, seeds, dried leaves, a box containing what looked like the skeletal remains of a bird.

At first, she tried to remember what her mother had told her about remedies for the flux. But as she thought about it, there at the work table, she realized that she wasn't at all interested in curing Mrs. Grinshaw's ailment. After all, her entire purpose was to enter the bedchamber and look for the little pewter box. She could mix up anything at all and Mrs. Grinshaw would eagerly take it, no doubt willing to try anything to feel better. She would have to be careful, of course, not to poison the woman, but surely a simple combining of herbs and a powder or two would do no harm. She would avoid the shelf below the window. This held several jars that, as her mother had explained to her, could be useful in minute amounts but which, if mixed in sufficient quantity, could sicken or even kill the patient. She had always been fascinated by them. Especially the container of belladonna, the dried leaves and root seemingly so innocent, like any other jar in her mother's work chamber, but so dangerous. Her mother had told her how some said the Roman Empress Livia had done away with Augustus through the use of belladonna.

She would stay away from the bird skeleton, as interesting as it was. She had to be careful not to use up anything that her mother would notice. This was an act of deception, pure and simple.

Slowly she circled the room, indecisive, finally coming to rest near a small group of jars filled with powders of different colors. Choosing one at random, a light gray powder, she poured a little into a cup, and then mixed it with a spoonful of a sludge-like substance from a bottle that seemed to be of sufficient quantity that a small amount would not be missed. Into this mixture she added some cinnamon. Crushing a small bit of nutmeg, she added this as well, stirring it all with authority. It was really very enjoyable, she thought, without a care as to the result. It did have to taste good, so she would pour this substance into a small cup of ale in the kitchen and then bottle it up for Mrs. Grinshaw. Once she had completed her recipe, she looked about the room to make sure that everything was as she had found it. Someday, if successful, she might want to tell her mother about this, but not just yet.

The flux. She was glad that she was not yet tormented by that, the way it took over your body, the endless rags to tie around oneself, one must feel as infants feel, swaddled in their own filth. Her mother, ever practical and forward-looking, had told her of it, so that she would not be frightened the first time. She told her that at first it would just be a little, a few red spots on her clothing, but then it would come in quantity and she might feel pain. This, several days of discomfort, every few weeks. She knew too that it had to do with her ability to bear a child, and thus with her womanhood. It made her want to remain a girl forever. She felt almost angry at the thought, the vision of that first drop of blood. Womanhood, with its babies and fluxes and misery. Women so earthbound, tied to their bodies in a way that men never were, like animals, unable to free themselves from their lot. Nappies, filth, restraint. Her thoughts wandered to her Samuel, out in the world, making something of himself, while she moldered away here in the country surrounded by women.

Keeping the little jar concealed in her skirts, Jane made her way down into the cellar where the ale was kept. This would be a good, likely time to find the kitchen and cellar deserted. The cook would be out in the garden, tending the sweet peas and carrots. It was lovely and cool in the cellar. Most of the year Jane avoided its chilly dampness but on a warm summer's day its shadowy cool came as a relief. The ale was kept in large casks in one corner of the storeroom but there was also a small collection of bottles. She took a bottle and up the stairs she went, into the kitchen.

The shabbiness of the dwelling was expected, but still Frances paused before she could bring herself to enter the little house. Her travels in London had brought her from the charming comfort of her sister-in-law's home in Finch Lane to the worn sadness of Mother Bright's lodging, but now she found herself in St. Botolph's parish, looking for Boo Lane. It was a busy, dirty part of London that defied any easy summary. She and Stephen made their way through streets of tall narrow houses contrasting with mean alleys where the habitations almost seemed to tumble into the street, poor and ill-built. Sarah and Nathaniel had begun to build a life together on Boo Lane, a life already fallen apart by the time Sarah travelled to Chalfont St. James. She had given over her son John Edward to neighbors who seemed trustworthy, after her own mother and brother had died. The husband had worked with Nathaniel on the docks, and the wife had two young children of her own, and so Sarah felt this could be a family for her son, should she never return. Sometimes, she told Frances, she thought the boy would be better off if she stayed away.

So when Frances had Stephen tap at the front door of the narrow, half-timbered house with its tidy front steps, she felt this would be the easiest of her London tasks, to make sure the boy was well and to let the family know that Sarah Kidd was in Chalfont St. James. He had to tap several times and Frances began to wonder if the family was entirely gone from the house. But eventually the door opened a small crack and a young face peered out at them. As Stephen came back to help her down from her horse—he was learning—Frances could see something was wrong. The little girl standing on the stoop was thin and her dress was damp with sweat. She almost seemed to be swaying as she stood there in the doorway, silently watching Frances make her way to the stairs.

"I am Frances Bright," she said to the girl. "I am here to see young John Edward Kidd, who I understand is a ward of your parents. May I come in?" She tried a cheery smile. The child held on to the doorway and her eyes were glassy, unfocused.

"We are sick here," she said, her voice dull and low, pleading. "Do you have some medicine for us?"

Stephen, afraid, moved back towards the horses, and Frances nodded at him. "Stephen, I will go in and see what is wrong. Please wait here." Used to sickrooms, she was uneasy about going into the home but relatively sure about what she would find. Of course, she had no medicine with her, but she might be able to be of help, and she had to see to John Edward. So in she went.

The house had been closed up for some time, she thought as she moved into the hallway after the girl. The air was dank and had many layers of odor to it, everything from human sweat to a pungent odor of sick. Frances had to concentrate to keep herself from fleeing. She asked the girl her name.

"My name is Patience," the child said as they moved further down the hall. "My father died and we had to bury him."

"And is your mother sick?"

"Oh yes she is very sick, ma'am, will you help her?" Again the pleading look as they went up some dusty stairs to the next floor. Everyone must be in their beds, thought Frances. Looking at the girl she thought it might be the dreaded typhus, which brought high fever, delirium, and a dry cough. More died than survived of this illness, though those who survived were often the children.

Upstairs the smells were even stronger, of course, and Frances took out a handkerchief to put over her nose and mouth. There were two rooms on either side of the landing. In one, Frances could discern a bed in the shadows. The room was dark, the shutters pulled against the afternoon light. Everything was in disarray, bedclothes on the floor, an overflowing chamber pot in one corner, its contents dripping and soaking into the rug beneath. The fireplace was cold and nothing had burned there for some time. A solitary figure lay in the bed, unmoving. The scene reminded her so much of the death of James Lyndal that Frances felt dizzy for a moment. Patience went ahead of her, stood by the bed and touched her mother's damp forehead.

"You see, ma'am, she's so sick," she said with a soft voice. She didn't want to wake the woman, whose eyes were closed. The sickly pallor to the woman's face gave Frances pause. To see this was to see death close at hand. Her breathing was shallow and faint. There was a dull rash across her collarbone.

"Where are—let's see how the others are, shall we?" she said to the girl, trying to sound cheerful and strong. Patience led the way to the other chamber, which reeked even worse than the first. Here too the shutters were closed to the warmth of the day, and the grate was cold. There was a bed pushed against the wall. On it were two little figures and to see them so small, so defenseless and weak, made Frances cry out. Neither moved as they lay there in the turmoil of soiled bedclothes.

"I feel better today," said Patience, "though I wish there were food here in the house. I'm so hungry. I found something to drink though. But John Edward and Christian, they are still sick, like Mother."

Frances crept closer to the bed and sat down on its edge. The two boys were nestled next to each other, similar in size, their little bodies thin and wasted from fever. One shared the light brown hair and freckles of the little girl, the other was darker with a swarthier cast to his skin. She touched first one and then the other, and sat back. The brother to the girl was dead, very recently so. He was still soft and pliable to the touch. Sarah Kidd's boy lived. His breathing was slow and calm, and she felt he would survive.

"John Edward," she whispered into his ear and his eyelids fluttered in response. She touched his forehead, which was warm but not feverish. As she sat there the little girl came and touched her arm.

"Tell me how they are," she said quietly, with reverence, as though she were in church. "How are they? I have been praying for them. I have prayed for Mother too, that is what she told me to do."

Frances did not want to answer her. A child and her prayers the only thing between this family and death. No food, no water, no care. She took a deep breath and looked at the girl. "That is good, that you pray for them. God loves them and they will be with Him. Now, you must be quiet as I tell you this, Patience. Your brother Christian has left this world and is with your father. He is no longer suffering. We must take care of his body, and look after the two that are here for us to care for."

Patience did as she was told and was quiet for a long moment, her gaze first darting to Christian's body and then back to Frances. Her eyes filled with tears and she wiped them away with one dirty hand. "I thought he was dead, he hadn't moved in such a long time," she finally said. "All I could do was pray."

"You are well," said Frances firmly. "You will stay with us awhile, Patience. Let us take care of Christian's body and see to his burial, and look after these other two. We have much to do. I will send my boy to get us some supplies for the household and we will see to things. Did you not have anyone to look in on you during this illness?"

Patience shook her head. "We have friends from the church who have come by now and again but I have not seen anyone for many days. They talk of the bad air here on this street and that that is the cause of the sickness. Nobody wants to be here in this air." Frances made the girl show her the larder, which was bare, and sent Stephen off for food and water from the well. She was not afraid of the air, sure that the disease had spent itself and that there was nothing left to fear. Stephen then went off to Mrs. Bright's house and gathered Frances' things. She would be lodging with John Edward's foster mother until they were well. She could not in good conscience leave John Edward, not until she was certain of his survival. This would delay her return to Chalfont St. James, but there was nothing for it. The evening was spent washing the body of poor little Christian, to ready him for burial.

Sarah Kidd was not thinking of her son that afternoon. She spent much of her time in the room that Frances had made for her at the Grove. Today she felt a need to move about, walk to the village. The quiet of the country grated. She left behind her cloak, for the day was warm, and made her way out the back door into the garden. She walked around by a side path past the chicken coop and back towards the front of the house, sheltered by a grove of elms as she made her way to the road to the village.

Perhaps the walk would do her good. She had felt trapped in her room, on this hot afternoon, without Frances at home to converse and sit with. She did not take to the embroidery and sewing that took up Jane's time. She had always been clumsy and impatient with the needle. She found herself sitting in the chair by her bed, her eyes closed, simply listening to the sounds of the house and thinking through, for yet another time, the chain of events that had led to this moment. It seemed that time had stopped, and nothing more would happen, that her husband would remain in the ground without revenge, his fortune still in the greedy hands that had taken it from him in cold blood.

Now, walking along towards the village in the bright glare of a summer afternoon, she felt lighter, her limbs loose and free. Frances had provided her with some clothes, which Sarah recognized to have been of the London fashion ten years before. She wore them gladly, the brown skirt swirling thick about her ankles, the bodice cream-colored and not unattractive. Even though she made love with a ghost, she was not dead yet.

She encountered the occasional villager as she approached the town, but while there was the required nod of greeting no one really looked at her. She had become used to this. Really it was no different from London where strangers surrounded one, a profound lack of curiosity being the townsman's signature. This studied ignorance was far better than the hostile stares she had received when she first entered Chalfont St. James. She had become something in the background of these peoples' lives.

The village felt somehow lazy with the heat of the afternoon, the bustle of the morning giving way to a slower pace, few people about. Even the High Street was unpopulated except for a few shopkeepers chatting with customers in doorways. Sarah made her way along the road, almost aimlessly. As she turned on to the market road, she came upon the Stroud couple. They were promenading, she felt, as fancy people, lord and lady.

The three nodded uncomfortably as they passed. A moment later, as Sarah began to round the corner towards the narrow lane that ran by the church, she heard Mr. Stroud's voice cheerily summoning her. She could not ignore it.

Turning, she saw the pair standing before her, the man's hat tipped in respect. "Dear lady, I know we have not been introduced," Mr. Stroud said in a hearty voice, "but I feel as though we know one another. I hope you will forgive this impertinence, introducing ourselves to you here on the street. I am John Stroud, and this is my wife, Mrs. Katherine Stroud. We are glad to make your acquaintance."

Sarah recognized Mr. Stroud as the man who stood next to Grinshaw when she asked for a room. "We have met before," she said with her usual honesty. "At the inn."

"Of course, of course," said Mr. Stroud. "Though we were not introduced at that time. I have heard of your case, Mrs. Kidd, and you have my sympathy. It is no easy thing for a lady such as yourself to be alone in the world, with a child, and having to make your way with little in your purse. Mrs. Stroud and I hope that God will see to your needs and those of your child. Do we not, Mrs. Stroud?"

Here the wife was compelled to speak, and it took a moment. "Yes," she said slowly, "yes, Mrs. Kidd, we do pray that God see to you and your child. We are most, most concerned for your well-being." Her face was without expression, still as the millpond on a hot summer's day. Sarah did not know what to say in reply.

"It seems shameful," said Mr. Stroud with feeling, "that you should be reduced to these circumstances, all because of a lack of fortune. I wonder if I can be of help. Now that you have buried your husband, Mrs. Kidd, your duty as a widow has been fulfilled. As to the fortune, need it be that of your poor husband? Could we, perhaps, provide you with at least a small portion, so that you may return to your child in London?"

Sarah could hardly believe her ears.

"You do not know me, Mr. Stroud," she said severely. "And so this offer, generous as it might be, I cannot accept. I do not accept coin from strangers, as kindly intended as it might be. I do not like to accuse, but your—friendship with Mr. Grinshaw makes your offer all the more troublesome to me."

"You misunderstand me, dear Mrs. Kidd," urged Mr. Stroud. "Mr. Grinshaw is my innkeeper and no more. What I see here is a lady who is away from her small child who needs her, and who waits here for the fortune that will give him the life he deserves. While I cannot supply that fortune, dear lady, and do not pretend to, I can provide for your safe travel back to your home and a sum that will keep you through next winter in comfort. That I can give you, as one good Christian to another."

"Do you not want to see your baby?" blurted out Mrs. Stroud. "Are you not afraid for him?"

Sarah Kidd could not help it: the image of her son rose before her eyes, as she had handed him to her neighbor. The green eyes, so like her husband's, the wild curly hair. He had been an easy baby, one could turn him from tears to laughter with just a look. She remembered the softness of his cheek against hers.

"Ah," said Sarah Kidd, "know then how I must pray for my son every day. It is his fortune I come to find. As kind as your offer is, my son will need more than that to get through next winter. I cannot accept such a gift from you, we do not know each other in that way." And then she nodded and turned from them, starting off down the road at a pace that precluded their company.

Chapter Fourteen

———— • ◆ • ————

The room smelled of blood and sweat. Ellin Grinshaw lay amongst the bedclothes, swaddled with linens, her face a constant grimace from cramping. The shutters were closed, as Mrs. Grinshaw had complained of a headache, making the room all the more close and airless. As much as the innkeeper's wife had always seemed intimidating and fearsome to Jane, she was filled with sympathy for her now.

Jane entered the room quietly, carrying her small jar of medicine, and walked slowly over to the bed. Pushing aside the clutter that always covers tables near a sickbed, she set down the jar and smiled at Mrs. Grinshaw. She enjoyed this moment, the smile pure artifice, easing her way closer.

"Dear Mrs. Grinshaw," she said, "I bring you something for what ails you. It should help. If it doesn't, you will need to let me know, so that I can make adjustments to the recipe. At the very least you should find it tasty. Let me find a spoon with which to give it to you"—and she began opening and closing drawers in the cabinet, in search of her utensil.

Mrs. Grinshaw lay there softly groaning, her eyes closed, one hand ineffectually rubbing her forehead, oblivious to all around her. Jane set down the jar and expanded her search to a nearby bureau. "Where is it?" she whispered to herself, as she opened drawers filled with underthings and stockings. Mrs. Grinshaw's only response was a groan. She thought she heard footsteps in the hall, but they stopped, so she continued her work. She would have to be quick.

Suddenly the door opened, and she looked up to see the inn-keeper. Her hands filled with handkerchiefs and ribbon, she then dropped everything and rushed over to the bed. She lifted the top off the jar and administered, a bit roughly, a dose of the medicine. It dribbled down Ellin Grinshaw's chin.

"Ah see," she said wildly, turning to face Daniel Grinshaw, "she's better already!"

"What's this?" he cried, moving towards Jane, who backed away into a corner, her jar of medicine tightly in her grasp.

Jane gathered herself and smoothed her skirts as she spoke. "Mr. Grinshaw, I was but following my duty and providing your wife with some comfort in her illness. I meant no harm, and as you can see she is sleeping well now." Indeed, as she pointed to Mrs. Grinshaw, she was pleased to see that the woman's face was peaceful and her breathing steady. Jane herself was surprised by this result, a little, and wondered if perhaps she shared her mother's gift.

Grinshaw was breathing heavily as he stood there, glaring at the girl. "You are all after us," he said with violence. "There is never a moment's peace with you or with that widow, charging me with murder, no matter the truth of it. I won't have you in my house, you are not welcome here. And take your vile drink with you." He suddenly grabbed at Jane's hand and wrested the jar away, walk-ing firmly over to the window, wrenching open the shutters, and throwing the offending vial out with all his force.

Jane stood very still as Grinshaw turned to look at her. She knew now that her visit had been an utter failure. There was no pewter box in sight. This—Mr. Grinshaw's angry face close to hers—was not how she had imagined this moment. A small twinge of uncer-tainty crept in to her thinking: perhaps the Grinshaws were not to blame for the death of Nathaniel Kidd. Perhaps this anger she saw in front of her was righteousness, pure and simple.

She fled the room and he did not try to stop her. As she half-ran, half-walked her way home along the lane, praying that she would not see anyone she knew, Jane considered how much easier these adventures were when they just existed in her mind. The real moment—the anger, the hurled jar, the lowered brow—was something else again. And, if the little pewter box were not among Mrs. Grinshaw's things, where was it?

Frances felt an ache in her back from having sat by Mary Clark's bed for the past three hours, soothing the woman's sweating forehead with a cool cloth. The daughter, Patience, ran back and forth with a neat pile of damp cloths, freshly dipped in water that Stephen had brought from the local well. John Edward hardly moved on his bed, which he now had entirely to himself. His eyes were open, but might as well have been shut—they looked at nothing. Frances dreaded the news she might have to bring back to Sarah.

The house was woefully lacking in anything of comfort. There was little food. The air was bad, refuse piled in the lane, cooked by the summer's heat. Frances spent what time she could cleaning. The place was infested with all manner of bugs and small rodents. She used lard to address the lice on the children's heads, and thought regretfully about the many ointments in her work chamber at home that could have provided some relief from the itching and scabbing that troubled the entire family. Frances wetted the lips of her patients and watched anxiously for any improvement.

On the third day, there was a knock at the door, and Frances had a wild hope that the family's church friends were going to reappear and provide some help. But on the stoop stood the two old women, Mrs. Bright and her servant Margaret. She couldn't help it: her heart sank, for what good were these frail, ancient women? Just two more to care for, she thought, as she rearranged her face into an expression of welcome.

Margaret spoke for them both. "Dear Frances, we've come to provide what help we can. When Stephen told us of your care for this family, how could we not come? We have brought with us some food that we could spare." She turned and pointed to a large basket at the bottom of the stairs. "We walked all this way," she added, perhaps sensing some hesitation from Frances.

"Of course, of course," Frances cried, trying to make up for what was clearly perceived as a lukewarm welcome. "I am not sure that you should come in, Mother Bright. There is much sickness here. But your basket is so very welcome."

Mrs. Bright looked uncertainly past Frances to the gloom of the house. "I have nursed many in my time. It is my Christian duty," she said. "Christ requires us to be of help to our neighbors. I cannot turn away, when you are here, Frances, alone with this family, nursing them back to health." The force of her words was belied by her delicate look. Frances saw how her hands shook.

"The sickness has not passed here, quite yet," said Frances. "And you could fall ill yourselves. There is no need. I am in good health and can see to things here. I am so thankful, of course, for your offer."

As she spoke, there was a cry. She thought it was John Edward. She turned from the women and rushed to the boy's sickroom. John Edward was sitting on the edge of the bed, trembling. Surrounding him was a puddle, his bowels having emptied themselves before he could get himself to the bucket. Tears were running down his wasted face as he looked at Frances.

She stood him up. Behind her came old Margaret, who found a pail of water over by the fire, with some rags. They both set to cleaning the boy as Mrs. Bright rolled up the soiled bedding and placed it carefully over by the fire, to be cleaned later, or possibly thrown away. Frances gestured to the nearby wardrobe, in which there was a none-too-clean but serviceable quilt to place on the bed.

"It is all well," she said to the boy, "you need not fear. This is the last of it, John Edward." She did not believe her own words, but the boy did, giving her a look of relief. She wrapped him in the quilt as he lay back down on the bed, exhausted.

Margaret had brought in the basket, and Frances could see that it had been packed with care. Useful things, like jars of meat broth, and a loaf of good bread, with a small container of honey. A bottle of ale, a cheese. Frances had not had much of an appetite since she entered this house, and suddenly felt famished at the sight of nourishment.

"You must keep up your strength, Frances," said Mrs. Bright.

"This is for them, but also for you. We can bring more. Let us be of help to you." Her soft tone was a surprise. Frances had never known her to be so gentle.

"This boy, John Edward, is the son of someone who is a guest in my home," said Frances, nodding towards the figure on the bed. "I will see him back to health, for her sake."

Mrs. Bright looked around the room. "We can set this home to rights," she said, nodding to Margaret. Frances, remembering the state of Mother Bright's own home, had her doubts. Old eyes did not see the same filth that she saw all around her. Nonetheless, the two old women slowly moved around the rooms, rags in hand, wiping down the kitchen table and chairs, moving on to the shelving with its own layers of grime and dust. Frances, meanwhile, sat down next to John Edward and allowed herself a moment of quiet. She could hear, in the other room, Patience softly talking to her mother in a sing-song voice. For the first time since she had arrived here, she felt some ease, a sense that all might, after all, be well.

The next week was overcast, day in and day out, the sky white and flat. Jane, back in the classroom with Eliza, tried to listen to Mr. Brown but his words meant nothing to her. She knew she was supposed to be writing, for that was what Eliza was doing, following the dictation, and she knew that Mr. Brown was well aware that her pen was still. He seemed to be studiously ignoring her, his voice droning on, the sound of Eliza's pen scratching across the paper in synchrony with the brisk adages of Seneca.

A knock at the door, then Deborah entered. "Young ladies," she said to the two girls, "your mother has just arrived home...."

And with that, Eliza threw down her pen and ran for the stairs. Jane sat where she was, in a mix of emotions. She looked up at Mr. Brown, who gave her a weak smile of encouragement. "We will give up on old Seneca for today," he said in an effort to be light, "you must go and greet your mother." She had no choice then but to push in her chair and make her way to the front entry, to be on hand as her mother made her grand entrance.

There was noise and hubbub, she could hear the rough breathing of the horses outside and the crunch of the gravel. Eliza's voice, high-pitched with excitement, talking with someone—Sarah Kidd?—as she waited for her mother. The thrum between her ears was loud as she made her way down the stairs. She thought about her mother's workroom, how she left everything just so. Really, she could have left the room as disordered as she liked, since no doubt the Grinshaws would be speaking with Mrs. Bright. It had all turned into something other than what she had planned, and yet she could not understand how it had all happened. She dreaded her mother's smiling face.

Mrs. Kidd stood next to Eliza, wearing a fragile smile, disarmed by Eliza's joy. Jane moved to stand beside her, feeling herself to be at this moment a dutiful daughter welcoming her beloved mother home. But as she glanced at Sarah, she saw her smile dissolve into tears as Frances Bright entered the hall, holding in her arms a small boy.

The wait for the witness seemed interminable. Nathaniel thought he might fall asleep in front of this assembly of villagers as they whispered amongst themselves, punctuated by occasional glances in his direction. He was hungry and tired and struggled with a feeling of hopelessness, a conviction that he would end up in some dreary chamber at the constable's home.

For a while, the villagers kept up the questioning. They asked where he was from, and who his people were. The names he listed meant nothing to any of them, which did not strengthen his case. The constable at one point turned to the very old woman and asked, "Mother Grime, do you know of this man's people?" Everyone was perfectly silent as they waited for her reply. She sat there for a short time, staring at Nathaniel but, he was convinced, not really seeing him.

"Ah, no," she finally croaked. "I know none of his people, none at all. He's a stranger to us." This seemed to have a very gloomy effect on the group who nodded at each other and gave Nathaniel long, hard looks.

"I have no people hereabouts," Nathaniel admitted readily. "I am new to these parts. I have never pretended otherwise. I have no one here to speak to my character. But that does not make me a robber. I am as you are, an honest Christian, unlucky to have been on the road at night. All I ask for is a bed for the night and then I will be on my way."

The watchman laughed. "Ah, so you say. You had a skulking, secret way about you when I came upon you in the dark. You and your bag of coin. I knew you to be up to no good." He laughed again, a cold, hard laugh, and was joined by the anxious gray man and the tall fellow. "We'll get to the truth of this, and then it will be off to the constable's with you. I'm not one to let a robber make his bed in our village."

"Well, if I be a robber, would I have just walked along the market road, for the watchman to see me?" asked Nathaniel reasonably. "Would I not have continued my skulking, and hidden myself away?"

This only infuriated the watchman. "Stop with your impudence! You'll not make fools of us. I know a thief when I see one." This set everyone else to nodding in agreement, even Mother Grime. The old woman fell into a prolonged cough, with spittle dripping down her chin. The gray man reached over with his handkerchief and gently wiped her face.

"Mother Grime knows everyone hereabouts," said the gray man, "and if she don't know you, then you're a stranger, out at night, with a bag of silver. You're a rough sort of man, we can see that just by looking at you."

Nathaniel remained silent at this. He saw no purpose in arguing with his captors. The room fell into silence again as the night deepened. He let his eyes close for a moment, just a moment, until the sound of approaching footsteps brought him to attention. The door opened with violence, slamming against the wall as a man strode into the room, followed by the boy who had been sent to fetch him.

It was the tutor, Samuel Prosper.

The assizes were to be held at a common room at the inn, an arrangement that brought the Grinshaws some much-welcomed business. The judge and his assistants were lodged upstairs and seemed constantly in need of food and drink. The maidservant was kept busy, running up and down stairs in answer to each fresh demand. The proceedings brought a certain number of villagers as well, curious onlookers and jurors both, all of whom required a quantity of ale to sustain them through the long days. Grinshaw himself could be seen, towel over his shoulder and pitcher in his hand, ready to make sure of the comfort of his guests. Of course, the prisoners who were to be tried at these hearings encountered none of this hospitality. They were brought from jail at the start of the day and returned at the end, or freed, once the sentence had been determined. So when Fox and his fellow Quakers were deposited before the judge, their emaciated and rough appearance was in sharp contrast to the well-fed villagers around them.

Frances Bright positioned herself as close to the front of the room as she possibly could, rubbing shoulders with the village blacksmith on one side and a farmer on the other. She did not mind. She had forbidden Jane from coming, and Sarah Kidd was at the Grove with her child. She thought about that, the way the little boy had reached out for Sarah, remembering her after all this time, and how the widow had held him tight. There had been much crying, until the two had taken themselves off to Sarah's room so that the boy could sleep, exhausted from both his long illness and the journey. If nothing else, thought Frances, going to London had accomplished this one good thing. She had seen to the needs of little Patience, and stayed long enough, several days, to make sure of the recovery of the girl's mother. Weak but sitting up, her face warm with life and hope, the woman had given thanks to Frances and said her farewell to little John Edward.

She had also seen a new side of Mother Bright: the old lady came daily, her servant Margaret armed with yet another basket of food and clean linens. They did not converse during the visits, which were busy with sick care, but Frances felt a new bond that gave her hope.

Now, at the assizes, Frances watched as Fox and his fellow Quakers were marched into the room. Their odor, even amongst folk for whom the smell of manure was a familiar friend, made most of the audience turn away and cover their noses with handkerchiefs. The Friends themselves were used to their own smell and so blissfully unaware of their condition, and held their heads high, Fox with a quiet smile on his gaunt, grimy face. They were ready.

The room was noisy as people settled themselves on chairs and benches, and talked of the Friends as they sat there in the first row. Everyone had an observation to make, thought Frances with some irritation. The farmer and his wife talking of the mean appearance of the Quakers, their dirty clothes somehow representing their sinfulness. The blacksmith laughing as he poked his neighbor on the other side, what a sorry assortment of fools these Quakers be. Entertainment, to see someone worse off than oneself. Frances saw the incongruency of it, the ridicule to which these Friends were put and yet they were accused of being a danger to the realm. To her, they were not ridiculous, but she could see, indeed, the danger in Fox's eyes. He was a man who could turn a nation away from their King if he so chose. Covered in filth and yet she could feel his strength as she sat but ten feet from him. He would never take such a stand, of course: kings did not matter to him.

The judge, announced as George Adams, sat behind a table, absent-mindedly sipping a cup of Grinshaw's best, creamiest ale as he looked through some papers in front of him. He was a thick-set, middle-aged man, a fine dark gray mustache gracing his upper lip. His eyebrows seemed cast in a permanent look of surprise, which made him seem less intelligent than he probably was, thought Frances. His shirt and vest were not new but spotless. Frances did not think he would look kindly upon her friends.

Sitting next to him, but off to the side, to indicate some sort of legal status but not a dominant one, was the Justice of the Peace, John Stroud, at whose behest some of the cases were here to be heard. He looked at ease in his chair, his well-turned legs expensively hosed, his coat a rich, glossy burgundy, his wig freshly powdered.

Fox did not look in her direction. Perhaps he didn't even know she was there. She had told him, during her last visit to the barn, that she would be certain to be at the trial, but he had many things on his mind and she did not expect him to remember that detail. She could have reached out and touched him. His eyes were bright and his carriage straight, even as his fellow Friends looked bowed down by their privations, worn through with suffering. They all were quiet and attentive, waiting for the judge to speak.

The place was called to order, and the judge had his assistant bring forth the Quakers to stand before him. The accusation was read, declaring the group to have broken the law against the meeting of religious conventicles not of the Church of England. The grand jury having decided, the day before, that the case had merit, it was now to be heard by the judge and the convened jury, a group of local men seated on either side of the defendants. They were somewhat lacking in solemnity, thought Frances with disapproval and worry. There were some who pointed and grinned at the filthy Quakers, and who held their noses in mock disgust. She knew and recognized several, good merchants of the town and farmers, solid men of good reputation, and yet here in this strange atmosphere they behaved as though at a bear-baiting.

The judge's voice was nasal and high, which helped to carry it through the room. Frances felt the place to be a little close now. Her neighbor's sweat made her want to hold her breath. She knew that all would be over in a matter of minutes, and she was prepared.

"You are the leader of these people," said Mr. Adams to Fox. "You may speak in defense of yourself if you will take the oath here on the Book—to swear to the honesty of your statement."

Fox shook his head. "I cannot take this oath, Mr. Adams, as you well know. You will have to trust my statement as true, without it. I can assure you, as can my friends here, that I do speak in all truth and honesty." His voice was strong and unwavering.

"Ah then," said the judge with a note of resignation, "since you will not take the oath and so cannot enter a plea, you are found guilty of the charge, and must pay the fine of ten pounds, for each of you, or be sent to six months prison. I cannot do else in this case."

This was Frances' moment. She rose from her chair and approached the judge. "I will pay for him and for his fellow prisoners, sir, so that they can all be freed." She brought out her purse, heavy with coin. This would be costly but it was the only way in which she could be of service to Fox and the Friends. As for Fox himself, she had no doubt that he would happily serve his sentence without the fine. He would accept her offering only so that he could go out and preach and spread the Word. And he would insist, of course, that his fellow prisoners accept her payment and their freedom.

As she came forward Fox turned to look at her. She felt the pull of his spirit, a sensation of connection that was irresistible. His expression was inscrutable, watchful. A curt nod of his head and then he turned to his fellow prisoners and whispered his counsel, which Frances was sure was to agree to her payment. They would all be set free that day, and she could see the expressions of gratitude and relief flood their faces as they turned from Fox to her and her small purse, at rest on the judge's table. Fox's face remained neutral, still.

Suddenly there was a tumult in the room, and Frances turned to see Sarah Kidd shoving her way to the front. Without any attempt at ceremony or respect, she pushed her way past men and women alike. Not at home looking after her son, Frances thought with disapproval, but here in this courtroom, calling attention to herself. Following in her wake was Susan Harp, her head down, perhaps hoping that by looking at the floor and avoiding others' gaze she might make herself invisible. The widow, after a good deal of shoving and elbowing, had made her way to stand next to Frances by the judge's table. Her coif askew, her skirts dragging at her heels, out of breath with the effort, leaving disarray and annoyance in her wake. Susan looked up and gasped as she saw Frances, her face white. There were some rude comments from the jurors as the judge called for quiet.

Before he could address her, Sarah spoke. "Sir, please excuse my appearance here today. My name is Sarah Kidd. It would have been my preference for the local constable to have brought my case before you, but since no one will see to my claim, I had no choice but to approach you myself and ask for justice." Her voice carried as the room fell into silence. Frances held herself very still, next to the widow, knowing they were in this matter together.

"I request, with respect, your help, as someone in authority, who can compel this case to move forward," Sarah Kidd continued, and tried a small curtsey. "I have a case of murder, two murders that have been committed in this village and the murderer still among us. One was my dearly beloved husband, and the other a poor servant boy. I ask for justice, long delayed." Sarah's eyes were cold and furious even as her voice stayed firm. "No one in this village will listen to me"—Frances wondered at this—"they are all in alliance with the murderer. I trust, sir, the King's justice, and so I turn to you."

Adams looked Sarah up and down as she spoke, his eyebrows even more arched than usual. She had been allowed to say her piece, thought Frances, only because she entertained the judge on what must be a dull day, persecuting Quakers. But nothing would come of it. She then saw emerging out of a dark corner the constable Notkin, his face red and his eyes bright, moving as quickly as his short legs would carry him to the Judge's table.

"Sir, judge sir," he said with force, "this woman here is disturbing the peace. It is her that should be in jail, not any 'murderer' she cries about. She goes about our village, accusing, interfering with people's business, crying up murder and such. There's no end to it, sir. If I could, I'd ban her from our village."

They made an odd pair, standing there together next to Frances, the thin widow in Frances' castoffs, holding herself erect and still, her eyes entirely on the judge, and the short constable with his hands flailing in the air as he spoke. Susan Harp had moved so that she stood just behind Sarah Kidd's right shoulder. The judge's eyebrows moved ever higher.

"And who is this person standing behind you?" he asked the widow. "Is she your murderer, perhaps?" There was a certain amount of laughter at this, which only made poor Susan retreat.

Sarah Kidd turned and took her arm, pressing her to stand before the judge. Frances began to sense George Fox's restlessness. He and his Quaker companions had been standing very still during Sarah Kidd's entreaty but now he shifted and began to pace, no doubt annoyed at the removal of attention for his cause.

"This," said Sarah, taking her voice up a notch, "is Susan Harp. She is a good woman of this village, well-respected, a woman of faith and good works. She has never done anyone harm in her life. Here she stands before you, as a witness to murder."

"No, no," interjected the constable. "Sir judge, these foolish women and their stories, they are full of mischief. No man should listen to them. Sir judge, there is not a single man in our village— excepting perhaps the priest—who listens to their tales." He looked around at the crowd behind him, daring any man to say otherwise. The judge nodded and looked hard at Susan Harp.

"In my courtroom," he said, "we follow the law, and you women have disrupted the ways of the court. You have no right to speak here." A long pause, Susan Harp with tears in her eyes, Sarah Kidd standing very still. "But murder is a serious charge, and justice turns away no man. I will hear your statement, Susan Harp, and if your words give cause I will ask the grand jury to meet and consider whether a case need be brought. Speak, then, and tell me of the murder that you witnessed." The judge settled back in his chair, clearly enjoying himself and his power. Frances took the moment to retreat off to the side, where the Quakers stood, unsure whether they were now free to go with Frances' purse still on the judge's table.

Susan Harp closed her eyes and began to speak. She told the story of her moonlit walk, the cry for help from the inn, the figures in the doorway, her hurrying on home. She then spoke of her later shock when told of the discovery of the body, not far from the place where she had heard the scream. Her story was a small one and yet it held the attention of the crowd, curiosity keeping them silent. Freed from the fear of the oath, allowed to tell her story amongst her neighbors and friends, Susan found her voice and told her story in full.

As she finished, Sarah Kidd moved closer to the judge. "Sir, it was the voice of my poor husband that this woman heard, as he was murdered in his bed in the inn. My husband was due home, a fortune in his pocket, and was known to have come through this way. He disappeared, and no one has seen him in these years, while I and our son suffer and wait, the fortune lost to us. His body was found in the field near the inn, and we buried him here in the churchyard. That," she continued with some bitterness, "was all these people would do for me, allow my husband a Christian burial. But as to how he died and the loss of his fortune, no one thinks of that. Now with the death of the boy Tom, we should all be in fear for our lives. And yet this constable"—she gestured at Notkin without taking her eyes off the judge—"refuses to bring this murderer to justice. He cares not for the cries of the widow and orphan, for the cries of a young boy killed and thrown in the river. What is a constable for, but to do this work? Why must women do his job for him, sir judge?"

There was a murmuring in the crowd at this, some nodding and a bit of laughter, all at the constable's expense. No doubt, thought Frances, the judge feels the entertainment of this diversion has been quite worth the slowing of the court's business. And keeping Quakers waiting was an added benefit.

"So, Constable Notkin," said the judge with some pleasure, "there have been two murders in Chalfont St. James without the murderer being found out? This, besides these Quakers causing trouble and all the other small crimes I have had to listen to over these past hours, leads me to wonder what you do for your pay." He stared at the constable who went from red-faced to pale in a matter of seconds.

"I do my best," the little man said. "Sir, I do my best. There is no witness to any murder. This woman's words mean nothing—someone cried out one night years ago. Someone crying out in his sleep, no doubt, and she with her woman's fancies has made it into murder. As for the boy, sir judge, he was but a servant boy, he had no family here. He was always getting himself into the scrapes that most boys do—his death is a mischief, no more." He shrugged for effect.

Sarah Kidd could not contain herself at this. "A boy without family, perhaps, but a good Christian and deserving of a natural death," she said with feeling. "As was my husband, an orphan who made his way in the world. Who will be next, if we grant such permission, to end the lives of two innocent men? How can you be idle in the face of such evil?" She seemed to aim this last question directly at the judge, stepping forward to stand in front of his table.

The room was now silenced by Sarah's words. Even the half-drunk jury sat still in their seats, and Frances saw that Sarah had George Fox's full attention. It was as though they were all seeing the widow for the first time. There was a long pause as everyone waited for the judge's reply. He coughed and reached for his ale, then thought better of it. Frances could hear Susan Harp next to her breathing, deep soft breaths, as the stillness stretched on.

"This is something that requires some deliberation," said Adams. "Mr. Notkin, you have in the years I've known you served the village well. But two bodies have turned up, dead by unnatural means, and it is your duty as constable to preserve the peace in this village. So, murderers must be apprehended and tried and punished. That is the wish of the Crown, and the duty of the constable in his jurisdiction. If a person comes to you with such a complaint, and a witness, then you must put the accused in jail to be bound over for trial. Why have you not done these things, Mr. Notkin?"

The little man drew himself up, now on firmer ground as he faced the judge. "There be no witnesses, sir Judge, it is all in the mind of a deluded woman. What am I to do, when no one saw the murder, and no one has confessed?"

Now the crowd, having recovered from Sarah Kidd's oratory, began to murmur and move about, with this talk of witnesses and trials. It was common sense, surely, that without a witness, or a confession, who can say who the culprit is? Frances felt a hand on her arm: George Fox was now by her side, a free man. But his eyes were on Sarah Kidd. The widow was in distress, no doubt feeling that her moment was slipping away. She went right up to the judge and gazed into his eyes.

"I have given my life to find my husband's murderer and to gain the lost fortune for my son. I have travelled among the Dutch, the Scots, and made my way to every town or village here that might have news of my husband. Now that I have found his bones, after much suffering, I am here to see to his murderer's punishment, for the sake of my boy. I have starved, I have been cold, I have been among strangers so that I could see to justice. What harm will it do, to seek the truth in this matter?"

The judge looked over at John Stroud, who still sat comfortably in his chair. "Mr. Stroud, as Justice of the Peace for this community, what say you? What knowledge have you of this matter?"

Stroud shifted in his chair and nodded to the judge. "Sir Judge, I have left this to our constable and have no reason to doubt the good sense of his decision." A slight bow even as he remained seated. Known to be an enemy of the constable in matters big and small, his decision to agree with Notkin in this case was greeted with a respectful silence. George Adams nodded and turned back towards the widow.

"What is it you ask of me, Mrs. Kidd?" he asked with some sympathy. A groan escaped the lips of Notkin.

Sarah Kidd did not hesitate. "I ask that you bring Daniel Grinshaw, whose home was the place of my husband's murder, in fact this very inn, to this chamber, to be asked certain questions about the night my husband died. If he be innocent"—here a small grimace—"then he will walk free and no man shall say anything more against him. But if, with the proper questions, he confess to the crime, or show by his mien that he is guilty of it, then I will be at ease and can know that my husband rests in peace. My son will gain his inheritance." It was what she had been waiting for, asking for, all these months, and the widow permitted herself a chin high in the air as she gazed about her at the villagers, all of whom had stood in her way.

Frances turned to look about the room. Surely the innkeeper himself, so central to this drama, would have made his way here, busy as he was with looking after the jurors and keeping the judge in ale. She was not the only one with this thought—there was a general murmuring about her, and she could hear the whispers, "where is he?" as though Grinshaw would suddenly appear in a puff of smoke before Judge Adams. But the man was nowhere to be seen.

"Mr. Notkin," intoned the judge suddenly, and the little constable came scurrying forward to stand before the judge's table. Even Fox smiled at his discomfiture. "Mr. Notkin, in light of this woman's charges, when it is clear that this matter will not rest without further investigation, I ask that you bring Daniel Grinshaw, innkeeper of this village, to this court tomorrow morning to answer questions from the grand jury." A slight cough. "If there be any truth in this woman's accusations, then the safety of this village's residents is at stake. I know this will be a hardship for Mr. Grinshaw, but it may well clear his name, for which he should be thankful."

The crowd of villagers then exploded in a fury of talk, clear astonishment at the judge's ruling. Sarah Kidd stood silent among them, her eyes clear and her mouth set in a firm line of determination, Susan Harp at her side. She had finally achieved her aim.

"And so," said Frances as she poured a cup of bitter coffee for the priest, "this will bring the matter to a close. We shall hear from Daniel Grinshaw, he will be speaking before the entire village. What man could avoid the truth at such a moment?" She nodded approvingly as Brunskill took a guarded sip of the brew, his eyes closed in concentration.

He could not say it was good. Putting down the cup carefully, he ventured a smile as Frances poured a small cup for George Fox, seated next to her. The Quaker was a strange man. He did not speak and yet Brunskill felt he dominated the room, filled it with his quiet presence. He knew the man engaged in theological debates far and wide, and yet he did not, in spite of his own thorough training at Cambridge, feel inclined to argue religion with Fox. He knew that it was his duty, to put this Quaker in his place, but he could not bring himself to do it.

Frances herself was feeling quite fashionable, serving up coffee to her guests, and also a little frightened, with two such natural adversaries in her parlor. She had brought Fox home after his release from custody and made sure a bath was drawn immediately. While her late husband's clothes were a poor fit on such a lanky, slender frame, with the proper belting and wrapping it all looked decent and he certainly no longer smelled. Finding Brunskill on her doorstep as she arrived home, she had ushered the priest into the parlor for refreshment. By the time she had recited to him the day's events, Fox had joined them and the tenor of the conversation had altered.

"And where is Mrs. Kidd, now that she is on the eve of finding justice?" asked Brunskill, knowing he sounded somehow false. What he had wanted was to say, may I see her? Will she see me? Impossible.

"With her son, naturally," said Frances with equanimity, "on such a day, no doubt out of doors. The boy has not seen much sunshine in his life, I'm afraid." She thought of his pallid face, so pinched and unsmiling, when she had lifted him up on to her saddle to come home to the Grove. A boy who had spent his days in the dark alleys of London, in shadowy rooms and streets running with offal. Every time she saw Sarah smile at the boy, or take his hand, or usher him outside to play on the lawn, she rejoiced.

The other member of the small party spoke up. "I will hope that this matter is resolved with Mr. Grinshaw's testimony," said Mr. Brown with energy, having drunk all his coffee with much enthusiasm, "but what will happen if he is indeed not the culprit, and continues to deny his guilt? We all seem to be assuming here that it was he who murdered the late Mr. Kidd and also young Tom, and that he will admit to all tomorrow. What if he is not guilty?"

Frances thought that Mr. Brown must have a gift for causing discomfort unawares. And yet his question was an honest one, a good one. She had been so much alongside Sarah Kidd and Susan Harp that she hadn't given much thought to the possibility of Grinshaw's innocence. His inn was the source of the cry, near where Nathaniel Kidd's body had been found, and the boy had been his servant. Evil circled around him—how could he not be the source of it?

"If he is persuasive in his innocence," said Brunskill firmly, "then without testimony from Susan Harp—and she is not likely to testify under oath—there is nothing on which to base a conviction, I'm afraid. Even with her testimony, she did not see the act of murder, nor can she identify the person standing in the doorway, so she cannot speak to that. Mrs. Kidd will have to accept the outcome, and if there is no one else in this village who could plausibly be charged, surely that will be an end to her case. I know it will be hard for her, but she is a—a reasonable woman." This last said with less authority and in fact a blush.

Suddenly Fox shifted in his chair and looked straight at Brunskill. "Woe be to the shepherds of Israel that do feed themselves! Should not the shepherds feed the flocks? Ye eat the fat, and ye clothe ye with the wool, but ye feed not the flock." Then he sat back again, his eyes on the priest. Ezekiel, thought Brunskill with some alarm.

"Please, there is no need here for debate," said Frances, "dear George, Mr. Brunskill is not our adversary now. We are all of the godly here, and we seek only justice for our friend Sarah Kidd. I do not know if she will accept a verdict that is not in support of her belief, but we are her friends and we must be happy in this moment's victory." She surprised herself with her admonishment of Fox, but his response was mild.

"You were right, Frances, when you first told me of Mistress Kidd and her troubles. I could not see it, not then, but when I heard her speak with such strength and love in her heart, I could not but feel the spirit in her, even if she does not know it yet. She has suffered because one man is not treated like another, one man's death is ignored because he is not high and powerful, and yet we are all the same before God. The men in steeplehouses may not see it thus"—and here he let his gaze settle on the offensive priest— "with their princely pews and vestments and golden vessels, but in the eyes of God, Mistress Kidd is more powerful than the King."

Frances could see that the tutor was warming to this subject and had something to say, so she spoke quickly. "We can all agree, can we not, that at last justice will speak tomorrow, after such a long silence. Whatever result it brings, it is a satisfaction, is it not? Judge Adams did not have to take this step, but he allowed Mrs. Kidd's sorrow to influence him. I am glad of that, as we all should be, whether we be in cottages, manor-houses or—steeplehouses." She smiled at Brunskill. "I will counsel Mrs. Kidd that no matter what the outcome tomorrow, she must and should see it as the conclusion of her case."

They all nodded, even Fox, who was not ready to be done with the priest. "How is it, Mr. Brunskill, that the folk who come to your house and listen to your talk are as sleepwalkers, repeating back words that have no meaning for them, yet when I find myself in a room of Friends we are alive in the spirit and each man has words to speak that are fresh with love and with faith? The Lord is nowhere near your steeplehouse, but lives and breathes in our house. You are but among the dead. Think on it, Mr. Brunskill, and join the living, join us at Meeting."

This heretical thought was jarring and unsettling to the priest and for a moment he was silent, staring at Fox and wondering at his confidence. But he was saved from the need for a reply, inevitably combative, by the appearance of Sarah and her son.

"Oh, Mrs. Bright," cried Sarah Kidd, suddenly in the doorway, her face rosy and glistening with the heat, her voice full and happy. But as she entered she saw the company and the warmth left her face. She could not stop her little boy from darting in front of her, for he saw the cakes on the table and as a child of poverty was in the habit of seizing every opportunity for a meal. As he reached the table and put out his small hand for a cake, Sarah rushed forward and pulled him to her. Such a thin little boy, thought Frances with a pang, he has paid a price with his illness. She very much wanted to hand him a cake.

The boy did not cry. He never did. He simply folded into his mother's arms and looked at the strangers sitting around the cakes, none of them, inexplicably to him, eating anything. It was one of a daily array of puzzles that confounded him, ever since the lady had raised him up on to the saddle and brought him to this place. Every morning he prayed that he would be let to stay here.

"And how are you, Mrs. Kidd?" asked Arthur Brunskill, having stood at her entrance, now patiently waiting for her to sit before returning to his chair. With no choice, it seemed, the widow made her way to a small cushioned bench and sat her son beside her. Frances reached forward and gave the boy a cake. It was gone in less time than it took her to sit back again in her chair.

"I am well, thank you, Mr. Brunskill," Sarah said rather formally, not really looking in his direction. "I am quite well. I will go to the court tomorrow and see justice done. I will see Mr. Grinshaw asked questions that he must answer under oath. This is all I have asked, in all the time I have been here. Once the man has been judged, and the fortune found, I will be able to return to London with my son and return to our life there."

Her little boy looked at her and she nodded, their communication easy. He reached for another cake. They all sat in silence as the boy licked his fingers, not with the pleasure of satiety but rather with anxious urgency. Mr. Brown could not resist: he handed another cake to the boy, and smiled at the mother. Frances began to fear the child would be sick.

"Mrs. Kidd," the tutor said with the smile still on his face, "we were just talking about this case, and I have to say that I am impressed with your certitude. But what will happen if Mr. Grinshaw denies all tomorrow? Will that be the end of it?"

"He is guilty, sir," said Mrs. Kidd with finality. "If he denies it, he does it before God and he will be punished for it. My husband died in his house. He came to me in a vision there, so I know it to be true, true as can be."

"Ah," said Fox with interest, "surely if he takes the oath in vain he will be punished, punished before our very eyes. I have seen it many a time, the retribution, the punishment. God will strike down the false oath-taker. Paul says to the Romans: but if thou do that which is evil, be afraid; for he beareth not the sword in vain: for he is the priest of God, a revenger to execute wrath upon him that doeth evil. Mrs. Kidd, tell us of your vision."

Her son now nestled in her arms, finally at peace after three cakes, Sarah took a deep breath. "He came to me in the night, as I slept in the inn. I lay there and he came to me, suffering, dying, unable to breathe as he looked at me. In the dark of my room, and there was nothing I could do but look upon him as he died, imploring me for help." She caressed her son's curly black hair and looked bleakly at Fox.

Frances could see that Fox was moved by this. He reached out and took Sarah Kidd's hand, giving it a warm shake. "That is a moment to be prized," he said softly to her, as though they were alone in the room. "The Lord brought him to you, so that justice could be wrought." The widow's eyes filled with tears but she smiled at him.

Arthur Brunskill now stood and excused himself for the long walk home. He was distressed by the words of Fox, for now he could see with hard clarity what the man had that he had not, and why his congregation sat sleepy-eyed before his sermons. If one had to ask which of them was the man of God, surely that was Fox. With a hasty bow to his hostess, he made his way out of the crowded parlor, feeling nothing but relief as he made his way to the road. He would go and work on his sermon.

Frances could see the priest's distress but could do nothing for it. It pleased her to see that Fox had come round to the widow, and that he no longer counseled Frances to remove herself from Sarah Kidd's small circle of supporters. As she observed him continuing to talk with Sarah, Mr. Brown looking on with the attention of an acolyte, she could see that he was embarking on the process of conversion. Whether it would take, she did not know. She had her doubts. For Sarah Kidd, the vision of her husband did not indicate God's presence in the world but, pure and simple, a cry for earthly justice.

Chapter Fifteen

———•◆•———

The walk to the inn the next morning took less time than it usually did. Sarah Kidd set the pace, and she wanted to be there from the very start of the proceedings. Leaving her son in the care of Mr. Brown, who did not look pleased to be spending his day in the classroom with the three children, she kept a stride that made her impatience obvious. Frances, a smaller woman, found it hard to match, wondering if she would have to break into a run.

The place was in a tumult. People were crowding into the chamber, so many that the judge's table was pushed up against the far wall simply by the press of bodies. Frances found it hard to breathe in the crush, and she could see that there were many more curious onlookers than the day before. Frances saw Mrs. Grinshaw out of the corner of her eye, over in the hall, hissing fiercely at the cook who looked to be near tears. She brushed up against the priest Mr. Brunskill. He turned and smiled at her.

"Let us find some good seats," he said. "Good morning, Mrs. Kidd," with a tap to the hat. Sarah Kidd, her good mood holding firm, returned the greeting and turned to the ladies. "Mr. Brunskill will lead the way," she said with a flourish, as they all moved forward into the crowd. At first it seemed impossible, because what chairs and benches there were had been taken over by all manner of folk. But the priest persevered, and after a short time they reached a long bench. It was currently jammed with a family of six, but also with poor Susan Harp, almost falling off at one end. It took but a moment for Brunskill to persuade the family that the Grove party would need their seats. They glanced at Frances, and recognizing her station as far different from their own, quietly picked themselves up and merged back into the crowd of seat-seekers. Susan Harp smiled weakly as Frances sat down beside her.

"They say that Mr. Grinshaw cannot be found," she said, her voice softly trembling. "They say he's run away. They've all been looking for him since last night." She wiped a kerchief across her forehead. "I don't know what to think, Frances. He must be guilty if he's gone away." A long sigh and a sad look in Sarah Kidd's direction.

Frances could see that Sarah hadn't heard this news. She was turned instead to the drama of the crowd around her, feeling her moment of victory to be at hand. But Mr. Brunskill turned pale and frowned at Susan. "Are you certain, Mrs. Harp, this isn't just gossip?"

"Mr. Brunskill, people all around me are talking of it," Susan replied, her chin in the air. "Listen, you will hear people now, speaking of it. Perhaps he ran away out of shame, knowing he could not lie under the oath that he believes in. It is too bad, it will bring an end to our suit."

Now the widow turned in their direction, her face changed by the news. "They must go after him," she cried. "How else to restore my child's fortune? Are they searching for him? Where?" She reached out her hand and grasped Frances' own with a painful strength.

Suddenly the room was filled with the rap of the gavel and the cry of an officer of the court, standing tall by the judge's table. "The court is in session," and indeed it was, with Judge Adams seated quietly beside him, finishing off his first draught of ale for the day.

As the judge and his men set about the preliminaries, Frances took Sarah's hand and gave it a little pressure. "The Lord is here with us," she whispered, "you will be heard, Sarah Kidd."

The man standing to the side of the judge finally called for Daniel Grinshaw to come forward. The name was called once to a silent room, and then again. There was an exchange of looks, but the judge did not seem surprised. No doubt as a resident of the inn overnight he was well aware of Grinshaw's disappearance. Frances felt a flash of impatience. Why go through this, when everyone knew?

But then she saw Mrs. Grinshaw appear in the doorway and proceed to the front of the chamber as people made way for her. The room remained quiet, with only the sound of her light, brisk footsteps and the slight rustle of her skirt to accompany her as she finally stepped before the judge.

"Sir judge," she said in her mild, flavorless voice, "I am here in place of my husband, who had to travel to London unexpectedly, on business. If he had known he would be called here today, he would not have departed on his journey. I am but a poor substitute, being only a woman and of no consequence, but if there be anything I can say to get to the truth of this matter, I am here to do that." Mrs. Grinshaw's face was as bland as her words.

The judge took another swig of his ale and looked amused. "Ah, Mrs. Grinshaw, you are indeed but a poor fit for your husband. But in his absence, let us put you to the oath and then say what you must, as to your knowledge of this matter." He nodded to his assistant, who came forward with the book and made Ellin Grinshaw swear. Frances could hear a swift intake of breath next to her as Sarah Kidd shook her head with violence. "This is not what I asked for," she whispered fiercely. "Nothing but lies."

"Now, Mrs. Grinshaw," said the judge, "did you know Nathaniel Kidd?"

"Yes," said in the innkeeper's wife, which led directly to a loud murmuring in the crowd. The judge's eyebrows went up.

"How did you know him?"

"He was a traveler, who stopped here but a short time and then was on his way."

"Did he take a room at your inn, Mrs. Grinshaw?" The judge had to wave his arms to get silence restored in the room.

The woman stood unspeaking for a short time. Then, "No, he did not. As I said, he stopped, but then went on down the road as far as I know."

"And so, what sort of talk did you have with him? What was the manner of your meeting with him?" Adams' tone was more alert and interested.

"Well, it was very simple. The watchman brought him to our

inn, because he was out and about on a dark night, and there'd been a robbery. A few questions were asked, and we could see he was no robber, and so he was let go to be on his way. That's all I know, that the watchman took him back to the road and away from the village. I know naught else." Mrs. Grinshaw said this with the ease of an innocent, describing a passing encounter.

"Why have you not spoken of this before?" asked the judge.

"No one asked me," Mrs. Grinshaw replied with asperity. "No one asked. It's a simple matter, really, we spoke with the man and then he was led back to the road, I believe, by our watchman. We did not know him, not at all. We never did find the robber, but then there were no more roadside robberies after that, so maybe he was at fault after all."

This brought Sarah Kidd to her feet. "How dare you say such a thing, idly here in the courtroom, to blacken a man's memory and reputation, and he unable to say different! We know that my husband did not leave here, his body lies in its grave, so you have something to answer for, you and Mr. Grinshaw!"

The crowd began to talk amongst themselves, and the judge called for order. Frances could feel Sarah's anger. The widow was visibly trembling.

Ellin Grinshaw threw back her shoulders and stared at Sarah. "I do not know your husband," she said. "None of us knew him. He was a stranger, on a dark night, and even Mother Grime"—she crossed herself—"was suspicious of him. We were right to question him, as one of our villagers had been robbed, and he had a bag of coin with him. I did not see him once we finished our questioning. All I know is that my husband and I went off to bed, saying our prayers."

"And who was the watchman that night?" asked the judge, looking hard at Mrs. Grinshaw.

"It was Edward Lampitt," she replied with confidence. "He and Will Porter came and got my husband and me, to talk to the man and decide whether he was the robber or not. And so we did, and we let him go. Lampitt took him, along with our boy, back to where he found him."

"Well, let's have a talk with Edward Lampitt then," said the judge. "Have him be called. You are now excused, Mrs. Grinshaw. We thank you for your testimony. We have other matters today to finish, and so we will begin with Mr. Lampitt tomorrow."

Frances took hold of Sarah Kidd's hand and drew her back down to the bench. "We must be patient, Sarah," she said softly, "the truth is here."

When Nathaniel saw the tutor, he quickly surmised the story that had been told. To hear Samuel Prosper say it out loud was mere confirmation.

"This is he," the tutor said without any hesitation. "This is the one who robbed me of my fortune. My father's hard-earned coin, given to me to start a new life. This man came upon me as I walked, gained my trust and then took my fortune as I slept. I was left with nothing. I was fortunate in that he did not harm my person, but he took with him all my hope for a livelihood. This is the rascal!" He looked from one person to the next but avoided Nathaniel's eyes.

"So," said the watchman, feeling his vigilance freshly justified, "I was right, this man is a scoundrel and a thief. Our Samuel Prosper has called him such. Mr. Notkin, it is your task to keep this man for the assizes, when the judge can decide punishment."

"Wait," cried Nathaniel, "this man lies. I did indeed meet him— his name is Samuel Prosper and he is tutor to children at—what is the name, the Forest—at the Grove. We walked together, and he told me of his visit to his father. He told me that his father refused to give him the money he asked for, and he was bitter. Then we parted ways. This fortune is mine, not his, though he now seeks to rob *me*!"

The tutor still did not meet his eye but instead sat down next to the constable. He was pale and he hastily wiped the sweat from his brow with a handkerchief. "You know me," he said as he sat there, "you all know me, have you ever known me to lie or do anyone wrong?"

The villagers all looked at the tutor and then looked at Nathaniel. He felt he had to have a response to this that would turn things around, so he kept silent as he considered. The silence deepened in the room as he thought long and hard.

"You do indeed know Samuel Prosper better than you know me," he finally agreed. "No doubt you know him quite well. Surely you have known him to tell less than the truth, to make himself look better? In all this time, have you not known him ever to boast of something not quite true? To show himself better than he is? Or is he some saint, admired by all for his virtue?"

There was an awkward silence. Finally the man with the wife by his side spoke, with a short bark of a laugh.

"Ah, we all be fools now and then, but we know him better than we know you!"

Losing this line of argument, Nathaniel tried another. "If this fortune be his, then have him tell us how much the bag holds. I know it down to the last shilling. Does he?"

Heads turned to Samuel Prosper, who flushed with anger. "Of course he knows the amount, he stole it! I am not someone who thinks of money. I took what my father gave me with no questions. I don't sit about counting my coin."

Another long silence, broken by the tall man. "We could use another here, to help us sort this. I'll go fetch the Justice." The constable reddened at this but said nothing as the man left the room. He turned then to Nathaniel, resolved to finish the matter quickly.

"So, tell us the amount, man," he said to Nathaniel. "We all count our coin, now and then," with a side glance at the tutor.

Nathaniel smiled. "I have in my possession exactly three hundred pounds, some of it in gold coin at the bottom, plus eleven shillings and eight pence. Count it for yourself and see."

The constable took the bag and opened it, and carefully began removing the silver to count as everyone watched. Samuel Prosper shifted his weight uneasily, and as the man counted, loudly and clearly, finally finishing with the total predicted by Nathaniel, the tutor leaped forward and pointed at the bag.

"He is a careful thief who knows his theft," he said with some force, "no doubt he enjoyed counting it after he took it from me. Am I to be punished for being so unworldly, as to the amount of my fortune? And he so greedy, counting each and every shilling!"

"That's right," said the watchman, seeing his case now under attack. "This does not prove anything. The thief had the coin in his possession long enough to have counted it many times over."

Mother Grime suffered another coughing fit. "'Tis getting so very late," she said once the cough had eased. "So very late. Edward Lampitt has done his duty as watchman and brought this man before us, but we cannot answer this tonight—it should be left for the assizes. I trust the word of our Samuel Prosper more than I do some vagrant with a bag of silver and gold. The constable will keep the fortune in the meantime, and we can all go home to our beds." She pulled her cloak closer around her thin shoulders and her eyes closed.

"Ah, but then I am truly to be punished," cried the tutor, "for that fortune is mine to use! I have need of it, I cannot wait until the summer. Surely we can find the man guilty and allow me my silver!"

This made Nathaniel smile, to see the tutor so tortured by his greed. The constable wagged his finger at Samuel. "Know this, Samuel Prosper, the money isn't yours until the man is shown to be guilty. Mother Grime is right—we cannot judge this amongst ourselves, there is no way of knowing. But the judge will know how to settle this, and we must wait on his judgment."

"That doesn't seem right," opined Lampitt, taking Samuel Prosper's side. "If not for this robber, Mr. Prosper would have his estate, and to wait two months seems unfair. Constable Notkin, it seems to me that we are within our rights to pass judgment here, with the evidence before us, otherwise you have to keep this scoundrel in your house for the next two months. We punish him with a branding and send him away."

The mention of branding made Nathaniel shiver in spite of himself. The loss of his fortune was one thing, to be branded a thief for all to see made him rack his brains for another argument.

Mother Grime was beginning to shift in her chair, in preparation for leaving.

"Ah, Mother Grime," he said finally, desperation bringing a new thought to his tired brain, "where I was raised, in Leominster, I knew someone from these parts, from the Chalfonts, and he was a good friend to my father. The name might be one you know, with your great age and fine memory."

The old woman perked up her head and gave him a long look. "I don't know anyone in Leominster," she said definitively, tightening her wrap around herself.

"But yes, you do, madam," replied Nathaniel, ready to laugh with relief as he brought to mind his father's friend. "The man's name was Stringfellow, John Stringfellow. He came from a family that owned the mill hereabouts, but made his own way as a blacksmith in our town. He was a fine storyteller and a singer too, in my memory."

"The Stringfellows," echoed Mother Grime. "They are gone from here now, but I knew them. I knew a John Stringfellow when he was a boy, son of Harry. He was good-hearted, I remember how he would come round when my son was too sick to work, and help around the farm. And you say your father knew him?"

Nathaniel warmed to the topic, his eyes on the tutor. "Oh indeed, they were great friends. We took our horses and our oxen to John Stringfellow, he did the shoeing. He talked of growing up here in the Chalfonts, talked of fishing the chalk streams"—here Mother Grime's old face brightened with pleasure—"and how hard he worked at his father's mill, which later went to his older brother that died. I know it went out of the family after that. A good man, John Stringfellow." He felt like adding, and so am I, Mother Grime, far better than this Samuel Prosper.

"No, no," burst in the tutor, "I'm sure I spoke of the String-fellows as we walked, and that he learned a thing or two from my patter. He's a sly one, this thief!"

"How would you know that family, Mr. Prosper," replied Constable Notkin reasonably, "since they've been gone from these parts at least ten years?"

At this, the watchman intervened. "This is all well and good, but how does this man's knowledge of the Stringfellows alter the case? I caught him and his coin, that I did."

There was silence as they all turned to look at Mother Grime, who seemed refreshed and newly alert.

"This alters the case," she said with authority. "This man is of Leominster, and knew one of ours. He knows his coin. I am sorry to say it, but I cannot see the truth in what Samuel Prosper says. He's but a Quaker you know, and to my mind has only newly been in our village." Her tone was dark and she looked away from the tutor.

"Quakers are known for their honesty," said Lampitt with some desperation.

"We're done with this," said the man with the wife, suddenly standing. "We have no cause to hold this man now. Take him back to the road and be done with it. As for you, Samuel Prosper, you've caused good people much trouble this night."

Nathaniel thought that he might faint with relief. No branding, no being held until the assizes. His fortune remained his own, and the road to London, late as it was, beckoned. The moon was up, and he could make some distance. He felt a sudden warm energy and could not wait to leave. He turned to the tutor.

"Be ashamed of how you treated me. I did no harm to you. I was but a traveler on my way home to my wife and child. I earned my fortune. I will be on my way, thanks to the wisdom of these good people, but you will have to stay here in this village and suffer their disregard."

Samuel Prosper stared right at Nathaniel. "I have spoken but the truth. You have won them over with your own lies and deceit. This is a terrible injustice! It is you that have harmed my reputation in this village, not I. I have but sought my patrimony. Now all is lost." He turned and left the room, without looking at his fellow villagers. The watchman moved forward.

"I will see that you leave this village, with your fortune," he said, and gestured to Nathaniel to follow him.

The heat of the afternoon brought about a languor that Jane could not shake as she sat in the grass alongside the Misbourne, her mind lazy with sun. She had spent the morning in a high anger, left at home while everyone else hurried off to the assizes. She longed for the day when her mother's commands would not bear this same weight, when she could say instead that she would go too. Surely as a wife and mother she would be free of this duty. The anger fed her throughout the morning, as she paced the floor of her room, refusing to attend to her studies with her little sister. Mr. Brown could do nothing with her. Immediately as she saw the party returning, early, from the village, she rushed into her seat and opened her copybook as Eliza laughed at her. Mr. Brown studiously ignored her and when her mother appeared in the doorway said nothing to reveal that she had not been at her studies all the morning. No doubt more for his own pride than any compassion for her.

Now, in the afternoon, she had made her escape, her mother occupied in her own work with her various potions and salves. She knew that Frances found that activity comforting in times of strain. As for herself, she made her way to the river, to be away from them all and alone with her thoughts. That was what she thought she wanted, but as she lay there in the grass, drowsy and unhappy, she was irritated by the heat and breathlessness of high summer. Her bodice and skirts, snug about her, felt oppressive and damp. She took off her cap and freed her hair, holding its damp strands up off her neck with one hand as she arranged herself in the grass.

She felt the shadow first, a coolness that removed the sun from her skirts. Opening her eyes with a hand to shield them from the light, she saw the figure of a man standing over her and her natural inclination was to sit up and smooth her skirts. She could not help a small gasp that escaped her lips as he stepped back and bowed. It was Samuel Prosper in front of her, big as life.

He put his finger to his lips and then squatted down beside her. His face had thinned and sharpened, and she realized that she had misremembered the color of his eyes. His clothes were dirty from travel, but he looked solid and strong and not at all as she had seen him last. She smiled at him and waited, as she always did. He had this effect on her, quieting her, making her patient. He seemed to know this and to enjoy drawing out the silence.

A long moment as he looked at her, the barest of smiles on his lips. "Ah, Jane," he finally said, "I told you I would come back. I've been out in the world, I have, and there is much to say for it, but I've always meant to come back for you. Are you happy to see me?" He said this, fully aware of what her answer would be.

"Yes, yes, I am," cried the girl, tears coming to her eyes. Life would now become entirely different, and she was ready for it.

The kiss was slow to come. She felt a flush throughout her body as Samuel moved his lips against hers, something new. She had been but a child before, the touching and kissing had been a form of attention that she enjoyed but no more than that. Now she felt it reach into her in a way that was surprising and exciting. He sat back and reached out to touch her hair, running his fingers through it, softly brushing it away from her face.

"Let us go tell my mother," she said to him. "You've made your way now, she will approve of you. I am older now. We welcome you back home."

"That is what I want, more than anything, my Jane," Samuel said with passion. "To ask your family for your hand and to become man and wife. I ask you to be patient, dear girl, for a short time. Please do not tell your mother of our meeting. I must finish some business and then I will announce myself and we will be married, but right now we must keep this between us two. I would not have made myself known to you now, but I could not resist seeing you and telling you of my plan."

Jane was disappointed but mixed in with that was a strong feeling of being loved. He could not keep away, even as he knew it was too early. Their marriage would be like that of her own parents, one of young love and devotion. She had never known her father but her mother liked to tell her stories of their courtship and the short days of their married life. It had always been so sad, his death during the War, but she also felt she served in a way as her mother's memory of her father. Her own youth and Samuel's devotion to her seemed a restoration of what had been lost.

"Yes, Samuel," she replied, wanting so much to reach out to touch him but feeling that this was not what he wanted, that he wanted to see restraint in her. "I have waited for you and I will continue to wait."

He took her hand for a moment before letting it go and standing, looming over her as she sat there in the grass. "All will be well, Jane," he said reassuringly, and then moved away into the wood.

Making her way back to the house, Jane began to wonder if it had been a vision, some sort of prophecy but not real. To see him standing there, to feel her hand in his, the warm blood of it, made her stop midway and close her eyes. He had been there, it had been no pallid vision of desire. They would be married, her mother would allow her to go to London with her new husband, and her new life would begin. No more Mr. Brown, no more Eliza laughing as she stumbled over her lessons unprepared, no more waiting in the house while others went forth into the world. She could hardly bear it. Coming into the cool of the house on that summer afternoon, she wanted to shout out her news. She who had always loved secrets found this one hard to keep.

Chapter Sixteen

———•◆•———

Sleep would not come even though it was well into the night. Frances had long ago thrown off the bedclothes. It was a warm, close night and she couldn't bear the weight of them. Clouds had moved in, covering the stars, so she knew the weather was changing, but not soon enough for a good night's sleep. No rest for her tonight. She was too full of the day's events, too aware of the little family sleeping close by, their hopes gone. Thoughts too of Jane, who had appeared late in the day, hot and bedraggled, grass clinging to her skirts, without a word to say. Perhaps Frances was negligent with the children, so absorbed in her own worries that she did not rule them as she should. Tomorrow they would all go to Meeting and perhaps some answers would come to her there. The disappearance of Daniel Grinshaw, and the consequences for Sarah Kidd, seemed so inexcusable. For all of George Fox's signs of God's justice, she saw so many more of His absence.

That thought alone made her sit up in bed, astonished at herself. Who was she to know God's plan? She sat there in the dark, aware of her own breathing. She got up and shook out her coverlet and laid it on top, to cool the bed, and then climbed back in, determined to find slumber. No more of these thoughts. After a time she felt herself drifting, the pleasurable wandering before sleep invades, thoughts scattering, incomplete, blown about by a breeze, only to land in a soft field of green. Frances could see the field, warm with sunlight, a billowy wind loosening her hair. She was alone and her feet were bare, but she did not feel the grass. She seemed to be slightly suspended above the field, ever so slightly, her feet not quite grazing the tops of the blades. She could sense them, whispering beneath her. She felt an extraordinary comfort, felt God all around her in the light.

Frances looked up at the sky, which seemed fresh and clear. A darkening then took over and she felt a stab of fear as dark clouds rolled over the landscape. The light shifted and then was gone. She felt, suddenly, a tremendous loss, and a nakedness, without shelter. The air became close, and the clouds descended around her. She could not breathe.

When Sarah Kidd announced that she would like to attend Meeting that morning, Frances both rejoiced and wondered. The widow Kidd had said little since returning from the assizes, secreting herself away in her room with her son. Frances certainly allowed her that. The quick turn in events, from a moment of triumph to one of despair, was no doubt overwhelming for her. Still, it was good to see her at breakfast, helping herself to the bread and milk next to Jane and Eliza, making sure her son had a second helping. And to walk beside her in the cool of a summer morning as they made their way to the meeting house was also very satisfying. Frances was worried about her vision of the night before, very much in doubt of herself, and so to bring another to the Light seemed to be a good recompense for her questioning of God's justice.

Sarah Kidd walked beside her as they made their way to the meeting house, with Jane and Eliza walking behind. Mr. Brown, lost in his own thoughts, wandered ahead. Frances thought of how her walk to meeting changed with the seasons: the wintry dark mornings in her hood and cape, holding up her skirts from the cold, wet snow, and the mornings in early autumn when the leaves began to crunch beneath her feet. She remembered walking this way with Matthew, trying to keep pace with his long stride, little Jane's hand in hers. Would this be the last summer for them all, the Grove soon to be in Richard's hands?

As they approached the small meeting house, her daughters went ahead with Mr. Brown, tired of the leisurely pace. Frances had noticed that the gathering had been smaller ever since Fox's arrest. Some people had been afraid of joining him in his prison cell. By coming to this place every week, the rest quietly acknowledged their own risk, and accepted it. Frances did not blame those who absented themselves, but she felt a strong sense of community with those who remained. Moving to an empty corner of the room and gesturing to her wayward daughters to join her and Mrs. Kidd, she stood expectantly as the room slowly filled. Mr. Brown remained aloof, off by a window. She saw Susan Harp, her coif askew and her light summer cloak dragging behind her, standing next to a young couple who both smiled at something she said. Even as the air filled with expectation, there was the usual sort of initial friendliness that characterized the start of every Meeting. Gradually they fell into silence, without prompting, all eager to find the Light and let it open within them.

The silence went on for some time. Frances gazed at Jane and Eliza. The younger girl's eyes were squeezed shut, in intense effort, but Jane's were open, looking at the people around her. Frances began to wonder about the state of her daughter's soul, her faith, for she saw in those eyes a worldly curiosity rather than anything seeking or tender. Perhaps the good Mr. Brown, his gaze out the window, was not the influence she had hoped he would be. She would have to consult with him about his lessons. Purposely looking away from Jane, she willed herself to take a different path, to close her eyes gently and consider the Lord's presence in her life. This took her far afield and before very long she felt a kind of warmth, an embrace. But as she was just beginning to find the words to express it, the voice of Sarah Kidd rushed in and threw it all away.

"I do not feel God's presence anywhere among you," she said with quiet precision. "This room is empty, except for this crowd of sinners. You see yourselves as godly, as filled with Light, or so I hear. All I see are a people with blood on their hands. You have left a poor widow defenseless, you have starved a child, you have harbored a murderer whose sins go unaccounted for. You speak of love and peace and the light and yet it is so dark in here."

There were murmurings among the Friends as she paused. There was certainly the rule to let a Friend moved to speak finish their words, but nobody felt that God was speaking through Mrs. Kidd. Frances felt hot and cold all at once and stood very still.

"Not one of you has come to my aid, except for Mrs. Bright," continued the widow with sorrow making her voice soft. "My son and I will try to make our way in the world, without the fortune his father had made for him. The murderer may go unpunished, but you will all suffer for his crime, I am sure of that. From this day forward, you will suffer." She said the last words so softly that Frances thought she might be the only one to have heard them. The room felt very close, as if there were no air left.

It was then that Frances noticed that Edward Lampitt was across from her, standing very still. He was an occasional visitor who seemed to be interested in their worship but still held everyone at a careful distance. He turned and looked at her for a long moment, and then moved towards the door. After his exit, there were some whispers and surprised looks, followed by old Mrs. Brewster shushing the group. Frances could see that the entire group had been affected by both Mrs. Kidd's speech and the small disruption of Lampitt. Everyone was simply waiting out the time, hopeless for God.

Frances reached out her hand and grasped that of Sarah Kidd's, willing her to remain for the time. The widow looked shuttered, withdrawn, spent. But she let Frances hold her hand and responded to the gentle squeeze with a weak one of her own. The silence deepened and grew until finally farmer Robinson, the one designated to take on this task, cleared his throat and brought the Meeting to an end. People moved towards the door with some sense of relief, everyone avoiding Mrs. Kidd. She remained close by Frances' side as they went out into the field.

In her bed that night, after prayers, Jane lay perfectly still, willing Eliza to sleep. The little girl seemed to thwart her at every turn, delaying bedtime until the last possible moment and then begging for

Jane to tell her a story as they lay there in the dark. Jane's story was, this time, perfunctory, which did nothing to ease Eliza into slumber. Since this was not Jane's habit, to abbreviate the chosen story—usually a version of a favorite story from the New Testament, though lately Jane had found herself making up stories about Vercingetorix, bloody tales of war and barbarian victory, that sometimes made Eliza cry out in both surprise and horror—and refuse to tell another, Eliza was immediately suspicious and became even more demanding. Jane finally put her arms around her in an effort to lull the girl into sleep. Time passed, and Eliza's breathing became regular and soft. Jane slipped her arms out from beneath her sister and lay there, sharply attuned to the noises of nighttime.

She felt certain that Samuel Prosper would visit her that night. Surely, surely her lover would make his way to the house, drawn to her, unwilling to stay away. She herself would have eagerly gone out into the night to find him, if only she had the remotest idea as to where he might be. She was not afraid of the dark. She imagined him moving along a silent lane, carefully so as to avoid the night watchman, coming to take her away to London. They would marry there, she was sure of it, and she would see what he had built for himself since he had left Chalfont St. James. No mere tutor, but someone of consequence who could provide for a household. She would be the mistress of that household, and the thought made her sigh with contentment. The keys to the storeroom, the hiring of the kitchen maid, the airing of the linens, the walks in the park with her husband. She wanted it all.

The night deepened, quieted, and Jane thought back to that night when Samuel Prosper had left Chalfont St. James, just a couple of years before, swearing he would be back. He and the boy, a pebble thrown at her window. She had gone down to the two of them, waiting on the lawn, she in her thin wrapper and bare feet, but she didn't feel the cold. Samuel had been wild-eyed, the boy somehow trying to calm him, his hand on the tutor's arm. "All will be well," she heard him say, just a child and yet with such certainty, knowing what Samuel Prosper needed to hear. Seeing the state of Samuel's shirt, filthy, she had left them there for a moment, gone back in and fetched another from the chest in his room. She and the boy together, disrobing Samuel and putting his arms through the sleeves as though he were a dead man preparing to be buried. He had smiled at her then, a tremulous, frightened smile, reaching out to touch her hand before turning and moving off into the darkness. The boy stayed with her.

"He won't be back," said the boy.

"Oh, but he will," she had replied, with certainty. "He's made a promise."

Now all was changed. As Eliza lay breathing softly beside her, her eyelids fluttering in a dream, Jane pinched herself, hard, which calmed her for a moment. The night was warm and so she pushed the coverlet off and let herself lie there in her nightshirt, her mind full of rich imaginings. As her breathing slowed and then became regular, she found herself drifting into a wood, down a soft shadowy path, where a hand reached out for her and pulled her in.

It was clear to everyone the next morning that Mr. Lampitt was not an eager witness. The judge, plied with refreshments by the increasingly hospitable Mrs. Grinshaw, seemed comfortable enough as he waited for the farmer's appearance. As time went on, however, he saw it necessary to send one of his deputies out to find the man, and Lampitt duly made his appearance, followed closely by the deputy, about thirty minutes later. The crowd was restive and greeted his entrance with a sudden buzzing of comment. Lampitt was a small man, wiry and strong, a scruffy halo of gray hair settled around his mostly bare skull. His eyes darted back and forth, as though he were looking for, or possibly trying to avoid, someone. He was well known in the community and liked, with a solid reputation for helping out whenever and wherever there was a need. His wife might complain of neglect, but his neighbor could always count on Lampitt. So, as he made his way forward, the crowd parted respectfully, giving him plenty of room.

Frances, having come very early, sat near the front of the chamber, Sarah Kidd by her side. She saw the constable in his usual seat, and the Justice of the Peace Mr. Stroud next to the judge. Sarah kept her eyes on Lampitt, willing him to look at her. Her hands were tidily in her lap, fingers moving back and forth over a small, tattered handkerchief. Lately she had been taking better care of herself: her hair was combed, and her dress, another one of Frances' cast-offs, was clean at the cuffs and collar. Frances noted with satisfaction that it fit her better than it would have a few weeks before; the meals at the Grove evidently agreed with Sarah Kidd.

"Edward Lampitt," said the judge, "you are here to help clear up a matter of great importance. We have a body—that of Nathaniel Kidd—and we are attempting to find out what became of him, and his fortune. As you know, Mrs. Grinshaw testified that she met Nathaniel Kidd when he was brought in by the night watchman, to be questioned as to his purpose in Chalfont St. James. You were, according to Mrs. Grinshaw, the watchman on that particular night, and were the last to see Mr. Kidd, since he was freed and allowed to go on his way. No one has seen the man since. You must, then, tell us what you saw and what you know of Nathaniel Kidd's fate."

The farmer looked at the judge and then at the floor, where he kept his gaze as though his shoes were in need of thorough study. There was a long silence which the judge was intelligent enough not to fill. Sarah's right hand found its way into Frances' left.

The Bible was brought forward and the watchman took the oath. Not so much of a Quaker, thought Frances uncharitably.

"I will tell the truth of that night," said Edward Lampitt, his slight voice expanding to fill the room. "No one has asked me, sir judge, and so I have never said. Was not my place to talk of it. I came across the stranger as I did my rounds after dark, and there was a full moon. I am careful as a watchman, I don't just find a spot and lie myself down such as some people do." Here there was a small ripple of laughter in the courtroom. "As I was saying, I am a good watchman. And so I stopped this man, to see what he was about. I'd heard talk of a robber in the neighborhood. I asked the man his name and his business, and so he told me, Nathaniel Kidd, on his way to London. So he said. He had a bag with him, and I could see it was heavy. He allowed as it was his fortune, and that made me wonder, so I sent Will Porter to get folk together to get to the truth of the matter, as we do at such times." Here he took a breath and looked up at the judge.

"And who were these folk, that questioned Nathaniel Kidd?" asked the judge. The farmer shifted his weight from one foot to the other and gave the judge a long look.

"As you know, sir, Mrs. Grinshaw was there, as was her husband," he said. "Mother Grime—may she rest in peace—was there as well, as were the constable Mr. Notkin and Will Porter. I believe that Tom, the Grinshaws' boy, was one, and then there was Samuel Jewett though he didn't say nothing, as I remember. I think the Justice, Mr. Stroud, showed up late, after everything was settled. Of course, the tutor was there too, Samuel Prosper his name was. Gone away now. He that—that said he was robbed."

Frances dropped Sarah's hand and put it to her mouth in surprise, her breath gone. Sarah's arm went around her and she recovered herself. It all was but a moment. The crowd around her was murmuring, impatient to hear Lampitt continue. She could not think—Samuel Prosper, who had left so suddenly, somehow implicated in this matter of Nathaniel Kidd. She thought of Jane, who had wept so after Prosper's disappearance. She herself had felt nothing but relief, mixed with inconvenience. But now all was changed.

Jane felt a little foolish, retracing her steps to find the very place in the woods where Samuel Prosper had found her before. She sat herself down in the grass and waited, watching as the sun's movement played with the shadows around her. By late morning, hopeless, she brushed the grass from her skirts and began the trudge back to the Grove. She began to wonder if Samuel's visit had been a dream, something she had imagined to satisfy, in some small way, her longing for him and for a new life. Why would he not come forward, ask for her hand, and be together with her? Always, she thought to herself, she was captive to others and their concerns.

She could see, as she approached the house, Eliza and the widow Kidd's little boy playing with the chickens, running after them and squealing as the chickens clucked. The maidservant Deborah was close by, seeing to the herb garden and keeping watch. Jane had no place in the scene, and began to feel, as she turned away and walked around the house through the garden, that she had no place at the Grove. She made her way deep into the hollyhocks and cosmos, to a bench someone had brought outside and left. This was a more pleasant spot than the woods, a place where she could hide and think. She tried to imagine Samuel again as she had seen him, his eyes on her, the warmth of his hand. It had been real, surely.

And as Jane sat there she felt his presence. She closed her eyes and could almost feel his breath. She knew he was close by. She hoped that he would come for her, and soon.

The moon was like a lantern, lighting their way as they walked to the road leading out of Chalfont St. James. As much as he longed for a bed, Nathaniel had no wish to stay, and as he knew there to be no robbers about, a night spent under a tree in the nearby woods was all he needed. He said nothing to Lampitt as they made their way to the highway. Lampitt was clearly uncomfortable in his presence, embarrassed perhaps, thought Nathaniel. The man walked quickly and looked in every direction but at him. When they arrived at the highway, he finally turned to Nathaniel.

"Here's where I leave you," he said gruffly. "They made their decision. I cannot say that I agree—for all the Stringfellows in the world, you are still a stranger to us—but they listen to Mother Grime, they do." And off he went, disappearing into the shadows. Nathaniel had barely time to note the man's swift departure. He was about to clap him on the back in a friendly way and be off, ready to be quit of this village, when out of the shadows moved the tutor Samuel Prosper. Nathaniel was fully aware of the size of the man, his thickness and strength as he strode toward him.

"That money should be mine," the tutor said in a low voice as he came close. "Give it over, and begone with you, you're lucky with no branding this time!"

Nathaniel held tighter to the bag. "Lampitt, you're the night watchman, call out! This man is robbing me!" But Lampitt was nowhere to be seen, and if he heard anything he did not reply. Samuel Prosper grabbed hold of Nathaniel and began to pull at the strap of Nathaniel's bag.

Nathaniel could do nothing but fight back. He pulled as hard as the tutor did, with all his strength, but both men soon found themselves in the dirt of the highway as Prosper, the bigger man, put his weight to him. Nathaniel was able to place a well-aimed thrust at the man's crotch, which sent the attacker flying off him, but he knew this was only for a moment. Shoving hard at the tutor while struggling to hold on to the bag, he scrambled to his feet and began to run. He cared not what direction. He could hear feet behind him, but he kept running.

Then he felt a shove from behind, someone leaping at him and throwing all their weight against him. He fell forward, felt a sudden sharp blow to his head, and then nothing more.

"Continue," the judge said as the room quieted. "We are getting to the bottom of this matter."

Edward Lampitt took a deep breath. "Well, we did as we always do, we asked the man questions, seeing as how he was a stranger in our village. The tutor, Samuel Prosper, had told us that he'd been robbed that very day, on his return from visiting his father, and so we were afraid that this man was the robber. He had a foreign look, to me he looked like a Welshman, to tell the truth. So questions had to be asked."

"Of course," encouraged Judge Adams, nodding his head. "You but did your duty."

The farmer smiled and looked around. "That we did, we asked him questions, we didn't want any mischief in our village from a Welshman. He seemed a mischief-maker to us, not properly respectful. And he had a big bag of coin with him, had a story that he'd earned it, but any thief would say that."

This made Sarah Kidd stand up, and her voice could be heard through the chamber. "Nathaniel Kidd was an honest man, let it be said here, this man's insults are but a fool's words. He was no Welshman, he was an Englishman born and bred, come from Leominster, and he earned his money fairly. This must be said." And then she sat down. The judge seemed unperturbed by her contribution, but Lampitt turned pale.

"I meant no disrespect," he said, "only that we had reason for what was done. We did not know him. And the tutor, Samuel Prosper, he said the man was the thief that robbed him."

More noise from the crowd. The judge put up a hand to quiet everyone. "So, this Mr. Prosper said that this was the robber?"

"That he did, sir," replied the farmer. "And we thought the matter done with, so the constable would take the man to his house. But then it turns out that Mother Grime—may her soul rest in peace, sir—had some memory of folk he knew—if I remember rightly, don't remember more than that—and that changed things. They had people in common. And so that was the end of it, we let the man go."

"So, that was the last you saw of him, as watchman that night?" The judge looked closely at Lampitt.

There was a long silence. Frances felt Sarah trembling.

The man looked at the Bible on which he had sworn. "Well, no. I was told to take him back to the highway, so that he could make his way out of town with no further incident. So that I did. I—I left him there. Don't know any more about it."

"About what?"

"About anything, sir," which made some people laugh.

"Well then Mr. Lampitt, you were the last one to see this man alive, it seems. For he did indeed end up dead, by a blow to the head. You are saying now that you had naught to do with that?" Judge Adams frowned and began to tap his fingers on his table.

"Naught to do with that, nothing," said the man sturdily. "I did not touch the man. I've no more to say, sir judge."

"It seems we cannot proceed further," said the judge with finality, looking out at the crowd. "There is no telling who came upon

Nathaniel Kidd, killed him and buried him. Widow Kidd, there is nothing here to show Mr. Grinshaw had anything to do with your husband's death. It seems he spoke with the man, but then that was the end of it. Your husband never stayed at the inn. You must accept this conclusion and be on your way, now that your husband is buried. There is nothing more to be done."

Sarah Kidd stood once again and turned to face the crowd, away from the judge. "I will not leave until Daniel Grinshaw is questioned. He hides, he is a coward and hides behind his wife, he refuses to come forward and speak the truth. He knows the truth. He is keeping my son's fortune from him. How can I leave and give that up?" She asked this in search of an answer, her eyes moving from face to face in the crowd. "It is all I have. Mr. Grinshaw must answer, and so must—so must the man who accused my husband of thievery. My husband came to Chalfont St. James in search of a bed for the night. Instead, he was greeted with suspicion and accusations, unfounded, and was killed, his fortune stripped from him. I do not see how I can leave here without the justice I seek." A long pause as she turned and bowed her head to the judge. She dropped suddenly on to the bench, spent.

"Let us go home, Sarah," said Frances.

Chapter Seventeen

———◆———

I am here," he said.

Jane knew this to be true before he said it. She moved over on the garden bench so that he could sit next to her. It was a wonder to her that he had returned, and she felt a strong urge to reach out and touch him, to make sure he was real. She could see that his coat was of good quality: no doubt he had met with success in London. There was a slight warm scent about him, perhaps freshly bathed.

"I am very glad to see you," she said shyly, and she could feel a blush warm her face. She wanted him to say that he had come back for her, and yet she felt some fear too, of what this might mean, what would happen next.

He took her hand between both of his and gave it a gentle squeeze. "Of that I have no doubt, dear Jane, though it is good to hear you say it. Stuck here in the country, amongst these people, it is like being buried alive. I could not bear it. London, now with the King's return, is a place where a man can make something of himself. I have found myself a place, and it provides me with all I need and more. Jane"—and here he turned to her, his eyes meeting hers—"Jane, you must come with me. I will make you my wife. We will find us a priest to marry us, it will be all lawful, and we will be man and wife." He leaned down and kissed her hand, still cradled within his own.

"A priest?" she asked, even as she found herself almost speechless with excitement, her heart pounding.

"Yes, yes," Samuel said quickly, looking away. "A Friends marriage is too easy to dispute—you and me before Meeting, no priest. I want to know that our marriage is lawful and cannot be undone."

He turned towards her again and their knees touched. "No one can come between us. It is a small price to pay, to have some steeple-house priest marry us, so that we can be safe in our union. You must trust me about this." Jane lifted her face to his. The kiss was long and gentle. After they parted she smiled, even as she thought she might weep. "My mother will understand," she said, something she knew to be completely untrue.

"When we tell her of it, yes," agreed Samuel with a laugh. "We must go now, Jane, and see to the marrying. We will send word to your mother once we are in London. I have a horse, we can be there tonight, and find ourselves someone to marry us."

Up to this point everything that had transpired was so close to what Jane had always imagined that she had wondered, for a fleeting moment, whether this was the Devil's conjuring, a demon in place of Samuel to tempt her. But here was where her imagining and her present diverged. She had not thought of an elopement to London. Her imaginings had always included her mother, and a walk of the bridal pair through the meadow to Meeting, her hand in Samuel's as the Friends looked on. She did not see her mother approving, exactly, but rather bending to her daughter's will. The moment at Meeting where they were joined was at the center of her thought. It did not include a ride to London as an unmarried woman, with none of her family about her. And yet here he was, her lover, about to take her away. She was suddenly aware of his impatience—that, unlike her own pleasure in the moment, he had from the start been ready to leave. He sat tensely, forward on the bench, ready to stand at a moment's notice.

"I do not know, Samuel," she said slowly. "I cannot leave without telling someone. My mother would worry. It would be wrong. Perhaps we can have the priest here, Mr. Brunskill, marry us, once we have spoken with Mother? She likes and respects him, even if he is not one of us. I so want to be with you in London, I do, but I cannot travel with you as an unmarried woman." She did not know where her sudden propriety came from. Certainly it had not played a role in her nighttime thoughts about Samuel. But she felt it quite fiercely here and now.

"We do not have time for this concern," replied Samuel with some urgency, his hands freeing hers. "Of course I would want you to be married with family and friends nearby. I would. But right now we cannot wait. We can be in London, and married, before nightfall, *if we go now.* I do not think your mother would allow us to marry, Jane. She is friends with this priest, as you say, I've seen them together—he will do her bidding. She will come round, once it is done, but she will put you away if she discovers me here. I know this. You must come with me." He stood and began to pace in front of her.

"Please let me think," she cried, standing too, fully in his shadow. "If you can give me time, I will consider and be ready with my decision soon. I will tell no one, I only wish to pray and consider this. It is such a surprise, Samuel, I am overcome." Tears began to fall. Samuel reached out to her with both hands and wiped them gently from her cheeks. They stood like this for a long moment.

"Yes," he finally said, "I would never do anything to harm you, please know this. I am thinking of what is best for us, and how we can be together as man and wife. This is something I have thought long about. It is no hasty matter, thoughtless or reckless. I know you are overwrought and I have no wish to cause you more pain. I await your answer."

She thought to herself, he came here today to take me away. And I have changed his mind, I am the one who decides. She smiled through her tears and began to speak, but she could hear the sound of the children, laughing and talking, louder as she stood there.

"Goodby," was all she said as she turned and ran toward the house.

As they approached the Grove, Frances could hear the children's voices, and the sound made her glad. Even Sarah, lost in her thoughts, picked up her pace at the sound of her little boy's laugh. Deborah's voice was there too, mingled with the children's. It was a world away from the assizes, and the disappointment of the watchman's testimony. Frances followed the sound of the voices, around the side of the house and through the garden. There sat Eliza, a garland of daisies in her dark hair, the little boy John laughing and trying to make his own garland with Deborah's help. Twisting the green stems round and round, the daisies were pushed, prodded and sometimes crushed into a crown. Frances sat herself down with little ceremony to help the small fingers finish the job.

"Ah, there you are," cried Jane, emerging from the house, her voice high. "I have been so worried. You must tell me of the watchman's witnessing, what came of it." Flushed and nervous, she sat on the bench next to the children, her eyes traveling back and forth between them and the women.

Sarah shrugged. "Nothing came of it, Jane. He saw nothing, he says, he does not know what happened. I do not believe him, but I am a poor woman. The judge dismissed the matter, with no one to hear."

"The strangest thing," said Frances as she placed the crown on the little boy's head, the child suddenly somber with the ritual of it, "there was some talk then of a robbery, and how it was our tutor at the time, Samuel Prosper, who accused Nathaniel Kidd of robbing him. The watchman talked of that, how he came upon Nathaniel, and then he and some others examined Nathaniel and with Samuel there too. But he is gone, we cannot know more of that."

There was a long silence, as the children danced, pleased with their daisy crowns. Frances noted how Jane sat there, her hands twisted together, her eyes on her feet, completely separate from the playing children. Sarah, meanwhile, rose from the ground and brushed off her skirts.

"I will go in search of this man, this Mr. Prosper," she said with firmness. "He accused Nathaniel of stealing. Why would he do such a thing, and play so false? Was he an enemy of my husband, and how could that be, since they did not know each other?"

"Now, that is the puzzle of it," Frances said, nodding her head. "For that, if I remember rightly, was the time when Samuel Prosper left my employ. Quite abruptly, in fact, without taking leave. He went away, and we were left with no tutor. I'd had no sign that he planned to take his leave of us. He simply was gone. It is clear to me now that his leaving had something to do with Nathaniel."

Jane abruptly rose from her bench and went into the house without a word. Frances looked at Sarah. "I am her mother, but still I do not know the girl. Sarah, I understand your desire to find Samuel Prosper and so find your way closer to the truth, but he is gone and there is no telling where."

Sarah shook her head slowly. "I cannot free myself of this. It is my duty to Nathaniel and to my son."

"Well," said Frances with some practicality, "It is not only the tutor, but Daniel Grinshaw, who can tell us more. And surely he will return—this is his inn, and his wife, in Chalfont St. James. He will wait until the assizes are over and return from whatever business he claims to have elsewhere. I ask that you wait, Sarah, until he returns, to decide whether to go in search of Mr. Prosper."

At that moment Eliza reached over and pulled off John Edward's crown, insisting that hers was the only head to wear such a crown, which brought the childish idyll to a sudden end, John Edward bursting into tears. The two mothers gathered up their children and left the garden, child's play over.

"You shouldn't have brought him back here, for God's sakes," the gruff voice was low and urgent. Nathaniel, his head throbbing with a killing pain, kept his eyes closed. He was not dead, but felt that if he were to open his eyes he would see his peril, and he wished to stay clear of that. The soothing darkness of his eyelids, gray and soft, brought a small comfort. He knew himself to be lying on a wood floor, cold and hard. The other people were talking and moving about. He could feel their stepping back and forth.

"I saw him lying there, done in," said one voice, perhaps that of the tall man at the earlier meeting. "Our watchman nowhere to be found. Just lying there, his bag gone. Couldn't just leave him to be found in the morning by one and all, could I?" A pause.

"Weren't no easy thing, dragging him along, your inn being the closest, Daniel."

"Well, he's in my inn, so he's my concern," replied the first man. "I don't want a dead man here, nor some troublemaker who's bound to make a noise about his missing bag of silver. This will just cause more trouble." A long sigh and the squeak of a chair as someone sat down. Nathaniel held his eyes closed. There was a deep, throbbing pain throughout his head that made him want to cry out, but he kept still.

Then he heard approaching footsteps and someone else coming into the room. Another voice, unknown to him. Almost a laugh but not quite. Nathaniel could feel the man circling him, his feet heavy on the floor. "This will take some cleaning up, all this blood. The man looks to be near dead."

At that, Nathaniel became aware of wetness, sticky and slick, beneath his cheek, the one next to the floor. It was strange, how parts of him seemed completely numb while his head filled with pain. He felt himself calming even as the voices became more distant. It was as though they had moved away, to some other room, and yet he knew that they were all still there, next to him. He thought suddenly of his wife Sarah, and it was so easy to imagine her next to him, her face full of worry, her hand reaching out to him. He felt himself drifting.

"I think he's dyin', Mr. Stroud sir," said the first man. "All we got to do is bury him. Just wait it out. Look at all that blood, there's nothing we can do for him. He's on his way." There was a hopeful note in his voice.

Nathaniel felt her presence, knew Sarah, somehow, to be there. She would find him, he was sure of that, she had an unerring sense of direction. There she was, reaching out to him, pulling him to his feet, bringing him back to himself. He could feel her, and he wanted so much to see her. Opening his eyes took some effort, as it turned out, and he felt the spill of blood across his eyelids as he worked at it. They were still talking, all around him, ignoring the presence of his wife.

"God's blood, he's awake," said the man with the heavy brows. Nathaniel tried to hoist himself up, thrusting his head up in the hope that his body would follow. The pain in his head made him want to vomit. The other men's figures came and went in his vision, and he did not see Sarah, began to wonder if that had been his imagination. He threw one arm across his torso to be able to push himself up with his hands. Groaning with the effort, he was able to sit up, and cried out, he could hear his voice carrying across the room and beyond, "Sarah, help me, help me," just as one of the men, it was the man he hadn't seen before, pushed his head back down with a firm push of his boot. He felt the floor hit him hard. And that was all.

The assizes having come to an end, there was a small, respectful crowd to watch as Judge Adams mounted his horse and bowed his head towards Mrs. Grinshaw, his host for the past several days. Jane lingered towards the back of the crowd. She wasn't sure why she had come, what she expected to see, but it had seemed necessary. She had not asked her mother for permission, knowing what the answer would be. The constable Notkin was there, bowing and scraping before the judge, and the liberated grand jury, bidding farewell to their temporary master. It was a festive scene, even celebratory. The day was warm and dry, clouds of dust floating past, caught in the sunlight. On the other side of the crowd from her she saw Arthur Brunskill. He seemed distracted, his eyes on some distant mark, his form very still in the midst of the tumult around him. Making her way towards him, Jane reached out and touched the priest's arm. He startled and looked at her.

"Miss Jane," he said, bowing his head slightly. The judge had moved off and so the crowd was beginning to disperse.

"Mr. Brunskill," replied Jane, "It is good and timely to see you now. I have a question for you, perhaps we could walk and consider it?" She tried to smile but felt overcome for a moment.

"Of course, Jane, let us walk. The judge has now left, there is nothing more to see." The priest put out his arm and they began to walk in the direction of the Grove. For some time they walked in silence as Brunskill waited patiently for Jane's question.

As they left behind the village, she began. "This will be a strange question, I am afraid, Mr. Brunskill, coming as it does from a devout member of the Society of Friends. I have known no other religion, in all my life, nor do I ever intend to leave it. It is my own. But there are some—customs, I suppose—among the Friends that I am troubled by. I wonder what your opinion is of the rite of marriage as it is performed by our faith?"

Brunskill was truly puzzled. He did not expect to engage in a discussion of religion with this young girl and had to admit to himself that whatever the Friends considered a marriage rite was not troubling him at all. "I have to say, Jane, I do not know how a wedding is performed by your sect."

The girl looked surprised. "We do not have a priesthood, as you know, Mr. Brunskill, and so there is no one to lead the couple in their vows. Indeed, there are no vows. There are very simple words expressed, by the two, in front of Meeting, and thus the marriage is recognized. That is all. No one pronounces the couple to be wed."

"I have no quarrel with that," Brunskill said thoughtfully. "I say this as a Christian, not as a priest. If they speak before God of their commitment to marriage, in view of their community, then that would seem to me to satisfy. However, for the Church it is a sacrament and thus requires the presence of an authority and for certain words and vows to be said—so therein lies a difference."

"Would you perform the ceremony for Christians who are not of your faith?" Jane was almost whispering.

"No," he said firmly. "It is a sacrament, an act before God. It is in the church, there are banns to be said, the man and woman must be baptized of course and receive the Eucharist." He looked closely at her. "Why this question, Jane?"

"It is no matter," Jane said with a slight catch in her voice. "It is that I worry that any marriage made in Meeting might not be recognized in the world. My mother—her marriage to my step-father—that marriage has been questioned. Our uncle questions it. He wishes to disinherit my sister Eliza."

The priest and girl walked on for some time in silence, at a more leisurely pace. Brunskill, though he did not see himself as very adept at looking into the hearts of his parishioners, knew that Jane was in some sort of trouble. He tried comfort.

"Do not worry about that," he said with a studied heartiness. "Your mother will make sure of Eliza's inheritance. She is a lawful widow of her husband, and their marriage is viewed by one and all to be a lawful one. Mrs. Bright is respected by all her neighbors. Your uncle is foolish in this plan of his."

"Oh it's not about her, not at all," burst out Jane. "I must ask you, Mr. Brunskill, if you would marry me to the man who is already my husband in my heart, if not in the flesh. We are of the Friends, though we were both baptized into the Church as infants. We are not of your Church now, but I know if we do not marry in this way, we will be cast down and torn apart." She stopped in the path and stared at him.

Brunskill was stunned. He stared back at Jane for a long moment. He did not know what to say.

"Ah, Jane, you are but a child. How can you be ready for such things? Who is this man who is of your heart?"

"Does it matter who he is? Will you marry us?" cried Jane with a fierce look, her arms crossed.

"How can I do that, when you have as good as said your mother does not approve? That she would not allow you to marry at your Meeting? Why do you think she would approve a marriage in the Church, if she would not in her own faith? This is not sensible, Jane."

"If you do not, then we will be together without marriage. We will leave Chalfont St. James and not be heard from again. He has said that he will take me to London. I will be with him, even without anyone's permission, not even God's." The last words were almost a shout. Brunskill looked about; they were, thankfully, the only ones on the path.

"Surely this man would not agree to that," he said, with real surprise. "He would not allow you to ruin your reputation in such a way."

"There is no other way, Mr. Brunskill, please understand. Of course he is careful of me. We have done nothing wrong, and he waits patiently for my decision. He is a good man. With time, my mother will agree. But we must do this now, there is no waiting."

"Dear girl, if I cannot dissuade you from this path, then I will do as you ask. I cannot agree to your ruin. Let me know how I can help you." Brunskill felt surrounded by strong, stubborn women, and he was no match for them, far from it. If he allowed this marriage to take place, Frances Bright might never forgive him. But if he did not, the consequences could be far worse.

The pathways around Chalfont St. James had all become very familiar to him, thought Nick Brown as he made his way through the copse just south of the Grove's pond. It had begun to wear on him, these paths that all seemed to lead either to the village or the Misbourne and no further. Of course, there was the high road, and one could decide to make a journey to Aylesbury or to London, or perhaps to Seer Green if one really wanted to go there, but he felt perversely annoyed at the limits to his wanderings. He thought of his upbringing in Yorkshire, and the moors, and the endless exploration that seemed possible there, wild and open. Here, he was somehow constrained.

Perhaps it was that tutoring did not suit him as a profession. He thought he might talk with George Fox, and see whether he could instead join him on his travels. Go on a mission to the New World, perhaps. To tutor two little girls in remote Buckinghamshire seemed freshly unbearable to him. He began to walk faster and took the turn towards the village. The river was at its lowest ebb until the fall rains, and he had no wish to sit on the bank of a mostly dry riverbed. As he turned a corner and saw the village in the distance, he saw a familiar figure a bit ahead of him, on a gray horse.

"Dear Mr. Grinshaw," he called out, suddenly eager for company of a sort other than female. He thought he could share the news of the assizes with the innkeeper, and the opportunity pleased him.

Daniel Grinshaw turned his horse and stopped in the road, giving him a brief smile. "Oh, Mr. Brown," he said with a tired voice. "I have been traveling much of today. It's good to be home." He hesitated a moment, and then dismounted. "And how go things here in the village? I feel I have been gone too long."

"You have indeed," said Nick with some enthusiasm. "The assizes are over and done with now. Mrs. Kidd brought her case forward, and the judge called for you but your wife said you had business elsewhere. I suppose it all was resolved, though not to anyone's satisfaction." He hoped that this tantalizing phrase would lead to questions from the innkeeper.

"That woman," said Grinshaw, spitting on the ground. "I'm sure she found a way into Judge Adams' good graces. She's a wily one. I will not be questioned, not I. I earned the respect I have in this village. But the judge, he'd listen to that vagrant, with her false tears." He began to move forward again, the horse alongside.

"Indeed," agreed Nick, "that was the way of it. Mrs. Kidd's tears and then the calling of witnesses. Not just Mrs. Grinshaw but Lampitt as well, he that was watchman that night and met Mr. Kidd." Here he hoped he was sufficiently mysterious to invite more questions and even astonishment from Grinshaw. He was not disappointed.

"God's blood!" cried the innkeeper, stopping again in the road and staring at the tutor. "What are you telling me, man? What sort of story got told to the judge?"

Nick felt quite happy in this moment. He provided a thorough and occasionally, he felt, witty summary of the events at the assizes, as Grinshaw picked up his pace to move towards the inn. The tale was told by the time they reached the front steps, the innkeeper shooing chickens away and handing his tired horse over to the newly hired boy. He did not object as Nick followed him up the steps and into the inn.

The place had gone back to its usual form with the departure of the assizes. No more crowds in the front rooms, instead the usual small cluster of folk talking over mugs of ale. They looked up as one as Grinshaw made his appearance, followed closely by the tutor. Mrs. Grinshaw came bustling out of the kitchen and, grabbing her husband's arm, led him back through the kitchen door. "I am glad to see you, Mr. Grinshaw," was all she said. Nick, still very interested and not feeling disinvited, followed.

The kitchen was close and warm. Pots were steaming on the hearth, and the aroma of freshly baked bread was cloying and slightly sickening. He rather hoped that Grinshaw would turn to him and ask him to repeat his story for the benefit of his wife, but the two ignored him. Looking around the kitchen, he went in search of some water, and after some exploring found a jug in a cupboard at the back of the kitchen. He was no longer in view of the Grinshaws but he could hear their conversation.

"Wife," said Grinshaw, "tell me what was said at the Assizes."

Mrs. Grinshaw sighed and smoothed her skirts. "It was a good thing you were—off on business, you know—you just missed Judge Adams who left this morning—but I am very glad to have you home. All's well, Mr. Grinshaw."

There was a moment of silence and then footsteps. He heard Mr. Stroud, though his voice lacked its usual heartiness.

"So, a convenient absence, Grinshaw?"

"There's nothing more to be said. The assizes are over," said Grinshaw with finality. "We will think no more of this, we are finished with it."

"Oh, so just because Judge Adams has left for the next town, you are finished? How will this ever be finished, Grinshaw? You were there, you saw everything, and yet you did nothing beyond bury a stranger in a shallow grave without so much as a prayer to send him on his way. Let me ride right now, to follow the assizes, and I am sure the judge will give his attention to what I have to say."

"You have no mind to your own destruction, then?" cried Mrs. Grinshaw. "For you were the one with the heavy boot! Mayhap there were two men that ambushed the poor traveler—methinks it was you alongside Prosper, Mr. Stroud, claiming that tutor's gambling debt. The poor man might have lived, but for you."

Nick felt faint and grabbed on to the table in the center of the room. Here he was, not in an inn's warm kitchen but rather a den of robbers, bloody with crime. He thought suddenly of his own safety and wished he had not accosted the innkeeper in the road.

Stroud's voice only deepened. "Dear lady, you needn't worry about me. You were not there when the man met his end. I'm sure that if the Judge would like to compare your husband's story and mine, he will vastly prefer my version."

Grinshaw laughed. "Judge Adams is well acquainted with my wife and myself. It does no good to threaten us, Stroud. We tell you now to leave our inn."

Nick moved away from the cupboard and tried to slip out the door to the kitchen garden. As he turned to grasp the door handle, he saw Stroud look up and their eyes met. There was a poisonous air of violence about Stroud, no matter his gentleman's manner, and the room felt close and dangerous. Suddenly the door to the front room opened and one of those whom Nick had seen enjoying a mug of ale came through. "Man, there's no one to see to my ale," he said with a swagger, looking from one to the other. "What's keeping you all in the kitchen? Where's Sally?"

Mrs. Grinshaw hustled forward and smiled at the villager. "Let me see to it," she said, with a smile that seemed more like a grimace to Nick. As she moved the customer back towards the door, the tutor decided this was a good moment for him to flee. He knew himself to be in grave danger and could only think of returning to the Grove. As he made his way to the door, Stroud turned on him.

"And you heard nothing, did you, tutor?"

It was a cool evening for late summer, and so a fire was laid in Frances' favorite parlor. She and Jane sat side by side companionably, working on their embroidery. Frances thought about her odd conversation with Mr. Brown before the evening's supper. He had declined joining the family for the meal and had abruptly informed her that he would be leaving the Grove the next morning. She had been surprised but he had refused to say more, except to share with her that teaching was no longer his calling. He hoped to go on a mission with Fox, perhaps to the New World. He was not meant for the classroom and felt, quite strongly, that Frances should seek a better tutor for her daughters.

It had been a surprise, but Frances could see that his mind was made up. She could not say that she would regret his leaving. She had had her own doubts about his teaching skills, especially concerning Jane. The girl worried her, very much. As they sat there working, Frances tried to draw her out.

"Your embroidery has much improved of late, daughter," she said, hoping the praise might bring a smile to Jane's face. "I see that you have improved in both speed and detail."

Jane looked down at the handkerchief in her lap, the small light-blue stitches delicately circling in a pleasing pattern. "Thank you, Mother." Her narrow face did not change expression. She seemed thinner to Frances, the waist of her dress loose about her.

More silence. Then Jane looked up at Frances as a log shifted position in the fireplace with a crack. "Mother, tell me about my father and how it was between you." She laid down her embroidery on a small table. "Tell me how it was then."

Frances was surprised. "It was such a long time ago, Jane, and the world was different then. It was before the War. I had not found my faith, all was different. It is hard to think of those times." But she too set aside her embroidery. "I have told you some of this before. Your father was of mild manner, gentle and kind. He was several years my senior, much wiser in the ways of the world, and yet he spoke generously to me, never minding my ignorance or simplicity. I knew him from the time I was a very young girl. He was much respected in our household, never did I hear a word against him from anyone. He was often out in society, and well-liked. When we agreed to marry, my happiness was greater than I had ever known."

Her daughter looked into the fire. "And you knew it to be right, the pledging of your troth? Was there no doubt in your mind? That he would be a good husband to you?" There was a note of something in her voice that made Frances uneasy.

"My Aunt Preston thought I was too young," she replied. "And I knew her to be right. My marriage to your father was not at all as my marriage to Mr. Bright. I was a child, I was not the helpmeet that your father needed and expected. Perhaps our very separation, with the War, was provided by God to allow me to grow and become thereby more useful to him. For surely in the early days of our marriage I was a silly thing, of no use to anybody." She laughed, thinking of that little girl. "We remained with my aunt and uncle, and so there was little for me to do in managing a household. But even so, I was charged with my husband's care, and yet he went about with torn hose and badly mended gloves. I did not even notice, I was just a child. He said nothing to me, he showed nothing to me but love and affection."

She thought for a moment of James Lyndal, the way he would look at her, and how she had known herself to be more an ornament, a pretty child, than a true wife to him. Aunt Preston, gently chiding her, and then James coming to her defense. It was, indeed, something of a relief in the midst of sorrow when he went off to war, allowing her to retreat into childhood for a time.

"But there was nothing about my father that made you hesitate to marry him?" asked Jane with some persistence.

Frances laughed. "Ah, no! I am sure he had his own hesitation, but I had none. I was certain. He was a good man and always did right by me. He honored and took care of me. He served our country with courage, known by all to be a good soldier, leading his men into battle. I was honored to be his wife and will always remember him. You look a little like him, Jane." Her voice softened as she looked at her daughter. In reality Jane took after Aunt Preston more than anyone, with her red-gold hair and green eyes. Still, there was something about her expression, pensive and serious, that was James.

Jane was silent for a moment and then reached for her embroidery. "I have never been certain about anything in my life," she said. "I am always filled with such doubt and care. Even in Meeting

I am not sure. I love Mr. Fox but I do not know if I love his God. I—I do not know what to do."

"About what, Jane? It is natural to not feel the Light when at Meeting, sometimes." Frances thought of her own lengthy dry periods. "The important thing is to seek the Light, even when it hides from you."

"Oh, it is not just that," cried the girl, suddenly standing. "It is not just that. I know! But what if there is something one has wanted for such a long time, so much, and then one finds something wrong about it? Some small wrong, but there all the same?"

Frances looked closely at her daughter. "What is it, Jane? What is it that you want?"

"It doesn't matter, not now," said Jane. "Please excuse me, I will say good night." And she was gone.

Chapter Eighteen

———•◆•———

The preparations did not take very long. A tutor travels light. There was the inevitable satchel of books, and then his carry-all with his few items of clothing. Nick Brown felt the lack of it, the narrowness of his existence, in the paltry pile of Latin classics and the single pair of breeches. His beloved Cicero was gone, of course, washed down the Misbourne to land on someone else's shore, waterlogged and indecipherable. He folded the everyday pair of stockings, graying with age, and set them on top of the breeches. This was his entire patrimony. He had left his Caesar's *Gallic Wars* as a gift for Jane, who had labored so long in her translation. He knew she would appreciate his act of generosity, which gave him a pleasant feeling of doing good in the world.

As he finished loading the satchel his mind moved to the exchange between Stroud and the Grinshaws earlier that day. He was fortunate to get away with his life, and the sooner he left Chalfont St. James the better. He had no illusions about Mr. Stroud, who was a dangerous man and in fact murderous. He thought of Sarah and the child, sleeping nearby, innocent—what he could tell them would do no good. There was no fortune to return to them. There was no justice to be had. Mr. Stroud was a gentleman, with influence, and judges didn't listen to the likes of a Quaker tutor or, for that matter, a village innkeeper.

"Mr. Brown, may I speak with you?" It was Frances Bright at the door.

She moved into the chamber. She had on her cloak and hat. "We must move quickly," she said in almost a whisper. She picked up his coat from the bed. "Put this on and come with me, Mr. Brown. I would like you to accompany me to the church. Please keep silent."

He slipped on his coat without a word and they went out through the kitchen into the night. The moon was out and there was sufficient light to see, yet still they stumbled as they went along the path, and the tutor had to stifle his urge to complain with each stub of his toe. Within a quick moment he could see their object: about one hundred feet in front of them a small figure, cloaked and hooded, a woman walking swiftly off towards the village.

The path broadened as they turned towards the village, and so the way became easier. But as soon as Nick picked up his pace, Frances reached out and touched his arm to keep him back. "We must not be seen," she whispered finally to him, as if he were a dunce, unable to understand that. "Of course," he whispered back fiercely, which only seemed to annoy her. She turned away and kept her eyes on the figure.

After some time they could see the woman take another turn and move towards St. James, which had a light in one of its windows. Frances reached out and took the tutor's hand and squeezed it with feeling. She gestured to the side of the church as the figure entered the front door. They moved swiftly towards the lit window and crept beneath it. Following Frances' lead, the tutor slowly raised his head so that he could peer within.

The scene in the church surprised him. There stood Jane, her hood fallen away, her bright hair glowing in the candlelight, next to the priest, who was speaking with another man. The fellow looked familiar; Nick was sure he had seen him somewhere about the village or on the road within the past week or so. He had a nervous look about him, pale and distracted. Jane, however, looked extremely attentive to whatever Brunskill was saying, frowning with concentration. Nick could hear Frances' breathing, quick and shallow.

"This must be stopped," she whispered to Nick. "The priest warned me about this, he won't complete the task, but we are here to confront Mr. Prosper." He looked at her, puzzled. What did she expect him to do?

They could see, and hear in mumbling tones, a conversation between the man and Jane. Her frown had transformed into a more open look, almost pleading, as she spoke softly to the man.

"That man is Samuel Prosper," Frances said into his ear. The name meant nothing to Nick.

At that moment the man reached into his pocket and drew out a small pewter box. He slowly opened it to reveal, to Nick's eyes, a small silver band. Jane suddenly reached out and knocked the box from her lover's hand, crying out as she put herself behind the priest.

"Let us go in," said Frances. She took Nick's hand in hers and moved swiftly to the front of the church, flinging open the door. The priest, the couple and the witnesses turned to her as one.

"I do not understand," said Samuel. He stood close to Jane. The church was filled with shadows, lit by candles on this late summer night. He picked the small box, and the ring, off the floor and turned them over thoughtfully.

"I cannot," she repeated, this time with more urgency. "I cannot. That night, Samuel, that moment with you and the boy. That is when you came by the fortune that gave you a way to leave the Grove and go to London. You stole that fortune! If not for you, Sarah's husband would still be in the world. That little box, it belongs to Sarah Kidd." She willed her voice to steady. This moment was so very different from everything she had imagined.

"I did not kill him," replied Samuel, his eyes on hers. "I did not kill him."

The priest looked to him and then to Jane. "What is this?"

Jane could not speak. She turned to face her mother.

"I forbid this," cried Frances, "I will be obeyed in this." She let go, finally, of Nick's hand and ran to her daughter. "We will go home, Jane," she said, taking hold of the girl's hand.

Jane nodded with relief. "Yes, Mother, that is right, we will go home. I—I cannot marry him." She did not look at Prosper. The face she had spent hours conjuring up from memory was now monstrous to her. Frances gathered her in her arms.

"Good, good," declared Brunskill with relief. "You are far too young, Jane, and your mother is always right. Mr. Prosper"—he turned towards Samuel, who stood there, struck dumb—"it seems to me, in light of what has been said, that you have much to answer for, particularly concerning Nathaniel Kidd. This girl has made a wise decision, to hesitate to join in union with you, when it is clear that you had something to do with that terrible crime."

Samuel Prosper seemed to shrink before the words of the priest, and turned to look at Jane, who hid her face in response. He turned back towards Brunskill.

"I did have much to do with the fate of Nathaniel Kidd," he said slowly, "but I did not murder him. I swear that, I swear it, and if you wish me to swear it on the Bible I will. I am not that good a Quaker. I am not that good a man. It was an accident, all that I saw. I admit, I was dishonest in claiming robbery, it was all part of a way to find my way to London and to be free of my debts. But the constable and his fellows saw through my ruse and gave me no credence. I then agreed with another man to set upon Nathaniel as he made his way in the road, and to take his money from him, which I did. As I tore the bag from his arms, he fell back and hit his head against a stone, and lay there bleeding. But he was alive then. I am ashamed to say that I fled at that moment, left—I fled Chalfont St. James with the help of the boy. And with Jane's help as well"—he again turned to look at Jane, at which moment she looked up and met his gaze—"she knew nothing of what I'd done, only saw that I was in trouble and gave me aid. She had nothing to do with my crime."

"And so, if you did not kill the man, who did?" asked Frances, her arms still cradling her daughter as they sank together onto a bench.

"That is a question that I can answer," Nick heard himself saying. Suddenly all eyes were upon him. He coughed and took a moment to compose his thoughts. "I met with Daniel Grinshaw on his way home this afternoon, from his business abroad. We walked together and I joined him as he greeted his wife at the inn. She was, naturally, happy to see her husband, after his time away. It was there that we were joined by Mr. Stroud"—here he paused for effect—"and it was then that Mr. Stroud, in the midst of a heated talk with Mr. Grinshaw, admitted to the murder of Mr. Kidd. This I did hear with my own ears. We were interrupted, so I have no way of saying what came after, since I chose to leave and return to the Grove."

Samuel Prosper visibly shuddered. "Mr. Stroud protects himself," he said to Nick. "If he knows you heard his confession, he will murder you in your bed. He will stop at nothing. He and I were to share in the coin, for I owed it as my gambling debt. I took it all and ran. No honor among thieves."

Frances could not contain herself. "Oh, Mr. Brown, were you to keep this secret? To leave such a murderer among us, while you depart on your travels?"

The young man blushed. "I am in fear of my life, dear lady. I have no reason to believe that my words carry any weight in our village, or that the constable will act on anything I might say. I would be a fool to declare against Mr. Stroud. He is a man of consequence." He turned to Prosper. "You were right to stay in hiding, sir, this man would not hesitate to harm you. He is a gentleman, I am sure he has powerful friends, and we are but poor Quaker tutors, our word is nothing against his. We cannot swear on the Bible, as others do."

Jane felt her mother's arms tighten around her. "Such cowards," Frances said in a voice low with controlled anger. "Here is the priest of the village, a constant helpmeet to Sarah Kidd, and then there are you two, saving your own skins. You, Samuel Prosper, willing and able to include my daughter in your own dangerous peril, with a fortune built on the suffering and death of another. And you, Nicholas Brown, upon hearing the murderer's confession, allying yourself with him by your silence. I wonder at both of you, what you could have possibly heard in George Fox's words, because you are so far from the Truth."

Brunskill, who had sat himself down beside Frances, felt abashed as she spoke. "Not always such a helpmeet," he whispered softly, but then stood and looked at them all. A long pause. "We must see this through," he said finally, "for Mrs. Kidd and her son. Tomorrow we must go to Mr. Notkin, and present him with what has transpired here tonight. This may mean jail for you, Mr. Prosper, but if it was as you say, and from what Mr. Brown has told us, the true culprit for the murder of Mr. Kidd will be punished. With Mrs. Bright's help, we can stand up to even a gentleman of Mr. Stroud's stature. Mr. Brown, your testimony will be crucial, but we can hope that Mr. Stroud will confess, so that you will not have to do so with an oath in court. Are we all agreed?" He looked hopefully around the room.

Jane stood up, apart from her mother. Finally someone had said something that gave her hope. She looked at Samuel Prosper for a long moment. "I waited for you, Samuel, and never doubted you, not for a moment. But I had a child's understanding of you. I did not know your character until now. To set upon a traveler and take his fortune, without a backward glance! I cannot but despise such an act." She stared into Prosper's eyes until he looked away.

"Let us all go to our beds now," said Brunskill, ushering them all out of the church. "Tomorrow we will see Mr. Notkin."

As they walked along in the moonlight back to the Grove, Jane and Frances spoke in low voices. Frances had her own doubts about the consequences for the Justice. Mr. Stroud was a man of property, of stature, a member of the Church of England, with strong ties to powerful people in the district and beyond. The likelihood that he would be prosecuted for what seemed to have been the casual murder of an itinerant working man, or even the murder of a servant-boy, seemed very small. That was exactly why he did it, Jane said angrily: *because he could*.

"Jane, you will share my bed this night," said Frances as they went up the stairs, "so that you will not disturb your sister's sleep." She turned to Prosper and Nick Brown. "You two may share Mr. Brown's room for the night. We will sort this in the morning." She did not sound hopeful.

"I was so wrong," Jane said once she and Frances were in her mother's bedchamber, making their preparations for whatever sleep might come. "I am sorry, Mother, I have dishonored you and our family. I did not know his true character. I lost my faith, I lost my way. I was proud and wayward. I have caused much hurt. There is nothing I can do to be forgiven for this. I accept what punishment you feel I deserve, and even so it will not be enough."

Frances laid her hand on her daughter's head as she sat on the bed. "You must listen to the Light in your heart, Jane. That will direct you. You have closed yourself off to God. Now is the time to open yourself to him and seek his forgiveness, not mine."

Jane shuddered slightly. "Yes, I will. I will! But what will be done about Mr. Stroud?"

This was the hard question. Frances was quiet for a long moment. "I wish we could make sure of justice," she said to Jane. "The man is a murderer, we all know that. But he is also a very powerful man in our village, indeed in the county. We are but women and Quakers, as they call us. Jane, I ask that you not say anything to Sarah Kidd. Nothing at all. For she will only damage her cause by confronting Mr. Stroud and would be likely to find herself in Mr. Notkin's jail. I had thought we could see this through, my Jane, and restore Sarah's fortune, but not if Mr. Stroud is the culprit and your Mr. Prosper has spent the silver. We are, my dear, helpless in this matter, and it pains me to say so."

Jane stared at her mother. "But Mrs. Kidd *must* know. I will ask Samuel—Mr. Prosper—to tell her of his perfidy, and to make it right. He should restore her fortune, that is the least of it. As for Mr. Stroud, are we not placed on this earth to further God's justice, not man's? We Friends are not here to see to the interests of the Crown, but to God's will. How can we stand by and allow that man to live among us?"

Frances was tired. She removed her dress and slipped into bed. "Come, Jane," she said, patting the place next to her. "You must find some sleep this night. As for Mr. Stroud—well, you saw how much resistance Mrs. Kidd faced when she accused Mr. Grinshaw. It would be that a thousandfold with Mr. Stroud. This is my decision, tonight. We will talk no more of it."

But as they both lay there in the dark, Frances' mind continued to slip around the matter. As much as she portrayed her decision as final to Jane, she was uncertain and afraid. For God, as she looked within, was entirely silent.

Jane lay still, her breath shallow. Her sleeplessness before now had always been an act of will. Now it seemed a separate thing, refusing her the one refuge she craved. Perhaps it was the presence of her mother, just inches away, lying too still to be asleep. But part of it was grief, and part of it was anger. Grief at the loss of love: she saw, with painful clarity, her foolishness in loving a man of no character. She was no longer a child, so easily won by soft glances and a touch. Her past thoughts and actions galled her, and fed the anger, the frustration of helplessness in the face of Stroud's villainy.

Jane stole a glance at her mother in the dimness of the room. Frances' eyes were closed and her breathing even. Perhaps she had drifted off to sleep. The room felt close, dense with breath. Jane's imagination led her to picture Stroud at the assizes, his hands tied, facing justice. She imagined him being taken away, removed, an end to his mischief. She saw herself standing tall in the courtroom, perhaps noticed by others, an avenging angel, a witness to his downfall. It was a pleasing thought. George Fox's tales of godly retribution often involved an instrument, something or someone whose actions brought about a holy justice. She was to be this instrument, and as she gazed upon her mother she began to see a path.

As eagerly as they all greeted their beds in that early morning hour, none found much sleep. Nick Brown had a long, unsettling dream in which he was floating along the Misbourne, on a beautiful summer day, and then found himself drowning in the stream, fighting for his breath. He woke in a sweaty tangle in the blanket, his sleeping companion awake next to him, unmoving, staring at the ceiling, bearing an uncomfortable resemblance to a dead person.

In the kitchen, Frances was having her morning draught. She had listened through the dawn to Jane's uneven breathing, the deep sighs followed by small gasps and shudders. The hours passed. Frances spent most of those hours pondering her duties as a mother and considering where she had gone astray with Jane. To find her in a steeplehouse, at the point of exchanging vows before a Church of England clergyman with a man whose character was so very flawed, was so far from her understanding of her daughter that it lay everything open to question. Having finished her draught, she went into her parlor and sat in the quiet. She would have her own Meeting here, alone, and try to find the Light. Surely Jane's acquiescence was a good sign. She had gone up to the door but not gone through it. But how to address this with her daughter, both in word and action, was mysterious to Frances.

Sitting in the gray quiet of the room, she let her mind go inward, her eyes closed. There were no words to her prayer, only feeling. Yet even as she sought an answer, she knew that it was not there. The act of seeking had to be its own comfort.

"Ma'am," said Deborah from the doorway, "there is a gentleman come to see you. Shall I have him wait in the front parlor?"

Frances took a moment. "Yes, thank you, Deborah. It is very early for guests. Who is calling?"

The answer made Frances gasp in spite of herself. "It is Mr. Stroud, ma'am, come to call." Deborah's face was bland with boredom.

Frances caught her breath.

"I will be there presently," was all she said.

After Deborah's departure, she sat for a moment longer, to collect herself and think about what to say to Mr. Stroud. His appearance at the Grove this morning was surely to do with Mr. Brown's experience in the Grinshaws' kitchen. Would he be so rash as to attack her? Or was his visit possibly coincidental? Would he assume that she had knowledge of Mr. Brown's story?

Realizing that her train of thought was just heightening her fear, Frances stood, smoothed her skirts, and made her way to the other parlor. There stood Stroud in all his gentlemanly splendor, a blue waistcoat and creamy white shirt topping his black knee-breeches. His shoes looked freshly polished. She thought of the boot that had put an end to Nathaniel Kidd's life. Stroud stood and smiled warmly, his eyes bright with an alertness that frightened her even more.

"Ah, Mrs. Bright, so good of you to see me so early," he said, bowing his head slightly. "Your servant has made me quite comfortable and at ease. You are fortunate in your servants."

"I know that well," replied Frances, indicating with her hand that he should sit down. She had to resist the urge to sit on the edge of her chair, readying herself for flight. Sitting back, taking a deep breath, she smiled at her visitor. "Do tell me the purpose of your visit, Mr. Stroud. It is rather early for calls, which makes me think it is something in particular that brings you here." There was no need, in her mind, to extend the pleasantries.

He seemed of a like mind. "Of course! Your Mr. Brown is quite a promising young man, and I wish to encourage such promise as best I can. I want to speak with him of an opportunity. Young men these days have a time of it, trying to make their way in the world, and it is a satisfaction to help them. I would like to be of use to this particular young man. That is why I am here, dear Mrs. Bright." The man's eyes shone as he congratulated himself on his generosity.

"Well, you are too late, Mr. Stroud," said Frances. "Mr. Brown is leaving for London this morning, to pursue opportunities of his own. I am sorry, but surely you will be glad to know that he is in pursuit of a bright future."

"Ah, this is even better!" cried Stroud. "I am on my way to London this morn as well, and so perhaps we might travel together. I must say, I am rather surprised by his decision, given all that our village has to offer." He laughed and shook his head. "Ah, to be young again! The recklessness, the heedlessness, of youth, but also the excitement. I do miss it, don't you, Mrs. Bright?"

She felt he was babbling. "Ah, no, Mr. Stroud, I can't say that I do. These are the inexorable ages of man, and we each inhabit our age as best we can. Now, I do not know if Mr. Brown has even risen yet." She saw that events were outpacing her. Stroud could easily take the tutor off and dispatch him as he had his earlier victims, never to be seen again. She did not put it past him. She had no doubt that Nick Brown would never make it to London. But she did not know how to stop it, without revealing her knowledge of his crime to Stroud. "You may have to be on your way. I would not expect you to wait on Mr. Brown," she said desperately, aware that if he did leave, a visit to the constable would mean nothing.

At that moment she heard Brown's voice, greeting Deborah as he made his way through into the hall. He entered the parlor, and quickly took in the scene. Frances prayed that he would not give them away—she did not think much of Mr. Brown's discretion. His smile ossified, and he bowed his head slightly towards their guest.

"Good morning, Mr. Stroud," he said. He looked as though he were going to say more, yet thought better of it.

"Good morning, dear Mr. Brown," smiled Stroud, gesturing towards the one remaining chair in the room. "Please be seated. I was just telling your employer, Mrs. Bright, about my trip to London. I would like to propose that we travel together, since I hear you are leaving your employment here at the Grove. It will give us an opportunity to talk about your future."

Stroud's size combined with his confidence seemed to fill the room. Frances could feel the violence in him. The man was capable of anything. She looked over at Mr. Brown, small in his chair.

"So, man, what is your answer?" demanded Stroud loudly, with a laugh. "I've got a horse to spare. Surely a finer way of travel than what you could manage. I see wealth in your future, my boy, and you deserve it. Let us be on our way, before the sun gets any hotter."

Frances heard footsteps in the hall, but they stopped short of the door, which Brown had closed when he entered. Jane, or Deborah? She stared hard at the door, willing it to stay closed. The steps melted away as Stroud continued his talk.

"We'll reach London tonight if we leave now. What do you say, Brown?"

"Ah, but I've changed my mind," the tutor almost whispered. "I leave not for London. I will stay here." He was so pale that Frances thought he might faint.

"What sort of answer is this?" said Stroud after a pause. "Surely staying in Chalfont St. James is not in your best interest. I say this as a man of experience. I do not mean to inconvenience Mrs. Bright"—a friendly nod in her direction—"but tutoring never got anyone anywhere. And staying in the village—well, I can tell you, there is nothing here for you. I have a future to give you, my boy, a future in London. With sufficient funds to make your way. I see a man of promise, I do, and I want to be of service. So do let me ride with you, to explain my plan. Really, you have no choice in the matter, I insist."

Throwing a desperate look at Frances, one that she could not decipher, Brown shrugged. "As you wish, Mr. Stroud." He stood. "Let us be on our way, be done with it." He was on his way to his sure death, thought Frances, and I can do nothing here. Stroud stood, and smiled again. He had won.

Jane could hear Frances downstairs and recognized the voice of Mr. Stroud. Slipping back into her dress from the night before, she made her way into the hall, running almost headlong into Mr. Brown as he came up the stairs. His face held nothing but fear, bone-white, damp with perspiration.

"He's here," he whispered unnecessarily. "He is to take me away, he says to London, I am to ride with him directly." He spoke as though this were a death sentence.

"Don't go," said Jane.

"How can I not? He waits below. He will not accept my refusal."

Jane took his hand and moved with him into the shadow of the hall. "Then leave, Mr. Brown, but leave now. Go the other direction if you must. Surely you see that? Why throw yourself into harm's way?" She moved into her mother's workroom, over to the window. It looked out over the stable, Stroud's two horses waiting. "You see, there is a horse, perfectly ready for you! Just tell Stephen you've been asked by Mr. Stroud to run an errand. He will think nothing of it." She wondered at her own temerity, but then it seemed so obvious, to seek escape. Once the tutor had left, she could move forward with her plan, knowing that Stroud was not likely to leave while waiting for Mr. Brown.

The tutor brightened, as if she had solved an impossible problem. "Yes, I see that, I can get away to Aylesbury, away from here! I know someone there, my father's older brother, I can seek sanctuary." He looked down at the horse. "I will send it back, of course, I am not a thief."

"Of course you aren't. But you should not give yourself over to that man," Jane said fiercely. She felt a kind of equality between the two of them there, no longer teacher and reluctant pupil, plotting the escape. Brown took himself down the backstairs. She stood by the window and watched as he rode away, then turned to her task at hand.

As she rummaged through the cupboards, she reflected on God's plan for her. It was very possible that she would be found out, and that she might be martyred. The thought was unsettling, even exciting. As she extracted the belladonna from its hiding place, concealed in a drawer with other poisonous, dangerous herbs and potions, she imagined the suffering: the sitting in jail, rats and filth surrounding her, the shackles, the court where the judge would pass sentence, the entire village a witness to her disgrace. She longed for it. What she had done, everything she had done, was shameful. She put herself in God's hands for this final act, something she knew to be a crime in this world but, possibly, not in the next.

Downstairs, she met with Deborah in the hall. She took a deep breath, to keep her voice from shaking.

"Please fetch the stepony, Deborah. Our guest is in need of refreshment. Bring it to the kitchen and I will prepare it to serve."

Amazingly, Deborah did as she asked. Jane went to the kitchen and retrieved a small jug from the shelf. She was careful in her preparation of the belladonna, respectful of its danger. When Deborah arrived from the cellar with the stepony, Jane gave her a quick, dismissive smile—so easy, so dissembling—listening hard for the voice of her enemy in the parlor. Deborah nodded and went back to her chores. The liquid swirled into the jug, cool, surely irresistible to a man who had just had a hard ride over to the Grove.

"Ah, what's this, Miss Jane?" Mrs. Cathcart appeared in the doorway, a basket of fresh sage in her hands. "Helping out in the kitchen?" Her tone was light, amused. Normally Jane would have taken offense. "Stepony for our guest—Deborah can take that in."

"No, I wish to speak with Mr. Stroud, so I will take it in with me," said Jane, keeping her gaze direct. "No need to call for Deborah. Thank you, Mrs. Cathcart." She felt time passing, and feared that, whatever Mr. Stroud's errand here, he would depart before she could carry out her mission.

The cook acquiesced and Jane, triumphant, placed the jug with two cups on a tray, making her way to the parlor. She would see about justice.

While the unfortunate Brown returned to his room to gather his things, no doubt to commiserate with the concealed Prosper, Frances found the light talk she was forced to engage in with Stroud nearly unbearable. This, she thought, was to be her hell, the life-on-earth hell that Fox often spoke of, the hell we make for ourselves. This was her punishment for thinking that she, a widow, a woman, a member of a despised and persecuted religious sect, could have the power to effect justice in her village. To be imprisoned in her own parlor with a murderer, talking of the petty doings of the county as a young man prepared himself for nearly certain death. She hoped he had the wit to slip out the kitchen door and flee, but she had no confidence in that. Brown struck her as someone without imagination or ambition. A lamb to the slaughter. Or maybe there was a small part of him that believed Stroud and hoped to be bought off with a financial start in London.

Jane appeared, bearing a tray of cups with a pitcher of Frances' stepony. Where was Deborah? Frances gratefully nodded towards the small table between herself and Mr. Stroud. "Thank you, Jane." The girl looked half-witted, her face pale, and her hands shook as she poured out two cups and distributed them to Frances and Mr. Stroud.

"Please, Mother, Eliza needs you," Jane said. The paleness of her face and her trembling hands made Frances quickly rise and move to the doorway. "Do excuse me," she said to Mr. Stroud, "please enjoy your stepony while I see to Jane and Eliza." Before he could answer, she followed Jane out into the hall. The girl moved with some swiftness towards the kitchen, Frances following hard behind.

"Mr. Brown is gone," the girl whispered as they made their way into the kitchen. "Samuel—Mr. Prosper—still lingers, however, because he would like to speak with you before he goes. Mr. Stroud does not know he is here."

"Mr. Brown won't have got far," said Frances worriedly, "and it will be easy for Mr. Stroud to chase after him."

Jane allowed herself a small smile. "Oh, we have seen to that. He took the horse that Mr. Stroud so very kindly meant for him. I am certain all will be well for Mr. Brown, Mother." Frances heard a new note in her daughter's voice, a sureness that surprised her. The penitent, frightened girl of the night before was gone.

"Well, we must find some way to tell Mr. Stroud," replied Frances, feeling somehow that she was no longer in command of what was happening. "He will not be pleased, and he is a man of violence. He will call Mr. Brown a horse thief and send the constable after him. What will he do to us?"

"Let us go and talk with him," said Jane soothingly, turning towards the door. "What can he do? We did not help Mr. Brown escape. You were conversing with Mr. Stroud, you had no knowledge of what Mr. Brown was about. He can do nothing." Again, that quiet confidence. "And do not touch the stepony, I beg of you. It is not for you, but only for Mr. Stroud." Frances wondered at this but was soon caught by Mr. Stroud's appearance in the hall. He was red-faced and clearly irritated.

"The wait has been long enough," he said. "The man must have an entire wardrobe to pack. Perhaps he requires help. Shall we go see? Where is his chamber?" His voice shook slightly. Frances wondered if the morning's situation was bringing on a fit of some kind.

"We should not intrude on Mr. Brown," she said. How to keep him here?

Stroud closed his eyes briefly. "I have waited with patience," he said slowly, taking a long, slow breath. "Please lead me to him."

Jane spoke up, her voice full and strong. "He is gone, Mr. Stroud, and it seems he has taken the horse you intended for him. I saw him but a moment ago, going down the road." Again the small smile. "It seems he has decided to go to London on his own." Stroud stared at her.

"Stolen my horse? Where was your boy, with whom I left the creature? What sort of plot is this?"

"I assure you, Mr. Stroud," said Frances, "this was not my doing. I do not know why Mr. Brown would leave without you, taking your horse. There has been a misunderstanding."

The man seemed to stumble, overcome with anger, as he pushed his way past the women and out through the kitchen door. His own horse remained there, but there was no boy in sight. Stroud slowly mounted his horse, and turned to look at her and Jane.

"This is not right," he said, spittle lining his mouth. "You have done something here for which there will be no forgiveness, Mrs. Bright. You will find yourself friendless in this county, rest assured. You have allied yourself with a liar and a thief. I will expect payment for the mare, at the very least." Pulling back on the reins, he moved off, his body swaying in the saddle.

As Frances and Jane stood in the doorway and watched, the man on his horse moved ever more slowly down the path. As he approached the pond on the way to the road, they saw him sway violently, and then with a sudden movement fall from the horse and into the pond. Frances began to run, calling to Stephen, who now appeared from the direction of the garden. Jane seemed to hesitate a long moment and then followed her mother.

As they approached the pond, they could see that Stroud was floundering in the water, but in a way that suggested he had been injured in the fall. The two women relied on Stephen to do most of the pulling as they retrieved Stroud and pulled him out to lie on the grass. The whole exercise took a long time, the man by this time a dead weight. Frances, wet to her waist, began to slap Stroud's cheeks in an effort to bring him round. His eyes were closed and he was pale as a fish's belly. He was breathing, but it was ragged and slow. What had made him fall from the horse? Frances remembered Jane's warning about the stepony. She recognized the symptoms: this was belladonna.

Then Stroud opened his eyes and looked at Frances. "You have done it," he whispered, "you have seen to it, you have made an end to me—" then a gasp.

"Oh no, Mr. Stroud," replied Jane in a clear voice, looking at him with a tranquility that seemed very much out of place to Frances. "You have done this, it is your crimes that have brought this about. God smites you down, punishes you for your sins, so that you may serve as a lesson to others. That is the truth of it."

Frances looked at her daughter in disbelief. "Have you no mercy in you?"

Jane continued looking at Mr. Stroud. "Mr. Stroud, as you are fast approaching death, it seems, will you confess to the murders of Tom Maltman and Nathaniel Kidd?"

It was at that moment that Frances could see Sarah Kidd running across the lawn, her hair down around her shoulders, alongside Samuel Prosper. As the widow approached and could see the fallen Mr. Stroud, her hand went to her mouth and she stood very still. "What is this?"

"Say it, Mr. Stroud," insisted Jane, not to be deterred. "Say what you have done, as you are finished and will soon meet with your eternal punishment." She leaned her face close in, next to his.

"Ah," he cried, "I see the Devil chasing me, it is after me, there are snakes—" he shuddered, and his breathing became more labored. "Horrible! I did the deeds, murders, the traveler, and the boy, he was there, the widow was meddling—has to stop, has to stop…" He was staring at Jane. "You are the Devil, you torment me!"

Sarah Kidd stood stock-still. Frances could see that she was trembling but kept herself erect, listening to Stroud, to what seemed to be his death-bed confession. Samuel Prosper's expression, as he stood by her side, was a confusion of shock and relief. His nemesis was on the ground, prostrate, breathing his last as he confessed to the murders of Nathaniel and Tom.

"May the Lord keep you," whispered Frances, wishing to comfort the dying man. His whole body shuddered, his limbs jerking this way and that, until finally all was quiet. She reached out and closed his eyes.

Chapter Nineteen

———•◆•———

The funeral for John Stroud was well attended and brought the several orders of society together as they gathered in St. James that late summer day. Frances would not have gone, but Sarah Kidd insisted, and asked for her and Jane to accompany her. All the way to the church Sarah and Jane talked eagerly of stories of God's punishment on earth, many of Jane's examples coming from the writings of George Fox. Frances found the conversation a little bloody and tried to move it in a different direction, but the widow Kidd and Jane had found their common ground and would not leave it.

"There are many times," said Sarah with authority, "that God has smote down those who have done evil in this world. Judgment is given. Mr. Stroud has been judged, and has suffered. His convulsions were no doubt sent by God to show us his guilt."

Jane nodded. "He may use instruments to bring his Will about," she added. "It is not always the arm of the Lord himself, but nonetheless it comes from Him and shows us his power."

"But surely," interjected Frances, trying her best, "it is his shining of the Light in those of us who choose to receive, and not his punishment of wrongdoers, that should be our guide. His actions can be mysterious, but his Light clarifies and opens us to love. This talk of—of convulsions and horrible deaths is not the way for us to find our way to God."

Ever since the day of Stroud's death, she had wondered at it. Certainly Fox and others talked of convulsions and mysterious ailments as a way that God visited his judgment on the world. But this had happened so suddenly, and with such fortuitous timing (Frances felt especially troubled by this), that she could not stop thinking about it. She worried about Jane, who seemed newly distant, and felt there to be a link between this new manner and the death of Mr. Stroud. Jane had been so at ease, so fearless, as though she knew that Stroud would weaken and die before her very eyes. The warning about the stepony.

They found seats toward the back of the church, Frances feeling every moment like a betrayer of her faith. Sarah looked around her at the crowd.

"They know not what a beast he was," she said softly, "and those who did, said nothing. They let his crime be. If not for the silence about Nathaniel, that boy Tom might not have died. They are bloody with ignorance and cowardice. The only good thing in this room is that the man lies dead in his coffin." Her eyes were dry, but Frances could feel Sarah's grief for her husband as if it were a living thing.

Brunskill entered the nave and stepped up into the pulpit. His face was quiet with concentration. He kept his eyes on his text as he began his sermon.

"I will begin with Psalm 49:12," he said, his voice loud and clear throughout the church. "Nevertheless man being in honor stays not: he is like the beasts that perish."

The congregation was silent. Frances could see the back of Mrs. Stroud's head, immobile beneath her headdress. In the pew behind her sat the Grinshaws, their heads close together.

"And from Psalm 73:3, Jeremiah 12:1 and Job 21:7–10: A carnal man may thrive and prosper, and grow great here on earth. Those who pay close heed to God's word may, in contrary, suffer and be subject to endless trial. Joseph is put forth to keep sheep, while Esau, the hated, goes on hunting. And so we know that there are those among us who seem rich, who seem fortunate in all ways. And yet God knows their hearts, and they will meet with His justice in good time. For our worldly goods follow us not into the next world; they are but a moment's glory. The bodies of the worldly will be torn asunder, prey to other beasts. Their ill-gotten goods will molder and rot away. In God's sight, they will be unpleasing, as some rotting animal.

"Such is death, for the worldling. We bow down before him here on earth, but know this: he will meet with justice in his end. We must all tremble and shake before the power of God. We cannot know who among us may meet this fate; we know not the mind of God. But our fear of God, our absolute fear of our Lord, is to be our Salvation."

The church had become quiet, while Brunskill's voice filled the space. "We are gathered here this morning to mark the passing of John Stroud, gentleman. We cannot know what was in his heart while he did live, but know this: our Lord God saw into his heart, and John Stroud will meet with the fate his Creator has always meant for him. So will we all. A man of much wealth in our village, it is no longer of any use to him. His body will no longer require the raiment that made clear his position in our midst. He is alone before God's judgment. So will we all be."

A long pause. Frances looked again at Mrs. Stroud, but could only see her erect, motionless back. Brunskill looked up from his text, and shook his head slightly. Perhaps he had just changed his mind about something. His gaze moved into the congregation before him.

"For many in our village, John Stroud represented justice. As the local Justice of the Peace, he was to see to it that order was established and maintained. Many looked to him for authority, and his word was always taken to be right and true. His home was gracious and his hospitality well known. His wealth obvious to all. But I will say, to all here in this church today, that to be enthralled with the trappings of this world is to lose one's way to the next. Worldly pride is hateful to God. Psalm 10:4: The wicked, through the pride of his countenance, will not seek after God: God is not in all his thoughts."

Another long pause: there was some muttering in the front pews.

"At his end, John Stroud knew what he was. He could see the Lord opening before him, and this revelation led him to reveal the truth to those who witnessed it. He was heard to say that he was the murderer of Nathaniel Kidd and Tom Maltman." Brunskill's voice rose with each word until he was shouting the names of the victims, surrounded by the shouts of outrage from his congregation. Outrage, naturally, against the priest, for maligning a gentleman. Mrs. Stroud stood slowly, gathered her skirts close, and moved into the aisle to leave the church. As she passed by Frances, Sarah and Jane she stopped and threw them a look poisonous with hatred.

"It was not enough for these women to ruin the reputation of Mr. Grinshaw, but they must now attack my dead husband. Will they stop at nothing? Will no one stop their calumny?"

Sarah Kidd rose from her place. "I heard him say it," she said, her voice full in the church. "I am sorry for you, Mrs. Stroud, but I waste no mercy on your husband. These deaths did not matter to him. He ended their lives as he would that of a fly. And he had nothing to fear from anyone here. Nobody would challenge him. I refuse to leave this village without proclaiming the truth of it. Father Brunskill has spoken it." She turned and looked at the priest, who was still in his pulpit. They exchanged a long look.

"The truth will not be silenced," the priest declared, returning his gaze to the villagers, who had all stood up in their pews, unsure as to whether to follow Mrs. Stroud or stay out of curiosity. The priest continued: "This man will be laid to rest in the same cemetery as his victims. He will forever be a sign to us of our own sin, our refusal of the widow. She came to us for help, the stranger at the inn, a mother, and we refused her. There was no room for her. We turned away and ignored her pleas. We took the side of evil, we allowed a murderer free movement in our midst, we sought the bliss of ignorance. We refused to see what was right before our eyes. This small, small blemish of evil, an abomination in the eye of the Lord, that festered and grew as we remained asleep to our sin. Now we are awake, and we see, and the Lord has brought about the justice we refused to grant. We must take from this our lesson, my dear people, acknowledge our sin and go out to sin no more." Then Brunskill shook his head slowly and moved away from the pulpit. "There will be no communion this day," he said as he stepped down. Frances wondered if he would ever enter this pulpit again.

The villagers surged into the center aisle and slowly exited the church, chattering as they went. Frances could overhear angry denunciations of the priest mingled with both praise and denunciations of the deceased. She waited in her place while the Grinshaws walked by, dignified, quiet, looking neither to the right nor the left. Sarah Kidd leaned forward and spat on the ground as they passed.

"I am glad to be leaving this place," she said to Frances and Jane. "I have known nothing but misery here. I am sorry to leave my Nathaniel in this graveyard, with these evildoers."

"Well," said Frances, "I know that. But evildoers are everywhere, Mrs. Kidd." She turned toward the pulpit to see Brunskill, now that the villagers had gone, walking towards them.

"Dear Mrs. Bright," he said as he approached, his color high. "Miss Bright, Mrs. Kidd," the last said with some small hesitation. "This is a hard day. I do not know what comes next. It is possible that my congregation will see to my removal."

"Does that worry you, Mr. Brunskill?" asked Frances. "You spoke the truth, as hard as it was for these people to hear."

The priest shook his head slowly. "And yet they continue to deny it. I have no weight among them. If I must leave, it is not only because of what happened today. I am not the priest they want. I never have been."

"Perhaps too this isn't the church you were meant to serve," said Frances. "It will all be as it should be, but perhaps not how we would like it."

Sarah Kidd reached out her hand to the priest. "I thank you, most sincerely, for your action. I will be leaving Chalfont St. James tomorrow morning, and am not sorry to be leaving. You have been one of my few friends in this village." She spoke slowly, each word precious. "I wish you well."

The priest flushed. "You thank me for something I had no choice in," he replied. "I wish you and your son well as you return to London. What about the lost fortune? How will you live, Mrs. Kidd?"

Here Jane spoke up. "It was Samuel Prosper that took it, and so it is he that will return it. He has a good living in London, having found his way into trade, and has promised Mrs. Kidd a monthly stipend from his earnings that will restore her fortune. He has given his word."

Sarah Kidd shrugged but the look on her face was determined. "John Edward must have what his father intended him to have. He is but a small child, but later he will need it to find his way in the world. Mr. Prosper has said he will send us half his earnings of a month, for as long as it is necessary. He wishes to make amends for his crime, and for the sake of John Edward I accept his silver. We have arranged an intermediary to come with the stipend. I have no wish to ever see Mr. Prosper again."

"Please join us at home for dinner, Mr. Brunskill," said Frances generously. "We must be on our way. Will you come?"

The priest smiled, a burden lifted from his shoulders. "Yes, with pleasure, Mrs. Bright." They made their way out of the church to find the day had turned warm, an autumnal warmth that had a chill edge to it. Frances led the way with Jane, Brunskill and Mrs. Kidd following behind.

"Now, Jane," said Frances, "I remember our talk, how strongly you spoke of Mr. Stroud's guilt and the requirement of punishment. I know that this was not the same: while Mr. Brunskill, at great cost to himself, spoke of the man's crime, so that forever more Mr. Stroud will be thought of as the murderer of Nathaniel Kidd and Tom Maltman, it is not as it should have been, a decision in a court of law."

Jane took her mother's hand. "I know, I know. I have learned how the world works. We live in a flawed shadow-world and see as through a glass darkly. We are weak and limited. But I am content, Mother, I am content. God has worked his will through the means at his disposal. For those who care to see, the truth has been revealed. I am content."

This surprised Frances. She could hear the voices of Brunskill and Mrs. Kidd, soft and low, behind her as they walked through the wood towards home. She, herself, was not content. She had to admit to that. The world's injustice pained her. It was not only the matter of the murders, but also her brother-in-law Richard's suit and the refusal of his family to help her. And yet she knew that to feel righteous, to feel that only she knew what was right, was but false pride and selfishness. Jane's clarity, her certainty, was what Frances longed for and yet could not find. She wondered at it, that such a young girl, so passionate and fierce, would have come to such an equanimity so suddenly.

As they approached the house she could see her boy taking away a horse to stabled. Richard must have arrived for another of his visits, she thought sourly, another outrage to be visited upon her against her will. The day took on a gloomy cast as she ushered everyone into the hall and went directly to her parlor. There stood Richard, his back to the fire. He was as finely dressed as ever, his dark brown coat spotless, his boots gleaming with oil.

"Dear Richard," she said, "we have guests for dinner, so you are just in time for our party. It is, as always, good to see you."

"Thank you for the invitation, Frances," Richard replied. There was a long pause. He seemed to be looking somewhere over the top of her head.

"Shall we go?"

Shaking himself out of his reverie, he directed his gaze to her. "In a moment. I have something to tell you. I know you will find it to be good news, though I have to say that I never thought my proposal would be to your disadvantage. Nonetheless, it seems that your campaign, with my mother and sister, has reaped rewards. Mother came to me and asked me to drop my suit."

Frances sat down. She was tempted to ask why Mrs. Bright would have done such a thing but opted for silence instead.

"It was a surprise to me," continued Richard. "I will follow her wishes, for I honor my mother in all things. It wasn't always so, and I am in arrears, so must follow her wishes as best I can. She has said that my father intended this house for Matthew and you, with no thought as to your manner of wedding, and that I must step aside. I do not know what prompted her decision, other than your visit with her. You are a persuasive woman, Frances."

It took a long, quiet moment for Frances to absorb what Richard had said. She could not help herself; tears came too easily at this time in her life. Frantically wiping at her cheeks with one hand, she took a deep breath and looked up at her brother-in-law.

"We women," she said with a laugh, "we need not persuasion, Richard. We are all widows, you see, we know what it is to be on our own in the world. Your mother and I. You will marry, and find a house, and your heirs will share in it. This house is all that I have. I am glad to be able to keep it, for Eliza's sake."

He bowed his head and reached out his hand to her. She took it.

"And now let us go, and join the others," she said.

Acknowledgments

The length of time it took to write *The Bailiff's Wife* means that I have many people, over the course of its creation, to thank.

Many thanks to my sister Jan Halvorsen, who while helping me with my dissertation research came across the broadsheet that is the cornerstone of my novel. She was there at the ground floor, so to speak, of its construction, and then again at the end, when she contributed the art that serves as the book's cover. She and I had many satisfying conversations about Sarah Kidd as we imagined the cover together.

I would like to thank Maria Semple and my classmates in Semple's Hugo House writing class, several years ago, for reading the first twenty pages of my manuscript and encouraging me to go further.

I am grateful to my editor and publisher, Martha Hoffman at Cuidono Press, for her editorial skill, appreciation of what I was trying to do in *The Bailiff's Wife*, and wise advice. She made it a better book.

While not directly involved in the writing of this novel, I would like to thank some other people for helping me grow as a writer: Charles Baxter, who took time outside of our writing workshop to problem-solve a story's ending, and my fellow writers Rhoda Berlin, Harriet Cannon, Susan Nolen, and Jody Harwood for our many deep and useful conversations about characters and plot and novel structure. Thanks too to Laura Dushkes, for all her support over the years.

Finally, deepest thanks to my husband Jamie and son Reese, who serve as role models in how they pursue their creative passions, with courage and confidence.

Maren Halvorsen is a historian, and a former college lecturer and administrator. She lives with her husband and dog in a small town on the Olympic Peninsula of Washington, where she is active within the local writing community. She has written for *Chiron Review*, *October Hill Magazine*, and *Tidepools Magazine*. As a historian and writer she is moved by how people of the past thought about and experienced the details of their daily life and community, especially how women negotiated their status, and how religion conflicted with the world and its demands. *The Bailiff's Wife* grew out of the discovery of a broadsheet during her scholarly research on the early English Quakers. Maren is currently working on a novel about Margaret of Anjou and the Wars of the Roses.